Bridget Jones's Diary

Helen Fielding was born in Yorkshire. She worked for many years in London as a newspaper and TV journalist, travelling as wildly and as often as possible to Africa, India and Central America. She has written five novels, *Cause Celeb* (1994), *Bridget Jones's Diary* (1996), *Bridget Jones: The Edge of Reason* (1999), *Olivia Joules and the Overactive Imagination* (2003) and *Bridget Jones: Mad About the Boy* (2013). She also co-wrote the screenplays for the movies *Bridget Jones's Diary*, *The Edge of Reason* and *Bridget Jones's Baby*. She now works full-time as a novelist and screenwriter, and lives in London and Los Angeles.

HELEN FIELDING

Bridget Jones's Diary (And Other Writing)

25th Anniversary Edition

PICADOR

First published 1996 by Picador

First published in paperback 1997 by Picador

This edition published 2021 by Picador
an imprint of Pan Macmillan
The Smithson, 6 Briset Street, London EC1M 5NR
EU representative: Macmillan Publishers Ireland Limited,
Mallard Lodge, Lansdowne Village, Dublin 4
Associated companies throughout the world
www.panmacmillan.com

ISBN 978-1-5290-5707-2

The Permissions Acknowledgements on p. 438
constitute an extension of this copyright page.

Printed and bound by CPI Group (UK) Ltd, Croydon, CR0 4YY

Visit **www.picador.com** to read more about all our books
and to buy them. You will also find features, author interviews and
news of any author events, and you can sign up for e-newsletters
so that you're always first to hear about our new releases.

Contents

INTRODUCTION

Monday 14 September 2020

11am. Right, am going to write the introduction now.

11.05am. Will just google coronavirus update.

Noon. Right! Time to start the introduction now.

12.05 Ooh! Lunchtime!

2pm. Right. Am just going to unselfconsciously get on with the introduction.

'No, I'm not Bridget Jones!' is something I've been insisting since I first wrote 'The Diary of Bridget Jones' anonymously in London's Independent *newspaper in 1995.*

2.05pm. Oh no, though. Even as I write this I am struck by self-doubt and multiple thoughts. Isn't it odd, and perhaps somehow vainglorious, to be writing an introduction to your own book? Isn't that something somebody else is supposed to do? And crucially, aren't they supposed to do it after you're dead?

2.30pm. It's completely wrong. I'm going to come across as boasty or disingenuous.

2.45pm. Also I've been procrastinating again. I was supposed to hand it in on July the 7th. And then August the 19th. And then I – rather brilliantly I feel – claimed that I'd been 'having a difficult time' (hasn't everyone? It's 2020) and, even more brilliantly, burst out with the confident yet random statement that I would finish on (for literally no reason) September the 16th. This seemed to satisfy everyone. The only drawback is, it is now September the 14th, and any second now I am going to get an email asking 'How are we getting along?' for all the world as if we are back in 1995 at the *Independent* and it is time to hand the column in again.

3pm. Look. I just need to get on and write it.

Ah! So much has both changed and not changed in the 25 years since I first wrote . . .

3.30pm. I do worry about the 25 years thing. I think it ages me. Am going to call Tom.

4pm. Tom agrees it is ageing: 'I mean, if we'd said 25 years of Bridget Jones 25 years ago, we'd all have thought it was a HILARIOUS joke and imagined ourselves with tight grey perms and Zimmer frames whereas obviously nothing could be *further from the truth.*'

4pm. Well anyway.

I think if Bridget Jones is about anything, it's about the gap between how you feel you're expected to be and how you actually are. That gap has only grown bigger over time, as the world becomes saturated in social media.

4.15pm. 'Saturated' in social media. *Saturated?*

4.30pm.

In this social media age, the futility of 'front' becomes ever clearer, as opposed to the things that really matter: kindness, emotional honesty, fun, laughter, friendship, community, the ability to find humour in one's own flaws and to tackle the difficulties of life and . . .

4.45pm. You see? Sanctimonious and annoying.

Also feel like I've told the story of how Bridget started and what it might mean too many times for it to be plausible anymore. It's the opposite of how, when people tell a lie so many times – e.g. with OJ Simpson, Bill Clinton or Lance Armstrong – it starts to seem like the truth. If you tell the truth too many times it starts to seem like a lie.

5pm. OK: this is my idea. Instead of writing an introduction I am simply going to say 'here is the book', and then afterwards put a selection of my other works of journalism and let them tell the story quite naturally, while simultaneously bringing a pleasing sense of 'added value'.

5.10pm. Jolly good then.

5.55pm.

Here is the book.

6pm. Ooh goody, time for a little drinky.

Helen Fielding
September 2020

Bridget Jones's Diary

To my mum, Nellie, for not being like Bridget's

Acknowledgements

With particular thanks to Charlie Leadbeater for first suggesting the column at the *Independent*. Thanks too to Gillon Aitken, Richard Coles, Scarlett Curtis, the Fielding family, Piers, Paula and Sam Fletcher, Emma Freud, Georgia Garrett, Sharon Maguire, Jon Turner and Daniel Woods for inspiration and support, and especially, as ever, to Richard Curtis.

New Year's Resolutions

I WILL NOT

Drink more than fourteen alcohol units a week.

Smoke.

Waste money on: pasta-makers, ice-cream machines or other culinary devices which will never use; books by unreadable literary authors to put impressively on shelves; exotic underwear, since pointless as have no boyfriend.

Behave sluttishly around the house, but instead imagine others are watching.

Spend more than earn.

Allow in-tray to rage out of control.

Fall for any of following: alcoholics, workaholics, commitment phobics, people with girlfriends or wives, misogynists, megalo-maniacs, chauvinists, emotional fuckwits or freeloaders, perverts.

Get annoyed with Mum, Una Alconbury or Perpetua.

Get upset over men, but instead be poised and cool ice-queen.

Have crushes on men, but instead form relationships based on mature assessment of character.

Bitch about anyone behind their backs, but be positive about everyone.

Obsess about Daniel Cleaver as pathetic to have a crush on boss in manner of Miss Moneypenny or similar.

Sulk about having no boyfriend, but develop inner poise and authority and sense of self as woman of substance, complete *without* boyfriend, as best way to obtain boyfriend.

I WILL

Stop smoking.

Drink no more than fourteen alcohol units a week.

Reduce circumference of thighs by 3 inches (i.e. 1½ inches each), using anti-cellulite diet.

Purge flat of all extraneous matter.

Give all clothes which have not worn for two years or more to homeless.

Improve career and find new job with potential.

Save up money in form of savings. Poss start pension also.

Be more confident.

Be more assertive.

Make better use of time.

Not go out every night but stay in and read books and listen to classical music.

Give proportion of earnings to charity.

Be kinder and help others more.

Eat more pulses.

Get up straight away when wake up in mornings.

Go to gym three times a week not merely to buy sandwich.

Put photographs in photograph albums.

Make up compilation 'mood' tapes so can have tapes ready with all favourite romantic/dancing/rousing/feminist etc. tracks assembled instead of turning into drink-sodden DJ-style person with tapes scattered all over floor.

Form functional relationship with responsible adult.

Learn to programme video.

JANUARY

An Exceptionally Bad Start

Sunday 1 January

9st 3 (but post-Christmas), alcohol units 14 (but effectively covers 2 days as 4 hours of party was on New Year's Day), cigarettes 22, calories 5424.

Food consumed today:

> 2 pkts Emmenthal cheese slices
> 14 cold new potatoes
> 2 Bloody Marys (count as food as contain Worcester sauce and tomatoes)
> ⅓ Ciabatta loaf with Brie
> coriander leaves – ½ packet
> 12 Milk Tray (best to get rid of all Christmas confectionery in one go and make fresh start tomorrow)
> 13 cocktail sticks securing cheese and pineapple
> Portion Una Alconbury's turkey curry, peas and bananas
> Portion Una Alconbury's Raspberry Surprise made with Bourbon biscuits, tinned raspberries, eight gallons of whipped cream, decorated with glacé cherries and angelica.

Noon. London: my flat. Ugh. The last thing on earth I feel physically, emotionally or mentally equipped to do is drive

7

to Una and Geoffrey Alconbury's New Year's Day Turkey Curry Buffet in Grafton Underwood. Geoffrey and Una Alconbury are my parents' best friends and, as Uncle Geoffrey never tires of reminding me, have known me since I was running round the lawn with no clothes on. My mother rang up at 8.30 in the morning last August Bank Holiday and forced me to promise to go. She approached it via a cunningly circuitous route.

'Oh, hello, darling. I was just ringing to see what you wanted for Christmas.'

'*Christmas?*'

'Would you like a surprise, darling?'

'No!' I bellowed. 'Sorry. I mean . . .'

'I wondered if you'd like a set of wheels for your suitcase.'

'But I haven't got a suitcase.'

'Why don't I get you a little suitcase *with wheels attached*. You know, like air hostesses have.'

'I've already got a bag.'

'Oh, darling, you can't go around with that tatty green canvas thing. You look like some sort of Mary Poppins person who's fallen on hard times. Just a little compact case with a pull-out handle. It's amazing how much you can get in. Do you want it in navy on red or red on navy?'

'Mum. It's eight thirty in the morning. It's summer. It's very hot. I don't want an air-hostess bag.'

'Julie Enderby's got one. She says she never uses anything else.'

'Who's Julie Enderby?'

'You know *Julie*, darling! Mavis Enderby's daughter. Julie! The one that's got that super-dooper job at Arthur Andersen . . .'

'Mum . . .'

'Always takes it on her trips . . .'

'I don't want a little bag with wheels on.'

'I'll tell you what. Why don't Jamie, Daddy and I all club together and get you a proper new big suitcase *and* a set of wheels?'

Exhausted, I held the phone away from my ear, puzzling about where the missionary luggage-Christmas-gift zeal had stemmed from. When I put the phone back she was saying: '. . . in actual fact, you can get them with a compartment with bottles for your bubble bath and things. The other thing I thought of was a shopping trolley.'

'Is there anything *you'd* like for Christmas?' I said desperately, blinking in the dazzling Bank Holiday sunlight.

'No, no,' she said airily. 'I've got everything *I* need. Now, darling,' she suddenly hissed, 'you will be coming to Geoffrey and Una's New Year's Day Turkey Curry Buffet this year, won't you?'

'Ah. Actually, I . . .' I panicked wildly. What could I pretend to be doing? '. . . think I might have to work on New Year's Day.'

'That doesn't matter. You can drive up after work. Oh, did I mention? Malcolm and Elaine Darcy are coming and bringing Mark with them. Do you remember Mark, darling? He's one of those top-notch barristers. Masses of money. Divorced. It doesn't start till eight.'

Oh God. Not another strangely dressed opera freak with bushy hair burgeoning from a side-parting. 'Mum, I've told you. I don't need to be fixed up with . . .'

'Now come along, darling. Una and Geoffrey have been holding the New Year Buffet since you were running round

9

the lawn with no clothes on! Of course you're going to come. And you'll be able to use your new suitcase.'

11.45 p.m. Ugh. First day of New Year has been day of horror. Cannot quite believe I am once again starting the year in a single bed in my parents' house. It is too humiliating at my age. I wonder if they'll smell it if I have a fag out of the window. Having skulked at home all day, hoping hangover would clear, I eventually gave up and set off for the Turkey Curry Buffet far too late. When I got to the Alconburys' and rang their entire-tune-of-town-hall-clock-style doorbell I was still in a strange world of my own – nauseous, vile-headed, acidic. I was also suffering from road-rage residue after inadvertently getting on to the M6 instead of the M1 and having to drive halfway to Birmingham before I could find anywhere to turn round. I was so furious I kept jamming my foot down to the floor on the accelerator pedal to give vent to my feelings, which is very dangerous. I watched resignedly as Una Alconbury's form – intriguingly deformed through the ripply glass door – bore down on me in a fuchsia two-piece.

'Bridget! We'd almost given you up for lost! Happy New Year! Just about to start without you.'

She seemed to manage to kiss me, get my coat off, hang it over the banister, wipe her lipstick off my cheek and make me feel incredibly guilty all in one movement, while I leaned against the ornament shelf for support.

'Sorry. I got lost.'

'Lost? Durr! What are we going to do with you? Come on in!'

She led me through the frosted-glass doors into the lounge, shouting, 'She got lost, everyone!'

'Bridget! Happy New Year!' said Geoffrey Alconbury, clad in a yellow diamond-patterned sweater. He did a jokey Bruce Forsyth step then gave me the sort of hug which Boots would send straight to the police station.

'Hahumph,' he said, going red in the face and pulling his trousers up by the waistband. 'Which junction did you come off at?'

'Junction nineteen, but there was a diversion . . .'

'Junction nineteen! Una, she came off at Junction nineteen! You've added an hour to your journey before you even started. Come on, let's get you a drink. How's your love-life, anyway?'

Oh *God*. Why can't married people understand that this is no longer a polite question to ask? We wouldn't rush up to *them* and roar, 'How's your marriage going? Still having sex?' Everyone knows that dating in your thirties is not the happy-go-lucky free-for-all it was when you were twenty-two and that the honest answer is more likely to be, 'Actually, last night my married lover appeared wearing suspenders and a darling little Angora crop-top, told me he was gay/a sex addict/a narcotic addict/a commitment phobic and beat me up with a dildo,' than, 'Super, thanks.'

Not being a natural liar, I ended up mumbling shamefacedly to Geoffrey, 'Fine,' at which point he boomed, 'So you *still* haven't got a feller!'

'Bridget! What *are* we going to do with you!' said Una. 'You career girls! I don't know! Can't put it off for ever, you know. Tick-tock-tick-tock.'

'Yes. How does a woman manage to get to your age without being married?' roared Brian Enderby (married to Mavis, used to be president of the Rotary in Kettering),

11

waving his sherry in the air. Fortunately my dad rescued me.

'I'm very pleased to see you, Bridget,' he said, taking my arm. 'Your mother has the entire Northamptonshire constabulary poised to comb the county with toothbrushes for your dismembered remains. Come and demonstrate your presence so I can start enjoying myself. How's the be-wheeled suitcase?'

'Big beyond all sense. How are the ear-hair clippers?'

'Oh, marvellously – you know – *clippy*.'

It was all right, I suppose. I would have felt a bit mean if I hadn't turned up, but Mark Darcy . . . Yuk. Every time my mother's rung up for weeks it's been, 'Of course you remember the *Darcys*, darling. They came over when we were living in Buckingham and you and Mark played in the paddling pool!' or, 'Oh! Did I mention Malcolm and Elaine are bringing Mark with them to Una's New Year's Day Turkey Curry Buffet? He's just back from America, apparently. Divorced. He's looking for a house in Holland Park. Apparently he had the most terrible time with his wife. Japanese. Very cruel race.'

Then next time, as if out of the blue, 'Do you remember Mark Darcy, darling? Malcolm and Elaine's son? He's one of these super-dooper top-notch lawyers. Divorced. Elaine says he works all the time and he's terribly lonely. I think he might be coming to Una's New Year's Day Turkey Curry Buffet, actually.'

I don't know why she didn't just come out with it and say, 'Darling, do shag Mark Darcy over the turkey curry, won't you? He's *very* rich.'

'Come along and meet Mark,' Una Alconbury sing-songed before I'd even had time to get a drink down me.

Being set up with a man against your will is one level of humiliation, but being literally dragged into it by Una Alconbury while caring for an acidic hangover, watched by an entire roomful of friends of your parents, is on another plane altogether.

The rich, divorced-by-cruel-wife Mark – quite tall – was standing with his back to the room, scrutinizing the contents of the Alconburys' bookshelves: mainly leather-bound series of books about the Third Reich, which Geoffrey sends off for from Reader's Digest. It struck me as pretty ridiculous to be called Mr Darcy and to stand on your own looking snooty at a party. It's like being called Heathcliff and insisting on spending the entire evening in the garden, shouting 'Cathy' and banging your head against a tree.

'Mark!' said Una, as if she was one of Santa Claus's fairies. 'I've got someone nice for you to meet.'

He turned round, revealing that what had seemed from the back like a harmless navy sweater was actually a V-neck diamond-pattern in shades of yellow and blue – as favoured by the more elderly of the nation's sports reporters. As my friend Tom often remarks, it's amazing how much time and money can be saved in the world of dating by close attention to detail. A white sock here, a pair of red braces there, a grey slip-on shoe, a swastika, are as often as not all one needs to tell you there's no point writing down phone numbers and forking out for expensive lunches because it's never going to be a runner.

'Mark, this is Colin and Pam's daughter, Bridget,' said Una, going all pink and fluttery. 'Bridget works in publishing, don't you, Bridget?'

'I do indeed,' I for some reason said, as if I were taking

part in a Capital radio phone-in and was about to ask Una if I could 'say hello' to my friends Jude, Sharon and Tom, my brother Jamie, everyone in the office, my mum and dad, and last of all all the people at the Turkey Curry Buffet.

'Well, I'll leave you two young people together,' said Una. 'Durr! I expect you're sick to death of us old fuddy-duddies.'

'Not at all,' said Mark Darcy awkwardly with a rather unsuccessful attempt at a smile, at which Una, after rolling her eyes, putting a hand to her bosom and giving a gay tinkling laugh, abandoned us with a toss of her head to a hideous silence.

'I. Um. Are you reading any, ah . . . Have you read any good books lately?' he said.

Oh, for God's sake.

I racked my brain frantically to think when I last read a proper book. The trouble with working in publishing is that reading in your spare time is a bit like being a dustman and snuffling through the pig bin in the evening. I'm halfway through *Men are from Mars*, *Women are from Venus*, which Jude lent me, but I didn't think Mark Darcy, though clearly odd, was ready to accept himself as a Martian quite yet. Then I had a brainwave.

'*Backlash*, actually, by Susan Faludi,' I said triumphantly. Hah! I haven't exactly read it as such, but feel I have as Sharon has been ranting about it so much. Anyway, completely safe option as no way diamond-pattern-jumpered goody-goody would have read five-hundred-page feminist treatise.

'Ah. Really?' he said. 'I read that when it first came out. Didn't you find there was rather a lot of special pleading?'

'Oh, well, not *too* much . . .' I said wildly, racking my

brains for a way to get off the subject. 'Have you been staying with your parents over New Year?'

'Yes,' he said eagerly. 'You too?'

'Yes. No. I was at a party in London last night. Bit hungover, actually.' I gabbled nervously so that Una and Mum wouldn't think I was so useless with men I was failing to talk to even Mark Darcy. 'But then I do think New Year's resolutions can't technically be expected to begin on New Year's Day, don't you? Since, because it's an extension of New Year's Eve, smokers are already on a smoking roll and cannot be expected to stop abruptly on the stroke of midnight with so much nicotine in the system. Also dieting on New Year's Day isn't a good idea as you can't eat rationally but really need to be free to consume whatever is necessary, moment by moment, in order to ease your hangover. I think it would be much more sensible if resolutions began generally on January the second.'

'Maybe you should get something to eat,' he said, then suddenly bolted off towards the buffet, leaving me standing on my own by the bookshelf while everybody stared at me, thinking, 'So that's why Bridget isn't married. She repulses men.'

The worst of it was that Una Alconbury and Mum wouldn't leave it at that. They kept making me walk round with trays of gherkins and glasses of cream sherry in a desperate bid to throw me into Mark Darcy's path yet again. In the end they were so crazed with frustration that the second I got within four feet of him with the gherkins Una threw herself across the room like Will Carling and said, 'Mark, you must take Bridget's telephone number before you go, then you can get in touch when you're in London.'

I couldn't stop myself turning bright red. I could feel it

climbing up my neck. Now Mark would think I'd put her up to it.

'I'm sure Bridget's life in London is quite full enough already, Mrs Alconbury,' he said. Humph. It's not that I wanted him to take my phone number or anything, but I didn't want him to make it perfectly obvious to everyone that he didn't want to. As I looked down I saw that he was wearing white socks with a yellow bumblebee motif.

'Can't I tempt you with a gherkin?' I said, to show I had had a genuine reason for coming over, which was quite definitely gherkin-based rather than phone-number-related.

'Thank you, no,' he said, looking at me with some alarm.

'Sure? Stuffed olive?' I pressed on.

'No, really.'

'Silverskin onion?' I encouraged. 'Beetroot cube?'

'Thank you,' he said desperately, taking an olive.

'Hope you enjoy it,' I said triumphantly.

Towards the end I saw him being harangued by his mother and Una, who marched him over towards me and stood just behind while he said stiffly, 'Do you need driving back to London? I'm staying here but I could get my car to take you.'

'What, all on its own?' I said.

He blinked at me.

'Durr! Mark has a company car and a driver, silly,' said Una.

'Thank you, that's very kind,' I said. 'But I shall be taking one of my trains in the morning.'

2 a.m. Oh, why am I so unattractive? Why? Even a man who wears bumblebee socks thinks I am horrible. Hate the

16

New Year. Hate everyone. Except Daniel Cleaver. Anyway, have got giant tray-sized bar of Cadbury's Dairy Milk left over from Christmas on dressing table, also amusing joke gin and tonic miniature. Am going to consume them and have fag.

Tuesday 3 January

9st 4 (terrifying slide into obesity – why? why?), alcohol units 6 (excellent), cigarettes 23 (v.g.), calories 2472.

9 a.m. Ugh. Cannot face thought of going to work. Only thing which makes it tolerable is thought of seeing Daniel again, but even that is inadvisable since am fat, have spot on chin, and desire only to sit on cushion eating chocolate and watching Xmas specials. It seems wrong and unfair that Christmas, with its stressful and unmanageable financial and emotional challenges, should first be forced upon one wholly against one's will, then rudely snatched away just when one is starting to get into it. Was really beginning to enjoy the feeling that normal service was suspended and it was OK to lie in bed as long as you want, put anything you fancy into your mouth, and drink alcohol whenever it should chance to pass your way, even in the mornings. Now suddenly we are all supposed to snap into self-discipline like lean teenage greyhounds.

10 p.m. Ugh. Perpetua, slightly senior and therefore thinking she is in charge of me, was at her most obnoxious and bossy, going on and on to the point of utter boredom about latest half-million-pound property she is planning to buy with her rich-but-overbred boyfriend, Hugo: 'Yars, yars, well it *is* north-facing but they've done something frightfully clever with the light.'

I looked at her wistfully, her vast, bulbous bottom swathed in a tight red skirt with a bizarre three-quarter-length striped waistcoat strapped across it. What a blessing to be born with such Sloaney arrogance. Perpetua could be the size of a Renault Espace and not give it a thought. How many hours, months, years, have I spent worrying about weight while Perpetua has been happily looking for lamps with porcelain cats as bases around the Fulham Road? She is missing out on a source of happiness, anyway. It is proved by surveys that happiness does not come from love, wealth or power but the pursuit of attainable goals: and what is a diet if not that?

On way home in end-of-Christmas denial I bought a packet of cut-price chocolate tree decorations and a £3.69 bottle of sparkling wine from Norway, Pakistan or similar. I guzzled them by the light of the Christmas tree, together with a couple of mince pies, the last of the Christmas cake and some Stilton, while watching *EastEnders*, imagining it was a Christmas special.

Now, though, I feel ashamed and repulsive. I can actually feel the fat splurging out from my body. Never mind. Sometimes you have to sink to a nadir of toxic fat envelopment in order to emerge, phoenix-like, from the chemical wasteland as a purged and beautiful Michelle Pfeiffer figure. Tomorrow new Spartan health and beauty regime will begin.

Mmmm. Daniel Cleaver, though. Love his wicked dissolute air, while being v. successful and clever. He was being v. funny today, telling everyone about his aunt thinking the onyx kitchen-roll holder his mother had given her for Christmas was a model of a penis. Was really v. amusing about it. Also asked me if I got anything nice for Christmas in rather flirty way. Think might wear short black skirt tomorrow.

Wednesday 4 January

9st 5 (state of emergency now as if fat has been stored in capsule form over Christmas and is being slowly released under skin), alcohol units 5 (better), cigarettes 20, calories 700 (v.g.).

4 p.m. Office. State of emergency. Jude just rang up from her portable phone in flood of tears, and eventually managed to explain, in a sheep's voice, that she had just had to excuse herself from a board meeting (Jude is Head of Futures at Brightlings) as she was about to burst into tears and was now trapped in the ladies' with Alice Cooper eyes and no make-up bag. Her boyfriend, Vile Richard (self-indulgent commitment phobic), whom she has been seeing on and off for eighteen months, had chucked her for asking him if he wanted to come on holiday with her. Typical, but Jude naturally was blaming it all on herself.

'I'm co-dependent. I asked for too much to satisfy my own neediness rather than need. Oh, if only I could turn back the clock.'

I immediately called Sharon and an emergency summit has been scheduled for 6.30 in Café Rouge. I hope I can get away without bloody Perpetua kicking up.

11 p.m. Strident evening. Sharon immediately launched into her theory on the Richard situation: 'Emotional fuckwittage', which is spreading like wildfire among men over thirty. As women glide from their twenties to thirties, Shazzer argues, the balance of power subtly shifts. Even the most outrageous minxes lose their nerve, wrestling with the first twinges of existential angst: fears of dying alone and being found three weeks later half-eaten by an Alsatian. Stereotypical notions of shelves, spinning wheels and sexual scrapheaps conspire to make you feel stupid, no matter how much time you spend thinking about Joanna Lumley and Susan Sarandon.

'And men like Richard,' fumed Sharon, 'play on the chink in the armour to wriggle out of commitment, maturity, honour and the natural progression of things between a man and a woman.'

By this time Jude and I were going, 'Shhh, shhh,' out of the corners of our mouths and sinking down into our coats. After all, there is nothing so unattractive to a man as strident feminism.

'How dare he say you were getting too serious by asking to go on holiday with him?' yelled Sharon. 'What is he *talking* about?'

Thinking moonily about Daniel Cleaver, I ventured that not all men are like Richard. At which point Sharon started on a long illustrative list of emotional fuckwittage in progress amongst our friends: one whose boyfriend of thirteen years refuses even to discuss living together; another who went out with a man four times who then chucked her because it was getting too serious; another who was pursued by a bloke for three months with impassioned proposals of marriage, only to find him ducking out

20

three weeks after she succumbed and repeating the whole process with her best friend.

'We women are only vulnerable because we are a pioneer generation daring to refuse to compromise in love and relying on our own economic power. In twenty years' time men won't even dare start with fuckwittage because we will just *laugh in their faces*,' bellowed Sharon.

At this point Alex Walker, who works in Sharon's company, strolled in with a stunning blonde who was about eight times as attractive as him. He ambled over to us to say hi.

'Is this your new girlfriend?' asked Sharon.

'Well. Huh. You know, she thinks she is, but we're not going out, we're just sleeping together. I ought to stop it really, but, well . . .' he said, smugly.

'Oh, that is just such crap, you cowardly, dysfunctional little schmuck. Right. I'm going to talk to that woman,' said Sharon, getting up. Jude and I forcibly restrained her while Alex, looking panic-stricken, rushed back, to continue his fuckwittage unrumbled.

Eventually the three of us worked out a strategy for Jude. She must stop beating herself over the head with *Women Who Love Too Much* and instead think more towards *Men are from Mars, Women are from Venus*, which will help her to see Richard's behaviour less as a sign that she is co-dependent and loving too much and more in the light of him being like a Martian rubber band which needs to stretch away in order to come back.

'Yes, but does that mean I should call him or not?' said Jude.

'No,' said Sharon, just as I was saying, 'Yes.'

After Jude had gone – because she has to get up at 5.45 to go to the gym and see her personal shopper before work starts at 8.30 (mad) – Sharon and I were suddenly filled with remorse and self-loathing for not advising Jude simply to get rid of Vile Richard because he is vile. But then, as Sharon pointed out, last time we did that they got back together and she told him everything we'd said in a fit of reconciliatory confession and now it is cripplingly embarrassing every time we see him and he thinks we are the Bitch Queens from Hell – which, as Jude points out, is a misapprehension because, although we have discovered our Inner Bitches, we have not yet unlocked them.

Thursday 5 January

9st 3 (excellent progress – 2lb of fat spontaneously combusted through joy and sexual promise), alcohol units 6 (v.g. for party), cigarettes 12 (continuing good work), calories 1258 (love has eradicated need to pig out).

11 a.m. Office. Oh my God. Daniel Cleaver just sent me a message. Was trying to work on CV without Perpetua noticing (in preparation for improving career) when **Message Pending** suddenly flashed up on top of screen. Delighted by, well, anything – as always am if is not work – I quickly pressed **RMS Execute** and nearly jumped out of my skin when I saw **Cleave** at the bottom of the message. I instantly thought he had been able to tap into the computer and see that I was not getting on with my work. But then I read the message:

```
Message Jones
You appear to have forgotten your skirt. As
I think is made perfectly clear in your
contract of employment, staff are expected
to be fully dressed at all times.
Cleave
```

Hah! Undeniably flirtatious. Thought for a little while whilst pretending to study tedious-beyond-belief manuscript from lunatic. Have never messaged Daniel Cleaver before but brilliant thing about messaging system is you can be really quite cheeky and informal, even to your boss. Also can spend ages practising. This is what sent.

```
Message Cleave
Sir, am appalled by message. Whilst skirt
could reasonably be described as a little
on the skimpy side (thrift being ever our
watchword in editorial), consider it gross
misrepresentation to describe said skirt as
absent, and considering contacting union.
Jones
```

Waited in frenzy of excitement for reply. Sure enough. **Message Pending** quickly flashed up. Pressed RMS:

```
Will whoever has thoughtlessly removed the
edited script of KAFKA'S MOTORBIKE from my
desk PLEASE have the decency to return it
immediately.
Diane
```

Aargh. After that: zilch.

Noon. Oh God. Daniel has not replied. Must be furious. Maybe he was being serious about the skirt. Oh God oh

God. Have been seduced by informality of messaging medium into being impertinent to boss.

12.10. Maybe he has not got it yet. If only could get message back. Think will go for walk and see if can somehow go into Daniel's office and erase it.

12.15. Hah. All explained. He is in meeting with Simon from Marketing. He gave me a look when walked past. Aha. Ahahahaha. `Message Pending`:

```
Message Jones
If walking past office was attempt to
demonstrate presence of skirt can only say
that it has failed parlously. Skirt is
indisputably absent. Is skirt off sick?
Cleave
```

`Message Pending` then flashed up again – immediately.

```
Message Jones
If skirt is indeed sick, please look into how
many days sick leave skirt has taken in prev-
ious twelvemonth. Spasmodic nature of recent
skirt attendance suggests malingering.
Cleave
```

Just sending back:

```
Message Cleave
Skirt is demonstrably neither sick nor
abscent. Appalled by management's
blatently sizist attitude to skirt.
Obsessive interest in skirt suggests
management sick rather than skirt.
Jones
```

Hmm. Think will cross last bit out as contains mild accusation of sexual harassment whereas v. much enjoying being sexually harassed by Daniel Cleaver.

Aaargh. Perpetua just walked past and started reading over shoulder. Just managed to press `Alt Screen` in nick of time but big mistake as merely put CV back up on screen.

'Do let me know when you've finished reading, won't you?' said Perpetua, with a nasty smirk. 'I'd hate to feel you were being *underused*.'

The second she was safely back on the phone – 'I mean frankly, Mr Birkett, what *is* the point in putting three to four bedrooms when it is going to be obvious the second we appear that bedroom four is an airing cupboard?' – I got back to work. This is what I am about to send.

```
Message Cleave
Skirt is demonstrably neither sick nor
abscent. Appalled by management's
blatantly sizist attitude to skirt.
Considering appeal to industrial tribunal,
tabloids, etc.
Jones.
```

Oh dear. This was return message.

```
Message Jones
Absent, Jones, not abscent. Blatantly, not
blatantly. Please attempt to acquire at
least perfunctory grasp of spelling. Though
by no means trying to suggest language fixed
rather than constantly adapting, fluctuat-
ing tool of communication (cf Hoenigswald)
computer spell check might help.
Cleave
```

Was just feeling crestfallen when Daniel walked past with Simon from Marketing and shot a very sexy look at my skirt with one eyebrow raised. Love the lovely computer messaging. Must work on spelling, though. After all, have degree in English.

Friday 6 January

5.45 p.m. Could not be more joyous. Computer messaging re: presence or otherwise of skirt continued obsessively all afternoon. Cannot imagine respected boss did stroke of work. Weird scenario with Perpetua (penultimate boss), since knew I was messaging and v. angry, but fact that was messaging ultimate boss gave self conflicting feelings of loyalty – distinctly un-level playing field where anyone with ounce of sense would say ultimate boss should hold sway.

Last message read:

```
Message Jones
Wish to send bouquet to ailing skirt over
weekend. Please supply home contact no asap
as cannot, for obvious reasons, rely on
given spelling of 'Jones' to search in file.
Cleave
```

Yesssss! Yessssss! Daniel Cleaver wants my phone no. Am marvellous. Am irresistible Sex Goddess. Hurrah!

Sunday 8 January

9st 2 (v. bloody g. but what is point?), alcohol units 2 (excellent), cigarettes 7, calories 3100 (poor).

2 p.m. Oh God, why am I so unattractive? Cannot believe I convinced myself I was keeping the entire weekend free to work when in fact I was on permanent date-with-Daniel standby. Hideous, wasted two days glaring psychopathically at the phone, and eating things. Why hasn't he rung? Why? What's wrong with me? Why ask for my phone number if he wasn't going to ring, and if he was going to ring surely he would do it over the weekend? Must centre myself more. Will ask Jude about appropriate self-help book, possible Eastern-religion-based.

8 p.m. Phone call alert, which turned out to be just Tom, asking if there was any telephonic progress. Tom, who has taken, unflatteringly, to calling himself a hag-fag, has been sweetly supportive about the Daniel crisis. Tom has a theory that homosexuals and single women in their thirties have natural bonding: both being accustomed to disappointing their parents and being treated as freaks by society. He indulged me while I obsessed to him about my unattractiveness crisis – precipitated, as I told him, first by bloody Mark Darcy then by bloody Daniel at which point he said, I must say not particularly helpfully, 'Mark Darcy? But isn't he that famous lawyer – the human-rights guy?'

Hmmm. Well, anyway. What about my human right not to have to wander round with fearsome unattractiveness hang-up?

11 p.m. It is far too late for Daniel to ring. V. sad and traumatized.

Monday 9 January

9st 2, alcohol units 4, cigarettes 29, calories 770 (v.g. but at what price?).

Nightmare day in office. Watched the door for Daniel all morning: nothing. By 11.45 a.m. I was seriously alarmed. Should I raise an alert?

Then Perpetua suddenly bellowed into the phone: 'Daniel? He's gone to a meeting in Croydon. He'll be in tomorrow.' She banged the phone down and said, 'God, all these bloody girls ringing him up.'

Panic stricken, I reached for the Silk Cut. Which girls? What? Somehow I made it through the day, got home, and in a moment of insanity left a message on Daniel's answer-phone, saying (oh no, I can't believe I did this), 'Hi, it's Jones here. I was just wondering how you are and if you wanted to meet for the skirt-health summit, like you said.'

The second I put the phone down I realized it was an emergency and rang Tom, who calmly said leave it to him: if he made several calls to the machine he could find the code which would let him play back and erase the message. Eventually he thought he'd cracked it, but unfortunately Daniel then answered the phone. Instead of saying, 'Sorry, wrong number,' Tom hung up. So now Daniel not only has the insane message but will think it's me who's rung his answerphone fourteen times this evening and then, when I did get hold of him, banged the phone down.

9st 1, alcohol units 2, cigarettes 0, calories 998 (excellent, v.g., perfect saint-style person).

Slunk into the office crippled with embarrassment about the message. I had resolved totally to detach myself from Daniel but then he appeared looking unnervingly sexy and started making everyone laugh so that I went all to pieces.

Suddenly, `Message Pending` flashed up on the top of my computer screen.

```
Message Jones
Thanks for your phone call.
Cleave.
```

My heart sank. That phone call was suggesting a date. Who replies by saying 'thanks' and leaves it at that unless they . . . but after a little thought, I sent back:

```
Message Cleave
Please shut up. I am very busy and
important.
Jones.
```

And after a few minutes more, he replied.

```
Message Jones
Sorry to interrupt, Jones, pressure must be
hellish. Over and out.
PS. I like your tits in that top.
Cleave
```

. . . And we were off. Frantic messaging continued all

week, culminating in him suggesting a date for Sunday night and me dizzyingly, euphorically, accepting. Sometimes I look around the office as we all tap away and wonder if anyone is doing any work at all.

(Is it just me or is Sunday a bizarre night for a first date? All wrong, like Saturday morning or Monday at 2 p.m.)

Sunday 15 January

9st (excellent), alcohol units 0, cigarettes 29 (v.v. bad, esp. in 2 hours), calories 3879 (repulsive), negative thoughts 942 (approx. based on av. per minute), minutes spent counting negative thoughts 127 (approx.).

6 p.m. Completely exhausted by entire day of date-preparation. Being a woman is worse than being a farmer – there is so much harvesting and crop spraying to be done: legs to be waxed, underarms shaved, eyebrows plucked, feet pumiced, skin exfoliated and moisturized, spots cleansed, roots dyed, eyelashes tinted, nails filed, cellulite massaged, stomach muscles exercised. The whole performance is so highly tuned you only need to neglect it for a few days for the whole thing to go to seed. Sometimes I wonder what I would be like if left to revert to nature – with a full beard and handlebar moustache on each shin, Dennis Healey eyebrows, face a graveyard of dead skin cells, spots erupting, long curly fingernails like Struwelpeter, blind as bat and stupid runt of species as no contact lenses, flabby body flobbering around. Ugh, ugh. Is it any wonder girls have no confidence?

7 p.m. Cannot believe this has happened. On the way to the bathroom, to complete final farming touches, I noticed the answerphone light was flashing: Daniel.

'Look, Jones. I'm really sorry. I think I'm going to have to give tonight a miss. I've got a presentation at ten in the morning and a pile of forty-five spreadsheets to get through.'

Cannot believe it. Am stood up. Entire waste of whole day's bloody effort and hydro-electric body-generated power. However, one must not live one's life through men but must be complete in oneself as a woman of substance.

9 p.m. Still, he is in top-level job. Maybe he didn't want to ruin first date with underlying work-panic.

11 p.m. Humph. He might have bloody well rung again, though. Is probably out with someone thinner.

5 a.m. What's wrong with me? I'm completely alone. Hate Daniel Cleaver. Am going to have nothing more to do with him. Am going to get weighed.

Monday 16 January

9 st 2 (from where? why? why?), alcohol units 0, cigarettes 20, calories 1500, positive thoughts 0.

10.30 a.m. Office. Daniel is still locked in his meeting. Maybe it *was* a genuine excuse.

1 p.m. Just saw Daniel leaving for lunch. He has not messaged me or anything. V. depressed. Going shopping.

11.50 p.m. Just had dinner with Tom in Harvey Nichols Fifth Floor, who was obsessing about a pretentious-sounding 'freelance film maker' called Jerome. Moaned to him about Daniel, who was in meetings all afternoon and only managed to say, 'Hi, Jones, how's the skirt?' at 4.30. Tom said not to be paranoid, give it time, but I could tell he was not concentrating and only wanted to talk about Jerome as suffused with sex-lust.

Tuesday 24 January

Heaven-sent day. At 5.30, like a gift from God, Daniel appeared, sat himself on the edge of my desk, with his back to Perpetua, took out his diary and murmured, 'How are you fixed for Friday?'

Yessssss! Yessssss!

Friday 27 January

9st 3 (but stuffed with Genoan food), alcohol units 8, cigarettes 400 (feels like), calories 875.

Huh. Had dream date at an *intime* little Genoan restaurant near Daniel's flat.

'Um . . . right. I'll get a taxi,' I blurted awkwardly as we stood in the street afterwards. Then he lightly brushed a hair from my forehead, took my cheek in his hand and kissed me, urgently, desperately. After a while he held me hard against him and whispered throatily, 'I don't think you'll be needing that taxi, Jones.'

The second we were inside his flat we fell upon each other like beasts: shoes, jackets, strewn in a trail across the room.

'I don't think this skirt's looking at all well,' he murmured. 'I think it should lie down on the floor.' As he started to undo the zip he whispered, 'This is just a bit of fun, OK? I don't think we should start getting involved.' Then, caveat in place, he carried on with the zip. Had it not been for Sharon and the fuckwittage and the fact I'd just drunk the best part of a bottle of wine, I think I would have sunk powerless into his arms. As it was, I leapt to my feet, pulling up my skirt.

'That is just such crap,' I slurred. 'How dare you be so fraudulently flirtatious, cowardly and dysfunctional? I am not interested in emotional fuckwittage. Goodbye.'

It was great. You should have seen his face. But now I am home I am sunk into gloom. I may have been right, but my reward, I know, will be to end up all alone, half-eaten by an Alsatian.

FEBRUARY

Valentine's Day Massacre

Wednesday 1 February

9st, alcohol units 9, cigarettes 28 (but will soon give up for Lent so might as well smoke self into disgusted smoking frenzy), calories 3826.

Spent the weekend struggling to remain disdainfully buoyant after the Daniel fuckwittage débâcle. I kept saying the words, 'Self-respect' and 'Huh' over and over till I was dizzy, trying to barrage out, 'But I lurrrve him.' Smoking was v. bad. Apparently there is a Martin Amis character who is so crazily addicted that he starts wanting a cigarette even when he's smoking one. That's me. It was good ringing up Sharon to boast about being Mrs Iron Knickers but when I rang Tom he saw straight through it and said, 'Oh, my poor darling,' which made me go silent trying not to burst into self-pitying tears.

'You watch,' warned Tom. 'He'll be gagging for it now. Gagging.'

'No, he won't,' I said sadly. 'I've blown it.'

On Sunday went for huge, lard-smeared lunch at my parents'. Mother is bright orange and more opinionated than ever, having just returned from week in Albufeira with Una Alconbury and Nigel Coles' wife, Audrey.

Mum had been to church and suddenly realized in a St Paul-on-road-to-Damascus-type blinding flash that the vicar is gay.

'It's just laziness, darling,' was her view on the whole homosexuality issue. 'They simply can't be bothered to relate to the opposite sex. Look at your Tom. I really think if that boy had anything about him he'd be going out with you properly instead of all this ridiculous, "friends" nonsense.'

'Mother,' I said. 'Tom has known he was a homosexual since he was ten.'

'Oh, darling! Honestly! You know how people get these silly ideas. You can always talk them out of it.'

'Does that mean if I talked to you really persuasively you'd leave Dad and start an affair with Auntie Audrey?'

'Now you're just being silly, darling,' she said.

'Exactly,' Dad joined in. 'Auntie Audrey looks like a kettle.'

'Oh, for heaven's sake, Colin,' Mum snapped, which struck me as odd as she doesn't usually snap at Dad.

My dad, somewhat bizarrely, insisted on giving my car a full service before I left, even though I assured him there was nothing wrong with it. I rather showed myself up by not remembering how to open the bonnet.

'Have you noticed anything odd about your mother?' he said in a stiff, embarrassed way as he fiddled around with the oil stick, wiping it with rags and plunging it back in a not unworrying manner, if one were a Freudian. Which I am not.

'You mean apart from being bright orange?' I said.

'Well yes, and ... well, you know, the usual, er *qualities*.'

'She did seem unusually aerated about homosexuality.'

'Oh no, that was just the Vicar's new vestments which set her off this morning. They *were* a little on the frou-frou side, to tell the truth. He's just come back from a trip to Rome with the Abbot of Dumfries. Dressed from head to toe in rose pink. No, I mean did you notice anything different from *usual* about Mummy?'

I racked my brains. 'I can't say I did, to be honest, other than seeming very sort of blooming and confident.'

'Hmmm,' he said. 'Anyway. Best get off before it gets dark. Send my love to Jude. How's she doing?'

Then he hit the bonnet in an off-you-go sort of way – but so hard that I had a feeling he might have broken his hand.

Thought all would be resolved with Daniel on Monday but he wasn't there. Nor yesterday. Work has become like going to a party in order to get off with someone and finding they haven't turned up. Worried about own ambition, career prospects and moral seriousness as seem to reduce everything to level of scout disco. Eventually managed to worm out of Perpetua that Daniel has gone to New York. He will clearly by now have got off with thin American cool person called Winona who puts out, carries a gun and is everything I am not.

On top of everything else, must go to Smug Married dinner party at Magda and Jeremy's tonight. Such occasions always reduce my ego to size of snail, which is not to say am not grateful to be asked. I love Magda and Jeremy. Sometimes I stay at their house, admiring the crisp sheets and many storage jars full of different kinds of pasta, imagining that they are my parents. But when they are together with their married friends I feel as if I have turned into Miss Havisham.

11.45 p.m. Oh God. It was me, four married couples and Jeremy's brother (forget it, red braces and face. Calls girls 'fillies').

'So,' bellowed Cosmo, pouring me a drink. 'How's your love-life?'

Oh no. Why do they do this? Why? Maybe the Smug Marrieds only mix with other Smug Marrieds and don't known how to relate to individuals any more. Maybe they really do want to patronize us and make us feel like failed human beings. Or maybe they are in such a sexual rut they're thinking, 'There's a whole other world out there,' and hoping for vicarious thrills by getting us to tell them the roller-coaster details of our sex lives.

'Yes, why aren't you married yet, Bridget?' sneered Woney (babytalk for Fiona, married to Jeremy's friend Cosmo) with a thin veneer of concern whilst stroking her pregnant stomach.

Because I don't want to end up like you, you fat, boring, Sloaney milch cow, was what I should have said, or, *Because if I had to cook Cosmo's dinner then get into the same bed as him just once, let alone every night, I'd tear off my own head and eat it*, or, *Because actually, Woney, underneath my clothes, my entire body is covered in scales*. But I didn't because, ironically enough, I didn't want to hurt her feelings. So I merely simpered apologetically, at which point someone called Alex piped up, 'Well, you know, once you get past a certain age . . .'

'Exactly . . . All the decent chaps have been snapped up,'

said Cosmo, slapping his fat stomach and smirking so that his jowls wobbled.

At dinner Magda had placed me, in an incestuous-sex-sandwich sort of way, between Cosmo and Jeremy's crashing bore of a brother. 'You really ought to hurry up and get sprogged up, you know, old girl,' said Cosmo, pouring a quarter of a pint of '82 Pauillac straight down his throat. 'Time's running out.'

By this time I'd had a good half-pint of '82 Pauillac myself. 'Is it one in three marriages that end in divorce now or one in two?' I slurred with a pointless attempt at sarcasm.

'Seriously, old girl,' he said, ignoring me. 'Office is full of them, single girls over thirty. Fine physical specimens. Can't get a chap.'

'That's not a problem I have, actually,' I breathed, waving my fag in the air.

'Ooh. Tell us more,' said Woney.

'So who is it, then?' said Cosmo.

'Getting a bit of a shag, old girl?' said Jeremy. All eyes turned to me, beadily. Mouths open, slavering.

'It's none of your business,' I said hoity-toitily.

'So she hasn't got a man!' crowed Cosmo.

'Oh my God, it's eleven o'clock,' shrieked Woney. 'The babysitter!' and they all leapt to their feet and started getting ready to go home.

'God, sorry about that lot. Will you be OK, hon?' whispered Magda, who knew how I was feeling.

'Want a lift or anything?' said Jeremy's brother, following it up with a belch.

'Actually, I'm going on to a nightclub.' I trilled, hurrying out into the street. 'Thanks for a super evening!'

Then I got into a taxi and burst into tears.

Midnight. Har har. Just called Sharon.

'You should have said "I'm not married because I'm a *Singleton*, you smug, prematurely ageing, narrow-minded morons,"' Shazzer ranted. '"And because there's more than one bloody way to live: one in four households are single, most of the royal family are single, the nation's young men have been proved by surveys to be *completely unmar-riageable*, and as a result there's a whole generation of single girls like me with their own incomes and homes who have lots of fun and don't need to wash anyone else's socks. We'd be as happy as sandboys if people like you didn't conspire to make us feel stupid just because you're jealous."'

'Singletons!' I shouted happily. 'Hurrah for the Singletons!'

Sunday 5 February

Still no word from Daniel. Cannot face thought of entire Sunday stretching ahead with everyone else in the world except me in bed with someone giggling and having sex. Worst of it is, only a week and a bit to go till impending Valentine's Day humiliation. No way will I get any cards. Toy with idea of flirting energetically with anyone I think might be induced to send me one, but dismiss as immoral. Will just have to take total indignity on the chin.

Hmm. I know. Think I'll go and see Mum and Dad again as am worried about Dad. Then will feel like caring angel or saint.

2 p.m. The last remaining tiny bathmat of security has been pulled from under my feet. Magnanimous offer to pay caring surprise visit met by odd-sounding Dad on end of phone.

'Er . . . I'm not sure, dear. Could you hang on?'

I reeled. Part of the arrogance of youth (well, I say 'youth') is the assumption that your parents will drop whatever they are doing and welcome you with open arms the second you decide to turn up. He was back. 'Bridget, look, your mother and I are having some problems. Can we ring you later in the week?'

Problems? What problems? I tried to get Dad to explain but got nowhere. What is going on? Is the whole world doomed to emotional trauma? Poor Dad. Am I to be the tragic victim of a broken home now, on top of everything else?

Monday 6 February

8st 12 (heavy internal weight completely vanished – mystery), alcohol units 1 (v.g.), cigarettes 9 (v.g.), calories 1800 (g.).

Daniel will be back in the office today. I shall be poised and cool and remember that I am a woman of substance and do not need men in order to be complete, especially not him. Am not going to message him or indeed take any notice of him whatsoever.

9.30 a.m. Humph. Daniel does not seem to be here yet.

9.35 a.m. Still no sign of Daniel.

9.36 a.m. Oh God, oh God. Maybe he's fallen in love in New York and stayed there.

9.47 a.m. Or gone to Las Vegas and got married.

9.50 a.m. Hmmm. think will go inspect make-up in case he does come in.

10.05 a.m. Heart gave great lurch when got back from loos and saw Daniel standing with Simon from Marketing at the photocopier. The last time I saw him he was lying on his sofa looking completely nonplussed while I fastened my skirt and ranted about fuckwittage. Now he was looking all sort of 'I've been away' – fresh faced and healthy-looking. As I passed he looked pointedly at my skirt and gave me a huge grin.

10.30 a.m. Message Pending flashed up on screen. Pressed RMS to pick up message.

Message Jones
Frigid cow.
Cleave.

I laughed. I couldn't help myself. When I looked across to his little glass office he was smiling at me in a relieved and fond sort of way. Anyway, am not going to message him back.

10.35 a.m. Seems rude not to reply, though.

10.45 a.m. God, I'm bored.

10.47 a.m. I'll just send him a tiny friendly message, nothing flirtatious, just to restore good relations.

11.00 a.m. Tee hee. Just logged on as Perpetua to give Daniel a fright.

> Message Cleave
> It is hard enough as it is, trying to meet
> your targets without people wasting my
> team's time with non-essential messages.
> Perpetua
> P.S. Bridget's skirt is not feeling at all
> well and have sent it home.

10 p.m. Mmmm. Daniel and I messaged each other all day. But there is no way I am going to sleep with him.

Rang Mum and Dad again tonight but no one answered. V. weird.

Thursday 9 February

9st 2 (extra fat presumably caused by winter whale blubber), alcohol units 4, cigarettes 12 (v.g.), calories 2845 (v. cold).

9 p.m. V. much enjoying the Winter Wonderland and reminder that we are at the mercy of the elements, and should not concentrate so hard on being sophisticated or hardworking but on staying warm and watching the telly.

This is the third time I have called Mum and Dad this week and got no reply. Maybe The Gables has been cut off by the snow? In desperation, I pick up the phone and dial my brother Jamie's number in Manchester, only to get one of his hilarious answerphone messages: the sound of running water and Jamie pretending to be President Clinton in the White House, then a toilet flushing and his pathetic girlfriend tittering in the background.

9.15 p.m. Just called Mum and Dad three times in a row, letting it ring twenty times each time. Eventually Mum picked it up sounding odd and saying she couldn't talk now but would call me at the weekend.

Saturday 11 February

8st 13, alcohol units 4, cigarettes 18, calories 1467 (but burnt off by shopping).

Just got home from shopping to message from my dad asking if I would meet him for lunch on Sunday. I went hot and cold. My dad does not come up to London to have lunch with me on his own on Sundays. He has roast beef, or salmon and new potatoes, at home with Mum.

'Don't ring back,' the message said. 'I'll just see you tomorrow.'

What's going on? I went round the corner, shaking, for some Silk Cut. Got back to find message from Mum. She too is coming to see me for lunch tomorrow, apparently. She'll bring a piece of salmon with her, and will be here about 1 o'clock.

Rang Jamie again and got 20 seconds of Bruce Springsteen and then Jamie growling, 'Baby, I was born to run . . . out of time on the answerphone.'

8st 13, alcohol units 5, cigarettes 23 (hardly surprising), calories 1647.

11 a.m. Oh God, I can't have them both arriving at the same time. It is too Brian Rix for words. Maybe the whole lunch thing is just a parental practical joke brought on by over-exposure of my parents to Noel Edmonds, popular television and similar. Perhaps my mother will arrive with a live salmon flipping skittishly on a lead and announce that she is leaving Dad for it. Maybe Dad will appear hanging upside-down outside the window dressed as a Morris dancer, crash in and start hitting Mum over the head with a sheep's bladder; or suddenly fall face downwards out of the airing cupboard with a plastic knife stuck in his back. The only thing which can possibly get everything back on course is a Bloody Mary. It's nearly the afternoon, after all.

12.05 p.m. Mum called. 'Let *him* come, then,' she said. 'Let him bloody well have his own way as usual.' (My mum does not swear. She says things like 'ruddy' and 'Oh my godfathers'.) 'I'll be all right on my bloody own. I'll just clean the house like Germaine sodding Greer and the Invisible Woman.' (Could she possibly, conceivably, have been drunk? My mum has drunk nothing but a single cream sherry on a Sunday night since 1952, when she got slightly tipsy on a pint of cider at Mavis Enderby's twenty-first and has never let herself or anyone else forget it. 'There's nothing worse than a woman drunk, darling.')

'Mum. No. Couldn't we all talk this through together over lunch?' I said, as if this were *Sleepless in Seattle* and lunch was going to end up with Mum and Dad holding hands and me winking cutely at the camera, wearing a luminous rucksack.

'Just you wait,' she said darkly. 'You'll find out what men are like.'

'But I already . . .' I began.

'I'm going out, darling,' she said. 'I'm going out to get *laid.*'

At 2 o'clock Dad arrived at the door with a neatly folded copy of the *Sunday Telegraph*. As he sat down on the sofa, his face crumpled and tears began to splosh down his cheeks.

'She's been like this since she went to Albufeira with Una Alconbury and Audrey Coles,' he sobbed, trying to wipe his cheek with his fist. 'When she got back she started saying she wanted to be paid for doing the housework, and she'd wasted her life being our slave.' (*Our* slave? I knew it. This is all my fault. If I were a better person, Mum would not have stopped loving Dad.) 'She wants me to move out for a while, she says, and . . . and . . .' He collapsed in quiet sobs.

'And what, Dad?'

'She said I thought the clitoris was something from Nigel Coles's lepidoptery collection.'

Monday 13 February

9st 1, alcohol units 5, cigarettes 0 (spiritual enrichment removes need to smoke – massive breakthrough), calories 2845.

Though heartbroken by my parents' distress, I have to admit parallel and shameful feeling of smugness over my new role as carer and, though I say it myself, wise counsellor. It is so long since I have done anything at all for anyone else that it is a totally new and heady sensation. This is what has been missing in my life. I am having fantasies about becoming a Samaritan or Sunday school teacher, making soup for the homeless (or, as my friend Tom suggested, darling mini-bruschettas with pesto sauce), or even retraining as a doctor. Maybe going out with a doctor would be better still, both sexually and spiritually fulfilling. I even began to wonder about putting an ad in the lonely hearts column of the *Lancet*. I could take his messages, tell patients wanting night visits to bugger off, cook him little goats cheese soufflés, then end up in a foul mood with him when I am sixty, like Mum.

Oh God. Valentine's Day tomorrow. Why? Why? Why is entire world geared to make people not involved in romance feel stupid when everyone knows romance does not work anyway. Look at royal family. Look at Mum and Dad.

Valentine's Day purely commercial, cynical enterprise, anyway. Matter of supreme indifference to me.

Tuesday 14 February

9st, alcohol units 2 (romantic Valentine's Day treat – 2 bottles Becks, on own, huh), cigarettes 12, calories 1545.

8 a.m. Oooh, goody. Valentine's Day. Wonder if the post has come yet. Maybe there will be a card from Daniel. Or a secret admirer. Or some flowers or heart-shaped chocolates. Quite excited, actually.

Brief moment of wild joy when discovered bunch of roses in the hallway. Daniel! Rushed down and gleefully picked them up just as the downstairs-flat door opened and Vanessa came out.

'Ooh, they look nice,' she said enviously. 'Who are they from?'

'I don't know!' I said coyly, glancing down at the card. 'Ah . . .' I tailed off. 'They're for you.'

'Never mind. Look, this is for you,' said Vanessa, encouragingly. It was an Access bill.

Decided to have cappuccino and chocolate croissants on way to work to cheer self up. Do not care about figure. Is no point as no one loves or cares about me.

On the way in on the tube you could see who had had Valentine cards and who hadn't. Everyone was looking round trying to catch each other's eye and either smirking or looking away defensively.

Got into the office to find Perpetua had a bunch of flowers the size of a sheep on her desk.

'Well, Bridget!' she bellowed so that everyone could hear. 'How many did you get?'

I slumped into my seat muttering, 'Shud-urrrrrrp,' out of the side of my mouth like a humiliated teenager.

'Come on! How many?'

I thought she was going to get hold of my earlobe and start twisting it or something.

'The whole thing is ridiculous and meaningless. Complete commercial exploitation.'

'I *knew* you didn't get any,' crowed Perpetua. It was only then that I noticed Daniel was listening to us across the room and laughing.

Wednesday 15 February

Unexpected surprise. Was just leaving flat for work when noticed there was a pink envelope on the table – obviously a late Valentine – which said, 'To the Dusky Beauty'. For a moment I was excited, imagining it was for me and suddenly seeing myself as a dark, mysterious object of desire to men out in the street. Then I remembered bloody Vanessa and her slinky dark bob. Humph.

9 p.m. Just got back and card is still there.

10 p.m. Still there.

11 p.m. Unbelievable. The card is still there. Maybe Vanessa hasn't got back yet.

Thursday 16 February

8st 12 (weight loss through use of stairs), alcohol units 0 (excellent), cigarettes 5 (excellent), calories 2452 (not v.g.), times gone down stairs to check for Valentine-type envelope 18 (bad psychologically but v.g. exercise-wise).

The card is still there! Obviously it is like eating the last Milk Tray or taking the last slice of cake. We are both too polite to take it.

Friday 17 February

8st 12, alcohol units 1 (v.g.), cigarettes 2 (v.g.), calories 3241 (bad but burnt off by stairs), checks on card 12 (obsessive).

9 a.m. Card is still there.

9 p.m. Still there.

9.30 p.m. Still there. Could stand it no longer. Could tell Vanessa was in as cooking smells emanating from flat, so knocked on door. 'I think this must be for you,' I said, holding out the card as she opened the door.

'Oh, I thought it must be for you,' she said.

'Shall we open it?' I said.

'OK.' I handed it to her, she gave it back to me, giggling. I gave it back to her. I love girls.

'Go on,' I said, and she slit open the envelope with the kitchen knife she was holding. It was rather an arty card – as if it might have been bought in an art gallery.

She pulled a face.

'Means nothing to me,' she said, holding out the card.

Inside it said, 'A piece of ridiculous and meaningless commercial exploitation – for my darling little frigid cow.'

I let out a high-pitched noise.

10 p.m. Just called Sharon and recounted whole thing to her. She said I should not allow my head to be turned by a cheap card and should lay off Daniel as he is not a very nice person and no good will come of it.

Called Tom for second opinion, particularly on whether I should call Daniel over the weekend. '*Noooooooo*!' he yelled. He asked me various probing questions: for example, what Daniel's behaviour had been like over the last few days when, having sent the card, he had had no response from me. I reported that he had seemed flirtier than usual. Tom's prescription was wait till next week and remain aloof.

Saturday 18 February

9st, alcohol units 4, cigarettes 6, calories 2746, correct lottery numbers 2 (v.g.).

At last I got to the bottom of Mum and Dad. I was beginning to suspect a post-Portuguese-holiday Shirley-Valentine-style scenario and that I would open the *Sunday People* to see my mother sporting dyed blonde hair and a leopardskin top sitting on a sofa with someone in stone-washed jeans called Gonzales and explaining that, if you really love someone, a forty-six-year age gap really doesn't matter.

Today she asked me to meet her for lunch at the coffee place in Dickens and Jones and I asked her outright if she was seeing someone else.

'No. There is no one else,' she said, staring into the distance with a look of melancholy bravery I swear she has copied from Princess Diana.

'So why are you being so mean to Dad?' I said.

'Darling, it's merely a question of realizing, when your father retired, that I had spent thirty-five years without a break running his home and bringing up his children—'

'Jamie and I are your children too,' I interjected, hurt.

'—and that as far as he was concerned his lifetime's work was over and mine was still carrying on, which is exactly how I used to feel when you were little and it got to the weekends. You only get one life. I've just made a decision to change things a bit and spend what's left of mine looking after me for a change.'

As I went to the till to pay, I was thinking it all over and trying, as a feminist, to see Mum's point of view. Then my eye was caught by a tall, distinguished-looking man with grey hair, a European-style leather jacket and one of those gentleman's handbag things. He was looking into the café, tapping his watch and raising his eyebrows. I wheeled round and caught my mother mouthing, 'Won't be a mo,' and nodding towards me apologetically.

I didn't say anything to Mum at the time, just said goodbye, then doubled back and followed her to make sure I wasn't imagining things. Sure enough, I eventually found her in the perfume department wandering round with the tall smoothie, spraying her wrists with everything in sight, holding them up to his face and laughing coquettishly.

Got home to answerphone message from my brother Jamie. Called him straight away and told him everything.

'Oh, for God's sake, Bridge,' he said, roaring with laughter. 'You're so obsessed with sex if you saw Mum taking communion you'd think she was giving the Vicar a blow-job. Get any Valentines this year, did you?'

'Actually, yes,' I breathed crossly. At which he burst out laughing again, then said he had to go because he and Becca were off to do Tai Chi in the park.

Sunday 19 February

8st 13 (v.g. but purely through worry), alcohol units 2 (but the Lord's Day), cigarettes 7, calories 2100.

Called Mum up to confront her about the late-in-life smoothie I saw her with after our lunch.

'Oh, you must mean Julian,' she trilled.

This was an immediate giveaway. My parents do not describe their friends by their Christian names. It is always Una Alconbury, Audrey Coles, Brian Enderby: 'You know David Ricketts, darling – married to Anthea Ricketts, who's in the Lifeboat.' It's a gesture to the fact that they know in their hearts I have no idea who Mavis Enderby is, even though they're going to talk about Brian and Mavis Enderby for the next forty minutes as if I've known them intimately since I was four.

I knew straight away that Julian would not turn out to be involved in any Lifeboat luncheons, nor would he have a wife who was in any Lifeboats, Rotaries or Friends of St George's. I sensed also that she had met him in Portugal, before the trouble with Dad, and he might well turn out to be not so much Julian but Julio. I sensed that, let's face it, Julio *was* the trouble with Dad.

I confronted her with this hunch. She denied it. She even came out with some elaborately concocted tale about 'Julian' bumping into her in the Marble Arch Marks and Spencer, making her drop her new Le Creuset terrine dish on her foot and taking her for a coffee in Selfridges from which sprang a firm platonic friendship based entirely on department store coffee shops.

Why, when people are leaving their partners because

they're having an affair with someone else, do they think it will seem better to pretend there is no one else involved? Do they think it will be less hurtful for their partners to think they just walked out because they couldn't stand them any more and then had the good fortune to meet some tall Omar Sharif-figure with a gentleman's handbag two weeks afterwards while the ex-partner is spending his evenings bursting into tears at the sight of the toothbrush mug? It's like those people who invent a lie as an excuse rather than the truth, even when the truth is better than the lie.

I once heard my friend Simon cancelling a date with a girl – on whom he was really keen – because he had a spot with a yellow head just to the right of his nose, and because, owing to a laundry crisis he had gone to work in a ludicrous late-seventies jacket, assuming he could pick his normal jacket up from the cleaner's at lunchtime, but the cleaners hadn't done it.

He took it into his head, therefore, to tell the girl he couldn't see her because his sister had turned up unexpectedly for the evening and he had to entertain her, adding wildly that he also had to watch some videos for work before the morning; at which point the girl reminded him that he'd told her he didn't have any brothers or sisters and suggested he come and watch the videos at her place while she cooked him supper. However, there were no work videos to take round and watch, so he had to construct a further cobweb of lies. The incident culminated with the girl, convinced he was having an affair with someone else when it was only their second date, chucking him, and Simon spending the evening getting hammered alone with his spot, wearing his seventies jacket.

I tried to explain to Mum that she wasn't telling the truth, but she was so suffused with lust that she had lost sight of, well, everything.

'You're really becoming very cynical and suspicious, darling,' she said. 'Julio' – aha!' ahahahahahaha! – 'is just a friend. I just need some *space*.'

So, it transpired, in order to oblige, Dad is moving into the Alconburys' dead granny's flat at the bottom of their garden.

Tuesday 21 February

V. tired. Dad has taken to ringing up several times in the night, just to talk.

Wednesday 22 February

9st, alcohol units 2, cigarettes 19, fat units 8 (unexpectedly repulsive notion: never before faced reality of lard splurging from bottom and thighs under skin. Must revert to calorie-counting tomorrow).

Tom was completely right. I have been so preoccupied with Mum and Dad, and so tired from taking Dad's distraught phone calls, I have hardly been noticing Daniel at all: with the miraculous result that he has been all over me. I made a complete arse of myself today, though. I got in the lift to go out for a sandwich and found Daniel in there with Simon from Marketing, talking about footballers being arrested for throwing matches. 'Have you heard about this, Bridget?' said Daniel.

'Oh yes,' I lied, groping for an opinion. 'Actually, I think it's all rather petty. I know it's a thuggish way to behave, but as long as they didn't actually set light to anyone I don't see what all the fuss is about.'

Simon looked at me as if I was mad and Daniel stared for a moment and then burst out laughing. He just laughed and laughed till he and Simon got out and then turned back and said, 'Marry me,' as the doors closed between us. Hmmmm.

Thursday 23 February

8st 13 (if only could stay under 9st and not keep bobbing up and down like drowning corpse – drowning in fat), alcohol units 2, cigarettes 17 (pre-shag nerves – understandable), calories 775 (last-ditch attempt to get down to 8st 7 before tomorrow).

8 p.m. Blimey. Computer messaging somehow whipped itself up to fever pitch. At 6 o'clock I resolutely put my coat on and left, only to meet Daniel getting into my lift on the floor below. There we were, just him and me, caught in a massive electrical-charge field, pulled together irresistibly, like a pair of magnets. Then suddenly the lift stopped and we broke apart, panting, as Simon from Marketing got in wearing a hideous beige raincoat over his fat frame. 'Bridget,' he said smirkily, as I involuntarily straightened my skirt, 'you look as if you've been caught throwing matches.'

As I left the building Daniel popped out after me and asked me to have dinner with him tomorrow. Yessss!

Midnight. Ugh. Completely exhausted. Surely it is not normal to be revising for a date as if it were a job interview? Suspect Daniel's enormously well-read brain may turn out to be something of a nuisance if things develop. Maybe I should have fallen for someone younger and mindless who would cook for me, wash all my clothes and agree with everything I say. Since leaving work I have nearly slipped a disc, wheezing through a step aerobics class, scratched my naked body for seven minutes with a stiff brush; cleaned the flat; filled the fridge, plucked my eyebrows, skimmed the papers and the *Ultimate Sex Guide*, put the washing in and waxed my own legs, since it was too late to book an appointment. Ended up kneeling on a towel trying to pull off a wax strip firmly stuck to the back of my calf while watching *Newsnight* in an effort to drum up some interesting opinions about things. My back hurts, my head aches and my legs are bright red and covered in lumps of wax.

Wise people will say Daniel should like me just as I am, but I am a child of *Cosmopolitan* culture, have been traumatized by supermodels and too many quizzes and know that neither my personality nor my body is up to it if left to its own devices. I can't take the pressure. I am going to cancel and spend the evening eating doughnuts in a cardigan with egg on it.

Saturday 25 February

8st 10 (miracle: sex proved indeed to be best form of exercise), alcohol units 0, cigarettes 0, calories 200 (at last have found the secret of not eating: simply replace food with sex).

6 p.m. Oh joy. Have spent the day in a state I can only describe as shag-drunkenness, mooning about the flat, smiling, picking things up and putting them down again. It was so lovely. The only down points were 1) immediately it was over Daniel said, 'Damn. I meant to take the car into the Citroën garage,' and 2) when I got up to go to the bathroom he pointed out that I had a pair of tights stuck to the back of my calf.

But as the rosy clouds begin to disperse, I begin to feel alarm. What now? No plans were made. Suddenly I realize I am waiting for the phone again. How can it be that the situation between the sexes after a first night remains so agonizingly imbalanced? Feel as if I have just sat an exam and must wait for my results.

11 p.m. Oh God. Why hasn't Daniel rung? Are we going out now, or what? How come my mum can slip easily from one relationship to another and I can't even get the simplest thing off the ground. Maybe their generation is just better at getting on with relationships? Maybe they don't mooch about being all paranoid and diffident. Maybe it helps if you've never read a self-help book in your life.

Sunday 26 February

9st, alcohol units 5 (drowning sorrows), cigarettes 23 (fumigating sorrows), calories 3856 (smothering sorrows in fat-duvet).

Awake, alone, to find myself imagining my mother in bed with Julio. Consumed with repulsion at vision of parental, or rather demi-parental sex; outrage on behalf of father; heady, selfish optimism at example of another thirty years of unbridled passion ahead of me (not unrelated to frequent thoughts of Joanna Lumley and Susan Sarandon); but mainly extreme sense of jealousy of failure and foolishness at being in bed alone on Sunday morning while my mother aged over sixty is probably just about to do it for the second . . . Oh my God. No. I can't bear to think about it.

MARCH

Severe Birthday-Related Thirties Panic

Saturday 4 March

9st (what is point of dieting for whole of Feb when end up exactly same weight at start of March as start of Feb? Huh. Am going to stop getting weighed and counting things every day as no sodding point).

My mother has become a force I no longer recognize. She burst into my flat this morning as I sat slumped in my dressing gown, sulkily painting my toenails and watching the preamble to the racing.

'Darling, can I leave these here for a few hours?' she trilled, flinging an armful of carrier bags down and heading for my bedroom.

Minutes later, in a fit of mild curiosity, I slobbed after her to see what she was doing. She was sitting in front of the mirror in an expensive-looking coffee-coloured bra-slip, mascara-ing her eyelashes with her mouth wide open (necessity of open mouth during mascara application great unexplained mystery of nature).

'Don't you think you should get dressed, darling?'

She looked stunning: skin clear, hair shining. I caught sight of myself in the mirror. I really should have taken my make-up off last night. One side of my hair was plastered to my head, the other sticking out in a series of peaks and horns. It is as if the hairs on my head have a life of their own, behaving perfectly sensibly all day, then waiting till I drop off to sleep and starting to run and jump about childishly, saying, 'Now what shall we do?'

'You know,' said Mum, dabbing Givenchy II in her cleavage, 'all these years your father's made such a fuss about doing the bills and the tax – as if that excused him from thirty years of washing-up. Well, the tax return was overdue, so I thought, sod it, I'll do it myself. Obviously I couldn't make head nor tail of it so I rang up the tax office. The man was really quite overbearing with me. "Really, Mrs Jones," he said. "I simply can't see what the difficulty is." I said, "Listen, can *you* make a brioche?" He took the point, talked me through it and we had it done inside fifteen minutes. Anyway, he's taking me out to lunch today. A tax man! Imagine!'

'What?' I stammered, grabbing at the door frame. 'What about Julio?'

'Just because I'm "friends" with Julio doesn't mean I can't have other "friends",' she said sweetly, slipping into a yellow two-piece. 'Do you like this? Just bought it. Super lemon, don't you think? Anyway, must fly. I'm meeting him in Debenhams coffee shop at one fifteen.'

After she'd gone I ate a bit of muesli out of the packet with a spoon and finished off the dregs of wine in the fridge.

I know what her secret is: she's discovered power. She has power over Dad: he wants her back. She has power over Julio, and the tax man, and everyone is sensing her power and wanting a bit of it, which makes her even more irresistible. So all I've got to do is find someone or something to have power over and then . . . oh God. I haven't even got power over my own hair.

I am so depressed. Daniel, though perfectly chatty, friendly, even flirty all week, has given me no hint as to what is going on between us, as though it is perfectly normal to sleep with one of your colleagues and just leave it at that. Work – once merely an annoying nuisance – has become an agonizing torture. I have major trauma every time he disappears for lunch or puts his coat on to go at end of day: to where? with whom? whom?

Perpetua seems to have managed to dump all her work on to me and spends the entire time in full telephonic autowitter to Arabella or Piggy, discussing the half-million-pound Fulham flat she's about to buy with Hugo. 'Yars. No. Yars. No, I *quite* agree. But the question is: does one want to pay another thirty grand for a fourth bedroom?'

At 4.15 on Friday evening Sharon rang me in the office. 'Are you coming out with me and Jude tomorrow?'

'Er . . .' I silently panicked, thinking, *Surely Daniel will ask to see me this weekend before he leaves the office?*

'Call me if he doesn't ask,' said Shazzer drily after a pause.

At 5.45 saw Daniel with his coat on heading out of the door. My traumatized expression must have shamed even him because he smiled shiftily, nodded at the computer screen and shot out.

Sure enough, Message Pending was flashing. I pressed RMS. It said:

Message Jones
Have a good weekend. Pip pip.
Cleave

Miserably, I picked up the phone and dialled Sharon.

'What time are we meeting tomorrow?' I mumbled sheepishly.

'Eight thirty. Café Rouge. Don't worry, we love you. Tell him to bugger off from me. Emotional fuckwit.'

2 a.m. Argor sworeal brilleve with Shazzan Jude. Dun stupid care bout Daniel stupid prat. Feel sicky though. Oops.

Sunday 5 March

8 a.m. Ugh. Wish was dead. Am never, ever going to drink again for the rest of life.

8.30 a.m. Oooh. Could really fancy some chips.

11.30 a.m. Badly need water but seems better to keep eyes closed and head stationary on pillow so as not to disturb bits of machinery and pheasants in head.

Noon. Bloody good fun but v. confused re: advice re: Daniel. Had to go through Jude's problems with Vile Richard first as clearly they are more serious since they have been going out for eighteen months rather than just shagged once. I waited humbly, therefore, till it was my turn to recount the latest Daniel instalment. The unanimous initial verdict was, 'Bastard fuckwittage.'

Interestingly, however, Jude introduced the concept of Boy Time – as introduced in the film *Clueless*: namely five days ('seven', I interjected) during which new relationship is left hanging in air after sex does not seem agonizing lifetime to males of species, but a normal cooling-down period in which to gather emotions, before proceeding. Daniel, argued Jude, was bound to be anxious about work situation, etc., etc., so give him a chance, be friendly and flirty: so as to reassure him that you trust him and are not going to become needy or fly off the handle.

At this Sharon practically spat into the shaved Parmesan and said it was inhuman to leave a woman hanging in air for two weekends after sex and an appalling breach of confidence and I should tell him what I think of him. Hmmm. Anyway. Going to have another little sleep.

2 p.m. Just triumphantly returned from heroic expedition to go downstairs for newspaper and glass of water. Could feel water flowing like crystal stream into section of head where most required. Though am not sure, come to think of it, if water can actually get in your head. Possibly it enters through the bloodstream. Maybe since hangovers are caused by dehydration water is drawn into the brain by a form of capillary action.

2.15 p.m. Story in papers about two-year-olds having to take tests to get into nursery school just made me jump out of skin. Am supposed to be at tea party for godson Harry's birthday.

6 p.m. Drove at breakneck speed feeling like I was dying, across grey, rain-sodden London to Magda's, stopping at Waterstone's for birthday gifts. Heart was sinking at thought of being late and hungover, surrounded by ex-career-girl mothers and their Competitive Child Rearing.

Magda, once a commodity broker, lies about Harry's age, now, to make him seem more advanced than he is. Even the conception was cut-throat, with Magda trying to take eight times as much folic acid and minerals as anyone else. The birth was great. She'd been telling everyone for months it was going to be a natural childbirth and, ten minutes in, she cracked and started yelling, 'Give me the drugs, you fat cow.'

Tea party was nightmare scenario: me plus a roomful of power mothers, one of whom had a four-week-old baby.

'Oh, isn't he *sweet*?' cooed Sarah de Lisle, then snapped, 'How did he do in his APGAR?'

I don't know what the big deal is about tests for two – this APGAR is a test they have to do at two minutes. Magda embarrassed herself two years ago by boasting at a dinner party that Harry got ten in his, at which one of the other guests, who happens to be a nurse, pointed out that the APGAR test only goes up to nine.

Undaunted, however, Magda has started boasting around the nanny circuit that her son is a defecational prodigy, triggering off a round of boast and counter-boast. The toddlers, therefore, clearly at the age when they should be securely swathed in layers of rubberware, were teetering around in little more than Baby Gap G-strings. I hadn't been there ten minutes before there were three turds on the carpet. A superficially humorous but vicious dispute ensued about who had done the turds, followed by a tense stripping off of towelling pants, immediately sparking another contest over the size of the boys' genitals and, correspondingly, the husbands'.

'There's nothing you can do, it's a hereditary thing. Cosmo doesn't have a problem in that area, does he?'

Thought head was going to burst with the racket. Eventually made my excuses and drove home, congratulating myself on being single.

Monday 6 March

11 a.m. Office. Completely exhausted. Last night was just lying in nice hot bath with some Geranium essential oil and a vodka and tonic when the doorbell rang. It was my mother, on the doorstep in floods of tears. It took me some time to establish what the matter was as she flopped all over the kitchen, breaking into ever louder outbursts of tears and saying she didn't want to talk about it, until I began to wonder if her self-perpetuating sexual power surge had collapsed like a house of cards, with Dad, Julio and the tax man losing interest simultaneously. But no. She had merely been infected with 'Having It All' syndrome.

'I feel like the grasshopper who sang all summer,' she (the second she sensed I was losing interest in the breakdown) revealed. 'And now it's the winter of my life and I haven't stored up anything of my own.'

I was going to point out that three potential eligible partners gagging for it plus half the house and the pension schemes wasn't exactly nothing, but I bit my tongue.

'I want a career,' she said. And some horrible mean part of me felt happy and smug because I had a career. Well – a job, anyway. I was a grasshopper collecting a big pile of grass, or flies, or whatever it is grasshoppers eat ready for the winter, even if I didn't have a boyfriend.

Eventually I managed to cheer Mum up by allowing her

to go through my wardrobe and criticize all my clothes, then tell me why I should start getting everything from Jaeger and Country Casuals. It worked a treat and eventually she was so much back on form she was actually able to call up Julio and arrange to meet him for a 'nightcap'.

By the time she left it was after ten so I called Tom to report the hideous news that Daniel had not rung all weekend and asked him what he thought about Jude and Sharon's conflicting advice. Tom said I should listen to neither of them, not flirt, not lecture but merely be an aloof, coolly professional ice-queen.

Men, he claims, view themselves as permanently on some sort of sexual ladder with all women either above them or below them. If the woman is 'below' (i.e. willing to sleep with him, very keen on him) then in a Groucho Marx kind of way he does not want to be a member of her 'club'. This whole mentality depresses me enormously but Tom said not to be naïve and if I really love Daniel and want to win his heart I have to ignore him and be as cold and distant to him as possible.

Eventually got to bed at midnight, v. confused, but was woken three times in the night by phone calls from Dad.

'When someone loves you it's like having a blanket all round your heart,' he said, 'and then when it's taken away . . .' and he burst into tears. He was speaking from the granny flat at the bottom of the Alconburys' garden, where he's staying, as he says hopefully, 'Just till things are sorted out.'

I suddenly realize everything has shifted and now I am looking after my parents instead of them looking after me, which seems unnatural and wrong. Surely I am not that old?

Monday 6 March

8st 12 (v.v.g. – have realized secret of dieting is not weighing oneself).

Can officially confirm that the way to a man's heart these days is not through beauty, food, sex, or alluringness of character, but merely the ability to seem not very interested in him.

Took no notice of Daniel whatsoever all day at work and pretended to be busy (try not to laugh). Message Pending kept flashing but I just kept sighing and tossing my hair about as if I were a very glamorous, important person under a great deal of pressure. By the end of the day I realized, like a school chemistry lab miracle (phosphorus, litmus test or similar), it was working. He kept staring at me and giving me meaningful glances. Eventually, when Perpetua was out, he walked past my desk, stopped for a moment and murmured, 'Jones, you gorgeous creature. Why are you ignoring me?'

In a rush of joy and affection I was just about to blurt out the whole story of Tom, Jude and Shazzer's conflicting theories, but the heavens were smiling on me and the phone rang. I rolled my eyes apologetically, picked it up, then Perpetua bustled up, knocking a pile of proofs off the desk with her bottom, and bellowed, 'Ah, Daniel. Now . . .' and swept him away, which was fortunate because the phone call was Tom, who said I had to keep up the ice-queen act and gave me a mantra to repeat when I felt myself weakening. 'Aloof, unavailable ice-queen; Aloof, unavailable ice-queen.'

Tuesday 7 March

9st 4, 2 or 5?? alcohol units 0, cigarettes 20, calories 1500, Instants 6 (poor).

9 a.m. Aargh. How can I have put on 3lb since the middle of the night? I was 9st 4 when I went to bed, 9st 2 at 4 a.m. and 9st 5 when I got up. I can understand weight coming *off* – it could have evaporated or passed out of the body into the toilet – but how could it be put *on*? Could food react chemically with other food, double its density and volume, and solidify into ever heavier and denser hard fat? I don't look fatter. I can fasten the button, though not, alas, the zipper on my '89 jeans. So maybe my whole body is getting smaller but denser. The whole thing smacks of female body-builders and makes me feel strangely sick. Call up Jude to complain about diet failure, who says write down everything you've eaten, honestly, and see if you stuck to the diet. Here is list.

> **Breakfast:** hot-cross bun (Scarsdale Diet – slight variation on specified piece of wholemeal toast); Mars Bar (Scarsdale Diet – slight variation on specified half grapefruit)
> **Snack:** two bananas, two pears (switched to F-plan as starving and cannot face Scarsdale carrot snacks). Carton orange juice (Anti-Cellulite Raw-Food Diet)
> **Lunch:** jacket potato (Scarsdale Vegetarian Diet) and hummus (Hay Diet – fine with jacket spuds as all starch, and breakfast and snack were all alkaline-forming with exception of hot-cross bun and Mars: minor aberration)
> **Dinner:** four glasses of wine, fish and chips (Scarsdale Diet and also Hay Diet – protein forming); portion tiramisu; peppermint Aero (pissed)

I realize it has become too easy to find a diet to fit in with whatever you happen to feel like eating and that diets are not there to be pick and mixed but picked and stuck to, which is exactly what I shall begin to do once I've eaten this chocolate croissant.

Tuesday 14 March

Disaster. Complete disaster. Flushed with the success of Tom's ice-queen theory I began to rather brim over, as it were, into Jude's, and starting messaging Daniel again, to reassure him that I trust him and am not going to become needy or fly off the handle without just cause.

By mid-morning, so successful was the ice-queen combined with *Men are from Mars, Women are from Venus* approach that Daniel walked right up to me by the coffee machine and said, 'Will you come to Prague next weekend?'

'What? Er hahahaha, you mean the weekend after this one?'

'Yeeeeees, next weekend,' he said, with an encouraging, slightly patronizing air, as if he had been teaching me to speak English.

'Oooh. *Yes, please,*' I said, forgetting the ice-queen mantra in the excitement.

Next thing he came up and asked if I wanted to come round the corner for lunch. We arranged to meet outside the building so no one would suspect anything and it was all rather thrilling and clandestine until he said, as we walked towards the pub, 'Listen, Bridge, I'm really sorry, I've fucked up.'

'Why? what?' I said, even, as I spoke, remembering my mum and wondering if I ought to be saying 'Pardon?'

'I can't make Prague next weekend. I don't know what I was thinking about. But maybe we'll do it another time.'

A siren blared in my head and a huge neon sign started flashing with Sharon's head in the middle going, 'FUCK-WITTAGE, FUCKWITTAGE'.

I stood stock still on the pavement, glowering up at him.

'What's the matter?' he said, looking amused.

'I'm fed up with you,' I said furiously. 'I told you quite specifically the first time you tried to undo my skirt that I am not into emotional fuckwittage. It was very bad to carry on flirting, sleep with me then not even follow it up with a phone call, and try to pretend the whole thing never happened. Did you just ask me to Prague to make sure you could still sleep with me if you wanted to as if we were on some sort of ladder?'

'A ladder, Bridge?' said Daniel. 'What sort of ladder?'

'Shut up,' I bristled crossly. 'It's all chop-change chop-change with you. Either go out with me and treat me nicely, or leave me alone. As I say, I am not interested in fuckwittage.'

'What about you, this week? First you completely ignore me like some Hitler Youth ice-maiden, then you turn into an irresistible sex kitten, looking at me over the computer with not so much 'come-to-bed' as just 'come' eyes, and now suddenly you're Jeremy Paxman.'

We stared at each other transfixed like two African animals at the start of a fight on a David Attenborough programme. Then suddenly Daniel turned on his heel and walked off to the pub, leaving me to stagger, stunned, back to the office, where I dived to the loo, locked the door and sat down, staring crazily at the door with one eye. Oh God.

5 p.m. Har har. Am marvellous. Feeling v. pleased with self. Had top-level post-works crisis meeting in Café Rouge with Sharon, Jude and Tom, who were all delighted with the Daniel outcome, each convinced it was because I had followed their advice. Also Jude had heard survey on the radio that by the turn of the millennium a third of all households will be single, therefore proving that at last we are no longer tragic freaks. Shazzer guffawed and said, 'One in three? Nine out of ten, more like.' Sharon maintains men – present company (i.e. Tom) excepted, obviously – are so catastrophically unevolved that soon they will just be kept by women as pets for sex, therefore presumably these will not count as shared households as the men will be kept outside in kennels. Anyway, feeling v. empowered. Tremendous. Think might read bit of Susan Faludi's *Backlash*.

5 a.m. Oh God, am so unhappy about Daniel. I love him.

Wednesday 15 March

9st, alcohol units 5 (disgrace: urine of Satan), cigarettes 14 (weed of Satan – will give up on birthday), calories 1795.

Humph. Have woken up v. fed up. On top of everything, only two weeks to go until birthday, when will have to face up to the fact that another entire year has gone by, during which everyone else except me has mutated into Smug Married, having children plop, plop, plop, left right and

77

centre and making hundreds of thousands of pounds and inroads into very hub of establishment, while I career rudderless and boyfriendless through dysfunctional relationships and professional stagnation.

Find self constantly scanning face in mirror for wrinkles and frantically reading *Hello!*, checking out everyone's ages in desperate search for role models (Jane Seymour is forty-two!), fighting long-impacted fear that one day in your thirties you will suddenly, without warning, grow a big fat crimplene dress, shopping bag, tight perm and face collapsing in manner of movie special-effect, and that will be it. Try to concentrate hard on Joanna Lumley and Susan Sarandon.

Also worried about how to celebrate birthday. Size of flat and bank balance prohibits actual party. Maybe dinner party? But then would have to spend birthday slaving and would hate all guests on arrival. Could all go out for meal but then feel guilty asking everyone to pay, selfishly presuming to force costly and dull evening on others merely to celebrate own birthday – yet cannot afford to pay for everyone. Oh God. What to do? Wish had not been born but immaculately burst into being in similar, though not identical, manner to Jesus, then would not have had to have birthday. Sympathize with Jesus in sense of embarrassment he must, and perhaps should, feel over two-millennium-old social imposition of own birthday on large areas of globe.

Midnight. Have had v.g. idea about birthday. Am going to ask everyone round for cocktails, perhaps Manhattans. Will then have given to guests something in manner of grand society hostess, and if everyone wishes to go to dinner afterwards: why, they may do so. Not sure what Manhattan is, come to think of it. But could buy book of cocktails maybe. Probably won't, to be perfectly honest.

Thursday 16 March

9st 1, alcohol units 2, cigarettes 3 (v.g.), calories 2140 (but mainly fruit), minutes spent doing party guest list 237 (bad).

Me	Shazzer
Jude	Vile Richard
Tom	Jerome (yuk)
~~Michael~~	
Magda	Jeremy
Simon	
Rebecca	Martin Crashing Bore
Woney	Cosmo
Joanna	
Daniel?	Perpetua? (eek) and Hugo?

Oh no. Oh no. What am I going to do?

Friday 17 March

Just called Tom who says, very wisely, 'It is your birthday and you should invite exactly and only who you want.'

So am just going to ask the following:

> Shazzer
> Jude
> Tom
> Magda and Jeremy

– and cook supper for everyone myself.

Called Tom back to tell him the plan and he said, 'and Jerome?'

'What?'

'And Jerome?'

'I thought, like we said, I'd just ask who I . . .' I tailed off, realizing if I said 'wanted' it would mean I didn't 'want' i.e. 'like' Tom's insufferable, pretentious boyfriend.

'Oh!' I said, over-compensating madly. 'You mean *your* Jerome? *Course* Jerome's invited, yer ninny. Chuh! But do you think it's OK not to ask Jude's Vile Richard? And Sloaney Woney – even though she had me to her birthday last week?'

'She'll never know.'

When I told Jude who was coming she said perkily, 'Oh, so we're bringing other halves?' which means Vile Richard. Also now that it's not just six I will have to ask Michael. Oh well. I mean nine is fine. Ten. It'll be fine.

Next thing Sharon rang. 'I hope I haven't put my foot in it. I just saw Rebecca and asked her if she was coming to your birthday and she looked really offended.'

Oh no, I'll have to ask Rebecca and Martin Crashing Bore now. But that means I'll have to ask Joanna as well. Shit. shit. Now I've said I'm cooking I can't suddenly announce we're going out to a restaurant or I'll seem both bone idle and mean.

Oh God. Just got home to icy offended-sounding answer-phone message from Woney.

'Cosmo and I were wondering what you'd like for your birthday this year. Would you call us back, please?'

Realize I am going to spend my birthday cooking food for sixteen people.

Saturday 18 March

8st 13, alcohol units 4 (fed up), cigarettes 23 (v.v. bad, esp. in two hours), calories 3827 (repulsive).

2 p.m. Humph. Just what I needed. My mother burst into my flat, last week's Grasshopper Who Sang All Summer crisis miraculously forgotten.

'My godfathers, darling!' she said breathily, steaming through my flat and heading for the kitchen. 'Have you had a bad week or something? You look dreadful. You look about ninety. Anyway, guess what, darling,' she said, turning, holding the kettle, dropping her eyes modestly, then looking up, beaming like Bonnie Langford about to embark upon a tap-dancing routine.

'What?' I muttered grumpily.

'I've got a job as a TV presenter.'

I'm going shopping.

Sunday 19 March

8st 12, alcohol units 3, cigarettes 10, calories 2465 (but mainly chocolate).

Hurray. Whole new positive perspective on birthday. Have been talking to Jude about book she has been reading about festivals and rites of passage in primitive cultures and am feeling happy and serene.

Realize it is shallow and wrong to feel that flat is too small to entertain nineteen, and that cannot be arsed to spend birthday cooking and would rather dress up and be taken to posh restaurant by sex-god with enormous gold credit card. Instead am going to think of my friends as a huge, warm, African, or possibly Turkish, family.

Our culture is too obsessed with outward appearance, age and status. Love is what matters. These nineteen people are my friends; they want to be welcomed into my home to celebrate with affection and simple homely fare – not to judge. Am going to cook shepherd's pie for them all – British Home Cooking. It will be a marvellous, warm, Third-World-style ethnic family party.

Monday 20 March

9st, alcohol units 4 (getting into mood), cigarettes 27 (but last day before giving up), calories 2455.

Have decided to serve the shepherd's pie with Chargrilled Belgian Endive Salad, Roquefort Lardons and Frizzled Chorizo, to add a fashionable touch (have not tried before but sure it will be easy), followed by individual Grand Marnier soufflés. V. much looking forward to the birthday. Expect to become known as brilliant cook and hostess.

Tuesday 21 March: Birthday

9st, alcohol units 9*, cigarettes 42*, calories 4295*.

6.30 p.m. Cannot go on. Have just stepped in a pan of mashed potato in new kitten-heel black suede shoes from

* If can't splash out on birthday, when can I?

82

Pied à terre (Pied-à-pomme-de-terre, more like), forgetting that kitchen floor and surfaces were covered in pans of mince and mashed potato. It is already 6.30 and have to go out to Cullens for Grand Marnier soufflé ingredients and other forgotten items. Oh my God – suddenly remembered tube of contraceptive jelly might be on side of washbasin. Must also hide storage jars with embarrassing un-hip squirrel design and birthday card from Jamie with picture of little lamb on front which says 'Happy Birthday, Guess which one is you?' Then inside, 'You're the one over the hill.' Humph.

Schedule:

6.30. Go to shop.
6.45. Return with forgotten groceries.
6.45–7. Assemble shepherd's pie and place in oven (oh God, hope will all fit).
7–7.05. Prepare Grand Marnier soufflés. (Actually think will have a little taste of Grand Marnier now. It is my birthday, after all.)
7.05–7.10. Mmm. Grand Marnier delicious. Check plates and cutlery for tell-tale signs of sluttish washing-up and arrange in attractive fan shape. Ah, must buy napkins also (or is it serviettes? Can never remember which one is common).
7.10–7.20. Tidy up and move furniture to sides of room.
7.20–7.30. Make frisse lardon frizzled chorizo thing.

All of which leaves a clear half-hour to get ready so no need to panic. Must have a fag. Aargh. It's quarter to seven. How did that happen? Aargh.

7.15 p.m. Just got back from shop and realize have forgotten butter.

7.35 p.m. Shit, shit shit. The shepherd's pie is still in pans all over the kitchen floor and have not yet washed hair.

7.40 p.m. Oh my God. Just looked for milk and realized have left the carrier bag behind in the shop. Also had the eggs in it. That means . . . Oh God, and the olive oil . . . so cannot do frizzy salad thing.

7.40 p.m. Hmm. Best plan, surely, is to get into the bath with a glass of champagne then get ready. At least if I look nice I can carry on cooking when everyone is here and maybe can get Tom to go out for the missing ingredients.

7.55 p.m. Aargh. Doorbell. Am in bra and pants with wet hair. Pie is all over floor. Suddenly hate the guests. Have had to slave for two days, and now they will all swan in, demanding food like cuckoos. Feel like opening door and shouting, 'Oh, go *fuck* yourselves.'

2 a.m. Feeling v. emotional. At door were Magda, Tom, Shazzer and Jude with bottle of champagne. They said to hurry up and get ready and when I had dried hair and dressed they had cleaned up all the kitchen and thrown away the shepherd's pie. It turned out Magda had booked a big table at 192 and told everyone to go there instead of my flat, and there they all were waiting with presents, planning to buy me dinner. Magda said they had had a weird, almost spooky sixth sense that the Grand Marnier soufflé and frizzled lardon thing were not going to work out. Love the friends, better than extended Turkish family in weird headscarves any day.

Right: for coming year will reactivate New Year's Resolutions, adding the following:

I will
Stop being so neurotic and dreading things.
I will not
Sleep with, or take any notice of, Daniel Cleaver any more.

APRIL

Inner Poise

Sunday 2 April

9st, alcohol units 0 (marvellous), cigarettes 0, calories 2250.

I read in an article that Kathleen Tynan, late wife of the late Kenneth, had 'inner poise' and, when writing, was to be found immaculately dressed, sitting at a small table in the centre of the room sipping at a glass of chilled white wine. Kathleen Tynan would not, when late with a press release for Perpetua, lie fully dressed and terrified under the duvet, chain-smoking, glugging cold *sake* out of a beaker and putting on make-up as a hysterical displacement activity. Kathleen Tynan would not allow Daniel Cleaver to sleep with her whenever he felt like it but not be her boyfriend. Nor would she become insensible with drink and be sick. Wish to be like Kathleen Tynan (though not, obviously, dead).

Lately, therefore, whenever things have risked ranging out of control, I have repeated the phrase 'inner poise' and imagined myself wearing white linen and sitting at a table with flowers on it. 'Inner poise.' No fags for six days now. Have assumed air of dignified hauteur with Daniel and not messaged, flirted or slept with him for three weeks. Only three alcohol units consumed over the last week as grudging concession to Tom, who complained that spending the evening with the new vice-free me was like going out for dinner with a whelk, scallop or other flaccid sea-creature.

My body is a temple. I wonder if it's time to go to bed yet? Oh no, it's only 8.30. Inner poise. Ooh. Telephone.

9 p.m. It was my father, speaking in a weird, disconnected voice, almost as if he were a dalek.

'Bridget. Turn your television set to BBC1.'

I switched channels and lurched in horror. It was a trailer for the Anne and Nick show and there, frozen in a video-effect diamond between Anne and Nick on the sofa, was my mother, all bouffed and made-up, as if she were Katie Bloody Boyle or someone.

'Nick,' said Anne pleasantly.

'. . . and we'll be introducing our new Springtime Slot,' said Nick, "Suddenly Single" – a dilemma being faced by a growing number of women. Anne.'

'And introducing spanking new presenter Pam Jones,' said Anne. '"Suddenly Single" herself and making her TV debut.'

While Anne was speaking my mother unfroze within the diamond, which started whooshing towards the front of the screen, obscuring Anne and Nick, and revealing, as it did so, that my mother was thrusting a microphone under the nose of a mousy-looking woman.

'Have you had suicidal thoughts?' boomed my mother.

'Yes,' said the mousy woman and burst into tears at which point the picture froze, turned on its end and whizzed off into one corner to reveal Anne and Nick on the sofa again looking sepulchral.

Dad was devastated. Mum hadn't even told him about the TV-presenting job. It seems he is in denial and has convinced himself Mum is just having an end-of-life crisis and that she already realizes she has made a mistake but is too embarrassed to ask to come back.

Actually, I'm all for denial. You can convince yourself of any scenario you choose and it keeps you as happy as a sandboy – as long as your ex-partner doesn't pop up on your television screen forging a new career out of not being married to you any more. I tried to pretend it didn't mean there was no hope, and that Mum might be planning their reunion as a really grabby end to the series, but it didn't wash. Poor Dad. I don't think he knows anything about Julio or the man from the tax office. I asked him if he'd like me to come up tomorrow and we could go out and have a nice supper together on Saturday night and maybe go for a walk on Sunday, but he said he was all right. The Alconburys are holding an Olde English supper on Saturday night for the Lifeboat.

Tuesday 4 April

Determined, now, to tackle constant lateness for work and failure to address in-tray bulging with threats from bailiffs, etc. Resolve to begin self-improvement programme with time-and-motion study.

7 a.m. Get weighed.
7.03 a.m. Return to bed in sulk over weight. Head-state bad. Sleeping or getting up equally out of question. Think about Daniel.

7.30 a.m. Hunger pangs force self out of bed. Make coffee, consider grapefruit. Defrost chocolate croissant.

7.35–7.50 a.m. Look out of window.

7.55 a.m. Open wardrobe. Stare at clothes.

8 am. Select shirt. Try to find black Lycra mini-skirt. Pull clothes out of bottom of wardrobe in quest for skirt. Go through drawers and search behind bedroom chair. Go through ironing basket. Go through dirty linen basket. Skirt has vanished. Have cigarette to cheer self up.

8.20 a.m. Dry skin brushing (anti-cellulite), bath and hairwash.

8.35 a.m. Begin selection of underwear. Laundry crisis means only available pants are vast white cotton. Too unattractive to contemplate, even for work (psychological damage). Go back to ironing basket. Find unsuitably small black lacy pair – prickly but better than giant Mummy-pant horror.

8.45 a.m. Start on black opaque tights. Pair one seems to have shrunk – crotch is three inches above knees. Get second pair on and find hole on back of leg. Throw away. Suddenly remember had Lycra mini-skirt on when returned home with Daniel last time. Go to living room. Triumphantly locate skirt between cushions on sofa.

8.55 a.m. Return to tights. Pair three have hole only in toe. Put on. Hole transforms into ladder which will protrude tellingly from shoe. Go to ironing basket. Locate last pair of black opaque tights twisted into rope-like object speckled with bits of tissue. Untangle and purge of tissue.

9.05 a.m. Have got tights on now. Add skirt. Begin ironing shirt.

9.10 a.m. Suddenly realize hair is drying in weird shape. Search for hairbrush. Locate in handbag. Blow-dry hair. Will not go right. Spray with plant spray and blow some more.

9.40 a.m. Return to ironing and discover stubborn stain on front of shirt. All other possible shirts dirty. Panic about time. Try to wash out stain. Entire shirt now soaking wet. Iron dry.

9.55 a.m. V. late now. In despair, have fag and read holiday brochure for calming five minutes.

10 a.m. Try to find handbag. Handbag has vanished. Decide to see if anything nice has come in the mail.

10.07 a.m. Access letter only, about non-payment of minimum payment. Try to remember what was looking for. Restart quest for handbag.

10.15 a.m. Beyond lateness now. Suddenly remember had handbag in bedroom when looking for hairbrush but cannot find. Eventually locate under clothes from wardrobe. Return clothes to wardrobe. Put on jacket. Prepare to leave house. Cannot find keys. Scour house in rage.

10.25 a.m. Find keys in handbag. Realize have forgotten hairbrush.

10.35 a.m. Leave house.

Three hours and thirty-five minutes between waking and leaving house is too long. In future must get straight up when wake up and reform entire laundry system. Open paper to read that convicted murderer in America is convinced the authorities have planted a microchip in his buttocks to monitor his movements, so to speak. Horrified by thought of similar microchip being in own buttocks, particularly in the mornings.

Wednesday 5 April

8st 13, alcohol units 5 (Jude's fault), cigarettes 2 (sort of thing that could happen to anyone – does not mean have started smoking again), calories 1765, Instants 2.

Told Jude today about the inner poise thing and she said, interestingly, that she'd been reading a self-help book about Zen. She said, when you looked at life, Zen could be applied to anything – Zen and the art of shopping, Zen and the art of flatbuying, etc. She said that it was all a question of Flow rather than struggle. And if, for example, you had a problem or things were not working out, instead of straining or becoming angry you should just relax and feel your way into the Flow and everything would work out. It is, she said, rather like when you can't get a key to open a lock and if you wiggle it furiously it gets worse, but take it out, stick a bit of lip gloss on it, then just sort of sense your way and Eureka! But not to mention idea to Sharon because she thought it was bollocks.

Thursday 6 April

Went to meet Jude for quiet drink to talk about Flow some more and noticed a familiar besuited figure with knitting-pattern dark good looks sitting in a quiet corner having dinner: it was Magda's Jeremy. Waved at him and just for split second saw expression of horror cross his face, which instantly made me look to his companion who was a) not Magda b) not yet thirty c) wearing a suit which I have tried on twice in Whistles and had to take off as too expensive. Bloody witch.

I could tell Jeremy was going to try to get away with the sort of quick 'Hello not now' look which acknowledges your close, old and enduring friendship but at the same time demonstrates that this is not the moment to affirm it with kisses and an in-depth chat. I was about to play along with it but then I thought, hang on a minute! Sisters! Under the skin! Magda! If Magda's husband has nothing to be ashamed of in dining with this worthless trollop in *my* suit, he will introduce me.

I altered my path to pass his table, at which he immersed himself deep in conversation with the trollop, glancing up as I walked past and giving me a firm, confident smile as if to say 'business meeting'. I gave him a look which said, 'Don't you business meeting me,' and strutted on.

What should I do now, though? Oh dear, oh dear. Tell Magda? Not tell Magda? Ring Magda and ask if everything's OK? Ring Jeremy and ask him if everything's OK? Ring Jeremy and threaten to tell Magda unless he drops the witch in my suit? Mind my own business?

Remembering Zen, Kathleen Tynan and Inner Poise, I did a version of Salute to the Sun I remembered from distant Yogacise class and centred myself, concentrating on the inner wheel, till the Flow came. Then I resolved serenely to tell no one, as gossip is a virulent spreading poison. Instead I will ring Magda a lot and be there for her so if anything is amiss (which she is bound, with woman's intuition, to sense), she will tell me. Then if, through Flow, it seems the right thing to do, I will tell her what I saw. Nothing of value comes through struggle; it is all about Flow. Zen and the art of life. Zen. Flow. Hmmm, but then how did I happen to bump into Jeremy and the worthless trollop if not through Flow? What does that mean, then?

Tuesday 11 April

8st 11, alcohol units 0, cigarettes 0, Instants 9 (this must stop).

All seems normal with Magda and Jeremy so maybe it was just a business meeting. Maybe the Zen and Flow notion is correct, for there is no doubt that by relaxing and going with the vibes I have done the right thing. Am invited to a glittering literati launch of *Kafka's Motorbike* next week at the Ivy. Determined, instead of fearing the scary party, panicking all the way through and going home pissed and depressed, am going to improve social skills, confidence and Make Parties Work for Me – as guided by article have just read in magazine.

Apparently, Tina Brown of the *New Yorker* is brilliant at dealing with parties, gliding prettily from group to group, saying, 'Martin Amis! Nelson Mandela! Richard Gere!' in a tone which at once suggests, 'My God, I have never been more enchanted to see anyone in my entire life! Have you met the most dazzling person at the party apart from you? Talk! Talk! Must network! Byeee!' Wish to be like Tina Brown, though not, obviously, quite so hardworking.

The article is full of useful tips. One should never, apparently, talk to anyone at a party for more than two minutes. When time is up, you simply say, 'I think we're expected to circulate. Nice to meet you,' and go off. If you get lost for words after asking someone what they do to which they reply 'Undertaker' or 'I work for the Child Support Agency', you must simply ask, 'Do you enjoy that?' When introducing people add a thoughtful detail or two about each person so that their interlocutor has a conversational kicking-off point. E.g., 'This is John – he's from New Zealand and enjoys windsurfing.' Or, 'Gina is a keen skydiver and lives on a barge.'

Most importantly, one must never go to a party without a clear objective: whether it be to 'network', thereby adding to your spread of contacts to improve your career; to make friends with someone specific; or simply 'clinch' a top deal. Understand where have been going wrong by going to parties armed only with objective of not getting too pissed.

Monday 17 April

8st 12, alcohol units 0 (v.g.), cigarettes 0 (v.g.), Instants 5 (but won £2 so total Instants expenditure only £3).

Right. Tomorrow is *Kafka's Motorbike*. Am going to work out clear set of objectives. In a minute. Will just watch adverts then ring up Jude.

Right

1) Not to get too pissed.
2) To aim to meet people to network with.

Hmmm. Anyway, will think of some more later.

11 p.m. Right.

3) To put the social skills from the article into action.
4) ~~To make Daniel think I have inner poise and want to get off with me again. No. No.~~
4) ~~To meet and sleep with sex god.~~
4) To make interesting contacts in the publishing world, possibly even other professions in order to find new career.

97

Oh God. Do not want to go to scary party. Want to stay home with bottle of wine and watch *EastEnders*.

Tuesday 18 April

9st 0, alcohol units 7 (oh dear), cigarettes 30, calories (cannot bear to think about it), Instants 1 (excellent).

Party got off to a bad start when could not see anyone that I knew to introduce to each other. Found myself a drink then spotted Perpetua talking to James from the *Telegraph*. Approached Perpetua confidently, ready to swing into action but instead of saying 'James, Bridget comes from Northamptonshire and is a keen gymnast' (am going to start going to gym again soon), Perpetua just carried on talking – well beyond the two-minute mark – and ignored me.

I hung around for a while feeling a total git, then spotted Simon from Marketing. Cunningly pretending I had not intended to join Perpetua's conversation at all, I bore down purposefully upon Simon, preparing to say, 'Simon Barnett!' in the style of Tina Brown. When I was almost there, however, I noticed that, unfortunately, Simon from Marketing was talking to Julian Barnes. Suspecting that I might not be able to fully pull off crying, 'Simon Barnett! Julian Barnes!' with quite the required gaiety and *tone*, I hovered indecisively then started to sidle away, at which point Simon said in an irritated superior voice (one you, funnily enough, never hear him use when he is trying to get off with you by the photocopier), 'Did you want something, Bridget?'

'Ah! Yes!' I said, panicking wildly about what it was I could possibly want. 'Ahm.'

'Yeees?' Simon and Julian Barnes looked at me expectantly.

'Do you know where the toilets are?' I blurted. Damn. Damn. Why? Why did I say that? I saw a faint smile hover over the thin-but-attractive lips of Julian Barnes.

'Ah, actually I think they're over there. Jolly good. Thanks,' I said, and made for the exit. Once out of the swing doors I slumped against the wall, trying to get my breath back, thinking, 'inner poise, inner poise'. It was not going particularly well so far, there were no two ways about it.

I looked wistfully at the stairs. The thought of going home, putting my nighty on and turning on the telly began to seem irresistibly attractive. Remembering the Party Objectives, though, I breathed in deeply through my nose, murmured, 'inner poise' and pushed through the doors back into the party. Perpetua was still by the door, talking to her ghastly friends Piggy and Arabella.

'Ah, Bridget,' she said. 'Are you going to get a drink?' and held out her glass. When I returned with three glasses of wine and a Perrier they were in full autowitter.

'I have to say, I think it's disgraceful. All it means in this day and age is that a whole generation of people only get to know the great works of literature – Austen, Eliot, Dickens, Shakespeare, and so on – through the television.'

'Well, quite. It's absurd. Criminal.'

'Absolutely. They think that what they see when they're "channel hopping" between *Noel's House Party* and *Blind Date* actually *is* Austen or Eliot.'

'*Blind Date* is on Saturdays,' I said.

'I'm sorry?' said Perpetua.

'Saturdays. *Blind Date* is on Saturdays at seven fifteen, after *Gladiators*.'

'So?' said Perpetua sneerily, with a sideways glance at Arabella and Piggy.

'Those big literary adaptations don't tend to go out on Saturday nights.'

'Oh look, there's Mark,' interrupted Piggy.

'Oh God, yah,' said Arabella, beadily. 'He's left his wife, hasn't he?'

'What I meant was, there isn't anything any good like *Blind Date* on the other side during the literary master-pieces, so I don't think that many people would be channel hopping.'

'Oh, *Blind Date* is "good", is it?' sneered Perpetua.

'Yes, it's very good.'

'And you do realize *Middlemarch* was originally a book, Bridget, don't you, not a soap?'

I hate Perpetua when she gets like this. Stupid old fartarse bag.

'Oh, I thought it was a soap of a shampoo,' I said, sulkily grabbing a handful of passing saté sticks and shoving them into my mouth. As I looked up I saw a dark-haired man in a suit straight in front of me.

'Hello, Bridget,' he said. I nearly opened my mouth and let all the saté sticks fall straight out. It was Mark Darcy. But without the Frank Bough-style diamond-pat-terned sweater.

'Hello,' I said through my mouthful, trying not to panic. Then, remembering the article, turned towards Perpetua.

'Mark. Perpetua is . . .' I began and then paused, frozen. What to say? Perpetua is very fat and spends her whole time bossing me around? Mark is very rich and has a cruel-raced ex-wife.

'Yes?' said Mark.

'. . . is my boss and is buying a flat in Fulham, and Mark is,' I said, turning desperately to Perpetua, 'a top human-rights lawyer.'

'Oh, hello, Mark. I know *of* you, of course,' gushed Perpetua as if she were Prunella Scales in *Fawlty Towers* and he were the Duke of Edinburgh.

'Mark, hi!' said Arabella, opening her eyes very wide and blinking in a way she presumably thought was very attractive. 'Haven't seen you for yonks. How was the Big Apple?'

'We were just talking about hierarchies of culture,' boomed Perpetua. 'Bridget is one of these people who thinks the moment when the screen goes back on *Blind Date* is on a par with Othello's "hurl my soul from heaven" soliloquy,' she said, hooting with laughter.

'Ah. Then Bridget is clearly a top post-modernist,' said Mark Darcy. 'This is Natasha,' he said, gesturing towards a tall, thin, glamorous girl beside him. 'Natasha is a top family-law barrister.'

I had the feeling he was taking the piss out of me. Bloody cheek.

'I must say,' said Natasha, with a knowing smile, 'I always feel with the Classics people should be made to prove they've read the book before they're allowed to watch the television version.'

'Oh, I *quite* agree,' said Perpetua, emitting further gales of laughter. 'What a marvellous idea!'

I could see her mentally fitting Mark Darcy and Natasha in with an array of Poohs and Piggies round the dinner table.

'They should have refused to let anyone listen to the World Cup tune,' hooted Arabella, 'until they could prove they'd listened to *Turandot* all the way through!'

'Though in many respects, of course,' said Mark's Natasha, suddenly earnest, as if concerned the conversation was going quite the wrong way, 'the democratization of our culture is a *good thing*—'

'Except in the case of Mr Blobby, who should have been punctured at birth,' shrieked Perpetua. As I glanced involuntarily at Perpetua's bottom thinking, 'That's a bit rich coming from her,' I caught Mark Darcy doing the same thing.

'What I *resent*, though' – Natasha was looking all sort of twitchy and distorted as if she were in an Oxbridge debating society – 'is this, this sort of, arrogant individualism which imagines each new generation can somehow create the world afresh.'

'But that's exactly what they *do*, do,' said Mark Darcy gently.

'Oh well, I mean if you're going to look at it at that level . . .' said Natasha defensively.

'What level?' said Mark Darcy. 'It's not a level, it's a perfectly good point.'

'No. No. I'm sorry, you're *deliberately* being obtuse,' she said, going bright red. 'I'm not talking about a ventilating deconstructionalistic freshness of vision. I'm talking about the ultimate *vandalization* of the cultural framework.'

Mark Darcy looked as if he was going to burst out laughing.

'What I mean is, if you're taking that sort of cutesy, morally relativistic, "*Blind Date* is brilliant" sort of line . . .' she said with a resentful look in my direction.

'I wasn't, I just really like *Blind Date*,' I said. 'Though I do think it would be better if they made the pickees make up their own replies to the questions instead of reading out those stupid pat answers full of puns and sexual innuendos.'

'Absolutely,' interjected Mark.

'I can't stand *Gladiators*, though. It makes me feel fat,' I said. 'Anyway, nice to meet you. Bye!'

I was just standing waiting for my coat, reflecting on how much difference the presence or absence of a diamond-patterned sweater can make to someone's attractiveness, when I felt hands lightly on my waist.

I turned round. 'Daniel!'

'Jones! What are you doing skulking off so early?' He leaned over and kissed me. 'Mmmmmm, you smell nice,' then offered me a cigarette.

'No thank you, I have found inner poise and given up smoking,' I said, in a pre-programmed, Stepford Wife sort of way, wishing Daniel wasn't quite so attractive when you found yourself alone with him.

'I see,' he smirked, 'inner poise, eh?'

'Yes,' I said primly. 'Have you been at the party? I didn't see you.'

'I know you didn't. I saw you, though. Talking to Mark Darcy.'

'How do you know Mark Darcy?' I said, astonished.

'Cambridge. Can't stand the stupid nerd. Bloody old woman. How do you know him?'

'He's Malcolm and Elaine Darcy's son,' I began, almost going on to say, 'You know Malcolm and *Elaine*, darling. They came over when we lived in Buckingham—'

'Who in the—'

'They're friends of my parents. I used to play with him in the paddling pool.'

'Yes, I bet you did, you dirty little bitch,' he growled. 'Do you want to come and have supper?'

Inner poise, I told myself, inner poise.

'Come on, Bridge,' he said, leaning towards me seductively. 'I need to have a serious discussion about your blouse. It's extremely thin. Almost, when you examine it, thin to the point of transparency. Has it ever occurred to you that your blouse might be suffering from . . . *bulimia*?'

'I've got to meet someone,' I whispered desperately.

'Come on, Bridge.'

'No,' I said with a firmness that rather surprised me.

'Shame,' he said softly. 'See you Monday,' and gave me a look so dirty I felt like throwing myself after him shouting, 'Shag me! Shag me!'

11 p.m. Just called Jude and told her about Daniel incident, also about Malcolm and Elaine Darcy's son, whom Mum and Una had tried to get me off with at the Turkey Curry Buffet, turning up at the party looking rather attractive.

'Wait a minute,' said Jude. 'You don't mean *Mark* Darcy, do you? The lawyer?'

'Yes. What – do you know him as well?'

'Well, yes. I mean, we've done some work with him. He's incredibly nice and attractive. I thought you said the chap at the turkey curry buffet was a real geek.'

Humph. Bloody Jude.

Saturday 22 April

8st 7, cigarettes, 0, alcohol units 0, calories 1800.

Today is an historic and joyous day. After eighteen years of trying to get down to 8st 7 I have finally achieved it. It is no trick of the scales, but confirmed by jeans. I am thin.

There is no reliable explanation. I have been to the gym twice in the last week, but that, though rare, is not freakish. I have eaten normally. It is a miracle. Rang Tom, who said maybe I have a tapeworm. The way to get rid of it, he said, is to hold a bowl of warm milk and a pencil in front of my mouth. (Tapeworms love warm milk, apparently. They love it.) Open my mouth. Then, when the worm's head appears, wrap it carefully round the pencil.

'Listen,' I told him, 'this tapeworm is staying.' I love my new tapeworm. Not only am I thin, but I no longer want to smoke or glug wine.

'Are you in love?' asked Tom in a suspicious, jealous tone. He's always like this. It's not that he wants to be with me, because, obviously, he is a homosexual. But if you are single the last thing you want is your best friend forming a functional relationship with somebody else. I racked my brains, then stopped, shocked by a sudden, stunning realization. I am not in love with Daniel any more. I am free.

Tuesday 25 April

8st 7, alcohol units 0 (excellent), cigarettes 0 (v.v.g.), calories 995 (continuing good work).

Humph. Went to Jude's party tonight in tight little black dress to show off figure feeling v. full of myself.

'God, are you all right?' asked Jude when I walked in. 'You look really tired.'

'I'm fine,' I said, crestfallen. 'I've lost half a stone. What's the matter?'

'Nothing. No, I just thought . . .'

'What? What?'

'Maybe you've lost it a bit quickly off your . . . face,' she trailed off, looking at my admittedly somewhat deflated cleavage.

Simon was the same.

'Bridgiiiiiiit! Have you got a fag?'

'No, I've given up.'

'Oh blimey, no wonder you look so . . .'

'What?'

'Oh, nothing, nothing. Just a bit . . . drawn.'

It continued all evening. There's nothing worse than people telling you you look tired. They might as well have done with it and say you look like five kinds of shit. I felt so pleased with myself for not drinking but as the evening wore on, and everyone got drunker, I began to feel so calm and smug that I was even irritating myself. I kept finding myself in conversations when I actually couldn't be bothered to say a single word, and just looked on and nodded in a wise, detached manner.

'Have you got any camomile tea?' I said to Jude at one

point as she lurched past, hiccupping happily, at which point she collapsed into giggles, put her arm round me and fell over. I decided I'd better go home.

Once there, I got into bed, put my head on the pillow but nothing happened. I kept putting my head in one place, then another place, but still it wouldn't go to sleep. Normally I would be snoring by now and having some sort of traumatized paranoid dream. I put the light on. It was only 11.30. Maybe I should do something, like, well, er . . . mending? Inner poise. The phone rang. It was Tom.

'Are you all right?'

'Yes. I feel great. Why?'

'You just seemed, well, flat tonight. Everyone said you weren't your usual self.'

'No, I was fine. Did you see how thin I am?' Silence.

'Tom?'

'I think you looked better before, hon.'

Now I feel empty and bewildered – as if a rug has been pulled from under my feet. Eighteen years – wasted. Eighteen years of calorie and fat-unit-based arithmetic. Eighteen years of buying long shirts and jumpers and leaving the room backwards in intimate situations to hide my bottom. Millions of cheesecakes and tiramisus, tens of millions of Emmenthal slices left uneaten. Eighteen years of struggle, sacrifice and endeavour – for what? Eighteen years and the result is 'tired and flat'. I feel like a scientist who discovers that his life's work has been a total mistake.

Thursday 27 April

Alcohol units 0, cigarettes 0, Instants 12 (v.v. bad, but have not weighed self or thought about dieting all day; v.g.).

Must stop doing the Instants but the trouble is I do quite often win. The Instants are much better than the Lottery itself, because the numbers no longer come up during *Blind Date* (it is not on at the moment) and all too often do not have a single one of yours among them, leaving you feeling both impotent and cheated with nothing to be done except screw your ticket up and throw it defiantly on the floor.

Not so with the Instants, which is very much a participation thing, with six cash figures to be scratched off – often quite a hard and skilled job – and never giving you the feeling that you didn't have a chance. Three amounts the same secures a win, and in my experience you always get very close, often with as many as two matching pairs for amounts as great as £50,000.

Anyway, you can't deny yourself all pleasures in life. I'm only on about four or five a day and, besides, I'm going to stop soon.

Friday 28 April

Alcohol units 14, cigarettes 64, calories 8400 (v.g., though bad to have counted. Slimming obsession v. bad), Instants 0.

At 8.45 last night I was running a relaxing aromatherapy bath and sipping camomile tea when a car burglar alarm started up. I have been waging a campaign in our street against car burglar alarms which are intolerable and counter-productive since you are more likely to get your car broken into by an angry neighbour trying to silence the burglar alarm than by a burglar.

This time, however, instead of raging and calling the police, I merely breathed in through flared nostrils and murmured, 'inner poise'. The doorbell rang. I picked up the intercom. A v. posh sheep-voice bleated, 'He's having a *fucking* affair.' Then there was hysterical sobbing. I rushed downstairs, where Magda was outside the flat in floods of tears fiddling under the steering wheel of Jeremy's Saab convertible, which was emitting a 'dowee-dowee-doowee' of indescribable loudness, all lights flashing, while the baby screamed as if being murdered by a domestic cat in the car seat.

'Turn it off!' somebody yelled from an upstairs window.

'I bloody well can't!' shrieked Magda, tugging at the car bonnet.

'Jerrers!' she yelled into the portable phone. 'Jerrers, you fucking adulterous bastard! How do you open the bonnet on the Saab!'

Magda is very posh. Our street is not very posh. It is of the kind which still has posters in the windows saying 'Free Nelson Mandela'.

'I'm not bloody coming back, you bastard!' Magda was yelling. 'Just tell me how to open the fucking bonnet.'

Magda and I were both in the car now, pulling every lever we could find, Magda swigging intermittently at a bottle of Laurent-Perrier. By this time an angry mob was gathering. Next thing, Jeremy roared up on his Harley-Davidson. But instead of turning off the alarm, he started trying to grab the baby out of the back seat with Magda screaming at him. Then the Australian guy, Dan, who lives below me, opened his window.

'Oy, Bridgid,' he shouted. 'There's water pouring through my ceiling.'

'Shit! The bath!'

I ran upstairs, but when I got to my door I realized I'd shut it behind me with the key inside. I started banging my heard against it, yelling, 'Shit, shit!'

Then Dan appeared in the hall. 'Chrisd,' he said. 'You'd biddah have one of these.'

'Thanks,' I said, practically eating the proffered fag.

Several cigarettes and a lot of fiddling with a credit card later we were in, to find water flooding everywhere. We couldn't turn the taps off. Dan rushed downstairs, returning with a spanner and a bottle of Scotch. He managed to turn off the taps, and started helping me to mop up. Then the burglar alarm stopped and we rushed to the window just in time to see the Saab roar off, with the Harley-Davidson in hot pursuit.

We both started laughing – we'd had quite a lot of whisky by now. Then suddenly – I don't quite know how – he was kissing me. This was quite an awkward situation, etiquette-wise, because I had just flooded his flat and ruined his evening, so I didn't want to seem ungrateful. I know that didn't give him licence to sexually harass me, but the complication was quite enjoyable, really, after all the dramas and inner poise and everything. Then suddenly a man in motorbike leathers appeared at the open door holding a pizza box.

'Oh shit,' said Dan. 'I forgod I ordered pizza.'

'So we ate the pizza and had a bottle of wine and a few more cigarettes and some more Scotch and then he restarted trying to kiss me and I slurred, 'No, no, we mushn't,' at which point he went all funny and started muttering, 'Oh, Chrisd. Oh, Chrisd.'

'What is it?' I said.

'I'm married,' he said. 'But Bridged, I think I love you.'

When he'd finally gone I slumped on the floor, shaking, with my back to the front door, chain-smoking butt ends. 'Inner poise,' I said, half-heartedly. Then the doorbell rang. I ignored it. It rang again. Then it rang without stopping. I picked it up.

'Darling,' said a different drunken voice I recognized.

'Go away, Daniel,' I hissed.

'No. Lemme explain.'

'No.'

'Bridge . . . I wanna come in.'

Silence. Oh God. Why do I still fancy Daniel so much?

'I love you, Bridge.'

'Go away. You're drunk,' I said, with more conviction than I felt.

'Jones?'

'What?'

'Can I use your toilet?'

Saturday 29 April

Alcohol units 12, cigarettes 57, calories 8489 (excellent).

Twenty-two hours, four pizzas, one Indian takeaway, three packets of cigarettes and three bottles of champagne later, Daniel is still here. I am in love. I am also now between one and all of the following:

a) Back on thirty a day.
b) Engaged.
c) Stupid.
d) Pregnant.

11.45 p.m. Have just been sick, and as I slumped over the loo trying to do it quietly so Daniel wouldn't hear, he suddenly yelled out from the bedroom, 'There goes your inner poise, my plumptious. Best place for it, I say.'

MAY

Mother-to-Be

Monday 1 May

Alcohol units 0, cigarettes 0, calories 4200 (eating for two).

I seriously think I am pregnant. How could we have been so stupid? Daniel and I were so carried away with euphoria at being back together again that reality seemed to go out of the window – and once you've . . . oh look, I don't want to talk about it. This morning I definitely felt the beginnings of morning sickness, but that could be because I was so hungover after Daniel finally left yesterday that I ate the following things to try to make myself feel better:

2 packets Emmenthal cheese slices.
1 litre freshly squeezed orange juice.
1 cold jacket potato.
2 pieces unbaked lemon cheesecake (very light; also possibly
    eating for two).
1 Milky Way (125 calories only. Body's enthusiastic response
    to cheesecake suggested baby needed sugar).
1 chocolate Viennoise dessert thing with cream on top
    (greedy baby incredibly demanding).
Steamed broccoli (attempt to nourish baby and stop it
    growing up spoilt).

4 cold Frankfurter sausages, (only available tin in cupboard –
too exhausted by pregnancy to go out to shop again).

Oh dear. Am starting to get carried away with idea of self
as Calvin Klein-style mother figure, poss. wearing crop-top
or throwing baby in the air, laughing fulfilledly in advert
for designer gas cooker, feel-good movie or similar.

In the office today Perpetua was at her most obnoxious,
spending 45 minutes on the phone to Desdemona, discussing whether yellow walls would look nice with pink-and-
grey ruched blinds or whether she and Hugo should go for
Blood Red with a floral frieze. For one 15-minute interlude
she said nothing whatsoever except, 'Absolutely . . . no,
absolutely . . . absolutely,' then concluded, 'But of course,
in a sense, one could make exactly the same argument for
the red.'

Instead of wanting to staple things to her head, I merely
smiled in a beatific sort of way, thinking how soon all these
things were to be immaterial to me, alongside caring for
another tiny human being. Next I discovered a whole new
world of Daniel fantasies: Daniel carrying the baby in a
sling, Daniel rushing home from work, thrilled to find the
two of us pink and glowing in the bath, and, in years to
come, being incredibly impressive at parent/teacher
evenings.

But then Daniel appeared. I have never seen him look
worse. The only possible explanation was that on leaving
me yesterday he had carried on drinking. He looked over at
me, briefly, with the expression of an axe-murderer. Suddenly the fantasies were replaced by images from the film
Barfly, where the couple spent the whole time blind drunk,
screaming and throwing bottles at each other, or Harry

Enfield's The Slobs with Daniel yelling, 'Bridge. The baby. Is bawlin'. Its 'ead off.'

And me retorting, 'Daniel. I am *avin'* ay fag.'

Wednesday 3 May

9st 2* (Eek. Baby growing at monstrous unnatural rate), alcohol units 0, cigarettes 0, calories 3100 (but mainly potatoes, oh my God).*

Help. Monday and most of Tuesday I sort of thought I was pregnant, but knew I wasn't really – rather like when you're walking home late at night, and think someone is following you, but know they're not really. But then they suddenly grab you round the neck and now I'm two days late. Daniel ignored me all day Monday then caught me at 6 p.m. and said, 'Listen, I'm going to be in Manchester till the end of the week. I'll see you Saturday night, OK?' He hasn't called. Am single mother.

Thursday 4 May

9st 3, alcohol units 0, cigarettes 0, potatoes 12.

Went to the chemist to discreetly buy a pregnancy test. I was just shoving the packet at the girl on the till, with my head down, wishing I'd thought to put my ring on my wedding finger, when the chemist yelled, 'You want a pregnancy test?'

---

* Must keep eye on weight again, now, for Baby's sake.

'Shhh,' I hissed, looking over my shoulder.

'How late's your period?' he bellowed. 'You'd be better with the blue one. It tells you if you're pregnant on the *first day* after your period is due.'

I grabbed the proffered blue one, handed over the eight pounds sodding ninety-five and scuttled out.

For the first two hours this morning I kept staring at my handbag as if it was an unexploded bomb. At 11.30 I could stand it no longer, grabbed the handbag, got in the lift and went to the loos two floors down to avoid the risk of anyone I knew hearing suspicious rustling. For some reason, the whole business suddenly made me furious with Daniel. It was his responsibility too and he wasn't having to spend £8.95 and hide in the toilets trying to wee on a stick. I unwrapped the packet in a fury, shoving the box and everything in the bin and getting on with it, then put the stick upside down on the back of the loo without looking at it. Three minutes. There was no way I was going to watch my fate being sealed by a slowly forming thin blue line. Somehow I got through those hundred and eighty seconds – my last hundred and eighty seconds of freedom – picked up the stick and nearly screamed. There in the little window was a thin blue line, bold as brass. Aargh! Aargh!

After 45 minutes of staring blankly at the computer trying to pretend Perpetua was a Mexican cheeseplant whenever she asked me what was the matter, I bolted and went out to a phone booth to ring Sharon. Bloody Perpetua. If Perpetua had a pregnancy scare she's got so much English establishment behind her she'd be down the aisle in an Amanda Wakeley wedding dress in ten minutes flat. Outside, there was so much traffic noise I couldn't make Sharon understand.

'What? Bridget? I can't hear. Are you in trouble with the police?'

'No,' I snuffled. 'The blue line in the *pregnancy test*.'

'Jesus. I'll meet you in Café Rouge in fifteen minutes.'

Although it was only 12.45 I thought a vodka and orange wouldn't do any harm since it was a genuine emergency, but then I remembered that baby wasn't supposed to have vodka. I waited, feeling like a weird sort of hermaphrodite or Push-me-pull-you experiencing the most violently opposed baby sentiments of a man and a woman both at the same time. On the one hand I was all nesty and gooey about Daniel, smug about being a real woman – so irrepressibly fecund! – and imagining fluffy pink baby skin, a tiny creature to love, and darling little Ralph Lauren baby outfits. On the other I was thinking, oh my God, life is over, Daniel is a mad alcoholic and will kill me then chuck me when he finds out. No more nights out with the girls, shopping, flirting, sex, bottles of wine and fags. Instead I am going to turn into a hideous grow-bag-cum-milk-dispensing-machine which no one will fancy and which will not fit into any of my trousers, particularly my brand new acid-green Agnès B jeans. This confusion, I guess, is the price I must pay for becoming a modern woman instead of following the course nature intended by marrying Abnor Rimmington off the Northampton bus when I was eighteen.

When Sharon arrived I sulkily thrust the pregnancy test, with its tell-tale blue line, at her under the table.

'Is this it?' she said.

'Of course it's it,' I muttered. 'What do you think it is? A portable phone?'

'You,' she said, 'are a ridiculous human being. Didn't you read the instructions? There are supposed to be two lines. This line is just to show the test is working. One line means you're *not* pregnant – you ninny.'

Got home to an answerphone message from my mother saying, 'Darling, call me immediately. My nerves are shot to *ribbons*.'

Her nerves are shot to ribbons!

Friday 5 May

9st (oh sod it, cannot break weighing habit of lifetime, particularly after pregnancy trauma – will get therapy of some kind in future), alcohol units 6 (hurrah!), cigarettes 25, calories 1895, Instants 3.

Spent the morning mooning about in mourning for lost baby but cheered up a bit when Tom called to suggest a lunchtime Bloody Mary to get the weekend off to a healthy start. Got home to find a petulant message from Mother saying she's gone to a health farm and will call me later. I wonder what's the matter. Probably overwhelmed by too many Tiffany's boxes from love-sick suitors and TV presenter job offers from rival production companies.

11.45 p.m. Daniel just called from Manchester.

'Had a good week?' he said.

'Super, thanks,' I said brightly. Super, thanks. Huh! I read somewhere that the best gift a woman can bring to a man is tranquillity, so I could hardly, as soon as we've started properly going out, admit that the minute his back was turned I started having neurotic hysterics over a phantom pregnancy.

Oh well. Who cares. We're seeing each other tomorrow night. Hurray! Lalalala.

Saturday 6 May: VE Day

9st 1, alcohol units 6, cigarettes 25, calories 3800 (but celebrating anniversary of end of rationing), correct lottery numbers 0 (poor).

Awake on VE Day in unseasonable heatwave trying to whip up frenzy of emotion in self about end of war, freedom of Europe, marvellous, marvellous, etc. etc. Feel extremely miserable about whole business, to tell truth. In fact, 'left out' might be the expression I am groping towards. I do not have any grandpas. Dad has got all worked up about a party being hosted in the Alconburys' garden at which, for unexplained reasons, he will be tossing pancakes. Mum is going back to the street she was brought up in in Cheltenham for a whale-meat fritter party, probably with Julio. (Thank God she didn't run off with a German.)

None of my friends are organizing anything. It would seem embarrassingly enthusiastic and all wrong, somehow, suggesting a positive approach to life or that we were trying creepily to annex something that was nothing to do with us. I mean, I probably wasn't even an egg when the war ended. I was just nothing: while they were all fighting and making jam out of carrots or whatever they did.

I hate this idea and toy with calling Mum to see if she had started her periods when the war ended. Do eggs get produced one at a time, I wonder, or are they stored from birth in micro-form until they are activated? Could I have somehow sensed the end of the war as a stored egg? If only I had a grandpa I could have got in on the whole thing under the guise of being nice to him. Oh, sod it, I am going to go shopping.

7 p.m. The heat has made my body double in size, I swear. I am never going in a communal changing room again. I got a dress stuck under my arms in Warehouse while trying to lift it off and ended up lurching around with inside-out fabric instead of a head, tugging at it with my arms in the air, rippling stomach and thighs on full display to the assembled sniggering fifteen-year-olds. When I tried to pull the stupid dress down and get out of it the other way it got stuck on my hips.

I hate communal changing rooms. Everyone stares sneakily at each other's bodies, but no one ever meets anyone's eye. There are always girls who know that they look fantastic in everything and dance around beaming, swinging their hair and doing model poses in the mirror saying, 'Does it make me look fat?' to their obligatory obese friend, who looks like a water buffalo in everything.

It was a disaster of a trip, anyway. The answer to shopping, I know, is simply to buy a few choice items from Nicole Farhi, Whistles and Joseph but the prices so terrify me that I go scuttling back to Warehouse and Miss Selfridge, rejoicing in a host of dresses at £34.99, get them stuck on my head, then buy things from Marks & Spencer because I don't have to try them on, and at least I've bought something.

I have come home with four things, all of them unsuitable and unflattering. One will be left behind the bedroom chair in an M&S bag for two years. The other three will be exchanged for credit notes from Boules, Warehouse, etc., which I will then lose. I have thus wasted £119, which would have been enough to buy something really nice from Nicole Farhi, like a very small T-shirt.

It is all a punishment, I realize, for being obsessed by shopping in a shallow, materialistic way instead of wearing the same rayon frock all summer and painting a line down the back of my legs; also for failing to join in the VE Day celebrations. Maybe I should ring Tom and get a lovely party together for Bank Holiday Monday. Is it possible to have kitsch ironic VE day party – like for the Royal Wedding? No, you see, you can't be ironic about dead people. And then there's the problem of flags. Half of Tom's friends used to be in the Anti-Nazi league and would think the presence of Union Jacks meant we were expecting skinheads. I wonder what would have happened if our generation had had a war? Ah well, time for a little drinky. Daniel will be here soon. Best start preparations.

11.59 p.m. Blimey. Hiding in kitchen having a fag. Daniel is asleep. Actually, I think he's pretending to be asleep. *Completely* weird evening. Realized that our entire relationship so far has been based on the idea that one or other of us is supposed to be resisting having sex. Spending an evening together when the idea was that we were *supposed* to have sex at the end of it was nothing short of bizarre. We sat watching VE Day on television with Daniel's arm uncomfortably round my shoulders as if we were two fourteen-year-olds in the cinema. It was really digging into the back of my neck but I didn't feel I could ask him to move it. Then when it was getting impossible to avoid the subject of bedtime any longer we went all formal and English. Instead of tearing each other's clothes off like beasts, we stood there going, 'Do use the bathroom first.'

'No! After you!'

'No, no, no! After you!'

'Really! I insist.'

'No, no, I won't hear of it. Let me find you a guest towel and some miniature seashell-shaped soaps.'

Then we ended up lying side by side and not touching, like we were Morecambe and Wise or John Noakes and Valerie Singleton in the Blue Peter House. If there is a God I would like to humbly ask Him – whilst making it clear that I am deeply grateful for His suddenly turning Daniel inexplicably into a regular feature after so much fuckwittage – to stop him getting into bed at night wearing pyjamas and reading glasses, staring at a book for 25 minutes then switching off the light and turning over – and turn him back into the naked lust-crazed sex beast I used to know and love.

Thanking you for your kind attention, Lord, regarding this matter.

Saturday 13 May

9st 1lb 8oz, cigarettes 7, calories 1145, Instants 5 (won £2 therefore total Instants expenditure only £3, v.g.), Lottery proper £2, number of correct numbers 1 (better).

How come have put on only 8oz after last night's over-consumption orgy?

Maybe food and weight are the same as garlic and stenchful breath: if you eat several entire bulbs your breath doesn't smell at all, similarly if eat huge amount does not cause weight gain: strangely cheering theory but creates v. bad situation in head. Would welcome removal for thorough valeting. Still, was worth it for delicious night of drunken feminist ranting with Sharon and Jude.

An unbelievable amount of food and wine was consumed since the generous girls, as well as bringing a bottle of wine each, had all brought a little extra something from M&S. Therefore, in addition to the three-course meal and two bottles of wine (1 fizzy, 1 white) I had already bought from M&S (I mean prepared by entire day's slaving over hot stove) we had:

1 tub hummus & pkt mini-pittas.
12 smoked salmon and cream cheese pinwheels.
12 mini-pizzas.
1 raspberry pavlova.
1 tiramisu (party size).
2 Swiss Mountain Bars.

Sharon was on top form. 'Bastards!' she was already yelling by 8.35, pouring three-quarters of a glass of Kir Royale straight down her throat. 'Stupid, smug, arrogant, manipulative, self-indulgent bastards. They exist in a total Culture of Entitlement. Pass me one of those mini-pizzas, will you?'

Jude was depressed because Vile Richard, with whom she is currently split up, keeps ringing her, dropping little verbal baits suggesting he wants to get back together to make sure he keeps her interested, but protecting himself by saying he just wants to be 'friends' (fraudulent, poisoned concept). Then last night he made an incredibly assumptive, patronizing phone call, asking her if she was going to a mutual friend's party.

'Ah well, in that case I won't come,' he said. 'No. It really wouldn't be fair on you. You see, I was going to bring this, sort of, date with me. I mean, it's nothing. It's just some girl who's stupid enough to let me shag her for a couple of weeks.'

'What?' exploded Sharon, beginning to turn pink. 'That's the most repulsive thing I've ever heard anyone say about a woman. Arrogant little *prat*! How dare he give himself licence to treat you any way he likes under the name of friendship, then make himself feel clever by trying to upset you with his stupid new date. If he really minded about not hurting your feelings he'd just shut up and come to the party on his own instead of waving his stupid date under your nose.'

'"Friends?" Pah! The Enemy more like!' I shouted happily, tucking into another Silk Cut and a couple of salmon pinwheels. 'Bastard!'

By 11.30 Sharon was in full and splendid auto-rant.

'Ten years ago people who cared about the environment were laughed at as sandal-wearing beardy-weirdies and now look at the power of the green consumer,' she was shouting, sticking her fingers into the tiramisu and transferring it straight into her mouth. 'In years ahead the same will come to pass with feminism. There won't be any men leaving their families and post-menopausal wives for young mistresses, or trying to chat women up by showing off in a patronizing way about all the other women throwing themselves at them, or trying to have sex with women without any niceness or commitment, because the young mistresses and women will just turn round and tell them to sod off and men won't get any sex or any women unless they learn how to behave properly instead of cluttering up the sea-bed of women with their SHITTY, SMUG, SELF-INDULGENT, BEHAVIOUR!'

'Bastards!' yelled Jude, slurping on her Pinot Grigio.

'Bastards,' I yelled through a mouthful of raspberry pavlova mixed with tiramisu.

'Bloody bastards!' shouted Jude, lighting a Silk Cut with the butt end of the last one.

Just then the doorbell rang.

'I bet that's Daniel, the bloody bastard,' I said. 'What is it?' I yelled into the entryphone.

'Oh, hello, darling,' said Daniel in his gentlest, politest voice. 'I'm really sorry to bother you. I did ring earlier and leave a message on your answerphone. It's just I've been stuck in the most tedious board meeting you can imagine for the entire evening and I so much wanted to see you. I'll just give you a little kiss and then go, if you like. Can I come up?'

'Burr. All right, then,' I muttered grumpily, pressed the buzzer and lurched back to the table. 'Bloody bastard.'

'Culture of Entitlement,' growled Sharon. 'Cooking, succour, beautiful young girls' bodies when they're old and fat. Think women are there to give them what they're bloody entitled . . . Here, have we run out of wine?'

Then Daniel appeared up the stairs, smiling lovingly. He looked tired yet fresh-faced, clean-shaven and very neat in his suit. He was holding three boxes of Milk Tray.

'I bought you all one of these,' he said, one eyebrow raised sexily, 'to eat with your coffee. Don't let me interrupt. I've done the shopping for the weekend.'

He carried eight Cullens carrier bags into the kitchen and started putting everything away.

At that moment the phone rang. It was the mini-cab firm the girls had rung half an hour earlier saying there'd been a terrible multiple pile-up in Ladbroke Grove, plus all their cars had unexpectedly exploded and they weren't going to be able to come for another three hours.

'How far are you going?' said Daniel. 'I'll drive you home. You can't hang around the streets looking for cabs at this time of night.'

As the girls fluttered around finding their handbags and grinning stupidly at Daniel I started eating all the nut, praline, fudge or caramel-based chocolates out of my box of Milk Tray, feeling a bewildering mixture of smugness and pride over my perfect new boyfriend whom the girls clearly wished to have a go at shagging, and furious with the normally disgusting sexist drunk for ruining our feminist ranting by freakishly pretending to be the perfect man. Huh. We'll see how long that lasts, won't we? I thought, while I waited for him to come back.

When he came back he ran up the stairs, swept me up into his arms and carried me into the bedroom.

'You get an extra chocolate for being lovely even when you're squiffy,' he said, taking a foil-wrapped chocolate heart out of his pocket. And then . . . Mmmmmm.

Sunday 14 May

7 p.m. Hate Sunday night. Feels like homework night. Have got to write catalogue copy for Perpetua before tomorrow. Think I will just ring Jude first.

7.05 p.m. No reply. Hmmmph. Anyway, down to work.

7.10 p.m. Think will just call Sharon.

7.45 p.m. Shazzer was annoyed with me for ringing because she had just got in and was about to call 1471 to see if this guy she has been seeing had rung while she was out and now my number will be stored instead.

Consider 1471 to be brilliant invention, instantly telling you the number of the last person who called. It was ironic, really, because when the three of us first found out about 1471 Sharon said she was totally against it, considering it exploitation by British Telecom of the addictive personalities and relationship-breakdown epidemic among the British populace. Some people are apparently calling it upwards of twenty times a day. Jude, on the other hand, is strongly in favour of 1471, but does concede that if you have just split up with or started sleeping with someone it doubles misery potential when you come home: no - number - stored -on-1471-misery, to add to no-message-on-answerphone-misery, or number - stored - turning - out - to - be - Mother's - misery.

Apparently in America the 1471 equivalent tells you *all* the numbers that have rung you since last time you checked and *how many times*. Shudder with horror at the thought of own obsessive calling of Daniel's number in early days being exposed in this way. The good thing over here is that if you dial 141 before you ring, it stops your number being stored on the other person's phone. Jude says you have to be careful, though, because if you have an obsessive crush on someone and ring accidentally when they are in, then ring off and no number is stored they might guess it was you. Must make sure Daniel does not find out about any of this.

9.30 p.m. Decided to nip round corner for cigarettes. On way up stairs heard phone ringing. Suddenly realizing had forgotten to put answerphone back on when Tom rang, tore up stairs, emptied contents of handbag on floor to find key and threw self across room to phone at which point phone stopped. Had just gone into loo when phone rang again. Stopped when got to it. Then started ringing again when went away. Finally got it.

'Oh, hello, darling, guess what?' Mum.

'What?' I said, miserably.

'I'm taking you to have your colours done! And don't keep saying, "what", please, darling. Color Me Beautiful. I'm sick to death of you wandering round in all these dingy slurries and fogs. You look like something out of Chairman Mao.'

'Mum. I can't really talk, I'm expecting . . .'

'Now come along, Bridget. I don't want any silliness,' she said in her Genghis-Khan-at-height-of-evil voice. 'Mavis Enderby used to be all miserable in buffs and mosses, now she's had hers done she comes out in all these wonderful shocking pinks and bottle greens and looks twenty years younger.'

'But I don't want to come out in shocking pinks and bottle greens,' I said, through clenched teeth.

'Well, you see, darling, Mavis is Winter. And I'm Winter, but you might be Summer like Una and then you'll get your pastels. You can't tell till they get the towel on your head.'

'Mum, I'm not going to Color Me Beautiful,' I hissed, desperately.

'Bridget, I'm not listening to any more of this. Auntie Una

was just saying the other day: if you'd had something a bit more bright and cheerful on at the turkey curry buffet Mark Darcy might have shown a bit more interest. Nobody wants a girlfriend who wanders round looking like someone from Auschwitz, darling.' Thought better of boasting to her about having a boyfriend despite being dressed from head to toe in slurry but prospect of Daniel and self becoming hot topic for discussion precipitating relentless stream of feedback folk-wisdom from Mum dissuaded me. Eventually got her to shut up about Color Me Beautiful by telling her I would think about it.

Tuesday 17 May

9st 2 (hooray!), cigarettes 7 (v.g.), alcohol units 6 (so v.g. – v. pure).

Daniel is still being gorgeous. How could everyone have been so wrong about him? Head is full of moony fantasies about living in flats with him and running along beaches together with tiny offspring in manner of Calvin Klein advert, being trendy Smug Married instead of sheepish Singleton. Just off to meet Magda.

11 p.m. Hmmm. Thought-provoking supper with Magda, who is v. depressed about Jeremy. The night of the burglar alarm and screaming row in my street was a result of a remark from Sloaney Woney, who claimed she had seen Jeremy with a girl at the Harbour Club who sounded suspiciously like the witch I saw him with all those weeks ago. After that, Magda asked me at point blank range if I'd heard or seen anything so I told her about the witch in the Whistles suit.

Turned out Jeremy admitted there'd been a flirtation and he'd been very attracted to this girl. They hadn't slept together, he alleged. But Magda was really fed up.

'You should make the most of being single while it lasts, Bridge,' she said. 'Once you've got kids and you've given up your job you're in an incredibly vulnerable position. I know Jeremy thinks my life is just one big holiday, but basically it's extremely hard work looking after a toddler and a baby all day, and it doesn't stop. When Jeremy comes home at the end of the day he wants to put his feet up and be nurtured and, as I imagine all the time now, fantasize about girls in leotards at the Harbour Club.

'I had a proper job before. I know for a fact it's much more fun going out to work, getting all dressed up, flirting in the office and having nice lunches than going to the bloody supermarket and picking Harry up from playgroup. But there's always this aggrieved air that I'm some sort of ghastly Harvey Nichols-obsessed lady who lunches while he earns all the money.'

She's so beautiful, Magda. I watched her toying with her champagne glass despondently and wondered what the answer is for we girls. Talk about grass is always bloody greener. The number of times I've slumped, depressed, thinking how useless I am and that I spend every Saturday night getting blind drunk and moaning to Jude and Shazzer or Tom about not having a boyfriend; I struggle to make ends meet and am ridiculed as an unmarried freak, whereas Magda lives in a big house with eight different kinds of pasta in jars, and gets to go shopping all day. And yet here she is so beaten, miserable and unconfident and telling me I'm lucky . . .

'Ooh, by the way,' she said, brightening, 'talking of Harvey Nicks, I got the most wonderful Joseph shift dress in there today – red, two buttons at one side at the neck, very nicely cut, £280. God, I so much wish I was like you, Bridge, and could just have an affair. Or have bubble baths for two hours on Sunday morning. Or stay out all night with no questions asked. Don't suppose you fancy coming shopping tomorrow morning, do you?'

'Er. Well, I've got to go to work,' I said.

'Oh,' said Magda, looking momentarily surprised. 'You know,' she went on, toying with her champagne, 'once you get the feeling that there's a woman your husband prefers to you, it becomes rather miserable being at home, imagining all the versions of that type of woman he might run into out in the world. You do feel rather powerless.'

I thought about my mum. 'You could seize power,' I said, 'in a bloodless coup. Go back to work. Take a lover. Bring Jeremy up short.'

'Not with two children under three,' she said resignedly. 'I think I've made my bed, I'll just have to lie in it now.'

Oh God. As Tom never tires of telling me, in a sepulchral voice, laying his hand on my arm and staring into my eyes with an alarming look, 'Only Women Bleed.'

Friday 19 May

8st 12½ (have lost 3lb 8oz literally overnight – must have eaten food which uses up more calories to eat it than it gives off e.g. v. chewy lettuce), alcohol units 4 (modest), cigarettes 21 (bad), Instants 4 (not v.g.).

4.30 p.m. Just when Perpetua was breathing down my neck so she didn't end up late for her weekend in Gloucestershire at the Trehearnes' the phone rang.

'Hello, darling!' My mother. 'Guess what? I've got the most marvellous opportunity for you.'

'What?' I muttered sulkily.

'You're going to be on television,' she gushed as I crashed my head on to the desk.

'I'm coming round with the crew at ten o'clock tomorrow. Oh, darling, aren't you *thrilled*?'

'Mother. If you're coming round to my flat with a television crew, I won't be in it.'

'Oh, but you must,' she said icily.

'No,' I said. But then vanity began to get the better of me. 'Why, anyway? What?'

'Oh, darling,' she cooed. 'They're wanting someone *younger* for me to interview on "Suddenly Single": someone pre-menopausal and Suddenly Single who can talk about, well, you know, darling, the pressures of impending child-lessness, and so on.'

'I'm *not* pre-menopausal, Mother!' I exploded. 'And I'm not Suddenly Single either. I'm suddenly part of a couple.'

'Oh, don't be silly, darling,' she hissed. I could hear office noises in the background.

'I've got a boyfriend.'

'Who?'

'Never you mind,' I said, suddenly glancing over my shoulder at Perpetua, who was smirking.

'Oh, please, darling. I've told them I've found someone.'

'No.'

'Oh, pleeeeeease. I've never had a career all my life and

134

now I'm in the autumn of my days and I need something for myself,' she gabbled, as if reading from a cue card.

'Someone I know might see. Anyway, won't they notice I'm your daughter?'

There was a pause. I could hear her talking to someone in the background. Then she came back and said, 'We could blot out your face.'

'What? Put a bag over it?' Thanks a lot.'

'Silhouette, darling, silhouette. Oh, please, Bridget. Remember, I gave you the gift of life. Where would you be without me? Nowhere. Nothing. A dead egg. A piece of space, darling.'

The thing is I've always, secretly, rather fancied being on television.

Saturday 20 May

9st 3 (why? why? from where?), alcohol units 7 (Saturday), cigarettes 17 (positively restrained, considering), number of correct lottery numbers 0 (but v. distracted by filming).

The crew had trodden a couple of wine glasses into the carpet before they'd been in the house thirty seconds, but I'm not too fussed about that sort of thing. It was when one of them staggered in shouting, 'Mind your backs,' carrying an enormous light with flaps on it, then bellowed, 'Trevor, where do you want this brute?' overbalanced, crashed the light through the glass door of the kitchen cupboard and knocked an open bottle of extra virgin olive oil over on to my River Café cookbook that I realized what I'd done.

Three hours after they arrived, filming had still not begun and they were still boshing around saying, 'Can I just cheat you this way a bit, love?' By the time we finally got going, with Mother and I sitting opposite each other in semi-darkness, it was nearly half past one.

'And tell me,' she was saying in a caring, understanding voice I'd never heard before, 'when your husband left you, did you have' – she was almost whispering now – 'suicidal thoughts?'

I stared at her incredulously.

'I know this is painful for you. If you feel you're going to break down we can stop for a moment,' she said hopefully.

I was too livid to speak. What husband?

'I mean, it must be a terrible time, with no partner on the horizon and that biological clock ticking away,' she said, kicking me under the table. I kicked her back and she jumped and let out a little noise.

'Don't you want a child?' she said, handing me a tissue.

At this point there was a loud snort of laughter from the back of the room. I had thought it would be fine to leave Daniel asleep in the bedroom because he never wakes up till after lunch on Saturdays and I'd put his cigarettes on the pillow next to him.

'If Bridget had a child she'd lose it,' he guffawed. 'Pleased to meet you, Mrs Jones. Bridget, why can't you get all done up on Saturdays like your mum?'

Sunday 21 May

My mum is not speaking to either of us for humiliating her and exposing her as a fraud in front of her crew. At least she might leave us alone for a bit now. So much looking forward to the summer, anyway. Will be so lovely having a boyfriend when it is warm. We will be able to go on romantic mini-breaks. V. happy.

JUNE

Hah! Boyfriend

Saturday 3 June

8st 13, alcohol units 5, cigarettes 25, calories 600, minutes spent looking at brochures: long-haul 45, mini-break 87, 1471 calls 7 (g.).

Finding it impossible to concentrate on almost anything in the heat except fantasies about going on mini-breaks with Daniel. Head is filled with visions of us lying in glades by rivers, me in long white floaty dress, Daniel and I sitting outside ancient Cornish waterside pub sipping pints in matching striped T-shirts and watching the sun set over the sea; Daniel and I eating candlelit dinners in historic country-house-hotel courtyards then retiring to our room to shag all hot summer night.

Anyway. Daniel and I are going to a party tonight at his friend Wicksy's, then tomorrow I expect we will go to the park or out to a lovely pub in the country for lunch. It is marvellous having a boyfriend.

Sunday 4 June

9st, alcohol units 3 (g.), cigarettes 13 (g.), minutes spent looking at brochures: long-haul 30 (g.), mini-break 52, 1471 calls 3 (g.).

7 p.m. Humph. Daniel has just gone home. Bit fed up, actually. Was really lovely hot Sunday but Daniel did not want to go out or discuss mini-breaks and insisted on spending all afternoon with the curtains drawn, watching the cricket. Also the party was quite nice last night, but at one point we went over to join Wicksy and a very pretty girl he was talking to. I did notice, as we approached, that she looked rather defensive.

'Daniel,' said Wicksy, 'have you met Vanessa?'

'No,' said Daniel, putting on his most flirtatious seductive grin and holding out his hand. 'Nice to meet you.'

'Daniel,' said Vanessa, folding her arms and looking absolutely livid, 'We've *slept together*.'

God, it's hot. Quite like leaning out of the window. Someone is playing a saxophone in effort to pretend we are all in a film set in New York, and can hear voices all around because everyone's windows are open, and smell cooking from restaurants. Hmm. Think would like to move to New York: though probably, come to think of it, not v.g. area for mini-breaks. Unless mini-break actually is to New York, which would be pointless if one were already in New York.

Will just ring Tom then get down to work.

8 p.m. Just going round to Tom's for a quick drink. Just for half an hour.

9st 2, alcohol units 4, cigarettes 3 (v.g.), calories 1326, Instants 0 (excellent), 1471 calls 12 (bad), hours spent asleep 15 (bad, but not self's fault as heatwave).

Managed to persuade Perpetua to let me stay at home to work. Certain she only agreed because she wants to sunbathe too. Mmmm. Got lovely new mini-break brochure: 'Pride of Britain: Leading Country House Hotels of the British Isles'. Marvellous. Going through all pages one by one imagining Daniel and me being alternately sexual and romantic in all the bedrooms and dining rooms.

11 a.m. Right: am going to concentrate now.

11.25 a.m. Hmmm, got a bit of a scratchy nail.

11.35 a.m. God. I just started having paranoid fantasy for no reason about Daniel having an affair with someone else and thinking up dignified but cutting remarks to make him sorry. Now why should that be? Have I sensed with a woman's intuition that he is having an affair?

The trouble with trying to go out with people when you get older is that everything becomes so loaded. When you are partnerless in your thirties, the mild bore of not being in a relationship – no sex, not having anyone to hang out with on Sundays, going home from parties on your own all the time – gets infused with the paranoid notion that the reason you are not in a relationship is your age, you have had your last ever relationship and sexual experience ever, and it is all your fault for being too wild or wilful to settle down in the first bloom of youth.

You completely forget the fact that when you were twenty-two and you didn't have boyfriend or meet anyone you remotely fancied for twenty-three months you just thought it was a bit of a drag. The whole thing builds up out of all proportion, so finding a relationship seems a dazzling, almost insurmountable goal, and when you do start going out with someone it cannot possibly live up to expectations.

Is it that? Or is it that there is something wrong with me being with Daniel? Is Daniel having an affair?

11.50 a.m. Hmmm. Nail really *is* scratchy. Actually, if don't do something about it I'll start picking at it and next thing I'll have no fingernail left. Right, I'd better go and find an emery board. Come to think of it, this nail varnish generally is looking a bit scrotty. I really need to take it all off and start again. Might as well do it now while I think about it.

Noon. It is such a bloody bore when the weather is so hot and one's *soi-disant* boyfriend refuses to go anywhere nice with you. Feel he thinks I am trying to trap him into a mini-break; as if it were not a mini-break but marriage, three kids and cleaning out the toilet in house full of stripped pine in Stoke Newington. I think this is turning into a psychological crisis. I'm going to call Tom (can always do the catalogue stuff for Perpetua this evening).

12.30 p.m. Hmmm. Tom says if you go mini-breaking with somebody you are having a relationship with you spend the whole time worrying about how the relationship is going, so it is better just to go with a friend.

Apart from sex, I say. Apart from sex, he agrees. I'm going to meet Tom tonight with brochures to plan fantasy, or phantom mini-break. So I must work really hard this afternoon.

12.40 p.m. These shorts and T-shirt are too uncomfortable in this heat. I'm going to change into a long floaty dress.

Oh dear, my pants show through this dress now. I'd better put some flesh-coloured ones on in case someone comes to the door. Now, my Gossard Glossies ones would be perfect. I wonder where they are.

12.45 p.m. In fact think might put the Glossies bra on to match if I can find it.

12.55 p.m. That's better.

1 p.m. Lunchtime! At last a bit of time off.

2 p.m. OK, so this afternoon I am really going to work and get everything done before the evening, then can go out. V. sleepy, though. It's so hot. Maybe I'll just close my eyes for five minutes. Catnaps are said to be an excellent way of reviving oneself. Used to excellent effect by Margaret Thatcher and Winston Churchill. Good idea. Maybe I'll lie down on the bed.

7.30 p.m. Oh, Bloody Hell.

Friday 9 June

9st 2, alcohol units 7, cigarettes 22, calories 2145, minutes spent inspecting face for wrinkles 230.

9 a.m. Hurrah! Night out with girls tonight.

7 p.m. Oh no. Turns out Rebecca is coming. An evening with Rebecca is like swimming in sea with jellyfish: all will be going along perfectly pleasantly then suddenly you get painful lashing, destroying confidence at stroke. Trouble is, Rebecca's stings are aimed so subtly at one's Achilles' heels, like Gulf War missiles going 'Fzzzzzz whoossssh' through Baghdad hotel corridors, that never see them coming. Sharon says am not twenty-four any more and should be mature enough to deal with Rebecca. She is right.

Midnight. Argor es wororrible. Am olanpassit. Face collapsin.

Saturday 10 June

Ugh. Woke up this morning feeling happy (still drunk from last night), then suddenly remembered horror of how yesterday's girls' night had turned out. After first bottle of Chardonnay was just about to broach subject of constant mini-break frustration when Rebecca suddenly said, 'How's Magda?'
   'Fine,' I replied.
   'She's incredibly attractive, isn't she?'
   'Mmm,' I said.

'And she's amazingly young-looking – I mean she could easily pass for twenty-four or twenty-five. You were at school together, weren't you, Bridget? Was she three or four years below you?'

'She's six months older,' I said, feeling the first twinges of horror.

'Really?' said Rebecca, then left a long, embarrassed pause. 'Well, Magda's lucky. She's got really good skin.'

I felt the blood draining from my brain as the horrible truth of what Rebecca was saying hit me.

'I mean, she doesn't smile as much as you do. That's probably why she hasn't got so many lines.'

I grasped the table for support, trying to get my breath. I am ageing prematurely, I realized. Like a time-release film of a plum turning into a prune.

'How's your diet going, Rebecca?' said Shazzer.

Aargh. Instead of denying it, Jude and Shazzer were accepting my premature ageing as read, tactfully trying to change the subject to spare my feelings. I sat, in a spiral of terror, grasping my sagging face.

'Just going to the ladies,' I said through clenched teeth like a ventriloquist keeping my face fixed, to reduce the appearance of wrinkles.

'Are you all right, Bridge?' said Jude.

'Fn,' I replied stiffly.

Once in front of the mirror I reeled as the harsh overhead lighting revealed my thick, age-hardened, sagging flesh. I imagined the others back at the table, chiding Rebecca for alerting me to what everyone had long been saying about me but I never needed to know.

Was suddenly overwhelmed by urge to rush out and ask all the diners how old they thought I was: like at school once, when I conceived private conviction that I was mentally subnormal and went round asking everyone in the playground, 'Am I mental?' and twenty-eight of them said, 'Yes.'

Once get on tack of thinking about ageing there is no escape. Life suddenly seems like holiday where, halfway through, everything starts accelerating towards the end. Feel need to do something to stop ageing process, but what? Cannot afford face-lift. Caught in hideous cleft stick as both fatness and dieting are in themselves ageing. Why do I look old? Why? Stare at old ladies in street trying to work out all tiny processes by which faces become old not young. Scour newspapers for ages of everyone, trying to decide if they look old for their age.

11 a.m. Phone just rang. It was Simon, to tell me about the latest girl he has got his eye on. 'How old is she?' I said, suspiciously.

'Twenty-four.'

Aargh aargh. Have reached the age when men of my own age no longer find their contemporaries attractive.

4 p.m. Going out to meet Tom for tea. Decided needed to spend more time on appearance like Hollywood stars and have therefore spent ages putting concealer under eyes, blusher on cheeks and defining fading features.

'Good God,' said Tom when I arrived.

'What?' I said. 'What?'

'Your face. You look like Barbara Cartland.'

I started blinking very rapidly, trying to come to terms with the realization that some hideous time-bomb in my skin had suddenly, irrevocably, shrivelled it up.

'I look really old for my age, don't I?' I said, miserably.

'No, you look like a five-year-old in your mother's make-up,' he said. 'Look.'

I glanced in the mock Victorian pub mirror. I looked like a garish clown with bright pink cheeks, two dead crows for eyes and the bulk of the white cliffs of Dover smeared underneath. Suddenly understood how old women end up wandering around over-made-up with everyone sniggering at them and resolved not to snigger any more.

'What's going on?' he said.

'I'm prematurely ageing,' I muttered.

'Oh, for God's sake. It's that bloody Rebecca, isn't it?' he said. 'Shazzer told me about the Magda conversation. It's ridiculous. You look about sixteen.'

Love Tom. Even though suspected he might have been lying still feel hugely cheered up as even Tom would surely not say looked sixteen if looked forty-five.

Sunday 11 June

8st 13 (v.g., too hot to eat), alcohol units 3, cigarettes 0 (v.g., too hot to smoke), calories 759 (entirely ice-cream).

Another wasted Sunday. It seems the entire summer is doomed to be spent watching the cricket with the curtains drawn. Feel strange sense of unease with the summer and not just because of the drawn curtains on Sundays and mini-break ban. Realize, as the long hot days freakishly repeat themselves, one after the other, that whatever I am doing I really think I ought to be doing something else. It comes from the same feeling *family* as the one which periodically makes you think that just because you live in central London you should be out at the RSC/Albert Hall/ Tower of London/Royal Academy/Madame Tussauds, instead of hanging around in bars enjoying yourself.

The more the sun shines the more obvious it seems that others are making fuller, *better* use of it elsewhere: possibly at some giant softball game to which everyone is invited except me; possibly alone with their lover in a rustic glade by waterfalls where Bambis graze, or at some large public celebratory event, probably including the Queen Mother and one or more of the football tenors, to mark the exquisite summer which I am failing to get the best out of. Maybe it is our climatic past that is to blame. Maybe we do not yet have the mentality to deal with a sun and cloudless blue sky, which is anything other than a freak incident. The instinct to panic, run out of the office, take most of your clothes off and lie panting on the fire escape is still too strong.

But there, too, is confusion. It is not the thing to go out courting malignant growths any more so what should you do? A shady barbecue, perhaps? Starve your friends while you tamper with fire for hours then poison them with burnt yet still quivering slices of underdone suckling pig? Or organize picnics in the park and end up with all the women scraping squashed gobbets of mozzarella off tinfoil and yelling at children with ozone asthma attacks; while the men swig warm white wine in the fierce midday sun, staring at the nearby softball games with left-out shame.

Envy summer life on the Continent, where men in smart lightweight suits and designer sunglasses glide around calmly in smart air-conditioned cars, maybe stopping for a *citron pressé* in a shady pavement café in an ancient square, totally cool about the sun and ignoring it because they know for a fact that it will still be shining at the weekend, when they can go and lie quietly on the yacht.

Feel certain this has been factor behind our waning national confidence ever since we started to travel and notice it. I suppose things might change. More and more tables are on pavements. Diners are managing to sit calmly at them, only occasionally remembering the sun and turning their faces to it with closed eyes, breaking into huge excited grins at passer-by – 'Look, look, we're enjoying a refreshing drink in a pavement café, we can do it too' – their expressions of angst merely brief and fleeting which say, 'Ought we to be at an outdoor performance of *A Midsummer Night's Dream?*'

Somewhere at the back of my mind is a new-born, tremulous notion that maybe Daniel is right: what you are supposed to do when it's hot is go to sleep under a tree or watch cricket with the curtains drawn. But to my way of thinking, to actually get to sleep you'd have to know that the next day would be hot as well, and the one after that, and that enough hot days lay in store in your lifetime to do all conceivable hot-day activities in a calm and measured manner with no sense of urgency whatsoever. Fat chance.

Monday 12 June

9st 1, alcohol units 3 (v.g.), cigarettes 13 (g.), minutes spent trying to programme video 210 (poor).

7 p.m. Mum just rang. 'Oh, hello, darling. Guess what? Penny Husbands-Bosworth is on *Newsnight*!!!'

'Who?'

'You know the Husbands-Bosworths, dar*ling*. Ursula was in the year above you at the High School. Herbert died of leukaemia . . .'

'What?'

'Don't say "what", Bridget, say "pardon". The thing is I'm going to be out because Una wants to see a slide show of the Nile so Penny and I wondered if you'd record it . . . Ooh, better dash – there's the butcher!'

8 p.m. Right. Ridiculous to have had video for two years and never to have been able to make it record anything. Also is marvellous FV 67 HV VideoPlus. Simple matter of following operating instructions, locating buttons, etc., certain.

8.15 p.m. Humph. Cannot locate operating instructions.

8.35 p.m. Hah! Found operating instructions under *Hello!*. Right. 'Programming your video is as easy as making a phone call'. Excellent.

8.40 p.m. 'Point the remote control at the video recorder.' V. easy. 'Turn to Index.' Aargh, horror list with 'Timer controlled simultaneous HiFi sound recordings', 'the decoder needed for encoded programmes', etc. Merely wish to record Penny Husbands-Bosworth's rant, not spend all evening reading treatise on spying techniques.

8.50 p.m. Ah. Diagram. 'Buttons for IMC functions'. But what are IMC functions?

8.55 p.m. Decide to ignore that page. Turn to 'Timer-controlled recordings with VideoPlus': '1. Meet the requirements for VideoPlus.' What requirements? Hate the stupid video. Feel exactly the same as feel when trying to follow signposts on roads. Know in heart that signposts and video manual do not make sense but still cannot believe authorities would be so cruel as to deliberately dupe us all. Feel incompetent fool and as if everyone else in world understands something which is being kept from me.

9.10 p.m. 'When you turn your recorder on you must adjust the clock and the calendar for precise TIMER-controlled recording (don't forget to use the quick-adjust options to switch between summer and winter time). Clock menus called with red and digital number 6.'

Press red and nothing happens. Press numbers and nothing happens. Wish stupid video had never been invented.

9.25 p.m. Aargh. Suddenly main menu is on TV saying 'Press 6'. Oh dear. Realize was using telly remote control by mistake. Now news has come on.

Just called Tom and asked him if he could record Penny Husbands-Bosworth but he said he didn't know how to work his video either.

Suddenly there is clicking noise within video and the news is replaced, incomprehensibly, by *Blind Date*.

Just called Jude and she can't work hers either. Aaargh. Aargh. Is 10.15. *Newsnight* in 15 minutes.

10.17 p.m. Cassette will not go in.

10.18 p.m. Ah, *Thelma and Louise* is in there.

10.19 p.m. *Thelma and Louise* will not come out.

10.21 p.m. Frenziedly press all buttons. Cassette comes out and goes back in again.

10.25 p.m. Have got new cassette in now. Right. Turn to 'Recording'.

'Recording will start when in Tuner Mode when any button is pressed (apart from Mem).' What, though, is Tuner Mode? 'When recording from a camcorder or similar press AV prog source 3 x during a bilingual transmission press 1/2 and hold for 3 seconds to make your choice of language.'

Oh God. Stupid manual reminds me of Linguistics professor had at Bangor, who was so immersed in finer points of language that could not speak without veering off into analysis of each individual word: 'This morning I would . . . now "would" you see, in 1570 . . .'

Aargh aargh. *Newsnight* is starting.

10.31 p.m. OK. OK. Calm. Penny Husbands-Bosworth's asbestos leukaemia item is not on yet.

10.33 p.m. Yesss, yesss. RECORDING CURRENT PROGRAMME. Have done it!

Aaargh. All going mad. Cassette has started rewinding and now stopped and ejected. Why? Shit. Shit. Realize in excitement have sat on remote control.

10.35 p.m. Frantic now. Have rung Shazzer, Rebecca, Simon, Magda. Nobody knows how to programme their videos. Only person I know who knows how to do it is Daniel.

10.45 p.m. Oh God. Daniel fell about laughing when said I could not programme video. Said he would do it for me. Still, at least have done best for Mum. It is exciting and historic when one's friends are on TV.

11.15 p.m. Humph. Mum just rang. 'Sorry, darling. It isn't *Newsnight*, it's *Breakfast News* tomorrow. Could you set it for seven o'clock tomorrow morning. BBC1?'

11.30 p.m. Daniel just called. 'Er, sorry, Bridge. I'm not quite sure what went wrong. It's recorded Barry Norman.'

Sunday 18 June

8st 12, alcohol units 3, cigarettes 17.

After sitting in semi-darkness for the third weekend running with Daniel's hand down my bra, fiddling with my nipple as if it were a sort of worry bead and me occasionally feebly saying, 'Was that a run?' I suddenly blurted out, '*Why* can't we go on a mini-break? Why? *Why? Why?*'

'That's a good idea,' said Daniel, mildly, taking his hand out of my dress. 'Why don't you book somewhere for next weekend? Nice country house hotel. I'll pay.'

Wednesday 21 June

8st 11 (v.v.g.), alcohol units 1, cigarettes 2, Instants 2 (v.g.), minutes spent looking at mini-break brochures 237 (bad).

Daniel has refused to discuss the mini-break any more, or look at the brochure, and has forbidden me from mentioning it until we actually set off on Saturday. How can he expect me not to be excited when I have been longing for this for so long? Why is it that men have not yet learnt to fantasize about holidays, choose them from brochures and plan and fantasize about them in the way that they (or some of them) have learnt to cook or sew? The single-handed mini-break responsibility is hideous for me. Wovingham Hall seems ideal – tasteful without being over-formal, with four-poster beds, a lake and even a fitness centre (not to go in), but what if Daniel doesn't like it?

Sunday 25 June

8st 11, alcohol units 7, cigarettes 2, calories 4587 (ooops).

Oh dear. Daniel decided the place was nouveau from the moment we arrived, because there were three Rolls-Royces parked outside, and one of them yellow. I was fighting a sinking realization that it was suddenly freezing cold and I had packed for 90° heat. This was my packing:

Swimsuits 2.
Bikinis 1.
Long floaty white dress 1.

Sundress 1.

Trailer-park-trash pink jelly mules 1 pair.

Tea-rose-pink suede mini dress 1.

Black silk teddy.

Bras, pants, stockings, suspenders (various).

There was a crack of thunder as I teetered, shivering, after Daniel to find the foyer stuffed with bridesmaids and men in cream suits and to discover that we were the only guests staying in the hotel who were not in the wedding party.

'Chuh! Isn't it dreadful what's happening in Srebrenica,' I chattered maniacally to try to put out problems in proportion. 'To be honest, I never feel I've quite *pinned down* what's going on in Bosnia. I thought the Bosnians were the ones in Sarajevo and the Serbians were attacking them, so who are the Bosnian Serbs?'

'Well, if you spent a bit less time reading brochures and more time reading the papers you might know,' smirked Daniel.

'So what *is* going on?'

'God, look at that bridesmaid's tits.'

'And who are the Bosnian Muslims?'

'I cannot believe the size of that man's lapels.'

Suddenly I had the unmistakable feeling that Daniel was trying to change the subject.

'Are the Bosnian Serbs the same lot who were attacking Sarajevo?' I asked.

Silence.

'Whose territory is Srebrenica in, then?'

'Srebrenica is a *safe area*,' said Daniel in deeply patronizing tones.

'So how come the people from the safe area were attacking before?'

'Shut up.'

'Just tell me if the Bosnians in Srebrenica are the same lot as the ones in Sarajevo.'

'Muslims,' said Daniel triumphantly.

'Serbian or Bosnian?'

'Look, will you shut up?'

'You don't know what's going on in Bosnia either.'

'I do.'

'You don't.'

'I do.'

'You *don't*.'

At this point the commissionaire, who was dressed in knickerbockers, white socks, patent leather buckled shoes, a frock coat and a powdered wig, leaned over and said, 'I think you'll find the former inhabitants of Srebrenica and of Sarajevo are Bosnian Muslims, sir.' Adding pointedly, 'Will you be requiring a newspaper in the morning at all, sir?'

I thought Daniel was going to hit him. I found myself stroking his arm murmuring, 'OK now, easy, easy,' as if he were a racehorse that had been frightened by a van.

5.30 p.m. Brrr. Instead of lying side by side with Daniel in hot sun at the side of the lake wearing a long floaty dress, I ended up blue with cold in a rowing boat with one of the hotel bath towels wrapped round me. Eventually we gave up to retire to our room for a hot bath and Codis, discovering en route that another couple were to be sharing the non-wedding party dining room with us that evening, the female half of which was a girl called Eileen whom Daniel had slept with twice, inadvertently bitten dangerously hard on the breast and never spoken to since.

As I emerged from my bath Daniel was lying on the bed giggling. 'I've got a new diet for you,' he said.

'So you *do* think I'm fat.'

'OK, this is it. It's very simple. All you do is not eat any food which you have to pay for. So at the start of the diet you're a bit porky and no one asks you out to dinner. Then you lose weight and get a bit leggy and shag-me hippy and people start taking you out for meals. So then you put a few pounds on, the invitations tail off and you start losing weight again.'

'Daniel!' I exploded. 'That's the most appalling sexist, fattist, cynical thing I've ever heard.'

'Oh, don't be like that, Bridge,' he said. 'It's the logical extension of what you really think. I keep telling you nobody wants legs like a stick insect. They want a bottom they can park a bike in and balance a pint of beer on.'

I was torn between a gross image of myself with a bicycle parked in my bottom and a pint of beer balanced on it, fury at Daniel for his blatantly provocative sexism and suddenly wondering if he might be right about my concept of my body in relation to men, and, in which case, whether I should have something delicious to eat straight away and what that might be.

'I'll just pop the telly on,' said Daniel, taking advantage of my temporary speechlessness to press the remote-control button, and moving towards the curtains, which were those thick hotel ones with blackout lining. Seconds later the room was in complete darkness apart from the flickering light of the cricket. Daniel had lit a fag and was calling down to room service for six cans of Fosters.

'Do you want anything, Bridge?' he said, smirking. 'Cream tea, maybe? I'll pay.'

JULY

Huh

Sunday 2 July

8st 10 (continuing good work), alcohol units 0, cigarettes 0, calories 995, Instants 0: perfect.

7.45 a.m. Mum just rang. 'Oh, hello, darling, guess what?'

'I'll just take the phone in the other room. Hang on,' I said, glancing over nervously at Daniel, unplugging the phone, creeping next door and plugging it in again only to find my mother had not noticed my absence for the last two and a half minutes and was still talking.

'. . . So what do you think, darling?'

'Um, I don't know. I was bringing the phone into the other room like I said,' I said.

'Ah. So you didn't hear anything?'

'No.' There was a slight pause.

'Oh, hello, darling, guess what?' Sometimes I think my mother is part of the modern world and sometimes she seems a million miles away. Like when she leaves messages on my answerphone which just say, very loudly and clearly, 'Bridget Jones's mother.'

'Hello? Oh, hello, darling, guess what?' she said, again.

'What?' I said resignedly.

'Una and Geoffrey are having a Tarts and Vicars party in the garden on the twenty-ninth of July. Don't you think that's fun! Tarts and Vicars! Imagine!'

I tried hard not to, fighting off a vision of Una Alconbury in thigh boots, fishnet nights and a peephole bra. For sixty-year-olds to organize such an event seemed unnatural and wrong.

'Anyway, we thought it would be super if you and' – coy, loaded pause – 'Daniel, could come. We're all dying to meet him.'

My heart sank at the thought of my relationship with Daniel being dissected in close and intimate detail amongst the Lifeboat luncheons of Northamptonshire.

'I don't think it's really Daniel's—' Just as I said that the chair I had, for some reason, been balancing on with my knees while I leaned over the table fell over with a crash.

When I retrieved the phone my mother was still talking. 'Yes, super. Mark Darcy's going to be there, apparently, with someone, so . . .'

'What's going on?' Daniel was standing stark naked in the doorway. 'Who are you talking to?'

'My mother,' I said, desperately, out of the corner of my mouth.

'Give it to me,' he said, taking the phone. I like it when he is authoritative without being cross like this.

'Mrs Jones,' he said, in his most charming voice. 'It's Daniel here.'

I could practically hear her going all fluttery.

'This is very bright and early on a Sunday morning for a phone call. Yes, it is an absolutely beautiful day. What can we do for you?'

He looked at me while she chattered for a few seconds then turned back to the receiver.

'Well, that'll be lovely. I shall put that in the diary for the twenty-ninth and look out my dog collar. Now, we'd better get back and catch up on our sleep. You take care of yourself, now. Cheerio. Yes. Cheerio,' he said firmly, and put the phone down.

'You see,' he said smugly, 'a firm hand, that's all it needs.'

Saturday 22 July

8st 11 (hmm must get 1lb off), alcohol units 2, cigarettes 7, calories 1562.

Actually I am really excited about Daniel coming to the Tarts and Vicars party with me next Saturday. It will be so lovely for once not to have to drive up on my own, arrive on my own and face all that barrage of inquisition about why I haven't got a boyfriend. It will be a gorgeous hot day. Maybe we could even make a mini-break of it and stay in a pub (or other hotel without televisions in the bedroom). I'm really looking forward to Daniel meeting my dad. I hope he likes him.

2 a.m. Woke up in floods of tears from a hideous dream I keep having where I'm sitting A-level French and realize as I turn over the paper that I have forgotten to do any revision and I'm wearing nothing except my Domestic Science apron, trying desperately to pull it round me so Miss Chignall won't see that I'm wearing no pants. I expected Daniel to at least be sympathetic. I know it's all to do with my worries about where my career is leading me but he just lit himself a cigarette and asked me to run over the bit about the Domestic Science apron again.

'It's all right for you with your bloody Cambridge First.' I whispered, sniffing. 'I'll never forget the moment when I looked at the notice board and saw a D next to French and knew I couldn't go to Manchester. It altered the course of my whole life.'

'You should thank your lucky stars, Bridge,' he said, lying on his back and blowing smoke at the ceiling. 'You'd probably have married some crashing Geoffrey Boycott character and spent the rest of your life cleaning out the whippet cage. Anyway . . .' he started laughing, '. . . there's nothing wrong with a degree from . . . from . . .' (he was *so* amused now he could hardly speak) '. . . Bangor.'

'Right, that's it. I'm sleeping on the sofa,' I yelled, jumping out of bed.

'Hey, don't be like that, Bridge,' he said, pulling me back. 'You know I think you're a . . . an intellectual *giant*. You just need to learn how to interpret dreams.'

'What's the dream telling me, then?' I said sulkily. 'That I haven't fulfilled my potential intellectually?'

'Not exactly.'

'What, then?'

'Well, I think the pantless apron is a pretty obvious symbol, isn't it?'

'What?'

'It means that the vain pursuit of an intellectual life is getting in the way of your true purpose.'

'Which is what?'

'Well, to cook all my meals for me, of course, darling,'

he said, beside himself at his own amusingness again. 'And walk around my flat with no pants on.'

Friday 28 July

8st 12 (must do diet before tomorrow), alcohol units 1 (v.g.), cigarettes 8, calories 345.

Mmmm. Daniel was really sweet tonight and spent ages helping me choose my outfit for the Tarts and Vicars. He kept suggesting different ensembles for me to try on while he weighed it up. He was quite keen on a dog collar and black T-shirt with black lace-topped hold-ups as a cross between a tart and a vicar but in the end, after I'd walked about for quite a while in both of them, he decided the best one was a black lacy Marks and Spencer body, with stockings and suspenders, a French maid's-style apron which we'd made out of two hankies and a piece of ribbon, a bow-tie, and a cotton-wool rabbit's tail. It was really good of him to give up the time. Sometimes I think he really is quite caring. He seemed particularly keen on sex tonight as well.

Ooh, I am so looking forward to tomorrow.

Saturday 29 July

8st 11 (v.g.), alcohol units 7, cigarettes 8, calories 6245 (sodding Una Alconbury, Mark Darcy, Daniel, Mum, everybody).

2 p.m. Cannot believe what has happened. By 1 p.m. Daniel had still not woken up and I was starting to worry because the party starts at 2.30. Eventually I woke him with a cup of coffee and said, 'I thought you needed to wake up because we're supposed to be there at two-thirty.'

'Where?' he said.

'The Tarts and Vicars.'

'Oh God, love. Listen, I've just realized, I've got so much work to do this weekend. I'm really going to have to stay at home and get down to it.'

I couldn't believe it. He *promised* to come. Everyone knows when you are going out with someone they are supposed to support you at hideous family occasions, and he thinks if he so much as mentions the word 'work' he can get out of anything. Now all the Alconburys' friends will spend the entire time asking me if I've got a boyfriend yet and no one will believe me.

10 p.m. Cannot believe what I have been through. I drove for two hours, parked at the front of the Alconburys' and, hoping I looked OK in the bunny girl outfit, walked round the side to the garden where I could hear voices raised in merriment. As I started to cross the lawn they all went quiet, and I realized to my horror that instead of Tarts and Vicars, the ladies were in Country Casuals-style calf-length floral two-pieces and the men were in slacks and V-necked sweaters. I stood there, frozen, like, well, a rabbit. Then while everyone stared, Una Alconbury came flapping across the lawn in pleated fuchsia holding out a plastic tumbler full of bits of apple and leaves.

'Bridget!! Super to see you. Have a Pimm's,' she said.

'I thought it was supposed to be a Tarts and Vicars party,' I hissed.

'Oh dear, didn't Geoff call you?' she said. I couldn't believe this. I mean, did she think I dressed as a bunny girl normally or something? 'Geoff,' she said. 'Didn't you telephone Bridget? We're all looking forward to meeting your new boyfriend,' she said, looking around. 'Where is he?'

'He had to work,' I muttered.

'How's-my-little-Bridget?' said Uncle Geoffrey, lurching over, pissed.

'Geoffrey,' said Una coldly.

'Yup, yup. All present and correct, orders obeyed, Lieutenant,' he said, saluting, then collapsing on to her shoulder giggling. 'But it was one of those ruddy answerphone thingummajigs.'

'Geoffrey,' hissed Una. 'Go-and-see-to-the-barbecue. I'm sorry, darling, you see we decided after all the scandals there've been with vicars around here there'd be no point having a Tarts and Vicars party because . . .' she started to laugh, '. . . because everyone thought vicars *were* tarts anyway. Oh dear,' she said, wiping her eyes. 'Anyway, how's this new chap, then? What's he doing working on a Saturday? Durrrr! That's not a very good excuse, is it? How are we going to get you married off at this rate?'

'At this rate I'm going to end up as a call girl,' I muttered, trying to unpin the bunny tail from my bottom.

I could feel someone's eyes on me and looked up to see Mark Darcy staring fixedly at the bunny tail. Beside him was the tall thin glamorous top family-law barrister clad in a demure lilac dress and coat like Jackie O. with sunglasses on her head.

The smug witch smirked at Mark and blatantly looked

me up and down in a most impolite manner. 'Have you come from another party?' she breathed.

'Actually, I'm just on my way to work,' I said, at which Mark Darcy half smiled and looked away.

'Hello, darling, can't stop. Shooting.' trilled my mother, hurrying towards us in a bright turquoise pleated shirtwaister, waving a clapper board. 'What on earth do you think you're wearing, darling? You look like a common prostitute. Absolute quiet, please, everyone, aaaaand . . .' she yelled in the direction of Julio, who was brandishing a video camera, 'action!'

In alarm I quickly looked round for Dad but couldn't see him anywhere. I saw Mark Darcy talking to Una and gesturing in my direction then Una, looking purposeful, hurried across to me.

'Bridget, I am *so sorry* about the mix-up over the fancy dress,' she said. 'Mark was just saying you must feel dreadfully uncomfortable with all these older chaps around. Would you like to borrow something?'

I spent the rest of the party wearing, over my suspender outfit, a puff-sleeved, floral-sprig Laura Ashley bridesmaid dress of Janine's with Mark Darcy's Natasha smirking and my mother periodically rushing past going, 'That's a pretty dress, darling. Cut!'

'I don't think much of the girlfriend, do you?' said Una Alconbury loudly, nodding in Natasha's direction as soon as she got me alone. 'Very much the Little Madam. Elaine thinks she's desperate to get her feet under the table. Oh, hello, Mark! Another glass of Pimm's? What a shame Bridget couldn't bring her boyfriend. He's a lucky chap, isn't he?' All this was said very aggressively as if Una was taking as a personal insult the fact that Mark had chosen a

girlfriend who was a) not me and b) had not been introduced to him by Una at a turkey curry buffet. 'What's his
name, Bridget? Daniel, is it? Pam says he's one of these
sooper-dooper young publishers.'

'Daniel Cleaver?' said Mark Darcy.

'Yes, it is, actually,' I said, jutting my chin out.

'Is he a friend of yours, Mark?' said Una.

'Absolutely not,' he said, abruptly.

'Oooh. I hope he's good enough for our little Bridget,'
Una pressed on, winking at me as if this was all hilarious
fun instead of hideous.

'I think I could say again, with total confidence, absolutely not,' said Mark.

'Oh, hang on a tick, there's Audrey. Audrey!' said Una,
not listening, and tripping off, thank God.

'I suppose you think that's clever,' I said furiously, when
she'd gone.

'What?' said Mark, looking surprised.

'Don't you "What?" me, Mark Darcy,' I muttered.

'You sound just like my mother,' he said.

'I suppose you think it's all right to slag people's boyfriends off to their parents' friends behind their back when
they're not even there for no reason just because you're
jealous,' I flailed.

He stared at me, as if distracted by something else.
'Sorry,' he said. 'I was just trying to figure out what you
mean. Have I . . .? Are you suggesting that I am jealous of
Daniel Cleaver? Over you?'

'No, not over me,' I said, furious because I realized it did
sound like that. 'I was just assuming you must have some
reason to be so horrible about my boyfriend other than
pure malevolence.'

'Mark, darling,' cooed Natasha, tripping prettily across the lawn to join us. She was so tall and thin she hadn't felt the need to put heels on, so could walk easily across the lawn without sinking, as if designed for it, like a camel in the desert. 'Come and tell your mother about the dining furniture we saw in Conran.'

'Just take care of yourself, that's all,' he said quietly, 'and I'd tell your mum to watch out for herself too,' he said, nodding pointedly in the direction of Julio as Natasha dragged him off.

After 45 minutes more horror I thought I could decently leave, pleading work to Una.

'You career girls! Can't put it off forever you know: tick-tock-tick-tock,' she said.

I had to have a cigarette in the car for five minutes before I was calm enough to set off. Then just as I got back to the main road my dad's car drove past. Sitting next to him in the front seat was Penny Husbands-Bosworth, wearing a red lace underwired uplift basque, and two bunny ears.

By the time I got back to London and off the motorway I was feeling pretty shaky and back much earlier than I expected, so I thought, instead of going straight home, I'd go round to Daniel's for a bit of reassurance.

I parked nose to nose with Daniel's car. There was no answer when I rang, so I left it a while and rang again in case it was just in the middle of a really good wicket or something. Still no answer. I knew he must be around because his car was there and he'd said he was going to be working and watching the cricket. I looked up at his window and there was Daniel. I beamed at him, waved and pointed at the door. He disappeared, I assumed to press the buzzer, so I rang the bell again. He took a bit of time to answer: 'Hi, Bridge. Just on the phone to America. Can I meet you in the pub in ten minutes?'

'OK,' I said cheerfully, without thinking, and set off towards the corner. But when I looked round, there he was again, not on the phone, but watching me out of the window.

Cunning as a fox, I pretended not to see and kept walking, but inside I was in turmoil. Why was he watching? Why hadn't he answered the door first time? Why didn't he just press the buzzer and let me come up straight away? Suddenly it hit me like a thunderbolt. He was with a woman.

My heart pounding, I rounded the corner, then, keeping flat against the wall, I peered round to check he had gone from the window. No sign of him. I hurried back and assumed a crouching position in the porch next to his, observing his doorway between the pillars in case a woman came out. I waited, crouched in the position for some time. But then I started to think: if a woman did come out, how would I know it was Daniel's flat she had come out of and not one of the other flats in the building? What would I do? Challenge her? Make a citizen's arrest? Also, what was to stop him leaving the woman in the flat with instructions to stay there until he had had time to get to the pub?

I looked at my watch. 6.30. Hah! The pub wasn't open yet. Perfect excuse. Emboldened, I hurried back towards the door and pushed the buzzer.

'Bridget, is that you again?' he snapped.

'The pub isn't open yet.'

There was silence. Did I hear a voice in the background? In denial, I told myself he was just laundering money or dealing in drugs. He was probably trying to hide polythene bags full of cocaine under the floorboards helped by some smooth South American men with ponytails.

'Let me in,' I said.

'I told you, I'm on the phone.'

'Let me in.'

'What?' He was playing for time, I could tell.

'Press the buzzer, Daniel,' I said.

Isn't it funny how you can detect someone's presence, even though you can't see, hear or otherwise discern them? Oh, of *course* I'd checked the cupboards on the way up the stairs and there was no one in any of them. But I knew there was a woman in Daniel's house. Maybe it was a slight smell . . . something about the way Daniel was behaving. Whatever it was, I just *knew*.

We stood there warily at opposite sides of the sitting room. I was just desperate to start running around opening and closing all the cupboards like my mother and ringing 1471 to see if there was a number stored from America.

'What have you got on?' he said. I had forgotten about Janine's outfit in the excitement.

'A bridesmaid's dress,' I said, haughtily.

'Would you like a drink?' said Daniel. I thought fast. I needed to get him into the kitchen so I could go through all the cupboards.

'A cup of tea, please.'

'Are you all right?' he said.

'Yes! Fine!' I trilled. 'Marvellous time at the party. Only one dressed as a tart, had to put on a bridesmaid dress, Mark Darcy was there with Natasha, that's a nice shirt your wearing . . .' I stopped, out of breath, realizing I had turned (there was no 'was turning' about it) into my mother.

He looked at me for a moment, then set off into the

kitchen at which I quickly leapt across the room to look behind the sofa and the curtains.

'What are you doing?'

Daniel was standing in the doorway.

'Nothing, nothing. Just thought I might have left a skirt of mine behind the sofa,' I said, wildly plumping up the cushions as if I were in a French farce.

He looked suspicious and headed off to the kitchen again.

Deciding there was no time to dial 1471, I quickly checked the cupboard where he keeps the duvet for the sofabed – no human habitation – then followed him to the kitchen, pulling open the door of the hall cupboard as I passed at which the ironing board fell out, followed by a cardboard box full of old 45s which slithered out all over the floor.

'What are you doing?' said Daniel mildly again, coming out of the kitchen.

'Sorry, just caught the door with my sleeve,' I said. 'Just on my way to the loo.'

Daniel was staring at me as if I was mad, so I couldn't go and check the bedroom. Instead I locked the loo door and started frantically looking around for things. I wasn't exactly sure what, but long blonde hairs, tissues with lipstick marks on, alien hairbrushes – any of these would have been a sign. Nothing. Next I quietly unlocked the door, looked both ways, slipped along the corridor, pushed open the door of Daniel's bedroom and nearly jumped out of my skin. There was someone in the room.

'Bridge.' It was Daniel, defensively holding a pair of jeans in front of him. 'What are you doing in here?'

'I heard you come in here so . . . I thought . . . It was a

secret assignation,' I said, approaching him in what would have been a sexy way were it not for the floral sprig dress. I leaned my head on his chest and put my arms around him, trying to smell his shirt for perfume traces and get a good look at the bed, which was unmade as usual.

'Mmmm, you've still got the bunny girl outfit on underneath, haven't you?' he said, starting to unzip the bridesmaid dress and pressing against me in a way which made his intentions very clear. I suddenly thought this might be a trick and he was going to seduce me while the woman slipped out unnoticed.

'Oooh, the kettle must be boiling,' said Daniel suddenly, zipping my dress up again and patting me reassuringly in a way that was most unlike him. Usually once he gets going he will see things through to their logical conclusion come earthquake, tidal wave or naked pictures of Virginia Bottomley on the television.

'Ooh yes, better make that cuppa,' I said, thinking it would give me a chance to get a good look round the bedroom and scout the study.

'After you,' said Daniel, pushing me out and shutting the door so I had to walk ahead of him back into the kitchen. As I did so I suddenly caught sight of the door that led up to the roof terrace.

'Shall we go and sit down?' said Daniel.

That was where she was, she was on the bloody roof.

'What's the matter with you?' he said as I stared at the door suspiciously.

'No-thing,' I sing-songed gaily, flopping into the sitting room. 'Just a little tired from the party.'

I flung myself insouciantly on to the sofa, wondering whether to streak faster than the speed of light down to the study as the final place she might be or just go hell for leather for the roof. I figured if she wasn't on the roof it meant she must be in the study, in the bedroom wardrobe, or under the bed. If we then went up on the roof she would be able to escape. But if that was the case, surely Daniel would have suggested going up on the roof much sooner.

He brought me a cup of tea and sat down at his laptop, which was open and turned on. Only then did I start to think that maybe there was no woman. There was a document up on the screen – maybe he really had been working and on the phone to America. And I was making a complete prat of myself behaving like a madwoman.

'Are you sure everything's all right, Bridge?'

'Fine, yes. Why?'

'Well, coming round unannounced like this dressed as a rabbit disguised as a bridesmaid and burrowing into all the rooms in a strange way. Not meaning to pry or anything, I just wondered if there was an explanation, that's all.'

I felt a complete fool. It was bloody Mark Darcy trying to wreck my relationship by sowing suspicions in my mind. Poor Daniel, it was so unfair to doubt him in this way, because of the word of some arrogant, ill-tempered, top-flight human-rights lawyer. Then I heard a scraping noise on the roof above us.

'I think maybe I'm just a bit hot,' I said, watching Daniel carefully. 'I think maybe I'll go and sit on the roof for a while.'

'For God's sake, will you sit still for two minutes!' he yelled, moving to bar my path, but I was too quick for him. I dodged past, opened the door, ran up the stairs and opened the hatch out into the sunlight.

There, spread out on a sunlounger, was a bronzed, long-limbed, blonde-haired stark-naked woman. I stood there frozen to the spot, feeling like an enormous pudding in the bridesmaid dress. The woman raised her head, lifted her sunglasses and looked at me with one eye closed. I heard Daniel coming up the stairs behind me.

'Honey,' said the woman, in an American accent, looking over my head at him. 'I thought you said she was *thin*.'

AUGUST

Disintegration

Tuesday 1 August

8st 12, alcohol units 3, cigarettes 40 (but have stopped inhaling in order to smoke more), calories 450 (off food), 1471 calls 14, Instants 7.

5 a.m. I'm falling apart. My boyfriend is sleeping with a bronzed giantess. My mother is sleeping with a Portuguese. Jeremy is sleeping with a horrible trollop, Prince Charles is sleeping with Camilla Parker-Bowles. Do not know what to believe in or hold on to any more. Feel like ringing Daniel in hope he could deny everything, come up with plausible explanation for the clothes-free rooftop valkyrie – younger sister, friendly neighbour recovering from flood or similar – which would make everything all right. But Tom has taped a piece of paper to the telephone saying, 'Do not ring Daniel or you will regret it.'

Should have gone to stay with Tom as suggested. Hate being alone in middle of night, smoking and snivelling like mad psychopath. Fear Dan downstairs might hear and ring loony bin. Oh God, what's wrong with me? Why does nothing ever work out? It is because I am too fat. Toy with ringing Tom again but only called him 45 minutes ago. Cannot face going into work.

After rooftop encounter I didn't say a single word to Daniel: just put my nose in the air, slithered past him, marched down to the street into car and drove away. Went immediately to Tom's, who poured vodka straight down my throat from the bottle, adding the tomato juice and Worcester sauce afterwards. Daniel had left three messages when I got back, asking me to call him. Did not, following advice of Tom, who reminded me that the only way to succeed with men is to be really horrible to them. Used to think he was cynical and wrong but I think I was nice to Daniel and look what happened.

Oh God, birds have started singing. Have to go to work in three and a half hours. Can't do it. Help, help. Have suddenly had brainwave: ring Mum.

10 a.m. Mum was *brilliant*. 'Darling,' she said. 'Of course you haven't woken me. I'm just leaving for the studio. I can't believe you've got in a state like this over a stupid *man*. They're all completely self-centred, sexually incontinent and no use to man nor beast. Yes, that *does* include you, Julio. Now come along, darling. Brace up. Back to sleep. Go into work looking drop-dead gorgeous. Leave no one – especially Daniel – in any doubt that you've thrown him over and suddenly discovered how *marvellous* life is without that pompous, dissolute old *fart* bossing you around and you'll be fine.'

'Are *you* all right, Mum?' I said, thinking about Dad arriving at Una's party with asbestos-widow Penny Husbands-Bosworth.

'Darling, you are sweet. I'm under such terrible pressure.'

'Is there anything I can do?'

'Actually, there is something,' she said, brightening. 'Do any of your friends have a number for Lisa Leeson? You know, Nick Leeson's wife? I've been desperate to get her for days. She'd be perfect for "Suddenly Single".'

'I was talking about Dad, not "Suddenly Single,"' I hissed.

'Daddy? I'm not under pressure from Daddy. Don't be silly, darling.'

'But the party . . . and Mrs Husbands-Bosworth.'

'Oh, I know, hilarious. Made a complete silly fool of himself trying to attract my attention. What did she think she looked like, a hamster or something? Anyway, must run, I'm frighteningly busy but will you think who might have a number for Lisa? Let me give you my *direct line*, darling. And let's have no more of this silly whining.'

'Oh, but Mum, I have to work with Daniel, I—'

'Darling – wrong way round. He has to work with you. Give him hell, baby.' (Oh God, I don't know who she's been mixing with.) 'I've been thinking, anyway. It's high time you got out of that silly dead-end job where no one appreciates you. Prepare to hand in your notice, kid. Yes, darling . . . I'm going to get you a job in television.'

Am just off to work looking like Ivana bloody Trump wearing a suit and lip gloss.

Wednesday 2 August

8st 12, thigh circumference 18 inches, alcohol units 3 (but v. pure sort of wine), cigarettes 7 (but did not inhale), calories 1500 (excellent), teas 0, coffees 3 (but made with real coffee beans therefore less cellulite-inducing), total caffeine units 4.

Everything's fine. Am going to get down to 8st 7lb again and free thighs entirely of cellulite. Certain everything will be all right then. Have embarked on intensive detoxification programme involving no tea no coffee no alcohol no white flour no milk and what was it? Oh well. No fish, maybe. What you have to do is dry-skin brushing for five minutes every morning, then a fifteen-minute bath with anti-cellulite essential oils in it, during which one kneads one's cellulite as one would dough, followed by massaging more anti-cellulite oil into the cellulite.

This last bit puzzles me – does the anti-cellulite oil actually soak into the cellulite through the skin? In which case, if you put self-tanning lotion on does that mean you get suntanned cellulite inside? Or suntanned blood? Or a suntanned lymphatic drainage system? Urgh. Anyway . . . (Cigarettes. That was the other thing. No cigarettes. Oh well. Too late now. I'll do that tomorrow.)

Thursday 3 August

8st 11, thigh circumference 18 inches (honestly, what is bloody point), alcohol units 0, cigarettes 25 (excellent, considering), negative thoughts: approx. 445 per hour, positive thoughts 0.

Head state v. bad again. Cannot bear thought of Daniel with someone else. Mind is full of horrid fantasies about them doing things together. The plans to lose weight and change personality kept me aloft for two days, only to collapse around my ears. I realize it was only a complicated form of denial. Was believing could totally reinvent self in space of small number of days, thereby negating impact of Daniel's hurtful and humiliating infidelity, since it had happened to me in a previous incarnation and would never have happened to my new improved self. Unfortunately, I now realize the whole point of the aloof over-made-up ice-queen on anti-cellulite diet palaver was to make Daniel realize the error of his ways. Tom did warn me of this and said 90 per cent of plastic surgery was done on women whose husbands had run off with a younger woman. I said the rooftop giantess was not so much younger as taller but Tom said that wasn't the point. Humph.

Daniel kept sending me computer messages at work. 'We should talk,' etc., which I studiously ignored. But the more he sent the more I got carried away, imagining that the self-reinvention was working, that he realized he had made a terrible, terrible mistake, had only now understood how much he truly loved me, and that the rooftop giantess was history.

Tonight he caught up with me outside the office as I was leaving. 'Darling, please, we really need to talk.'

Like a fool I went for a drink with him to the American Bar at the Savoy, let him soften me up with champagne and 'I feel so terrible I really miss you blar blar blar.' Then the very second he got me to admit, 'Oh, Daniel, I miss you too,' he suddenly went all patronizing and businesslike and said, 'The thing is, Suki and I . . .'

'Suki? Pukey, more like,' I said, thinking he was about to say, 'are brother and sister,' 'cousins,' 'bitter enemies,' or 'history.' Instead he looked rather cross.

'Oh, I can't explain,' he said huffily. 'It's very special.'

I stared at him, astonished at the audacity of his volte-face.

'I'm sorry, love,' he said, taking out his credit card and starting to lean back to get the attention of the waiter, 'but we're getting married.'

Friday 4 August

Thigh circumference 18 inches, negative thoughts 600 per minute, panic attacks 4, crying attacks 12 (but both times only in toilets and remembered to take mascara), Instants 7.

Office. Third-floor toilets. This is just . . . just . . . intolerable. What on earth possessed me to think it was a good idea to have an affair with my boss? Cannot deal with it out there. Daniel has announced his engagement to the giantess. Sales reps who I didn't think even knew about our affair keep ringing up to congratulate me and I have to explain that actually he has got engaged to someone else. I keep remembering how romantic it was when we started and it was all secret computer messages and trysts in the lift. I heard Daniel on the phone arranging to meet Pukey tonight and he said in a Flopsy Bunny voice, 'Not too bad . . . so far,' and I knew he was talking about my reaction, as if I were Sara bloody Keays or someone. Am seriously considering face-lift.

Tuesday 8 August

9st, alcohol units 7 (har har), cigarettes 29 (tee hee), calories 5 million, negative thoughts 0, thoughts, general 0.

Just called Jude. I told her a bit about the tragedy with Daniel and she was horrified, immediately declared a state of emergency and said she would call Sharon and fix for us all to meet at nine. She couldn't come till then because she was meeting Vile Richard, who'd at last agreed to come to Relationship Counselling with her.

2 a.m. Gor es wor blurry goofun tonight though. Ooof. Tumbled over.

Wednesday 9 August

9st 2 (but in good cause), thigh circumference 16 inches (either miracle or hangover error), alcohol units 0 (but body still drinking units from last night), cigarettes 0 (ugh).

8 a.m. Ugh. In physically disastrous state but emotionally v. much cheered up by night out. Jude arrived in vixen-from-hell fury because Vile Richard had stood her up for the Relationship Counselling.

'The therapist woman obviously just thought he was an imaginary boyfriend and I was a very, very sad person.'

'So what did you do?' I said sympathetically, banishing a rogue disloyal thought from Satan that said, 'She was right.'

'She said I had to talk about the problems I had that were unrelated to Richard.'

'But you don't have any problems that are unrelated to Richard,' said Sharon.

'I know. I told her that, then she said I had a problem with boundaries and charged me fifty-five quid.'

'Why didn't he turn up? I hope the sadistic worm had a decent excuse,' said Sharon.

'He said he got tied up at work,' said Jude. 'I said to him, "Listen, you don't have a monopoly on commitment problems. Actually, I have a commitment problem. If you ever deal with your own commitment problem you might be brought up short by my commitment problem, by which time it'll be *too late*."'

'*Have* you got a commitment problem?' I said, intrigued, immediately thinking maybe I had a commitment problem.

'Of *course* I've got a commitment problem,' snarled Jude. 'It's just that nobody ever sees it because it's so submerged by Richard's commitment problem. Actually, my commitment problem goes much deeper than his.'

'Well, exactly,' said Sharon. 'But you don't go round wearing your commitment problem on your sleeve like every bloody man over the age of twenty does these days.'

'Exactly my point,' spat Jude, trying to light up another Silk Cut but having trouble with the lighter.

'The whole bloody world's got a commitment problem,' growled Sharon in a guttural, almost Clint Eastwood voice. 'It's the three-minute culture. It's a global attention-span deficit. It's typical of men to annex a global trend and turn it into a male device to reject women to make themselves feel clever and us feel stupid. It's nothing but fuckwittage.'

'Bastards!' I shouted happily. 'Shall we have another bottle of wine?'

9 a.m. Blimey. Mum just rang. 'Darling,' she said. 'Guess what? *Good Afternoon!* are looking for researchers. Current affairs, terribly good. I've spoken to Richard Finch, the editor, and told him all about you. I said you had a degree in politics, darling. Don't worry, he'll be far too busy to check. He wants you to come in on Monday for a chat.'

Monday. Oh my God. That only gives me five days to learn Current Affairs.

Saturday 12 August

9st 3 (still in very good cause), alcohol units 3 (v.g.), cigarettes 32 (v.v. bad, particularly since first day of giving up), calories 1800 (g.), Instants 4 (fair), no. of serious current affairs articles read 1.5, 1471 calls 22 (OK), minutes spent having cross imaginary conversations with Daniel 120 (v.g.), minutes spent imagining Daniel begging me to come back 90 (excellent).

Right. Determined to be v. positive about everything. Am going to change life: become well informed re: current affairs, stop smoking entirely and form functional relationship with adult man.

8.30 a.m. Still have not had fag. V.g.

8.35 a.m. No fags all day. Excellent.

8.40 a.m. Wonder if anything nice has come in post?

8.45 a.m. Ugh. Hateful document from Social Security Agency asking for £1452. What? How can this be? Have not got £1452. Oh God, need fag to calm nerves. Mustn't. Mustn't.

8.47 a.m. Just had fag. But no-smoking day does not start officially till have got dressed. Suddenly start thinking of

former boyfriend Peter with whom had functional relationship for seven years until finished with him for heartfelt,
agonizing reasons can no longer remember. Every so often
– usually when he has no one to go on holiday with – he
tries to get back together and says he wants us to get
married. Before know where am, am carried away with
idea of Peter being answer. Why be unhappy and lonely
when Peter wants to be with me? Quickly find telephone,
ring Peter and leave message on his answerphone – merely
asking him to give me call rather than whole plan of
spending rest of life together, etc.

1.15 p.m. Peter has not rung back. Am repulsive to all men
now, even Peter.

4.45 p.m. No-smoking policy in tatters. Peter finally rang.
'Hi, Bee.' (We always used to call each other Bee and
Waspy.) 'I was going to ring you anyway. I've got some
good news. I'm getting married.'

Ugh. V. bad feeling in pancreas area. Exes should never,
never go out with or marry other people but should remain
celibate to the end of their days in order to provide you
with a mental fallback position.

'Bee?' said Waspy. 'Bzzzzzzz?'

'Sorry,' I said, slumping dizzily against the wall. 'Just,
um, saw a car accident out of the window.'

I was evidently superfluous to the conversation, however,
as Waspy gushed on about the cost of marquees for about
twenty minutes, then said, 'Have to go. We're cooking
Delia Smith venison sausages with juniper berries tonight
and watching TV.'

Ugh. Have just smoked entire packet of Silk Cut as act

of self-annihilating existential despair. Hope they both become obese and have to be lifted out of the window by crane.

5.45 p.m. Trying to concentrate hard on memorizing names of Shadow Cabinet to avoid spiral of self-doubt. Have never met Waspy's Intended of course but imagine giant thin blonde rooftop giantess-type who rises at five each morning, goes to gym, rubs herself down with salt then runs international merchant bank all day without smudging mascara.

Realize with sinking humiliation that reason have been feeling smug about Peter all these years was that I finished with him and now he is effectively finishing with me by marrying Mrs Giant Valkyrie bottom. Sink into morbid, cynical reflection on how much romantic heartbreak is to do with ego and miffed pride rather than actual loss, also incorporating sub-thought that reason for Fergie's insane over-confidence may be that Andrew still wants her back (until he marries someone else, har har).

6.45 p.m. Was just starting to watch the 6 o'clock news, notebook poised, when Mum burst in bearing carrier bags.

'Now, darling,' she said sailing past me into the kitchen. 'I've brought you some nice soup, and some smart outfits of mine for Monday!' She was wearing a lime green suit, black tights and high-heeled court shoes. She looked like Cilla Black on *Blind Date*.

'Where *do* you keep your soup ladles?' she said, banging cupboard doors. 'Honestly, darling. What a mess! Now. Have a look through these bags while I heat up the soup.'

Deciding to overlook the fact that it was a) August

b) boiling hot c) 6.15 and d) I didn't want any soup, I peered cautiously into the first carrier bag, where there was something pleated and synthetic in bright yellow with a terracotta leaf design. 'Er, Mum . . .' I began, but then her handbag started ringing.

'Ah, that'll be Julio. Yup, yup.' She was balancing a portable phone under her chin now and scribbling. 'Yup, yup. Put it on, darling,' she hissed. 'Yup, yup. Yup. Yup.'

Now I have missed the news and she has gone off to a Cheese and Wine party, leaving me looking like Teresa Gorman in a bright blue suit with slithery green blouse underneath and blue eyeshadow right up to my eyebrows.

'Don't be silly, darling,' was her parting shot. 'If you don't do *something* about your appearance you'll never get a new job, never mind another boyfriend!'

Midnight. After she'd gone, called Tom, who took me to a party a friend of his from art school was having at the Saatchi Gallery to stop me obsessing.

'Bridget,' he muttered nervously as we walked into the white hole and sea of grunge youths. 'You know it's unhip to laugh at Installation, don't you?'

'OK, OK,' I said sulkily. 'I won't make any dead fish jokes.'

Someone called Gav said 'Hi': twenty-two maybe, sexy, in a shrunken T-shirt revealing a chopping-board-like midriff.

'It's really, really, really, *really* amazing,' Gav was saying. 'It's, like, a sullied Utopia with these really, really, *really* good echoes of, like, lost national identities.'

He led us excitedly across the big white space to a toilet roll: inside out with the cardboard outside the paper.

They looked at me expectantly. Suddenly I knew I was going to cry. Tom was now drooling over a giant bar of soap bearing the imprint of a penis. Gav was staring at me. 'Wow, that is, like, a really, really, *really* wild . . .' he whispered reverently as I blinked back tears, '. . . response.'

'Just going to the loo,' I blurted, rushing away past a configuration of sanitary-towel bags. There was a queue outside a Portaloo, and I joined it, shaking. Suddenly, just when it was almost my turn, I felt a hand on my arm. It was Daniel.

'Bridge, what are you doing here?'

'What does it look like?' I snapped. 'Excuse me, I'm in a hurry.' I burst into the cubicle and was just about to get on with it when I realized the toilet was actually a moulding of the inside of a toilet, vacuum-packed in plastic. Then Daniel put his head round the door.

'Bridge, don't wee on the Installation, will you?' he said, and closed the door again.

When I came out he had vanished. I couldn't see Gav, Tom or anyone I knew. Eventually I found the real toilets, sat down and burst into tears, thinking I wasn't fit to be in society any more, and just needed to get away till I stopped feeling like this. Tom was waiting outside.

'Come and talk to Gav,' he said. 'He's really, like, into you.' Then he took one look at my face and said. 'Oh shit, I'll take you home.'

It's no good. When someone leaves you, apart from missing them, apart from the fact that the whole little world you've created together collapses, and that everything you see or do reminds you of them, the worst is the thought that they tried you out and, in the end, the whole sum of parts which adds up to you got stamped REJECT

193

by the one you love. How can you not be left with the personal confidence of a passed-over British Rail sandwich?

'Gav likes you,' said Tom.

'Gav is ten. Anyway he only liked me because he thought I was crying about a toilet roll.'

'Well you were, in a way,' said Tom. 'Bloody git, Daniel. If that man turns out to be singlehandedly responsible for all the fighting in Bosnia, I wouldn't be in the least surprised.'

Sunday 13 August

V. bad night. On top of everything else, tried to read myself to sleep with new issue of *Tatler*, only to find Mark Bloody Darcy's face smouldering out from feature on London's fifty most eligible bachelors going on about how rich and marvellous he was. Ugh. Made me even more depressed in way cannot quite fathom. Anyway. Am going to stop feeling sorry for myself and spend morning learning newspapers off by heart.

Noon. Rebecca just rang, asking if I was 'all right'. Thinking she meant all right about Daniel I said, 'Chuh, well it's very depressing.'

'Oh, poor you. Yes, I saw Peter last night . . . (Where? What? Why wasn't I invited?) '. . . and he was telling everyone how upset you were about the wedding. As he said, it *is* difficult, single women do tend to get desperate as they get older . . .'

By lunchtime could no longer go on with Sunday, trying to pretend everything was OK. Rang up Jude and told her about Waspy, Rebecca, job interview, Mum, Daniel and general misery and arranged to meet at Jimmy Beez at two for a Bloody Mary.

6 p.m. As luck would have it, Jude had just been reading brilliant book called *Goddesses in Everywoman*. Apparently the book says that at certain times in your life everything goes wrong and you don't know which way to turn and it is as if everywhere around you stainless steel doors are clamping shut like in *Star Trek*. What you have to do is be a heroine and stay brave, without sinking into drink or self-pity and everything will be OK. And that all the Greek myths and many successful movies are all about human beings facing difficult trials and not being wimps but holding hard and thus coming out on top.

The book also says that coping with difficult times is like being in a conical shell-shaped spiral and there is a point at each turn that is very painful and difficult. That is your particular problem or sore spot. When you are at the narrow, pointy end of the spiral you come back to that situation very often as the rotations are quite small. As you go round, you will go through the troubled time less and less frequently but still you must come back to it, so you shouldn't feel when it happens that you are back to square one.

Trouble is now I have sobered up not sure I am 100 per cent sure what she was talking about.

Mum rang up and I tried to talk to her about how difficult it is being a woman and having a sell-by date for reproduction unlike men, but she just said, 'Oh, honestly, darling. You girls are just so picky and romantic these days: you've simply got too much choice. I'm not saying I didn't

195

love Dad but, you know, we were always taught, instead of waiting to be swept off our feet, to "expect little, forgive much". And to be honest, darling, having children isn't all it's built up to be. I mean, no offence, I don't mean this personally but given my chance again I'm not sure I'd have . . .'

Oh God. Even my own mother wishes I'd never been born.

Monday 14 August

9st 5 (great – turned into lard mountain for interview, also have spot), alcohol units 0, cigarettes many, calories 1575 (but threw up so effectively 400, approx.).

Oh God. Terrified about interview. I have told Perpetua I am at the gynaecologist – I know I should have said dentist but opportunities to torture the nosiest woman in the world must not be allowed to slip through the net. I am almost ready and merely need to complete my make-up while practising my opinions on Tony Blair's leadership. Oh my God, who's the Shadow Defence Secretary? Oh fuck, oh fuck. Is it someone with a beard? Shit: telephone. I can't believe it: terrifying telephonic teenager with patronizing South London sing-song going, 'Hel-lo, Bridget, Richard Finch's office here. Richard's in Blackpool this morning so he won't be able to make the meeting.' Rescheduled for Wednesday. Will have to pretend have recurring gynaecological condition. Might as well take rest of morning off anyway.

Wednesday 16 August

Horrible night. Kept waking up bathed in sweat, panicking about the difference between the Ulster Unionists and SDLP and which of them Ian Paisley was involved in.

Instead of being ushered into the office to meet the great Richard Finch, I was left pouring sweat in reception for forty minutes thinking Oh my God who's the Health Secretary? before being picked up by the sing-song personal assistant – Patchouli – who sported Lycra cycle shorts and a nose stud and blanched at my Jigsaw suit, as if, in a hideously misjudged attempt to be formal, I had turned up in a floor-length shot-silk Laura Ashley ballgown.

'Richard says to come to the conference, know what I'm sayin'?' she muttered, powering off down a corridor while I scurried after her. She burst through a pink door into a vast open-plan office strewn with piles of scripts, TV screens suspended from the ceiling, charts all over the walls, and mountain bikes propped against the desks. At the far end was a large oblong table where the meeting was in progress. Everyone turned and stared as we approached.

A plump, middle-aged man with curly blond hair, a denim shirt and red Christopher Biggins spectacles was jigging up and down at the end of the table.

'Come on! Come on!' he was saying, holding up his fists like a boxer. 'I'm thinking Hugh Grant. I'm thinking Elizabeth Hurley. I'm thinking how come two months on they're still together. I'm thinking how come he gets away with it. That's it! How does a man with a girlfriend with looks like Elizabeth Hurley have a blow-job from a prostitute on a public highway and get away with it? What happened to hell hath no fury?'

I couldn't believe this. What about the Shadow Cabinet? What about the Peace Process? He was obviously trying to work out how he could get away with sleeping with a prostitute himself. Suddenly, he was looking straight at me.

'Do *you* know?' The entire table of grunge youths stared. 'You. You must be Bridget!' he shouted impatiently. 'How does a man with a beautiful girlfriend manage to sleep with a prostitute, get found out and get away with it?'

I panicked. My mind went blank.

'Well?' he said. 'Well? Come on, say something!'

'Well, maybe,' I said, because it was the only thing I could think of, 'it was because somebody swallowed the evidence.'

There was a deathly hush, then Richard Finch started to laugh. It was the most repulsive laugh I've ever heard in my life. Then all the grunge youths started to laugh as well.

'Bridget Jones,' said Richard Finch eventually, wiping his eyes. 'Welcome to *Good Afternoon!* Take a seat, my darling,' and then he winked.

Tuesday 22 August

9st 2, alcohol units 4, cigarettes 25, Instants 5.

Still haven't heard anything from the interview. Don't know what to do for Bank Holiday as cannot face remaining alone in London. Shazzer is going to the Edinburgh Festival, as is Tom, I think, also lots of people from the office. Would like to go but not sure can afford it and fear presence of Daniel. Also everyone will be more successful and having a better time than me.

Wednesday 23 August

Definitely going to Edinburgh. Daniel is working in London so no danger of bumping into him on the Royal Mile. It will be good for me to get away instead of obsessing and waiting for *Good Afternoon!* letter.

Thursday 24 August

I'm staying in London. I always think I'm going to enjoy going to Edinburgh then end up only being able to get into the mime acts. Also you dress for summer, then it's freezing cold and you have to teeter shivering for miles up cobble-stone precipices thinking everyone else is at a big party.

Friday 25 August

7 p.m. I *am* going to Edinburgh. Today Perpetua said, 'Bridget, this is *absurdly* short notice, but it's just occurred to me. I've taken a flat up in Edinburgh – I'd adore it if you wanted to stay.' So generous and hospitable of her.

10 p.m. Just called Perpetua and told her I'm not coming. It's all stupid. I can't afford it.

Saturday 26 August

8.30 a.m. Right, I'm going to have a quiet, healthy time at home. Lovely. I might finish *The Famished Road*.

9.00 a.m. Oh God, I'm so depressed. Everybody's gone to Edinburgh except me.

9.15 a.m. I wonder if Perpetua's left yet?

Midnight. Edinburgh. Oh God. I must go to see something tomorrow. Perpetua thinks I'm mad. She spent the entire train journey with the portable phone pressed to her ear, bellowing at the rest of us. 'Arthur Smith's *Hamlet* is completely booked up so we could go to the Coen brothers instead at five but that means we'll be too late for Richard Herring. So shall we not go to Jenny Eclair – Chuh! I frankly don't know why she still *bothers* – and do *Lanark*, then try to get into Harry Hill or Bondages and Julian Clary? Hang on. I'll try the Gilded Balloon. No, Harry Hill's booked up, so shall we skip the Coen brothers?'

I said I'd meet them at the Pleasance at six because I wanted to go to the George Hotel and leave a message for Tom, and I bumped into Tina in the bar. I didn't realize how far it was to the Pleasance, and when I got there it had started and there were no seats left. Secretly relieved, I walked or rather abseiled back to the flat, picked up a lovely jacket potato with a chicken curry and watched *Casualty*. I was supposed to meet Perpetua at the Assembly Rooms at nine. By the time I was ready it was 8.45 but I didn't realize you couldn't ring out on the phone so I couldn't book a taxi and by the time I got there it was too late. I went back to the

George bar to look for Tina and find out where Shazzer was. I'd just got myself a Bloody Mary and was trying to pretend I didn't mind not having any friends when I noticed a flurry of lights and cameras in one corner and nearly screamed. It was my mother, done up like Marianne Faithfull and about to interview Alan Yentob.

'Absolute quiet, everyone!' she trilled in a Una Alconbury flower-arranging voice.

'Aaaaand action!!!! Tell me, Alan,' she said, looking traumatized, 'have you ever had . . . suicidal thoughts?'

The telly's been quite good tonight, actually.

Sunday 27 August, Edinburgh

No. of shows seen 0.

2 a.m. Can't get to sleep. I bet they're all at a really nice party.

3 a.m. Just heard Perpetua come in, giving her verdict on the alternative comedians: 'Puerile . . . completely childish . . . just silly.' I think she might have misunderstood something somewhere along the line.

5 a.m. There is a man in the house. I can just *tell*.

6 a.m. He's in Debby from Marketing's room. Blimey.

9.30 a.m. Woken by Perpetua bellowing, 'Anyone coming to the poetry reading?!' Then it all went quiet and I heard Debby and the man whispering and him going into the kitchen. Then Perpetua's voice boomed out, 'What are you doing here?!! I said NO OVERNIGHT GUESTS.'

2 p.m. Oh my God. I've overslept.

7 p.m. King's Cross train. Oh dear. Met Jude in the George at three. We were going to go to a Question and Answer session but we had a few Bloody Marys and remembered that Question and Answer sessions have a bad effect on us. You get hyper tense trying to think up a question, putting your hand up and down. You finally get to ask it, in a semi-crouching position and odd high-pitched voice, then sit frozen with embarrassment, nodding like a dog in the back of a car whilst a twenty-minute answer in which you had no interest in the first place is directed at you. Anyway, before we knew where we were it was 5.30. Then Perpetua appeared with a whole bunch of people from the office.

'Ah, Bridget,' she bellowed. 'What have you been to see?' There was a big silence.

'Actually, I'm just about to go to . . .' I began confidently '. . . get the train.'

'You haven't been to see anything at all, have you?' she hooted. 'Anyway, you owe me seventy-five pounds for the room.'

'What?' I stammered.

'Yes!' she yelled. 'It would have been fifty pounds, but it's 50 per cent extra if there are two people in the room.'

'But . . . but, there weren't . . .'

'Oh, come *on*, Bridget, we all knew you had a man in there,' she roared. 'Don't worry about it. It isn't love, it's only Edinburgh. I'll make sure it gets back to Daniel and teaches him a lesson.'

Monday 28 August

9st 6 (full of beer and jacket potatoes), alcohol units 6, cigarettes 20, calories 2846.

Got back to message from Mum asking me what I thought about an electric handwhisk for Christmas, and to remember Christmas Day was a Monday this year so was I coming home on the Friday night or the Saturday?

Considerably less annoyingly, there was a letter from Richard Finch, the editor of *Good Afternoon!* offering me a job, I think. This is all it said:

OK, my darling. You're on.

Tuesday 29 August

9st 2, alcohol units 0 (v.g.), cigarettes 3 (g.), calories 1456 (pre-new-job healthy eating).

10.30 a.m. Office. Just called Richard Finch's assistant Patchouli and it is a job offer but must start in a week. I don't know anything about television but sod it, I'm stuck in a dead-end here, and it is just too humiliating working with Daniel now. I had better go and tell him.

11.15 a.m. I can't believe this. Daniel stared at me, ashen-faced. 'You can't do this,' he said. 'Have you any idea how difficult the last few weeks have been for me?' Then Perpetua burst in – she must have been eavesdropping outside the door.

'Daniel,' she exploded. 'You selfish, self-indulgent, manipulative, emotional blackmailer. It was you – for God's sake – who chucked *her*. So you can just bloody well put up with it.'

Suddenly think I might love Perpetua, though not in a lesbian way.

SEPTEMBER

Up The Fireman's Pole

Monday 4 September

9st, alcohol units 0, cigarettes 27, calories 15, minutes spent having imaginary conversations with Daniel telling him what I think of him 145 (good, better).

8 a.m. First day at new job. Must begin as mean to go on, with new calm, authoritative image. And no smoking. Smoking is a sign of weakness and undermines one's personal authority.

8.30 a.m. Mum just rang, I assumed to wish me luck for the new job.

'Guess what, darling?' she began.

'What?'

'Elaine has invited you to their ruby wedding!' she said, pausing breathlessly and expectantly.

My mind went blank. Elaine? Brian - and - Elaine? Colin-and-Elaine? Elaine-married-to-Gordon-who-used-to-be-head-of-Tarmacadam-in-Kettering-Elaine?

'She thought it might be nice to have one or two young 'uns there to keep Mark company.'

Ah. *Malcolm* and Elaine. Begetters of the over-perfect Mark Darcy.

'Apparently he told Elaine he thought you were very attractive.'

'Durr! Don't lie,' I muttered. Pleased though.

'Well, I'm sure that's what he meant, anyway, darling.'

'What did he say?' I hissed, suddenly suspicious.

'He said you were very. . .'

'Mother. . .'

'Well, the word he actually used, darling, was "bizarre". But that's lovely, isn't it – "bizarrre"? Anyway, you can ask him all about it at the ruby wedding.'

'I'm not going all the way to Huntingdon to celebrate the ruby wedding of two people I have spoken to once for eight seconds since I was three, just to throw myself in the path of a rich divorcee who describes me as bizarre.'

'Now, don't be silly, darling.'

'Anyway, I've got to go,' I said, foolishly since she then, as always, began to gabble as if I were on death row and this was our last phone call before I was given a lethal injection.

'He was earning thousands of pounds an hour. Had a clock on his desk, tick-tock-tick-tock. Did I tell you I saw Mavis Enderby in the post office?'

'Mum. It's my first day at work today. I'm really nervous. I don't want to talk about Mavis Enderby.'

'Oh, my godfathers, darling!' What are you going to wear?'

'My short black skirt and a T-shirt.

'Oh, now you're not going to go looking like a *sloppy tramp* in dull colours. Put something smart and bright on. What about that lovely cerise two-piece you used to wear? Oh, by the way, did I tell you Una's gone down the Nile?'

Grrrr. Felt so bad when she put the phone down that smoked five Silk Cut in row. Non-v.g. start to day.

9 p.m. In bed, completely exhausted. I had forgotten how hideous it is starting a new job when nobody knows you, so your entire character becomes defined by every chance remark or slightly peculiar thing you say; and you can't even so much as go to put some make-up on without asking where the ladies' is.

I was late through no fault of my own. It was impossible to get into the TV studios as I had no pass and the door was run by the sort of security guards who think their job is to prevent the staff from entering the building. When I finally reached reception I wasn't allowed upstairs till someone came to get me. By this time it was 9.25 and the conference was at 9.30. Patchouli eventually appeared with two huge barking dogs, one of which started jumping up and licking my face while the other put its head straight up my skirt.

'They're Richard's. Aren't they, like, brilliant?' she said. 'I'll just take them to the car.'

'Won't I be late for the meeting?' I said desperately, holding on to the dog's head between my knees and trying to push it away. She looked me up and down as if to say, 'So?' and then disappeared, dragging the dogs.

By the time I got in to the office, therefore, the meeting had started and everyone stared except Richard, whose portly form was clad in a strange green woollen boilersuit.

'Come on, come on,' he was saying, jigging and beckoning the table towards him with both hands. 'I'm thinking

Nine o'clock Service. I'm thinking dirty vicars. I'm thinking sexual acts in church. I'm thinking, why do women fall for vicars? Come on. I'm not paying you for nothing. Have an idea.'

'Why don't you interview Joanna Trollope?' I said.

'A trollop?' he said, staring at me blankly. 'What trollop?'

'Joanna Trollope. The woman who wrote *The Rector's Wife* that was on the telly. *The Rector's Wife*. She should know.'

A leery smile spread across his face. 'Brilliant,' he said to my breasts. 'Absolutely fucking brilliant. Anyone got a number for Joanna Trollope?'

There was a long pause. 'Er, actually I have,' I said eventually, feeling walls of hate vibes coming from the grunge youths.

When the meeting was over I rushed to the loo to recover my composure where Patchouli was making herself up next to her friend, who was wearing a sprayed-on dress that showed her pants *and* midriff.

'This isn't too tarty, is it?' the girl was saying to Patchouli. 'You should have seen those bitch thirtysomethings' faces when I walked in . . . Oh!'

Both girls looked at me, horrified, with their hands over their mouths.

'We didn't mean you,' they said.

I am not sure if I am going to be able to stand this.

Saturday 9 September

8st 12 (v.g. advantage of new job with attendant nervous tension), alcohol units 4, cigarettes 10, calories 1876, minutes spent having imaginary conversations with Daniel 24 (excellent), minutes spent imagining re-run of conversations with mother in which I come out on top 94.

11.30 a.m. Why oh why did I give my mother a key to my flat? I was just – for the first time in five weeks – starting a weekend without wanting to stare at the wall and burst into tears. I'd got through a week at work. I was starting to think maybe it was all going to be OK, maybe I wasn't *necessarily* going to be eaten by an Alsatian when she burst in carrying a sewing machine.

'What on earth are you doing, silly?' she trilled. I was weighing out 100 grams of cereal for my breakfast using a bar of chocolate (the weights for the scales are in ounces which is no good because the calorie chart is in grams).

'Guess what, darling?' she said, beginning to open and shut all the cupboard doors.

'What?' I said, standing in my socks and nighty trying to wipe the mascara from under my eyes.

'Malcolm and Elaine are having the ruby wedding in London now, on the twenty-third, so you will be able to come and keep Mark company.'

'I don't want to keep Mark company,' I said through clenched teeth.

'Oh, but he's very clever. Been to Cambridge. Apparently he made a fortune in America . . .'

'I'm not going.'

'Now, come along, darling, let's not start,' she said, as if

I were thirteen. 'You see, Mark's completed on the house in Holland Park and he's throwing the whole party for them, six floors, caterers and everything . . . What are you going to wear?'

'Are you going with Julio or Dad?' I said, to shut her up.

'Oh, darling, I don't know. Probably both of them,' she said in the special, breathy voice she reserves for when she thinks she is Diana Dors.

'You can't do that.'

'But Daddy and I are still friends, darling. I'm just friends with Julio as well.'

Grr. Grrr. Grrrrrrr. I absolutely cannot deal with her when she's like this.

'Anyway, I'll tell Elaine you'd love to come, shall I?' she said, picking up the inexplicable sewing machine as she headed for the door. 'Must fly. Byee!'

I am not going to spend another evening being danced about in front of Mark Darcy like a spoonful of puréed turnip in front of a baby. I am going to have to leave the country or something.

8 p.m. Off to dinner party. All the Smug Marrieds keep inviting me on Saturday nights now I am alone again, seating me opposite an increasingly horrifying selection of single men. It is very kind of them and I appreciate it v. much but it only seems to highlight my emotional failure and isolation – though Magda says I should remember that being single is better than having an adulterous, sexually incontinent husband.

Midnight. Oh dear. Everyone was trying to cheer up the spare man (thirty-seven, newly divorced by wife, sample

view: 'I have to say, I do think Michael Howard is somewhat unfairly maligned.').

'Don't know what you're complaining about,' Jeremy
was holding forth to him. 'Men get more attractive when
they get older and women get less attractive, so all those
twenty-two-year-olds who wouldn't look at you when you
were twenty-five will be gagging for it.'

I sat, head down, quivering furiously at their inferences
of female sell-by dates and life as game of musical chairs
where girls without a chair/man when the music stops/they
pass thirty are 'out'. Huh. As if.

'Oh yes, I quite agree it's much the best to go for
younger partners,' I burst out, airily. 'Men in their thirties
are *such* bores with their hang-ups and obsessive delusions
that all women are trying to trap them into marriage. These
days I'm only *really* interested in men in their early twenties. They're so much better able to . . . well, you know . . .'

'*Really?*' said Magda, rather too eagerly. 'How . . .?'

'Yes, *you're* interested,' interjected Jeremy, glaring at
Magda. 'But the point is *they're* not interested in *you*.'

'Um. Excuse me. My current boyfriend is twenty-three,'
I said, sweetly.

There was a stunned silence.

'Well, in that case,' said Alex, smirking, 'you can bring
him to us next Saturday when you come to dinner, can't
you?'

Bugger. Where am I going to find a twenty-three-year-
old who will come to dinner with Smug Marrieds on a
Saturday night instead of taking contaminated Ecstasy
tablets?

Friday 15 September

9st, alcohol units 0, cigarettes 4 (v.g.), calories 3222 (British Rail sandwiches hideously impregnated), minutes spent imagining speech will make when resigning from new job 210.

Ugh. Hateful conference with bully-boss Richard Finch going, 'Right. Harrods one-pound-a-pee toilets. I'm thinking Fantasy Toilets. I'm thinking studio: Frank Skinner and Sir Richard Rogers on furry seats, armrests with TV screens, quilted loo paper. Bridget, you're Dole Youths Clampdown. I'm thinking the North. I'm thinking Dole Youths, loafing about, live down the line.'

'But . . . but . . .' I stammered.

'Patchouli!' he shouted, at which point the dogs under his desk woke up and started jumping about and barking.

'Wha'?' yelled Patchouli above the din. She was wearing a crocheted midi-dress with a floppy straw hat and an orange Bri-nylon saddle-stitched blouse on top. As if the things I used to wear in my teens were a hilarious joke.

'Where's the Dole Youths OB?'

'Liverpool.'

'Liverpool. OK, Bridget. OB crew outside Boots in the shopping centre, live at five thirty. Get me six Dole Youths.'

Later, as I was leaving to get the train, Patchouli yelled casually, 'Oh yeah, like, Bridget, it's not Liverpool, it's, like, Manchester, right?'

4.15 p.m. Manchester.

Number of Dole Youths approached 44, Number of Dole Youths agreed to be interviewed 0.

Manchester–London train 7 p.m. Ugh. by 4.45 I was running hysterically between the concrete flower tubs, gabbling.

'scuse me, are you employed? Never mind. Thanks!'

'What are we doing, then?' asked the cameraman with no attempt to feign interest. 'Dole Youths,' I said gaily. 'Back in a mo!' then rushed round the corner and hit myself on the forehead. I could hear Richard over my earpiece going, 'Bridget . . . where the *fuck*. . .? Dole Youths.' Then I spotted a cashpoint machine on the wall.

By 5.20 six youths claiming to be unemployed were neatly lined up in front of the camera, a crisp £20 note in each of their pockets while I flapped around trying to make oblique amends for being middle-class. At 5.30 I heard the signature tune bonging and crashing then Richard yelling, 'Sorry, Manchester, we're dropping you.'

'Urm . . .' I began, to the expectant faces. The youths clearly thought I had a syndrome that made me want to pretend I worked in TV. Worse, with working like a mad thing all week and coming up to Manchester I had been unable to do anything about the no-date trauma tomorrow. Then suddenly as I glanced across at the divine young whippersnappers, with the cashpoint machine in the background, the germ of an extremely morally suspect idea began to form itself in my mind.

Hmm. Think was right decision not to attempt to lure Dole Youth to Cosmo's dinner party. Would have been

215

exploitative and wrong. Doesn't answer question of what to do about it, though. Think will go have a fag in the smoking carriage.

7.30 p.m. Ugh. 'Smoking Carriage' turned out to be Monstrous Pigsty where smokers were huddled, miserable and defiant. Realize it is no longer possible for smokers to live in dignity, instead being forced to sulk in the slimy underbelly of existence. Would not have been in least surprised if carriage had mysteriously been shunted off into siding never to be seen again. Maybe privatized rail firms will start running Smoking Trains and villagers will shake their fists and throw stones at them as they pass, terrifying their children with tales of fire-breathing freaks within. Anyway, rang Tom from miracle-on-train-phone (How does it work? How? No wires. Weird. Maybe somehow connected through electric contact between wheels and tracks) to moan about the no-twenty-three-year-old-date crisis.

'What about Gav?' he said.

'Gav?'

'You know. The guy you met at the Saatchi Gallery.'

'D'you think he'd mind?'

'No. He was really into you.'

'He wasn't. Shut-urrrrp.'

'He was. Stop obsessing. Leave it to me.'

Sometimes feel without Tom I would sink without trace and disappear.

Tuesday 19 September

8st 12 (v.g.), alcohol units 3 (v.g.), cigarettes 0 (too shameful to smoke in presence of healthy young whippersnappers).

Blimey, must hurry. About to go on date with Diet Coke-esque young whippersnapper. Gav turned out to be completely divine, and behaved exquisitely at Alex's dinner party on Saturday, flirting with all the wives, fawning over me and fending all their trick questions over our 'relationship' with the intellectual dexterity of a Fellow of All Souls. Unfortunately, I was so overcome with gratitude* in the taxi on the way back I was powerless to resist his advances**. I did, however, manage to get a grip of myself*** and not accept his invitation to go in for coffee. Subsequently, however, I felt guilty about being a prick-teaser****, so when Gav rang and asked me round to his house for dinner tonight I accepted graciously*****.

Midnight. Feel like Old Woman of the Hills. Was so long since had been on a date that was completely full of myself and could not resist boasting to taxi driver about my 'boyfriend' and going round to my 'boyfriend's', who was cooking me supper.

Unfortunately, however, when I got there, Number 4 Malden Road was a fruit and vegetable shop.

* lust
** put my hand on his knee
*** my panic
**** could not stop self thinking 'Damn, damn, damn!'
***** could barely contain my excitement

'Do you want to use my phone, love?' said the taxi driver wearily.

Of course I didn't know Gav's number, so I had to pretend to ring Gav and find it engaged and then ring Tom and try to ask him for Gav's address in a way that wouldn't make the taxi driver think I had been lying about having a boyfriend. Turned out it was 44 Malden Villas and had not been concentrating when wrote it down. Conversation between me and the taxi driver had rather dried up as we drove to the new address. I'm sure he thought I was a prostitute or something.

By the time I arrived I was feeling less than assured. It was all very sweet and shy to start with – a bit like going round to a potential Best Friend's house for tea at junior school. Gav had cooked spag bog. The problem came when food preparation and serving were over and activities turned to conversation. We ended up, for some reason, talking about Princess Diana.

'It seemed such a fairytale. I remember sitting on that wall outside St Paul's at the wedding,' I said. 'Were you there?'

Gav looked embarrassed. 'Actually, I was only six at the time.'

Eventually we gave up on conversation and Gav, with tremendous excitement (this, I recall, the fabulous thing about twenty-two-year-olds) began to kiss me and simultaneously try to find entrances to my clothes. Eventually he managed to slide his hand over my stomach at which point he said – it was so humiliating – 'Mmm. You're all squashy.'

I couldn't go on with it after that. Oh God. It's no good. I am too old and will have to give up, teach religious knowledge in a girls' school and move in with the hockey teacher.

Saturday 23 September

9st, alcohol units 0, cigarettes 0 (v.v.g.), draft replies written to Mark Darcy's invitation 14 (but at least has replaced imaginary conversations with Daniel).

10 a.m. Right. I am going to reply to Mark Darcy's invitation and say quite clearly and firmly that I will be unable to attend. There is no reason why I should go. I am not a close friend or relation, and would have to miss both *Blind Date* and *Casualty*.

Oh God, though. It is one of those mad invitations written in the third person, as if everyone is so posh that to acknowledge directly in person that they were having a party and wondered if you would like to come would be like calling the ladies' powder room the toilet. Seem to remember from childhood am supposed to reply in same oblique style as if I am imaginary person employed by self to reply to invitations from imaginary people employed by friends to issue invitations. What to put?

Bridget Jones regrets that she will be unable . . .

Miss Bridget Jones is distraught, that she will be unable . . .

Devastated does not do justice to the feelings of Miss Bridget Jones . . .

It is with great regret that we must announce that so great was Miss Bridget Jones's distress at not being able to accept the kind invitation of Mr Mark Darcy that she has topped herself and will therefore, more certainly than ever, now, be unable to accept Mr Mark Darcy's kind . . .

Ooh: telephone.

It was Dad: 'Bridget, my dear, you are coming to the horror event next Saturday, aren't you?'

'The Darcys' ruby wedding, you mean.'

'What else? It's been the only thing that has distracted your mother from the question of who's getting the mahogany ornament cabinet and nesting coffee tables since she got the Lisa Leeson interview at the beginning of August.'

'I was kind of hoping to get out of it.'

The line went quiet at the other end.

'Dad?'

There was a muffled sob. Dad was crying. I think Dad is having a nervous breakdown. Mind you, if I'd been married to Mum for thirty-nine years I'd have had a nervous breakdown, even without her running off with a Portuguese tour operator.

'What's wrong, Dad?'

'Oh, it's just . . . Sorry. It's just . . . I was hoping to get out of it too.'

'Well, why don't you? Hurray. Let's go to the pictures instead.'

'It's . . .' he broke down again. 'It's the thought of her going with that greasy beperfumed bouffant wop, and all my friends and colleagues of forty years saying "cheers" to the pair of them and writing me off as history.'

'They won't . . .'

'Oh yes, they will. I'm determined to go, Bridget. I'm going to get on my glad rags and hold my head up high and . . . but . . .' Sobs again.

'What?'

'I need some moral support.'

11.30 a.m.

> *Miss Bridget Jones has great pleasure . . .*

> *Ms Bridget Jones thanks Mr Mark Darcy for his . . .*

> *It is with great pleasure that Miss Bridget Jones accepts . . .*

Oh, for God's sake.

> *Dear Mark,*
> *Thank you for your invitation to your ruby wedding party for Malcolm and Elaine. I would love to come.*
> *Yours,*
> > *Bridget Jones*

Hmmm.

> *Yours,*
> > *Bridget*

or just

> *Bridget*

> *Bridget (Jones)*

Right. Will just copy it out neatly and check spellings then send it.

Tuesday 26 September

8st 13, alcohol units 0, cigarettes 0, calories 1256, Instants 0, obsessive thoughts about Daniel 0, negative thoughts 0. Am perfect saint-style person.

It is great when you start thinking about your career instead of worrying about trivial things – men and relationships. It's going really well on *Good Afternoon!* I think I might have a gift for popular television. The really exciting news is that I am going to be given a try-out in front of the camera.

Richard Finch got this idea into his head at the end of last week that he wanted to do a Live Action Special with reporters attached to emergency services all over the capital. He didn't have much luck to start with. In fact people were going round the office saying he had been turned down by every Accident and Emergency unit, Police and Ambulance force in the Home Counties. But this morning when I arrived he grabbed me by the shoulders yelling, 'Bridget! We're on! Fire. I want you on-camera. I'm thinking mini-skirt. I'm thinking fireman's helmet. I'm thinking pointing the hose.'

Everything has been total mayhem ever since, with the everyday business of the day's news utterly forgotten and everyone gibbering down the phone about links, towers and OBs. Anyway, it is all happening tomorrow and I have to report to Lewisham fire station at 11 o'clock. I'm going to ring round everybody tonight and tell them to watch. Cannot wait to tell Mum.

Wednesday 27 September

8st 11 (shrunk with embarrassment), alcohol units 3, cigarettes 0 (no smoking in fire station) then 12 in 1 hour, calories 1584 (v.g.).

9 p.m. Have never been so humiliated in my life. Spent all day rehearsing and getting everything organized. The idea was that when they cut to Lewisham I was going to slide down the pole into shot and start interviewing a fireman. At five o'clock as we went on air I was perched at the top of the pole ready to slide down on my cue. Then suddenly in my earpiece I heard Richard shouting, 'Go, go, go go, go!' so I let go of the pole and started to slide. Then he continued, 'Go, go, go, Newcastle! Bridget, stand by in Lewisham. Coming to you in thirty seconds.'

I thought about dropping to the bottom of the pole and rushing back up the stairs but I was only a few feet down so I started to pull myself up again instead. Then suddenly there was a great bellow in my ear.

'Bridget! We're on you. What the fuck are you doing? You're meant to be sliding down the pole, not climbing up it. Go, go, go.'

Hysterically I grinned at the camera and dropped myself down, landing, as scheduled, by the feet of the fireman I was supposed to interview.

'Lewisham, we're out of time. Wind it up, wind it up, Bridget,' yelled Richard in my ear.

'And now back to the studio,' I said, and that was it.

Thursday 28 September

8st 12, alcohol units 2 (v.g.), cigarettes 11 (g.), calories 1850, job offers from fire service or rival TV stations 0 (perhaps not altogether surprising).

11 a.m. Am in disgrace and am laughing stock. Richard Finch humiliated me in front of the whole meeting flinging words like 'shambles', 'disgrace', and 'bleedin' bloody idiot' at me randomly.

'And now back to the studio,' seems to have turned into a new catchphrase in the office. Any time anyone gets asked a question they don't know the answer to they go. 'Errrr ... and now back to the studio,' and burst out laughing. Funny thing is, though, the grunge youths are being much more friendly to me. Patchouli (even!) came up and said, 'Oh, like, don't take any notice of Richard, right? He's, like, you know, really into control, right. You know what I'm sayin'? That fireman's pole thing was really like subversive and brilliant, right. Anyway, like ... now back to the studio, OK?'

Richard Finch now just either ignores me or shakes his head disbelieving whenever he comes anywhere near me, and I have been given nothing to do all day.

Oh God, I'm so depressed. I thought I'd found something I was good at for once and now it's all ruined, and on top of everything else it is the horrible ruby wedding party on Saturday and I have nothing to wear. I'm no good at anything. Not men. Not social skills. Not work. Nothing.

OCTOBER

Date with Darcy

Sunday 1 October

8st 11, cigarettes 17, alcohol units 0 (v.g., esp for party).

4 a.m. Startling. One of the most startling evenings of life.

After got depressed on Friday Jude came round and talked to me about being more positive about things, bringing with her fantastic black dress for me to borrow for party. Was worried that might split or spill on the dress but she said she had lots of money and dresses because of top job and did not matter so not to worry about it. Love Jude. Girls are so much nicer than men (apart from Tom – but homosexual). Decided to accessorize fantastic dress with black tights with Lycra and Light Shimmer (£6.95) and Pied à Terre kitten-heel black suede shoes (have got mashed potato off).

Had shock on arrival at the party as Mark Darcy's house was not a thin white terraced house on Portland Road or similar as had anticipated, but huge, detached wedding cake-style mansion on the other side of Holland Park Avenue (where Harold Pinter, they say, lives) surrounded by greenery.

He had certainly pushed the boat out for his mum and

dad. All the trees were dotted with red fairy lights and strings of shiny red hearts in a really quite endearing manner and there was a red and white canopied walkway leading all the way up the front path.

At the door things began to look even more promising as we were greeted by serving staff who gave us champagne and relieved us of our gifts (I had bought Malcolm and Elaine a copy of Perry Como love songs from the year they were married, plus a Bodyshop Terracotta Essential Oil Burner as an extra present for Elaine as she had been asking me about Essential Oils at the Turkey Curry Buffet). Next we were ushered down a dramatic curved pale wood stairway lit by red heart-shaped candles on each step. Downstairs was one vast room, with a dark wood floor and a conservatory giving on to the garden. The whole room was lit by candles. Dad and I just stood and stared, completely speechless.

Instead of the cocktail fancies you would expect at a parent-generational do – compartmentalized cut-glass dishes full of gherkins; plates sporting savoury doilies and half grapefruits bespined with cheese-and-pineapple-chunk-ladened cocktail sticks – there were large silver trays containing prawn won tons, tomato and mozzarella tartlets and chicken saté. The guests looked as though they couldn't believe their luck, throwing their heads back and roaring with laughter. Una Alconbury looked as though she had just eaten a lemon.

'Oh dear,' said Dad, following my gaze, as Una bore down on us. 'I'm not sure this is going to be Mummy and Una's cup of tea.'

'Bit showy, isn't it?' said Una the second she was with-in earshot, pulling her stole huffily around her shoulders.

'I think if you take these things too far it gets a bit common.'

'Oh, don't be absurd, Una. It's a sensational party,' said my father, helping himself to his nineteenth canapé.

'Mmm. I agree,' I said through a mouthful of tartlet, as my champagne glass was filled as if from nowhere, ''s bloody fantastic.' After psyching myself up for so long for Jaeger two-piece hell, I was euphoric. No one had even asked me why I wasn't married yet.

'Humph,' said Una.

Mum too was now bearing down on us.

'Bridget,' she yelled. 'Have you said hello to Mark?'

I suddenly realized cringing, that both Una and Mum must be coming up to their ruby weddings soon. Knowing Mum, it is highly unlikely she will let a trifling detail like leaving her husband and going off with a tour operator stand in the way of the celebrations and will be determined not to be outdone by Elaine Darcy at whatever price, even the sacrifice of a harmless daughter to an arranged marriage.

'Hold hard there, bigfeller,' said my dad, squeezing my arm.

'What a lovely house. Haven't you got a nice stole to put over your shoulders, Bridget? Dandruff!' trilled Mum, brushing Dad's back. 'Now, darling. Why on *earth* aren't you talking to Mark?'

'Um, well . . .' I mumbled.

'What do you think, Pam?' hissed Una tensely, nodding at the room.

'Showy,' whispered Mum, exaggerating her lip movements like Les Dawson.

'Exactly what I said,' mouthed Una triumphantly. 'Didn't I say so, Colin? Showy.'

I glanced around nervously and jumped in fright. There, looking at us, not three feet away, was Mark Darcy. He must have heard everything. I opened my mouth to say something – I'm not quite sure what – to try to improve matters, but he walked away.

Dinner was served in the 'Drawing Room' on the ground floor and I found myself in the queue on the stairs directly behind Mark Darcy.

'Hi,' I said, hoping to make amends for my mother's rudeness. He looked round, completely ignored me and looked back again.

'Hi,' I said again and poked him.

'Oh, hi, I'm sorry. I didn't see you,' he said.

'It's a great party,' I said. 'Thanks for inviting me.'

He stared at me for a moment. 'Oh, I didn't,' he said. 'My mother invited you. Anyway. Must see to the, er, *placement*. Very much enjoyed your Lewisham fire station report, by the way,' and he turned and strode upstairs, dodging between the diners and excusing himself while I reeled. Humph.

As he reached the top of the stairs Natasha appeared in a stunning gold satin sheath, grabbing his arm possessively and, in her haste, tripping over one of the candles which spilt red wax on the bottom of her dress. 'Fack,' she said. 'Fack.'

As they disappeared ahead I could hear her telling him off. 'I told you it was ridiculous spending all afternoon arranging candles in dangerous places for people to fall over. Your time would have been far better spent ensuring that the placement was . . .'

Funnily enough, the placement turned out to be rather brilliant. Mum was sitting next to neither Dad nor Julio but Brian Enderby, whom she always likes to flirt with. Julio had been put next to Mark Darcy's glamorous fifty-five-year-old aunt, who was beside herself with delight. My dad was pink with pleasure at sitting next to a stunning Shakira Caine look-alike. I was really excited. Maybe I would be sandwiched between two of Mark Darcy's dishy friends, top barristers or Americans from Boston, perhaps. But as I looked for my name on the chart a familiar voice piped up beside me.

'So how's my little Bridget? Aren't I the lucky one? Look, you're right next to me. Una tells me you've split up with your feller. I don't know! Durr! When are we going to get you married off?'

'Well I hope, when we do, I shall be the one to do the deed,' said a voice on my other side. 'I could do with a new vimper. Mmm. Apricot silk. Or maybe a nice thirty-nine-button souterne from Gamirellis.'

Mark had thoughtfully put me between Geoffrey Alconbury and the gay vicar.

Actually, though, once we all got a few drinks down us conversation was by no means stilted. I was asking the vicar what he thought about the miracle of Indian statues of Ganesh the Elephant God taking in milk. The vicar said the word in ecclesiastical circles was that the miracle was due to the effect on terracotta of a hot summer followed by cold weather.

As the meal broke up and people started to make their way downstairs for the dancing, I was thinking about what he said. Overcome with curiosity, and keen, also, to avoid having to do the twist with Geoffrey Alconbury, I excused myself, discreetly taking a teaspoon and milk jug from the table, and nipped into the room where the presents had –

rather proving Una's point about the showy element of things – already been unwrapped and put on display.

It took me a while to locate the terracotta oil burner, as it had been shoved near the back, but when I did I simply poured a little milk on to the teaspoon, tilted it and held it against the edge of the hole where you put the candle in. I couldn't believe it. The Essential Oil Burner was taking in milk. You could actually see the milk disappearing from the teaspoon.

'Oh my God, it's a miracle,' I exclaimed. How was I to know that was when Mark Darcy would be bloody well walking past?

'What are you doing?' he said, standing in the doorway.

I didn't know what to say. He obviously thought I was trying to steal the presents.

'Mmm?' he said.

'The Essential Oil Burner I bought your mother is taking in milk,' I muttered sulkily.

'Oh, don't be ridiculous,' he said, laughing.

'It *is* taking in milk,' I said indignantly. 'Look.'

I put some more milk on the teaspoon, tilted the spoon and sure enough the oil burner slowly started to take it in.

'You see,' I said proudly. 'It's a miracle.'

He was pretty impressed, I can tell you. 'You're right,' he said softly. 'It is a miracle.'

Just then Natasha appeared in the doorway. 'Oh, hi,' she said, seeing me. 'Not in your bunny girl outfit today, then,' and then gave a little laugh to disguise her bitchy comment as an amusing joke.

'Actually we bunnies wear these in the winter for warmth,' I said.

'John Rocha?' she said, staring at Jude's dress. 'Last autumn? I recognize the hem.'

I paused to think up something very witty and cutting to say, but unfortunately couldn't think of anything. So after a bit of a stupid pause I said, 'Anyway, I'm sure you're longing to circulate. Nice to see you again. Byee!'

I decided I needed to go outside for a little fresh air and a fag. It was a wonderful, warm, starry night with the moon lighting up all the rhododendron bushes. Personally, I have never been keen on rhododendrons. They remind me of Victorian country houses up North from D. H. Lawrence where people drown in lakes. I stepped down into the sunken garden. They were playing Viennese waltzes in a rather smart *fin de millennium* sort of way. Then suddenly I heard a noise above. A figure was silhouetted against the French windows. It was a blond adolescent, an attractive public schoolboy-type.

'Hi,' said the youth. He lit a cigarette unsteadily and stared, heading down the stairs towards me. 'Don't suppose you fancy a dance? Oh. Ah. Sorry,' he said, holding out his hand as if we were at the Eton open day and he was a former Home Secretary who had forgotten his manners: 'Simon Dalrymple.'

'Bridget Jones,' I said, holding out my hand stiffly, feeling as if I were a member of a war cabinet.

'Hi. Yah. Really nice to meet you. So *can* we have a dance?' he said, reverting to the public schoolboy again.

'Well, I don't know, I'm sure,' I said, reverting to pissed floozy and giving an involuntary raucous laugh like a prostitute in a Yates Wine Lodge.

'I mean out here. Just for a moment.'

I hesitated. I was flattered, to tell you the truth. What

with this and performing a miracle in front of Mark Darcy it was all starting to go to my head.

'Please,' pressed Simon. 'I've never danced with an older woman before. Oh, gosh, I'm sorry, I didn't mean. . .' he went on, seeing my face. 'I mean, someone who's left school,' he said, seizing my hand passionately. 'Would you mind? I'd be most awfully, awfully grateful.'

Simon Dalrymple had obviously been taught ballroom dancing from birth, so it was rather nice being expertly guided to and fro, but the trouble was, he seemed to have, well, not to put too fine a point on it, the most enormous erection I've ever had the good fortune to come across, and us dancing so close it was not the sort of thing one could pass off as a pencil case.

'I'll take over, now, Simon,' said a voice.

It was Mark Darcy.

'Come along. Back inside. You should be in bed now.'

Simon looked completely crushed. He blushed scarlet and hurried back into the party.

'May I?' said Mark, holding out his hand to me.

'No,' I said, furious.

'What's the matter?'

'Um,' I said, flailing for an excuse for being so angry. 'That was a horrible thing to do to a young whippersnapper, throwing your weight about and humiliating him like that at a sensitive age.' Then, noticing his baffled expression, I gabbled on. 'Though I do appreciate your asking me to your party. Marvellous. Thank you very much. Fantastic party.'

'Yes. I think you've said that,' he said, blinking fast. The truth is, he looked rather agitated and hurt.

'I . . .' He paused, then started pacing around the patio,

sighing and running his hand through his hair. 'How's the
. . . Have you read any good books lately?' Unbelievable.

'Mark,' I said. 'If you ask me once more if I've read any
good books lately I'm going to eat my head. Why don't you
ask me something else? Ring the changes a bit. Ask me if
I've got any hobbies, or a view on the single European
currency, or if I've had any particularly disturbing experiences with rubber.'

'I . . .' he began again.

'Or if I had to sleep with Douglas Hurd, Michael Howard
or Jim Davidson which one I'd choose. Actually, no contest,
Douglas Hurd.'

'Douglas Hurd?' said Mark.

'Mmm. Yes. So deliciously strict but fair.'

'Hmmm,' said Mark thoughtfully. 'You say that,
but Michael Howard's got an extremely attractive and
intelligent wife. He must have some sort of hidden
charms.'

'Like what, you mean?' I said, childishly, hoping he
would say something about sex.

'Well . . .'

'He might be a good shag, I suppose,' I supplied.

'Or a fantastically skilful potter.'

'Or a qualified aromatherapist.'

'Will you have dinner with me, Bridget?' he said
abruptly, and rather crossly, as if he was going to sit me
down at a table somewhere and tell me off.

I stopped and stared at him. 'Has my mum put you up
to this?' I said, suspiciously.

'No . . . I . . .'

'Una Alconbury?'

'No, no . . .'

Suddenly I realized what was going on. 'It's *your* mum, isn't it?'

'Well, my mother has . . .'

'I don't want to be asked out to dinner just because your mum wants you to. Anyway, what would we talk about? You'd just ask me if I've read any good books lately and then I'd have to make up some pathetic lie and—'

He stared at me in consternation. 'But Una Alconbury told me you were a sort of literary whizz-woman, completely obsessed with books.'

'Did she?' I said, rather pleased by the idea suddenly. 'What else did she tell you?'

'Well, that you're a radical feminist and have an incredibly glamorous life . . .'

'Oooh,' I purred.

'. . .with millions of men taking you out.'

'Huh.'

'I heard about Daniel. I'm sorry.'

'I suppose you did try to warn me,' I muttered sulkily. 'What have you got against him, anyway?'

'He slept with my wife,' he said. 'Two weeks after our wedding.'

I stared at him aghast as a voice above us shouted, 'Markee!' It was Natasha, silhouetted against the lights, peering down to see what was going on.

'Markee!' she called again. 'What are you doing down there?'

'Last Christmas,' Mark went on hurriedly, 'I thought if my mother said the words "Bridget Jones" just once more I would go to the *Sunday People* and accuse her of abusing me as a child with a bicycle pump. Then when I met you . . . and I was wearing that ridiculous diamond-patterned jumper that Una had bought me for Christmas . . . Bridget, all the other girls I know are so lacquered over. I don't know anyone else who would fasten a bunny tail to their pants or . . .'

'Mark!' yelled Natasha, heading down the stairs towards us.

'But you're going out with somebody,' I said, rather pointing out the obvious.

'I'm not any more, actually,' he said. 'Just dinner? Some time?

'OK,' I whispered. 'OK.'

Afterwards I thought I'd better go home: what with Natasha watching my every move as if she were a crocodile and I was getting a bit near to her eggs, and me having given Mark Darcy my address and phone number and having fixed to see him next Tuesday. On my way through the dancing room I saw Mum, Una and Elaine Darcy chatting animatedly to Mark – couldn't help imagining their faces if they knew what had just gone on. I suddenly had a vision of next year's Turkey Curry Buffet with Brian Enderby hitching up the waistband of his trousers going, 'Harumph. Nice to see the young people enjoying themselves, isn't it?' and Mark Darcy and me forced to do tricks for the assembled company, like rubbing noses, or having sex in front of them, like a pair of performing seals.

Tuesday 3 October

8st 12, alcohol units 3 (v.g.), cigarettes 21 (bad), number of times said word 'bastard' in last twenty-four hours 369 (approx.).

7.30 p.m. Complete panic stations. Mark Darcy is coming round to pick me up in half an hour. Just got home from work with mad hair and unfortunate laundry crisis outfit on. Help oh help. Was planning to wear white 501s but suddenly occurs to me he may be the type who will take me to a posh scary restaurant. Oh God, do not have anything posh to wear. Do you think he will expect me to put bunny tail on? Not that I'm interested in him or anything.

7.50 p.m. Oh God oh God. Still have not washed hair. Will quickly get into bath.

8.00 p.m. Drying hair now. V. much hope Mark Darcy is late as do not want him to find me in dressing gown with wet hair.

8.05 p.m. Hair is more or less dry now. Then just have to do make-up, get dressed and put mess behind sofa. Must prioritize. Consider make-up most important, then mess-disposal.

8.15 p.m. Still not here. V.g. Keen on a man who comes round late, in stark contrast to people who come round early, startling and panicking one and finding unsightly items still unhidden in the home.

8.20 p.m. Well, pretty much ready now. Maybe will put something different on.

8.30 p.m. This is weird. Does not seem like him to be more than half an hour late.

9.00 p.m. Cannot quite believe it. Mark Darcy has stood me up. Bastard!

Thursday 5 October

8st 13 (bad), chocolate items 4 (bad), number of times watched video 17 (bad).

11 a.m. In loos at work. Oh no. Oh no. On top of humiliating standing-up débâcle, found self horrible centre of attention at morning meeting today.

'Right, Bridget,' said Richard Finch. 'I'm going to give you another chance. The Isabella Rossellini trial. Verdict expected today. We think she's going to get off. Get yourself down to the High Court. I don't want to see you climbing up any poles or lamp-posts. I want a hard-headed interview. Ask her if this means it's OK for us all to murder people every time we don't fancy having sex with them. What are you waiting for, Bridget? Off you go.'

I had no idea, not even a glimmer of a clue as to what he was talking about.

'You have noticed the Isabella Rossellini trial, haven't you?' said Richard. 'You do read the papers, occasionally?'

The trouble with this job is that people keep flinging names and stories at you and you have a split second to decide whether or not to admit you have no idea what they're talking about, and if you let the moment go then you'll spend the next half hour desperately flailing for clues to what it is you are discussing in depth and at length with a confident air: which is precisely what happened with Isabella Rossellini.

And now I must set off to meet scary camera crew at the law courts in five minutes to cover and report on a story on the television without having the faintest idea what it is about.

11.05 a.m. Thank God for Patchouli. Just came out of the toilets and she was being pulled along by Richard's dogs straining at the leash.

'Are you OK?' she said. 'You look a bit freaked out.'

'No, no, I'm fine,' I said.

'Sure?' she stared at me for a moment. 'Listen, right, you realize he didn't mean Isabella Rossellini at the meeting, didn't you? He's thinking of Elena Rossini, right.'

Oh, thank God and all his angels in heaven above. Elena Rossini is the children's nanny accused of murdering her employer after he allegedly subjected her to repeated rape and effective house arrest for eighteen months. I grabbed a couple of newspapers to gen up and ran for a taxi.

3 p.m. Cannot believe what just happened. Was hanging around outside the High Court for ages with the camera crew and a whole gang of reporters all waiting for the trial to end. Was bloody good fun, actually. Even started to see the funny side of being stood up by Mr Perfect Pants Mark Darcy. Suddenly realized I'd run out of cigarettes. So I whispered to the cameraman, who was really nice, if he thought it would be OK if I nipped to the shop for 5 minutes and he said it would be fine, because you're always given warning when they're about to come out and they'd come and get me if it was about to happen.

When they heard I was going to the shop, a lot of reporters asked me if I'd bring them fags and sweets and so it took quite a while working it all out. I was just standing in the shop trying to keep all the change separate with the shopkeeper when this bloke walked in obviously in a real hurry and said, 'Could you let me have a box of Quality Street?' as if I wasn't there. The poor shopkeeper looked at me as if not sure what to do.

'Excuse me, does the word "queue" mean anything to you?' I said in a hoity-toity voice, turning round to look at him. I made a weird noise. It was Mark Darcy all dressed up in his barrister outfit. He just stared at me, in that way he has.

'Where in the name of arse were you last night?' I said.

'I might ask the same question of you,' he said, icily.

At that moment the camera assistant burst into the shop. 'Bridget!' he yelled. 'We've missed the interview. Elena Rossini's come out and gone. Did you get my Minstrels?'

Speechless, I grabbed the edge of the sweet counter for support.

'Missed it?' I said as soon as I could steady my breathing. 'Missed it? Oh God. This was my last chance after the fireman's pole and I was buying sweets. I'll be sacked. Did the others get interviews?'

'Actually, nobody got any interviews with her,' said Mark Darcy.

'Didn't they?' I said, looking up at him desperately. 'But how do you know?'

241

'Because I was defending her, and I told her not to give any,' he said casually. 'Look, she's out there in my car.'

As I looked, Elena Rossini put her head out of the car window and shouted in a foreign accent, 'Mark, sorry. You bring me Dairy Box, please, instead of Quality Street?' Just then our camera car drew up.

'Derek!' yelled the cameraman out of the window. 'Get us a Twix and a Lion Bar, will you?'

'So where were you last night?' asked Mark Darcy.

'Waiting for bloody you,' I said between clenched teeth.

'What, at five past eight? When I rang on your doorbell twelve times?'

'Yes, I was . . .' I said, feeling the first twinges of realization, 'drying my hair.'

'Big hairdryer?' he said.

'Yes, 1600 volts, Salon Selectives,' I said proudly. 'Why?'

'Maybe you should get a quieter hairdryer or begin your *toilette* a little earlier. Anyway. Come on,' he said laughing. 'Get your cameraman ready, I'll see what I can do for you.'

Oh God. How embarrassing. Am complete berk.

9 p.m. Cannot believe how marvellously everything has turned out. Have just played the *Good Afternoon!* headlines back for the fifth time.

'And a *Good Afternoon!* exclusive,' it says. '*Good Afternoon!*: the only television programme to bring you an exclusive interview with Elena Rossini, just minutes after today's not guilty verdict. Our home news correspondent, Bridget Jones, brings you this exclusive report.'

I *love* that bit: 'Our home news correspondent, Bridget Jones, brings you this exclusive report.'

I'll just play it back once more, then I'll definitely put it away.

Friday 6 October

9st (comfort eating), alcohol units 6 (drink problem), Instants 6 (comfort gambling), 1471 calls to see if Mark Darcy has rung 21 (curiosity only, obviously), number of times watched video 9 (better).

9 p.m. Humph. Left a message for Mum yesterday to tell her all about my scoop so when she rang tonight I assumed it would be to congratulate me, but no, she was just going on about the party. It was Una and Geoffrey this, Brian and Mavis that and how marvellous Mark was and why didn't I talk to him, etc., etc.? Temptation to tell her what happened almost overwhelming but managed to control myself by envisaging consequences: screaming ecstasy at the making of the date and brutal murder of only daughter when she heard the actual outcome.

Keep hoping he might ring me up and ask me for another date after the hairdryer débâcle. Maybe I should write him a note to say thank you for the interview and sorry about the hairdryer. It's not because I fancy him or anything. Simple good manners demands it.

Thursday 12 October

9st 1 (bad), alcohol units 3 (both healthy and normal), cigarettes 13, fat units 17 (wonder if it's possible to calculate fat unit content of entire body? Hope otherwise), Instants 3 (fair), 1471 calls to see if Mark Darcy has rung 12 (better).

Humph. Incensed by patronizing article in the paper by Smug Married journalist. It was headlined, with subtle-as-a-Frankie-Howerd-sexual-innuendo-style irony: 'The Joy of Single Life'.

'They're young, ambitious and rich but their lives hide an aching loneliness . . . When they leave work a gaping emotional hole opens up before them . . . Lonely style-obsessed individuals seek consolation in packeted comfort food of the kind their mother might have made.'

Huh. Bloody nerve. How does Mrs Smug Married-at-twenty-two think she knows, thank you very much?

I'm going to write an article based on 'dozens of conversations' with Smug Marrieds: 'When they leave work, they always burst into tears because, though exhausted, they have to peel potatoes and put all the washing in while their porky bloater husbands slump burping in front of the football demanding plates of chips. On other nights they plop, wearing unstylish pinnies, into big black holes after their husbands have rung to say they're working late again, with the sound of creaking leatherware and sexy Singletons tittering in the background.'

Met Sharon, Jude and Tom after work. Tom, too, was working on a furious imaginary article about the Smug Marrieds' gaping emotional holes.

'Their influence affects everything from the kind of

houses being built to the kind of food that stocks the supermarket shelves,' Tom's appalled article was going to rant. 'Everywhere we see Anne Summers shops catering for housewives trying pathetically to simulate the thrilling sex enjoyed by Singletons and ever-more exotic foodstuffs in Marks & Spencer for exhausted couples trying to pretend they're in a lovely restaurant like the Singletons and don't have to do the washing up.'

'I'm bloody sick of this arrogant hand-wringing about single life!' roared Sharon.

'Yes, yes!' I said.

'You forgot the fuckwittage,' burped Jude. 'We always have fuckwittage.'

'Anyway, we're not lonely. We have extended families in the form of networks of friends connected by telephone,' said Tom.

'Yes! Hurrah! Singletons should not have to explain themselves all the time but should have an accepted status – like geisha girls do,' I shouted happily, slurping on my tumbler of Chilean Chardonnay.

'Geisha girls?' said Sharon, looking at me coldly.

'Shut up, Bridge,' slurred Tom. 'You're drunk. You're just trying to escape from your yawning emotional hole into drunk.'

'Well, so's bloody well Shazzer,' I said sulkily.

'I's not,' said Sharon.

'You's blurr are,' I said.

'Look. Shuddup,' said Jude, burping again. 'Shagernoth-ebol Chardonnay?'

Friday 13 October

9st 3 (but have temporarily turned into wine bag), alcohol units 0 (but feeding off wine bag), calories 0 (v.g.)*.
*Actually might as well be honest here. Not really v.g. as only 0 because puked up 5876 calories immediately after eating.

Oh God, I'm so lonely. An entire weekend stretching ahead with no one to love or have fun with. Anyway, I don't care. I've got a lovely steamed ginger pudding from M&S to put in the microwave.

Sunday 15 October

9st (better), alcohol units 5 (but special occasion), cigarettes 16, calories 2456, minutes spent thinking about Mr Darcy 245.

8.55 a.m. Just nipped out for fags prior to getting changed ready for BBC *Pride and Prejudice*. Hard to believe there are so many cars out on the roads. Shouldn't they be at home getting ready? Love the nation being so addicted. The basis of my own addiction, I know, is my simple human need for Darcy to get off with Elizabeth. Tom says football guru Nick Hornby says in his book that men's obsession with football is not vicarious. The testosterone-crazed fans do not wish themselves on the pitch, claims Hornby, instead seeing their team as their chosen representatives, rather like parliament. That is precisely my feeling about Darcy and Elizabeth. They are my chosen representatives in the field of shagging, or, rather, courtship. I do not, however, wish to see any actual goals. I would hate to see Darcy and Elizabeth in bed, smoking a cigarette afterwards. That would be unnatural and wrong and I would quickly lose interest.

10.30 a.m. Jude just called and we spent twenty minutes growling, 'Fawaw, that Mr Darcy.' I love the way he talks, sort of as if he can't be bothered. *Ding-dong!* Then we had a long discussion about the comparative merits of Mr Darcy and Mark Darcy, both agreeing that Mr Darcy was more attractive because he was ruder but that being imaginary was a disadvantage that could not be overlooked.

Monday 23 October

9st 2, alcohol units 0 (v.g. Have discovered delicious new alcohol substitute drink called Smoothies – v. nice, fruity), cigarettes 0 (Smoothies removes need for cigarettes), Smoothies 22, calories 4265 (4135 of them Smoothies).

Ugh. Just about to watch *Panorama* on 'The trend of well qualified female breadwinners – stealing all the best jobs' (one of which I pray to the Lord in Heaven Above and all his Seraphims I am about to become): 'Does the solution lie in redesigning the educational syllabus?' When I stumbled upon a photograph in the *Standard* of Darcy and Elizabeth, hideous, dressed as modern-day luvvies, draped all over each other in a meadow: she with blonde Sloane hair, and linen trouser suit, he in striped polo neck and leather jacket with Shoestring-style moustache. Apparently they are already sleeping together. That is absolutely disgusting. Feel disorientated and worried, for surely Mr Darcy would never do anything so vain and frivolous as to be an actor and yet Mr Darcy *is* an actor. Hmmm. All v. confusing.

Tuesday 24 October

9st 3 (bloody Smoothies), alcohol units 0, cigarettes 0, Smoothies 32.

On marvellous roll with work. Ever since Elena whatserface interview, seems can do no wrong.

'Come on! Come on! Rosemary West!' Richard Finch was saying, when I got into the office (bit late, actually, sort of thing that could happen to anyone), holding up his fists like a boxer. 'I'm thinking lesbian rape victims, I'm thinking Jeanette Winterson, I'm thinking *Good Afternoon!* doctor, I'm thinking what lesbians actually *do*. That's it! What *do* lesbians actually *do* in bed?' Suddenly, he was looking straight at me.

'Do *you* know?' Everyone stared at me. 'Come on, Bridget-fucking-late-again,' he shouted impatiently. 'What do lesbians actually do in bed?'

I took a deep breath. 'Actually, I think we should be doing the off-screen romance between Darcy and Elizabeth.'

He looked me up and down slowly. 'Brilliant,' he said reverently. 'Absolutely fucking brilliant. OK. The actors who play Darcy and Elizabeth? Come on, come on,' he said, boxing at the meeting.

'Colin Firth and Jennifer Ehle,' I said.

'You, my darling,' he said to one of my breasts, 'are an absolute fucking genius.'

I always hoped I would turn out to be a genius, but I never believed it would actually happen to me – or *my left breast.*

NOVEMBER

A Criminal in the Family

Wednesday 1 November

8st 13lb 8oz (yesss! yesss!), alcohol units 2 (v.g.), cigarettes 4 (but could not smoke at Tom's in case set Alternative Miss World costume alight), calories 1848 (g.), Smoothies 12 (excellent progress).

Just went round to Tom's for top-level summit to discuss the Mark Darcy scenario. Found Tom, however, in a complete lather about the forthcoming Alternative Miss World contest. Having decided ages ago to go as 'Miss Global Warming', he was having a crisis of confidence.

'I haven't got a hope in hell,' he was saying, looking in the mirror, then flouncing to the window. He was wearing a polystyrene sphere painted like map of the globe but with the polar ice-caps melting and a large burn mark on Brazil. In one hand he was holding a piece of tropical hardwood and a Lynx aerosol, and in the other an indeterminate furry item which he claimed was a dead ocelot. 'Do you think I should have a melanoma?' he asked.

'Is it a beauty contest or a fancy dress contest?'

'That's just it, I don't know, no one knows,' said Tom, throwing down his headdress – a miniature tree which he was intending to set alight during the contest. 'It's both. It's everything. Beauty. Originality. Artistry. It's all ridiculously unclear.'

'Do you have to be a poof to enter?' I asked, fiddling with a bit of polystyrene.

'No. Anyone can enter: women, animals, anything. That's exactly the problem,' he said, flouncing back to the mirror. 'Sometimes I think I'd stand more chance trying to win with a really confident dog.'

Eventually we agreed that though the global warming theme *in itself* was faultless, the polystyrene sphere was not, perhaps, the most flattering shape for evening wear. In fact in the end we found we were thinking more towards a fluid sheath of shot-silk-effect Yves Klein blue, floating over smoke and earth shades to symbolize the melting of the polar ice-caps.

Deciding I wasn't going to get the best out of Tom over Mark Darcy just at the moment, I excused myself before it got too late, promising to think hard about Swim and Daywear.

When I got back I called Jude but she started telling me about a marvellous new oriental idea in this month's *Cosmopolitan* called Feng Shui, which helps you get everything you want in life. All you have to do, apparently, is clean out all the cupboards in your flat to unblock yourself, then divide the flat up into nine sections (which is called mapping the ba-gua), each of which represents a different area of your life: career, family, relationships, wealth, or offspring, for example. Whatever you have in that area of your house will govern how that area of your life performs. For example, if you keep finding you have no money it could be due to the presence of a wastepaper basket in your Wealth Corner.

V. excited by new theory as could explain a lot. Resolve to buy *Cosmo* at earliest opportunity. Jude says not to tell Sharon as, naturally, she thinks Feng Shui is bollocks. Managed, eventually, to bring conversation round to Mark Darcy.

'*Of course* you don't fancy him, Bridge, the thought never crossed my mind for a second,' said Jude. She said the answer was obvious: I should have a dinner party and invite him.

'It's perfect,' she said. 'It's not like asking him for a date, so it takes away all the pressure and you can show off like mad and get all your friends to pretend to think you're marvellous.'

'Jude,' I said, hurt, 'did you say, "pretend"?'

Friday 3 November

9st 2 (humph), alcohol units 2, cigarettes 8, Smoothies 13, calories 5245.

11 a.m. V. excited about dinner party. Have bought marvellous new recipe book by Marco Pierre White. At last understand the simple difference between home cooking and restaurant food. As Marco says, it is all to do with *concentration* of taste. The secret of sauces, of course, apart from taste concentration, lies in real stock. One must boil up large pans of fish bones, chicken carcasses, etc., then freeze them in form of ice-stockcubes. Then cooking to Michelin star standard becomes as easy as making shepherd's pie: easier, in fact, as do not need to peel potatoes, merely confit them in goose fat. Cannot believe have not realized this before.

This will be the menu:

Velouté of Celery (v. simple and cheap when have made stock).

Char-grilled Tuna on Velouté of Cherry Tomatoes Coulis with Confit of Garlic and Fondant Potatoes.

Confit of Oranges. Grand Marnier Crème Anglaise.

Will be marvellous. Will become known as brilliant but apparently effortless cook.

People will flock to my dinner parties, enthusing, 'It's really great going to Bridget's for dinner, one gets Michelin star-style food in a bohemian setting.' Mark Darcy will be v. impressed and will realize I am not common or incompetent.

Sunday 5 November

9st (disaster), cigarettes 32, alcohol units 6 (shop has run out of Smoothies – careless bastards), calories 2266, Instants 4.

7 p.m. Humph. Bonfire night and not invited to any bonfires. Rockets going off tauntingly left, right and centre. Going round to Tom's.

11 p.m. Bloody good evening at Tom's, who was trying to deal with the fact that the Alternative Miss World title had gone to Joan of Bloody Arc.

'The thing that makes me really angry is that they say it isn't a beauty contest but really it is. I mean, I'm sure if it wasn't for this nose . . .' said Tom, staring at himself furiously in the mirror.

'What?

'My nose.'

'What's wrong with it?'

'What's wrong with it? Chuh! *Look* at it.'

It turned out there was a very, very tiny bump where someone had shoved a glass in his face when he was seventeen. 'Do you see what I mean?'

My feeling was, as I explained, that the bump in itself couldn't be blamed for Joan of Arc snatching the title from directly beneath it, as it were, unless the judges were using a Hubble telescope, but then Tom started saying he was too fat as well and was going on a diet.

'How many calories are you supposed to eat if you're on a diet?' he said.

'About a thousand. Well, I usually aim for a thousand and come in at about fifteen hundred,' I said, realizing as I said it that the last bit wasn't strictly true.

'A thousand?' said Tom, incredulously. 'But I thought you needed two thousand just to survive.'

I looked at him nonplussed. I realized that I have spent so many years being on a diet that the idea that you might actually need calories to survive has been completely wiped out of my consciousness. Have reached point where believe nutritional ideal is to eat nothing at all, and that the only reason people eat is because they are so greedy they cannot stop themselves from breaking out and ruining their diets.

'How many calories in a boiled egg?' said Tom.

'Seventy-five.'

'Banana?'

'Large or small?'

'Small.'

'Peeled?'

'Yes.'

'Eighty,' I said, confidently.

'Olive?'

'Black or green?'

'Black.'

'Nine.'

'Hobnob?'

'Eighty-one.'

'Box of Milk Tray?'

'Ten thousand, eight hundred and ninety-six.'

'How do you know all this?'

I thought about it. 'I just do, as one knows one's alphabet or times tables.'

'OK. Nine eights,' said Tom.

'Sixty-four. No, fifty-six. Seventy-two.'

'What letter comes before J? Quick.'

'P. L, I mean.'

Tom says I am sick but I happen to know for a fact that I am normal and no different from everyone else, i.e. Sharon and Jude. Frankly, I am quite worried about Tom. I think taking part in a beauty contest has started to make him crack under the pressures we women have long been subjected to and he is becoming insecure, appearance-obsessed and borderline anorexic.

Evening climaxed with Tom cheering himself up letting off rockets from the roof terrace into the garden of the people below who Tom says are homophobic.

Thursday 9 November

8st 13 (better without Smoothies), alcohol units 5 (better than having huge stomach full of puréed fruit), cigarettes 12, calories 1456 (excellent).

V. excited about the dinner party. Fixed for a week on Tuesday. This is the guest list:

Jude	Vile Richard
Shazzer	
Tom	Pretentious Jerome
	(unless get v. lucky and it is off
	between him and Tom by Tuesday)
Magda	Jeremy
Me	Mark Darcy

Mark Darcy seemed very pleased when I rang him up.

'What are you going to cook?' he said. 'Are you good at cooking?'

'Oh, you know . . .' I said. 'Actually, I usually use Marco Pierre White. It's amazing how simple it can be if one goes for a concentration of taste.'

He laughed and then said, 'Well, don't do anything too complicated. Remember everyone's coming to see *you*, not to eat parfaits in sugar cages.'

Daniel would never have said anything nice like that. V. much looking forward to the dinner party.

Saturday 11 November

8st 12, alcohol units 4, cigarettes 35 (crisis), calories 456 (off food).

Tom has disappeared. First began to fear for him this morning when Sharon rang saying wouldn't swear on her mother's life but thought she'd seen him from the window of a taxi on Thursday night wandering along Ladbroke Grove with his hand over his mouth and, she thought, a black eye. By the time she'd got the taxi to go back he'd disappeared. She'd left two messages for him yesterday asking if he was OK but had had no reply.

I suddenly realized, as she spoke, that I had left a message for Tom myself on Wednesday asking if he was around at the weekend and he hadn't replied, which is not like him at all. Frantic phoning ensued. Tom's phone just rang and rang, so I called Jude who said she hadn't heard from him either. I tried Tom's Pretentious Jerome: nothing. Jude said she'd ring Simon, who lives in next street to Tom, and get him to go round. She called back 20 minutes later saying Simon had rung Tom's bell for ages and hammered on the door but no reply. Then Sharon rang again. She'd spoken to Rebecca, who thought Tom was supposed to be going to Michael's for lunch. I called Michael who said Tom had left a weird message talking in an odd distorted voice saying he wasn't going to be able to come and hadn't given a reason.

3 p.m. Starting to feel really panicky, at the same time enjoying sense of being at centre of drama. Am practically Tom's best friend so everyone is ringing me and am adopting calm yet deeply concerned air about whole thing.

Suddenly occurs to me that maybe he's just met someone new and is enjoying honeymoon-style shag hideaway for a few days. Maybe it wasn't him Sharon saw, or black eye is just product of lively enthusiastic young sex or post-modern-style ironic retrospective Rocky Horror Show make-up. Must make more phone calls to test new theory.

3.30 p.m. General opinion quashes new theory, since it is widely agreed to be impossible for Tom to meet new man, let alone start affair, without ringing everyone up to show off. Cannot argue with that. Wild thoughts ranging through head. No denying that Tom has been disturbed lately. Start to wonder whether am really good friend. We are all so selfish and busy in London. Would it be possible for one of my friends to be so unhappy that they . . . ooh, *that's* where I put this month's *Marie Claire*: on top of fridge!

As flicked through *Marie Claire* started fantasizing about Tom's funeral and what I would wear. Aaargh, have suddenly remembered MP who died in a bin liner with tubes round neck and chocolate orange in mouth or something. Wonder if Tom has been doing weird sexual practices without telling us?

5 p.m. Just called Jude again.

'Do you think we should call the police and get them to break in?' I said.

'I already rang them,' said Jude.

'What did they say?' I couldn't help feeling secretly annoyed that Jude had rung the police without clearing it with me first. I am Tom's best friend, not Jude.

'They didn't seem very impressed. They said to call them if we still couldn't find him by Monday. You can see their point. It does seem a bit alarmist to report that a twenty-nine-year-old single man is not in on Saturday morning and has failed to turn up for a lunch party he said he wouldn't be coming to anyway.'

'Something's wrong, though, I just know,' I said in a mysterious, loaded voice, realizing for the first time what an intensely instinctive and intuitive person I am.

'I know what you mean,' said Jude, portentiously. 'I can feel it, too. Something's definitely wrong.'

7 p.m. Extraordinary. After spoke to Jude could not face shopping or similar lighthearted things. Thought this might be the perfect time to do the Feng Shui so went out and bought *Cosmopolitan*. Carefully, using the drawing in *Cosmo*, I mapped the ba-gua of the flat. Had a flash of horrified realization. There was a wastepaper basket in my Helpful Friends Corner. No wonder bloody Tom had disappeared.

Quickly rang Jude to report same. Jude said to move the wastepaper basket.

'Where to, though?' I said. 'I'm not putting it in my Relationship or Offspring Corners.'

Jude said hang on, she'd go have a look at *Cosmo*.

'How about Wealth?' she said, when she came back.

'Hmm, I don't know, what with Christmas coming up and everything,' I said, feeling really mean even as I said it.

'Well, if that's the way you look at things. I mean you're probably going to have one less present to buy anyway . . .' said Jude accusingly.

In the end I decided to put the wastepaper basket in my Knowledge Corner and went out to the greengrocer to get some plants with *round leaves* to put in the Family and

Helpful Friends Corners (spiky-leaved plants, particularly cacti, are counter-productive). Was just getting plant pot out of the cupboard under sink when heard a jangling sound. I suddenly hit myself hard on the forehead. They were Tom's spare keys from when he went to Ibiza.

For a moment I thought about going round there *without Jude*. I mean, she rang the police without telling me, didn't she? But in the end it seemed too mean, so I rang her and we decided we'd get Shazzer to come as well, because she'd raised the alert in the first place.

As we turned into Tom's street, though, I came out of my fantasy about how dignified, tragic and articulate I would be when interviewed by the newspapers, along with a parallel paranoid fear that the police would decide it was me who had murdered Tom. Suddenly it stopped being a game. Maybe something terrible and tragic actually had happened.

None of us spoke or looked at each other as we walked up the front steps.

'Should you ring first?' whispered Sharon as I lifted the key to the lock.

'I'll do it,' said Jude. She looked at us quickly, then pressed the buzzer.

We stood in silence. Nothing. She pressed again. I was just about to slip the key in the lock when a voice on the intercom said, 'Hello?'

'Who's that?' I said tremulously.

'Who'd you think it is, you daft cow.'

'Tom!' I bellowed joyfully. 'Let us in.'

'Who's us?' he said suspiciously.

'Me, Jude and Shazzer.'

'I'd rather you didn't come up, hon, to be honest.'

'Oh, bloody hell,' said Sharon, pushing past me. 'Tom, you silly bloody queen, you've only had half London up in arms ringing the police, combing the metropolis for you because no one knows where you are. Bloody well let us in.'

'I don't want anyone except Bridget,' said Tom petulantly. I beamed beatifically at the others.

'Don't be such a prima bloody donna,' said Shazzer.

Silence.

'Come on, you silly sod. Let us in.'

There was a pause, then the buzzer went. 'Bzzz.'

'Are you ready for this?' came his voice as we reached the top floor and he opened the door.

All three of us cried out. Tom's whole face was distorted, hideous yellow and black, and encased in plaster.

'Tom, what's happened to you?' I cried, clumsily trying to embrace him and ending up kissing his ear. Jude burst into tears and Shazzer kicked the wall.

'Don't worry, Tom,' she growled. 'We'll find the bastards who did this.'

'What happened?' I said again, tears beginning to plop down my cheeks.

'Er, well . . .' said Tom, extracting himself awkwardly from my embrace, 'actually I, er, I had a nose job.'

Turned out Tom had secretly had the operation on Wednesday but was too embarrassed to tell us because we'd all been so dismissive about his minuscule nasal bump. He was supposed to have been looked after by Jerome, henceforth to be known a Creepy Jerome (it was going to be heartless Jerome but we all agreed that sounded too interesting). When, however, Creepy Jerome saw him after the operation he was so repulsed he said he was going away for a few days, buggered off and hasn't been seen or heard of since. Poor Tom was so depressed and traumatized and so weird from the anaesthetic that he just unplugged the phone, hid under the blankets and slept.

'Was it you I saw in Ladbroke Grove on Thursday night, then?' said Shazzer.

It was. Apparently he had waited till dead of night to go out and forage for food under cover of darkness. In spite of our high spirits that he was alive Tom was still very unhappy about Jerome.

'Nobody loves me,' he said.

I told him to ring my answerphone, which held twenty-two frantic messages from his friends, all distraught because he had disappeared for twenty-four hours, which put paid to all our fears about dying alone and being eaten by an Alsatian.

'Or not being found for three months . . . and *bursting* all over the carpet,' said Tom.

Anyway, we told him, how could one moody git with a stupid name make him think nobody loves him?

Two Bloody Marys later he was laughing at Jerome's obsessive use of the term 'self-aware', and his skintight calf-length Calvin-Klein underpants. Meanwhile, Simon, Michael, Rebecca, Magda, Jeremy and a boy claiming to be called Elsie had all rung to see how he was.

'I know we're all psychotic, single and completely dys-functional and it's all done over the phone,' Tom slurred sentimentally, 'but it's a bit like a family, isn't it?'

I *knew* the Feng Shui would work. Now – its task completed – I am going to quickly move the round-leaved plant to my Relationship Corner. Wish there was a Cookery Corner too. Only nine days to go.

Monday 20 November

8st 12 (v.g.), cigarettes 0 (v. bad to smoke when performing culinary miracles), alcohol units 3, calories 200 (effort of going to supermarket must have burnt off more calories than purchased, let alone ate).

7 p.m. Just returned from hideous middle-class Singleton guilt experience at supermarket, standing at checkout next to functional adults with children buying beans, fish fingers, alphabetti spaghetti, etc., when had the following in my trolley:

> 20 heads of garlic
> tin of goose fat
> bottle of Grand Marnier
> 8 tuna steaks
> 36 oranges
> 4 pints of double cream
> 4 vanilla pods at £1.39 each.

Have to start preparations tonight as working tomorrow.

8 p.m. Ugh, do not feel like cooking. Especially dealing with grotesque bag of chicken carcasses: completely disgusting.

10 p.m. Have got chicken carcasses in pan now. Trouble is, Marco says am supposed to tie flavour-enhancing leek and celery together with string but only string have got is blue. Oh well, expect it will be OK.

11 p.m. God, stock took bloody ages to do but worth it as will end up with over 2 gallons, frozen in ice-cube form and only cost £1.70. Mmm, confit of oranges will be delicious also. Now all have got to do is finely slice thirty-six oranges and grate zest. Shouldn't take too long.

1 a.m. Too tired to stay awake now but stock is supposed to cook for another two hours and oranges need another hour in oven. I know. Will leave the stock on v. low heat overnight, also oranges on lowest oven setting, so will become v. tender in manner of a stew.

Tuesday 21 November

8st 11 (nerves eat fat), alcohol units 9 (v. bad indeed), cigarettes 37 (v.v. bad), calories 3479 (and all disgusting).

9.30 a.m. Just opened pan. Hoped-for 2-gallon stock taste-explosion has turned into burnt chicken carcasses coated in jelly. Orange confit looks fantastic, though, just like in picture only darker. Must go to work. Am going to leave by four, then will think of answer to soup crisis.

5 p.m. Oh God. Entire day has turned into nightmare. Richard Finch gave me a real blowing-up at the morning meeting in front of everyone. 'Bridget, put that recipe book away for God's sake. Fireworks Burns Kids. I'm thinking maiming, I'm thinking happy family celebrations turned into nightmares. I'm thinking twenty years on. What about that kid who had his penis burnt off by bangers in his pockets back in the sixties? Where is he now? Bridget, find me the Fireworks Kid with no Penis. Find me the Sixties Guy Fawkes Bobbit.'

Ugh. I was just grumpily making my forty-eighth phone call to find out if there was a burnt-off-penis victims support group when my phone rang.

'Hello, darling, it's Mummy here.' She sounded unusually high-pitched and hysterical.

'Hi, Mum.'

'Hello, darling, just called to say 'bye before I go, and hope everything goes well.'

'Go? Go where?'

'Oh. Ahahahaha. I told you, Julio and I are popping over to Portugal for a couple of weeks, just to see the family and so on, get a bit of a suntan before Christmas.'

'You didn't tell me.'

'Oh, don't be a silly-willy, darling. Of course I told you. You must learn to listen. Anyway, do take care, won't you?'

'Yes.'

'Oh, darling, just one more thing.'

'What?'

'For some reason I've been so busy I forgot to order my travellers' cheques from the bank.'

'Oh, don't worry, you can get them at the airport.'

'But the thing is, darling, I'm just on my way to the airport now, and I've forgotten my banker's card.'

I blinked at the phone.

'Such a nuisance. I was wondering ... You couldn't possibly lend me some cash? I mean not much, just a couple of hundred quid or something so I can get some travellers' cheques.'

The way she said it reminded me of the way winos ask for money for a cup of tea.

'I'm in the middle of work, Mum. Can't Julio lend you some money?'

She went all huffy. 'I can't believe you're being so mean, darling. After all I've done for you. I gave you the gift of *life* and you can't even loan your mother a few pounds for some travellers' cheques.'

'But how am I going to get it to you? I'll have to go out to the cashpoint and put it on a motorbike. Then it will be stolen and it'll all be ridiculous. Where are you?'

'Oooh. Well, actually, as luck would have it I'm ever so close, so if you just pop out to the NatWest opposite I'll meet you there in five minutes,' she gabbled. 'Super, darling. Byee!'

'Bridget, where the *fuck* are you off to?' yelled Richard as I tried to sneak out. 'You found the Banger Bobbit Boy yet?'

'Got a hot tip,' I said, tapping my nose, then made a dash for it.

I was waiting for my money to come, freshly baked and piping hot, out of the cashpoint, wondering how my mother was going to manage for two weeks in Portugal on two hundred pounds, when I spotted her scurrying towards me, wearing sunglasses, even though it was pissing with rain, and looking shiftily from side to side.

'Oh, there you are, darling. You are sweet. Thank you very much. Must dash, going to miss the plane. Byee!' she said, grabbing the banknotes from my hand.

'What's going on?' I said. 'What are you doing outside here when it's not on your way to the airport? How are you going to manage without your banker's card? Why can't Julio lend you the money? Why? What are you up to? What?'

For a second she looked frightened, as if she was going to cry, then, her eyes fixed on the middle distance, she adopted her wounded Princess Diana look.

'I'll be fine, darling.' She gave her special brave smile.

269

'Take care,' she said in a faltering voice, hugged me quickly then was off, waving the traffic to a standstill and tripping across the road.

7 p.m. Just got home. Right. Calm, calm. Inner poise. Soup will be absolutely fine. Will simply cook and purée vegetables as instructed and then – to give concentration of flavour – rinse blue jelly off chicken carcases and boil them up with cream in the soup.

8.30 p.m. All going marvellously. Guests are all in living room. Mark Darcy is being v. nice and brought champagne and a box of Belgian chocolates. Have not done main course yet apart from fondant potatoes but sure will be v. quick. Anyway, soup is first.

8.35 p.m. Oh my God. Just took lid off casserole to remove carcasses. Soup is bright blue.

9 p.m. Love the lovely friends. Were more than sporting about the blue soup, Mark Darcy and Tom even making lengthy argument for less colour prejudice in the world of food. Why, after all, as Mark said – just because one cannot readily think of a blue vegetable – should one object to blue soup? Fish fingers, after all, are not naturally orange. (Truth is, after all the effort, soup just tasted like big bowl of boiled cream which Vile Richard rather unkindly pointed out. At which point Mark Darcy asked him what he did for a living, which was v. amusing because Vile Richard was sacked last week for fiddling his expenses.) Never mind, anyway. Main course will be v. tasty. Right, will start on velouté of cherry tomatoes.

9.15 p.m. Oh dear. Think there must have been something in the blender, e.g. Fairy Liquid, as cherry tomato purée seems to be foaming and three times original volume. Also fondant potatoes were meant to be ready ten minutes ago and are hard as rock. Maybe should put in microwave. Aargh aargh. Just looked in fridge and tuna is not there. What has become of tuna? What? What?

9.30 p.m. Thank God. Jude and Mark Darcy came in kitchen and helped me make big omelette and mashed up half-done fondant potatoes and fried them in the frying pan in manner of hash browns, and put the recipe book on the table so we could all look at the pictures of what chargrilled tuna would have been like. At least orange confit will be good. Looks fantastic. Tom said not to bother with Grand Marnier Crème Anglaise but merely drink Grand Marnier.

10 p.m. V. sad. Looked expectantly round table as everyone took first mouthful of confit. There was an embarrassed silence.

'What's this, hon?' said Tom eventually. 'Is it marmalade?'

Horror-struck, took mouthful myself. It was, as he said, marmalade. Realize after all effort and expense have served my guests:

    Blue soup
    Omelette
    Marmalade

Am disastrous failure. Michelin-star cookery? Kwik-fit, more like.

Did not think things could get any worse after the marmalade. But no sooner was the horrible meal cleared away than the phone went. Fortunately I took it in the bedroom. It was Dad.

'Are you on your own?' he said.

'No. Everyone's round here. Jude and everyone. Why?'

'I – wanted you to be with someone when . . . I'm sorry, Bridget. I'm afraid there's been some rather bad news.'

'What? What?'

'Your mother and Julio are wanted by the police.'

2 a.m. Northamptonshire in single bed in the Alconburys' spare room. Ugh. Had to sit down and get my breath back while Dad said, 'Bridget? Bridget? Bridget?' over and over again in manner of a parrot.

'What's happened?' I managed to get out eventually.

'I'm afraid they – possibly, and I pray, without your mother's knowledge – have defrauded a large number of people, including myself, and some of our very closest friends, out of a great deal of money. We don't know the scale of the fraud at the moment, but I'm afraid, from what the police are saying, it's possible that your mother may have to go to prison for a considerable period of time.'

'Oh my God. So that's why she's gone off to Portugal with my two hundred quid.'

'She may well be further afield by now.'

I saw the future unfolding before me like a horrible nightmare: Richard Finch dubbing me *Good Afternoon!*'s 'Suddenly Single's Jailbird's Daughter, and forcing me to do a live interview down the line from the Holloway visitors' room before being Suddenly Sacked on air.

'What did they do?'

'Apparently Julio, using your mother as – as it were – 'front man', has relieved Una and Geoffrey, Nigel and Elizabeth and Malcolm and Elaine' (oh my God, Mark Darcy's parents) 'of quite considerable sums of money – many, many thousands of pounds, as down payments on time-share apartments.'

'Didn't you know?'

'No. Presumably because they were unable to overcome some slight vestigial embarrassment about doing business with the greasy beperfumed wop who has cuckolded one of their oldest friends they omitted to mention the whole business to me.'

'So what happened?'

'The time-share apartments never existed. Not a penny of your mother's and my savings or pension fund remains. I also was unwise enough to leave the house in her name, and she has remortgaged it. We are ruined, destitute and homeless, Bridget, and your mother is to be branded a common criminal.'

After that he broke down. Una came to the phone, saying that she was going to give Dad some Ovaltine. I told her I'd be there in two hours but she said not to drive till I'd got over the shock, there was nothing to be done, and to leave it till the morning.

Replacing the receiver, I slumped against the wall cursing myself feebly for leaving my cigarettes in the living room. Immediately though, Jude appeared with a glass of Grand Marnier.

'What happened?' she said.

I told her the whole story, pouring the Grand Marnier straight down my throat as I did. Jude didn't say a word but immediately went and fetched Mark Darcy.

'I blame myself,' he said, running his hands through his hair. 'I should have made myself more clear at the Tarts and Vicars party. I knew there was something dodgy about Julio.'

'What do you mean?'

'I heard him talking on his portable phone by the herbaceous border. He didn't know he was being over-heard. If I'd had any idea that my parents were involved I'd . . .' He shook his head. 'Now I think about it, I do remember my mother mentioning something, but I got so aerated at the mere mention of the words "time-share" that I must have terrorized her into shutting up. Where's your mother now?'

'I don't know. Portugal? Rio de Janeiro? Having her hair done?'

He started to pace around the room firing questions like a top barrister.

'What's being done to find her?' 'What are the sums involved?' 'How did the matter come to light?' 'What is the police's involvement?' 'Who knows about it?' 'Where is your father now?' 'Would you like to go to him?' 'Will you allow me to take you?' It was pretty damn sexy, I can tell you.

Jude appeared with coffee. Mark decided the best thing would be if he got his driver to take him and me up to Grafton Underwood and, for a fleeting second, I experienced the totally novel sensation of being grateful to my mother.

It was all very dramatic when we got to Una and Geoffrey's, with Enderbys and Alconburys all over the shop, everyone in tears and Mark Darcy striding around making phone calls. Found myself feeling guilty, since part of self – despite horror – was hugely enjoying the fact of normal business being suspended, everything different from usual and everyone allowed to throw entire glasses of sherry and salmon-paste sandwiches down their throats in manner of Christmas. Was exactly the same feeling as when Granny turned schizophrenic and took all her clothes off, ran off into Penny Husbands-Bosworth's orchard and had to be rounded up by the police.

Wednesday 22 November

8st 10 (hurrah!), alcohol units 3, cigarettes 27 (completely understandable when Mum is common criminal), calories 5671 (oh dear, seem to have regained appetite), Instants 7 (unselfish act to try to win back everyone's money, though maybe would not give them all of it, come to think of it), total winnings £10, total profit £3 (got to start somewhere).

10 a.m. Back in flat, completely exhausted after no sleep. On top of everything else, have to go to work and get bollocking for being late. Dad seemed to be rallying a little when I left: alternating between moments of wild cheerfulness that Julio proved to be a bounder so Mum might come back and start a new life with him and deep depression that the new life in question will be one of prison-visiting using public transport.

Mark Darcy went back to London in small hours. I left a message on his answerphone saying thank you for helping and everything, but he has not rung me back. Cannot blame him. Bet Natasha and similar would not feed him blue soup and turn out to be the daughter of criminal.

Una and Geoffrey said not to worry about Dad as Brian and Mavis are going to stay and help look after him. Find myself wondering why it is always 'Una and Geoffrey' not 'Geoffrey and Una' and yet 'Malcolm and Elaine' and 'Brian and Mavis'. And yet, on the other hand, 'Nigel and Audrey Coles'. Just as one would never, never say 'Geoffrey and Una' so, conversely, one would never say 'Elaine and Malcolm'. Why? Why? Find self, in spite of self, trying out own name imagining Sharon or Jude in years to come, boring their daughters rigid by going 'You know Bridget and *Mark*, darling, who live in the big house in Holland Park and go on lots of holidays to the Caribbean.' That's it. It would be Bridget and Mark. Bridget and Mark Darcy. The Darcys. Not Mark and Bridget Darcy. Heaven forbid. All wrong. Then suddenly feel terrible for thinking about Mark Darcy in these terms, like Maria with Captain Von Trapp in *The Sound of Music*, and that I must run away and go to see Mother Superior, who will sing 'Climb Ev'ry Mountain' to me.

Friday 24 November

8st 13, alcohol units 4 (but drunk in police presence so clearly OK), cigarettes 0, calories 1760, 1471 calls to see if Mark Darcy has rung 11.

10.30 p.m. Everything is going from bad to worse. Had thought only silver lining in cloud of mother's criminality was that it might bring me and Mark Darcy closer together but have not heard a peep from him since he left the Alconburys'. Have just been interviewed in my flat by police officers. Started behaving like people who are inter-viewed on the television after plane crashes in their front gardens, talking in formulaic phrases borrowed from news broadcasts, courtroom dramas or similar. Found myself describing my mother as being 'Caucasian' and 'of medium build'.

Policemen were incredibly charming and reassuring, though. They stayed quite late, in fact, and one of the detectives said he'd pop round again when he was passing and let me know how everything was going. He was really friendly, actually.

Saturday 25 November

9st, alcohol units 2 (sherry, ugh), cigarettes 3 (smoked out of Alconburys' window), calories 4567 (entirely custard creams and salmon spread sandwiches), 1471 calls to see if Mark Darcy has rung 9 (g.).

Thank God. Dad has had a phone call from Mum. Appar-ently, she said not to worry, she was safe and everything was going to be all right, then hung up immediately. The police were at Una and Geoffrey's tapping the phone line as in *Thelma and Louise* and said she was definitely calling from Portugal but they didn't manage to get where. So much wish Mark Darcy would ring. Was obviously completely put off by culinary disasters and criminal element in family, but too polite to show it at time. Paddling-pool bonding evi-dently pales into insignificance alongside theft of parents' savings by naughty Bridget's nasty mummy. Am going to see Dad this afternoon, in manner of tragic spinster spurned by all men instead of in manner to which have been accustomed: in chauffeur-driven car with top barrister.

1 p.m. Hurrah! Hurrah! Just as I was leaving had phone call, but could not hear anything but beeping sound at the other end. Then the phone rang again. It was Mark, from Portugal. Just incredibly kind and brilliant of him. Apparently he has been talking to the police all week in between being top barrister and flew out to Albufeira yesterday. The police over there have found Mum, and Mark thinks she will get off because it will be pretty obvious she had no idea what Julio was up to. They've managed to track down some of the money, but haven't found Julio yet. Mum is coming back tonight, but will have to go straight to a police station for questioning. He said not to worry, it will probably all be OK, but he's made arrangements for bail if it turns out to be necessary. Then we got cut off before I even had time to say thank you. Desperate to ring Tom to tell him fantastic news but remember no one is supposed to know about Mum and, unfortunately, last time I spoke to Tom about Mark Darcy I think I might have implied he was a creepy mummy's boy.

Sunday 26 November

9st 1, alcohol units 0, cigarettes ½ (fat chance of any more), calories God knows, minutes spent wanting to kill mother 188 (conservative estimate).

Nightmare day. Having first expected Mum back last night, then this morning, then this afternoon and having almost set off to Gatwick a total of three times, it turned out she was arriving this evening at Luton, under police escort. Dad and I were preparing ourselves to comfort a very different person from the one we had last been told off by, naively assuming that Mum would be chastened by what she had gone through.

'Let go of me, you *silly billy*,' a voice rang out through the arrival lounge. 'Now we're on British soil I'm certain to be recognized and I don't want everyone seeing me being *manhandled* by a policeman. Ooh, d'you know? I think I've left my sunhat on the aeroplane under the seat.'

The two policemen rolled their eyes as Mum, dressed in a sixties-style black-and-white checked coat (presumably carefully planned to co-ordinate with the policemen), head-scarf and dark glasses, zoomed back towards the baggage hall with the officers of the law wearily tagging after her. Forty-five minutes later they were back. One of the police-men was carrying the sunhat.

There was nearly a stand-up fight when they tried to get her into the police car. Dad was sitting in the front of his Sierra in tears and I was trying to explain to her that she had to go to the station to see whether she was going to be charged with anything, but she just kept going, 'Oh, don't be silly, darling. Come here. What have you got on your face? Haven't you got a tissue?'

'Mum,' I remonstrated as she took a handkerchief out of her pocket and spat on it. 'You might be charged with a criminal offence,' I protested as she started to dab at my face. 'I think you should go quietly to the station with the policemen.'

'We'll see, darling. Maybe tomorrow when I've cleaned out the vegetable basket. I left 2 pounds of King Edwards in there and I bet they've sprouted. Nobody's touched the plants, apparently, the entire time I've been away, and I bet you anything Una's left the heating on.'

It was only when Dad came over and curtly told her the house was about to be repossessed, vegetable basket included, that she shut up and huffily allowed herself to be put in the back of the car next to the policeman.

Monday 27 November

9st 1, alcohol units 0, cigarettes 50 (yesss! yesss!), 1471 calls to see if Mark Darcy has rung 12, hours of sleep 0.

9 a.m. Just having last fag before going to work. Completely shattered. Dad and I were made to wait on a bench in the police station for two hours last night. Eventually we heard a voice approaching along the corridor. 'Yes, that's right it's mee! "Suddenly Single" every morning! Of course you can. Have you got a pen? On here? Who shall I put it to? Oh, you naughty man. Do you know I've been dying to try one of those on . . .'

'Oh, there you are, Daddy,' said Mum, appearing round the corner wearing a policeman's helmet. 'Is the car outside? Oof, d'you know – I'm dying to get home and get the kettle on. Did Una remember to turn on the timer?'

Dad looked rumpled, startled and confused and I didn't feel any less so myself.

'Have you walked free?' I said.

'Oh, don't be silly, darling. Walked free! I don't know!' said Mum rolling her eyes at the senior detective and bustling me out of the door ahead of her. The way the detective was blushing and fussing around her I wouldn't have been in the least surprised if she'd got herself off by giving him sexual favours in the interview room.

'So what happened?' I said, when Dad had finished putting all her suitcases, hats, straw donkey ('Isn't it super?') and castanets in the boot of the Sierra and had started the engine. I was determined she wasn't going to brazen this one out, sweep the whole thing under the carpet and start patronizing us again.

'All sorted out now, darling, just a silly misunderstanding. Has someone been smoking in this car?'

'What happened, Mother?' I said dangerously. 'What about everyone's money and the time-share apartments? Where's my two hundred quid?'

'Durr! It was just some silly problem with the planning permission. They can be very corrupt, you know, the Portuguese authorities. It's all backhanders and baksheesh like Winnie Mandela. So Julio's just paid all the deposits back. We had a super holiday, actually! The weather was very mixed, but . . .'

'Where is Julio?' I said, suspiciously.

'Oh, he's stayed behind in Portugal to sort out all this planning permission palaver.'

'What about my house?' said Dad. 'And the savings?'

'I don't know what you're talking about, Daddy. There's nothing wrong with the house.'

Unfortunately for Mum, however, when we got back to The Gables all the locks had been changed, so we had to go back to Una and Geoffrey's.

'Oof, do you know, Una, I'm so exhausted, I think I'm going to have to go straight to bed,' said Mum after one look at the resentful faces, wilting cold collation and tired beetroot slices.

The phone rang for Dad.

'That was Mark Darcy,' said Dad when he came back. My heart leapt into my mouth as I tried to control my features. 'He's is Albufeira. Apparently some sort of deal's been done with . . . with the filthy wop . . . and they've recovered some of the money. I think The Gables may be saved . . .'

At this a loud cheer went up from us all and Geoffrey launched into 'For He's a Jolly Good Fellow.' I waited for Una to make some remark about me but none was forthcoming. Typical. The minute I decide I like Mark Darcy, everyone immediately stops trying to fix me up with him.

'Is that too milky for you, Colin?' said Una, passing Dad a mug of tea decorated with apricot floral frieze.

'I don't know . . . I don't understand why . . . I don't know what to think,' Dad said worriedly.

'Look, there's absolutely no need to worry,' said Una, with an unusual air of calmness and control, which suddenly made me see her as the mummy I'd never really had. 'It's because I've put a bit too much milk in. I'll just tip a bit out and top it up with hot water.'

When finally got away from scene of mayhem, drove far too fast on way back to London, smoking fags all the way as act of mindless rebellion.

DECEMBER

Oh, Christ

Monday 4 December

9st 2 (hmm, must get weight off before Christmas gorging), alcohol units a modest 3, cigarettes a saintly 7, calories 3876 (oh dear), 1471 calls to see if Mark Darcy has called 6 (g.).

Just went to supermarket and found self unaccountably thinking of Christmas trees, firesides, carols, mince pies, etc. Then I realized why. The air vents by the entrance which usually pump out baking bread smells were pumping out baking mince pies smells instead. Cannot believe cynicism of such behaviour. Reminded of favourite poem by Wendy Cope which goes:

At Christmas little children sing and merry bells jingle.
The cold winter air make our hands and faces tingle.
And happy families go to church and cheerily they mingle,
And the whole business is unbelievably dreadful if you're single.

Still no word from Mark Darcy.

Tuesday 5 December

9st 2 (right, am really going to start dieting today), alcohol units 4 (start of festive season), cigarettes 10, calories 3245 (better), 1471 calls 6 (steady progress).

Repeatedly distracted by 'Stocking Filla' catalogues tumbling out of the newspapers. Particularly keen on the shield-shaped burnished metal 'funfur'-lined Spectacles Holder Stand: 'All too often spectacles are put down flat on a table, inviting an accident.' Couldn't agree more. The sleekly designed 'Black Cat' Key-Chain Light does indeed have a simple flip-down mechanism, as it 'casts a powerful red light on the keyhole of any cat lover.' Bonsai Kits! Hurrah. 'Practise the ancient art of Bonsai with this tub of pre-planted Persian Pink Silk Tree shoots.' Nice, very nice.

Cannot help but feel sad about the brutal trampling on the pink silk shoots of romance burgeoning between me and Mark Darcy by Marco Pierre White and my mother, but trying to be philosophical about it. Maybe Mark Darcy is too perfect, clean and finished off at the edges for me, with his capability, intelligence, lack of smoking, freedom from alcoholism, and his chauffeur-driven cars. Maybe it has been decreed that I should be with someone wilder, earthier and more of a flirt. Like Marco Pierre White, for example, or, just to pick a name totally at random, Daniel. Hmmm. Anyway. Must just get on with life and not feel sorry for self.

Just called Shazzer, who said it has not been decreed that I must go out with Marco Pierre White and certainly not with Daniel. The only thing a woman needs in this day and age is herself. Hurrah!

2 a.m. Why hasn't Mark Darcy rung me? Why? Why? Am going to be eaten by Alsatian despite all efforts to the contrary. Why me, Lord?

Friday 8 December

9st 5 (disaster), alcohol units 4 (g.), cigarettes 12 (excellent), Christmas presents purchased 0 (bad), cards sent 0, 1471 calls 7.

4 p.m. Humph. Jude just rang and just before we said goodbye she said, 'See you at Rebecca's on Sunday.'

'Rebecca's? Sunday? What Rebecca's? What?'

'Oh, hasn't . . .? She's just having a few . . . I think it's just a sort of pre-Christmas dinner party.'

'I'm busy on Sunday, anyway,' I lied. At last – a chance to get into those awkward corners with the duster. I *had* thought that Jude and I were equal friends of Rebecca so why should she invite Jude and not me?

9 p.m. Popped to 192 for refreshing bottle of wine with Sharon and she said, 'What are you wearing for Rebecca's party?'

Party? So it is a *party* party.

Midnight. Anyway. Must not get upset about it. This is just the sort of thing that is not important in life any more. People should be allowed to invite who they want to *their* parties without others pettily getting upset.

5.30 a.m. Why hasn't Rebecca invited me to her party?

Why? Why? How many more parties are going on that everyone has been invited to except me? I bet everyone is at one now, laughing and sipping expensive champagne. No one likes me. Christmas is going to be a total party-desert, apart from a three-party pile-up on December 20th, when I am booked into an editing session all evening.

Saturday 9 December

Christmas parties to look forward to 0.

7.45 a.m. Woken by Mum.

'Hello, darling. Just rang quickly because Una and Geoffrey were asking what you wanted for Christmas and I wondered about a Facial Sauna.'

How, after being totally disgraced and narrowly escaping several years in custody, can my mother just plop back into being exactly like she was before, flirting openly with policemen and torturing me.

'By the way, are you coming to . . .' for a moment my heart leapt with the thought that she was going to say 'turkey curry buffet' and bring up, in a manner of speaking, Mark Darcy, but no. '. . . the Vibrant TV party on Tuesday?' she continued brightly.

I shuddered with humiliation. I *work* for Vibrant TV, for God's sake.

'I haven't been invited,' I mumbled. There is nothing worse than having to admit to your mum that you are not very popular.

'Oh, darling, of course you've been invited. *Everyone*'s going.'

'I haven't been.'

'Well, maybe you haven't worked there long enough. Anyway—'

'But, Mum,' I interrupted, 'you don't work there at all.'

'Well, that's different, darling. Anyway, Must run. Byeee!'

9 a.m. Brief moment of party oasis when an invitation arrived in the post but turned out to be party mirage: invitation to a sale of designer eyewear.

11.30 a.m. Called Tom in paranoid desperation to see if he wanted to go out tonight.

'Sorry,' he chirped, 'I'm taking Jerome to the PACT party at the Groucho Club.'

Oh God, I hate it when Tom is happy, confident and getting on well with Jerome, much preferring it when he is miserable, insecure and neurotic. As he himself never tires of saying, 'It's always so nice when things go badly for other people.'

'I'll see you tomorrow, anyway,' he gushed on, 'at Rebecca's.'

Tom has only ever met Rebecca twice, both times at my house, and I've known her for nine years. Decided to go shopping and stop obsessing.

2 p.m. Bumped into Rebecca in Graham and Greene buying a scarf for £169. (What is going on with scarves? One minute they were stocking filler-type items which cost £9.99; next minute they have to be fancy velvet and cost as much as a television. Next year it will probably happen to socks or pants and we will feel left out if we are not wearing £145 English Eccentrics knickers in textured black velvet.)

'Hi,' I said excitedly, thinking at last the party night-mare would be over and she too would say, 'See you on Sunday.'

'Oh, hello,' she said coldly, not meeting my eye. 'Can't stop. I'm in a real rush.'

As she left the shop they were playing 'Chestnuts roasting on an open fire' and I stared hard at a £185 Philippe Starck colander, blinking back tears. I hate Christmas. Everything is designed for families, romance, warmth, emotion and presents, and if you have no boyfriend, no money, your mother is going out with a missing Portuguese criminal, and your friends don't want to be your friend any more, it makes you want to emigrate to a vicious Muslim regime, where at least *all* the women are treated like social outcasts. Anyway, I don't care. I am going to quietly read a book all weekend and listen to classical music. Maybe will read *The Famished Road*.

8.30 p.m. *Blind Date* was v.g. Just going for another bottle of wine.

Monday 11 December

Returned from work to icy answerphone message.

'Bridget. This is Rebecca. I know you work in TV now. I know you have much more glamorous parties to go to every night, but I would have thought you could at least have the courtesy to reply to an invitation from a friend, even if you are too grand to deign to come to her party.'

Frantically called Rebecca but no reply or answerphone. Decided to go round and leave a note and bumped into Dan on the stairs, the Australian guy from downstairs who I snogged in April.

'Hi. Merry Christmas,' he said leerily, standing too close. 'Did you get your mail?' I looked at him blankly. 'I've been putting it under your door so you don't have to get cold in your nighty in the mornings.'

I shot back upstairs, grabbed back the doormat and there, nestling underneath like a Christmas miracle, was a little pile of cards, letters and invitations all addressed to me. Me. Me. Me.

Thursday 14 December

9st 3, alcohol units 2 (bad, as did not drink any units yesterday – must make up extra tomorrow to avoid heart attack), cigarettes 14 (bad? or maybe good? Yes: a sensible level of nicotine units is probably good for you as long as do not binge-smoke), calories 1500 (excellent), Instants 4 (bad but would have been good if Richard Branson had won non-profit-making lottery bid), cards sent 0, presents purchased 0, 1471 calls 5 (excellent).

Parties, parties, parties! Plus Matt from the office just rang asking if I'm going to the Christmas lunch on Tuesday. He *can't* fancy me – I'm old enough to be his great-aunt – but then why did he ring me in the evening? And why did he ask me what I was wearing? Must not get over-excited and allow party casbah and phone call from feller-me-lad to go to self's head. Should remember old saying 'once bitten twice shy' as regards dipping pen in office ink. Also must remember what happened last time snogged whipper-snapper: ghastly 'Ooh, you're all squashy' humiliation with Gav. Hmmm. Sexually tantalizing Christmas lunch followed bizarrely by disco dancing in the afternoon (such being editor's idea of a good time) involves severe outfit choice complexity. Best ring Jude, I think.

Tuesday 19 December

9st 7 (but still nearly one week to lose half-stone before Christmas), alcohol units 9 (poor), cigarettes 30, calories 4240, Instants 1 (excellent), cards sent 0, cards received 11, but include 2 from paper boy, 1 from dustman, 1 from Peugeot garage and 1 from hotel spent night in for work four years ago. Am unpopular, or maybe everyone sending cards later this year.

9 a.m. Oh God, feel awful: horrible sick acidic hangover and today is office disco lunch. Cannot go on. Am going to burst with pressure of unperformed Christmas tasks, like revision for finals. Have failed to do cards or Christmas shopping apart from doomed panic-buy yesterday lunch-time as realized was going to see girls for last time before Christmas at Magda and Jeremy's last night.

Dread the exchange of presents with friends as, unlike with the family, there is no way of knowing who is and isn't going to give and whether gifts should be tokens of affection or proper presents, so all becomes like hideous exchange of sealed bids. Two years ago I bought Magda lovely Dinny Hall earrings, rendering her embarrassed and miserable because she hadn't bought me anything. Last year, therefore, I didn't get her anything and she bought me an expensive bottle of Coco Chanel. This year I bought her a big bottle of Saffron Oil with Champagne and a distressed wire soapdish, and she went into a complete grump muttering obvious lies about not having done her Christmas shopping yet. Last year Sharon give me bubble bath shaped like Santa, so last night I just gave her Body Shop Algae and Polyp Oil shower gel at which point she presented me with a handbag. I had wrapped up a spare bottle of posh olive oil as a generalized emergency gift which fell out of my coat and broke on Magda's Conran Shop rug.

Ugh. Would that Christmas could just *be*, without presents. It is just so stupid, everyone exhausting themselves, miserably haemorrhaging money on pointless items nobody wants: no longer tokens of love but angst-ridden solutions to problems. (Hmmm. Though must admit, pretty bloody pleased to have new handbag.) What is the point of entire nation rushing round for six weeks in a bad mood preparing for utterly pointless Taste-of-Others exam which entire nation then fails and gets stuck with hideous unwanted merchandise as fallout? If gifts and cards were completely eradicated, then Christmas as pagan-style twinkly festival to distract from lengthy winter gloom would be lovely. But if government, religious bodies, parents, tradition, etc. insist on Christmas Gift Tax to ruin everything why not make it that everyone must go out and spend £500 on themselves then distribute the items among their relatives and friends to wrap up and give to them instead of this psychic-failure torment?

9.45 a.m. Just had Mum on the phone. 'Darling, I've just rung to say I've decided I'm not doing presents this year. You and Jamie know there isn't a Santa now, and we're all far too busy. We can just appreciate each other's company.'

But we always get presents from Santa in sacks at the bottom of our beds. World seems bleak and grey. Won't seem like Christmas any more.

Oh God, better go to work – but will not have anything to drink at disco-lunch, just be friendly and professional to Matt, stay till about 3.30 p.m., then leave and do my Christmas cards.

2 a.m. *Course* is OK – everyone drunks office Christmas parties. Is a good fun. Must gust sleep – doen mattr about clothesoff.

Wed 20 December

5.30 a.m. Oh my God. *Oh my God*. Where am I?

Thursday 21 December

9st 3 (actually, in funny sort of way there is no reason why should not actually lose weight over Christmas since am so full that – certainly any time after Christmas dinner it is perfectly acceptable to refuse all food on grounds of being too full. In fact it is probably the one time of year when it is OK not to eat).

For ten days now have been living in state of permanent hangover and foraging sub-existence without proper meals or hot food.

Christmas is like war. Going down to Oxford Street is hanging over me like going over the top. Would that the Red Cross or Germans would come and find me. Aaargh. It's 10 a.m. Have not done Christmas shopping. Have not sent Christmas cards. Got to go to work. Right, am never, never going to drink again for the rest of life. Aargh – field telephone.

Humph. It was Mum but might as well have been Goebbels trying to rush me into invading Poland.

'Darling, I was just ringing to check what time you're arriving on Friday night.'

Mum, with dazzling bravado, has planned schmaltzy family Christmas, with her and Dad pretending the whole of last year never happened 'for the sake of the children' (i.e. me and Jamie, who is thirty-seven).

'Mum, as I *think* we've discussed, I'm not coming home on Friday, I'm coming home on Christmas Eve. Remember all those conversations we've had on the subject? That first one . . . back in August—'

'Oh, don't be *silly*, darling. You can't sit in the flat on your own all weekend when it's Christmas. What are you going to eat?'

Grrr. I hate this. It's as if, just because you're single, you don't have a home or any friends or responsibilities and the only possible reason you might have for not being at everyone else's beck and call for the entire Christmas period and happy to sleep bent at odd angles in sleeping bags on teenagers' bedroom floors, peel sprouts all day for fifty, and 'talk nicely' to perverts with the word 'Uncle' before their

295

name while they stare freely at your breasts is complete selfishness.

My brother, on the other hand, can come and go as he likes with everyone's respect and blessing just because he happens to be able to stomach living with a vegan Tai Chi enthusiast. Frankly, I would rather set fire to my flat all on my own than sit in it with Becca.

Cannot believe my mother is not more grateful to Mark Darcy for sorting everything out for her. Instead of which he has become part of That Which Must Not Be Mentioned, i.e. the Great Time-Share Rip-Off, and she behaves as if he never existed. Cannot help but think he must have coughed up a bit to get everyone their money back. V. nice good person. Too good for me, evidently.

Oh God. Must put sheets on bed. Disgusting to sleep on uncomfortable button-studded mattress. Where are sheets, though? Wish had some food.

Friday 22 December

Now it is nearly Christmas, find self feeling sentimental about Daniel. Cannot believe have not had Christmas card from him (though come to think of it have not managed to send any cards yet myself). Seems weird to have been so close during the year and now be completely out of touch. V. sad. Maybe Daniel is unexpectedly Orthodox Jew. Maybe Mark Darcy will ring tomorrow to wish me Happy Christmas.

Saturday 23 December

9st 4, alcohol units 12, cigarettes 38, calories 2976, friends and loved ones who care about self this festive tide 0.

6 p.m. So glad decided to be festive Home Alone Singleton like Princess Diana.

6.05 p.m. Wonder where everybody is? I suppose they are all with their boyfriends or have gone home to their families. Anyway, chance to get things done . . . or they have families of own. Babies. Tiny fluffy children in pyjamas with pink cheeks looking at the Christmas tree excitedly. Or maybe they are all at a big party except me. Anyway. Lots to do.

6.15 p.m. Anyway. Only an hour till *Blind Date*.

6.45 p.m. *Oh God, I'm so lonely.* Even Jude has forgotten about me. She has been ringing all week panicking about what to buy Vile Richard. Mustn't be too expensive: suggests getting too serious or an attempt to emasculate him (v.g. idea if ask self); nor anything to wear as taste-gaffe minefield and might remind Vile Richard of last girlfriend Vile Jilly (whom he does not want to get back with but pretends still to love in order to avoid having to be in love with Jude – creep). Latest idea was whisky but combined with other small gift so as not to seem cheapskate or anonymous – possibly combined with tangerines and chocolate coins, depending on whether Jude decided Christmas Stocking concept over-cute to point of nausea or terrifyingly smart in its Post-Modernity.

7 p.m. Emergency: Jude on phone in tears. Is coming round. Vile Richard has gone back to Vile Jilly. Jude blames gift. Thank God stayed home. Am clearly Emissary of Baby Jesus here to help those persecuted at Christmas by Herod-Wannabees, e.g. Vile Richard. Jude will be here at 7.30.

7.15 p.m. Damn. Missed start of *Blind Date* as Tom rang and is coming round. Jerome, having taken him back, has chucked him again and gone back with former boyfriend who is member of chorus in *Cats*.

7.17 p.m. Simon is coming round. His girlfriend has gone back to her husband. Thank God stayed at home to receive chucked friends in manner of Queen of Hearts or Soup Kitchen. But that's just the kind of person I am: liking to love others.

8 p.m. Hurrah! A magic-of-Christmas miracle. Daniel just called. 'Jonesh,' he slurred. 'I love you, Jonesh. I made tebble mishtake. Stupid Suki made of plastic. Breast point north at all times. I love you, Jonesh. I comin' round to check how your skirts is.' Daniel. Gorgeous, messy, sexy, exciting, hilarious Daniel.

Midnight. Humph. None of them turned up. Vile Richard changed his mind and came back to Jude, as did Jerome, and Simon's girlfriend. It was just over-emotional Spirit-of-Christmas-Past making everyone wobbly about ex-partners. And Daniel! He rang up at 10 o'clock.

'Listen, Bridge. You know I always watch the match on Saturday nights? Shall I come round tomorrow before the football?' Exciting? Wild? Hilarious? Huh.

1 a.m. Totally alone. Entire year has been failure.

5 a.m. Oh, never bloody mind. Maybe Christmas itself will not be awful. Maybe Mum and Dad will emerge radiantly shag-drunk in the morning, holding hands shyly and saying, 'Children, we've got something to tell you,' and I could be a bridesmaid at the reaffirming of vows ceremony.

Sunday 24 December: Christmas Eve

9st 4, alcohol units 1 measly glass of sherry, cigarettes 2 but no fun as out of window, calories 1 million, probably, number of warm festive thoughts 0.

Midnight. V. confused about what is and is not reality. There is a pillowcase at the bottom of my bed which Mum put there at bedtime, cooing, 'Let's see if Santa comes,' which is now full of presents. Mum and Dad, who are separated and planning to divorce, are sleeping in the same bed. In sharp contrast, my brother and his girlfriend, who have been living together for four years, are sleeping in separate rooms. The reason for all this is unclear, except that it may be to avoid upsetting Granny who is a) insane and b) not here yet. The only thing that connects me to the real world is that once again I am humiliatingly spending Christmas Eve alone in my parents' house in a single bed. Maybe Dad is at this moment attempting to mount Mum. Ugh, ugh. No, no. Why did brain think such thought?

Monday 25 December

9st 5 (oh God, have turned into Santa Claus, Christmas pudding or similar), alcohol units 2 (total triumph), cigarettes 3 (ditto), calories 2657 (almost entirely gravy), totally insane Christmas gifts 12, number of Christmas gifts with any point to them whatsoever 0, philosophical reflections on the meaning of the Virgin Birth 0, number of years since self was Virgin, hmmm.

Staggered downstairs hoping hair did not smell of fags to find Mum and Una exchanging political views while putting crosses in the end of sprouts.

'Oh yes, I think what's-his-name is *very* good.'

'Well, he is, I mean, he got through his what-do-you-mer-call-it clause that nobody thought he would, didn't he?'

'Ah, but then, you see, you've got to watch it because we could easily end up with a nutcase like what-do-you-mer-call-him that used to run the miners. Do you know? The problem I find with smoked salmon is that it repeats on me, especially when I've had a lot of chocolate brazils. Oh, hello, darling,' said Mum, noticing me. 'Now, what are you going to put on for Christmas Day?'

'This,' I muttered sulkily.

'Oh, don't be silly, Bridget, you can't wear that on *Christmas Day*. Now, are you going to come into the lounge and say hello to Auntie Una and Uncle Geoffrey before you change?' she said in the special bright, breathy isn't-everything-super? voice that means, 'Do what I say or I'll Magimix your face.'

'So, come on, then, Bridget! How's yer love-life!'

quipped Geoffrey, giving me one of his special hugs, then going all pink and adjusting his slacks.

'Fine.'

'So you still haven't got a chap. Durr! What are we going to do with you!'

'Is that a chocolate biscuit?' said Granny, looking straight at me.

'Stand up straight, darling,' hissed Mum.

Dear God, please help me. I want go home. I want my own life again. I don't feel like an adult, I feel like a teenage boy who everyone's annoyed with.

'So what *are* you going to do about babies, Bridget?' said Una.

'Oh look, a penis,' said Granny, holding up a giant tube of Smarties.

'Just going to change!' I said, smiling smarmily at Mum, rushed up to the bedroom, opened the window and lit up a Silk Cut. Then I noticed Jamie's head sticking out of window one floor below, also having fag. Two minutes later the bathroom window opened and an auburn-coiffed head stuck out and lit up. It was bloody Mum.

12.30 p.m. Gift exchange was nightmare. Always over-compensate for bad presents, yelping with delight, which means I get more and more horrid gifts each year. Thus Becca – who, when I worked in publishing, gave me a worsening series of book-shaped clothes-brushes, shoe-horns and hair ornaments – this year gave me a clapper-board fridge magnet. Una, for whom no household task must remain ungadgeted, gave me a series of mini-spanners to fit different jar or bottle lids in the kitchen. While my mum, who gives me presents to try and make my life more like hers, gave me a slo-cooker for one person: 'All you have to do is brown the meat before you go to work and stick a bit of veg in.' (Has she any idea how hard it is some mornings to make a glass of water without vomiting?)

'Oh look. It isn't a penis, it's a biscuit,' said Granny.

'I think this gravy's going to need sieving, Pam,' called Una, coming out of the kitchen holding a pan.

Oh no. Not this. Please not this.

'I don't think it will, dear,' Mum said already spitting, murderously through clenched teeth. 'Have you tried stirring it?'

'Don't patronize me, Pam,' said Una, smiling dangerously. They circled each other like fighters. This happens every year with the gravy. Mercifully there was a distraction: a great crash and scream as a figure burst through the French windows. Julio.

Everyone froze, and Una let out a scream.

He was unshaven and clutching a bottle of sherry. He stumbled over to Dad and drew himself up to his full height.

'You sleep with my woman.'

'Ah,' replied Dad. 'Merry Christmas, er . . . Can I get you a sherry – ah, got one already. Jolly good. Mince pie?'

'You sleep,' said Julio dangerously, 'with my woman.'

'Oh, he's so Latin, hahaha,' said Mum coquettishly while everyone else stared in horror. Every time I've met Julio he has been clean and coiffed beyond all sense and carrying a gentleman's handbag. Now he was wild, drunk, unkempt and, frankly, just the type I fall for. No wonder Mum seemed more aroused than embarrassed.

'Julio, you naughty person,' she cooed. Oh God. She was still in love with him.

'You sleep,' said Julio, 'with him.' He spat on the Chinese carpet and bounded upstairs, pursued by Mum, who trilled back at us, 'Could you carve, Daddy, please, and get everyone sitting down?'

Nobody moved.

'OK, everybody,' said Dad, in a tense, serious, manly sort of voice. 'There is a dangerous criminal upstairs using Pam as a hostage.'

'Oh, she didn't seem to mind, if you ask me,' piped up Granny in a rare and most untimely moment of clarity. 'Oh look, there's a biscuit in the dahlias.'

I looked out of the window and nearly jumped out of my skin. There was Mark Darcy slipping, lithe as a whipper-snapper, across the lawn and in through the French windows. He was sweating, dirty, his hair was unkempt, his shirt unbuttoned. *Ding-dong*!

'Everyone keep completely still and quiet, as if everything is normal,' he said softly. We were all so stunned, and he so thrillingly authoritative, that we started doing as he said as if hypnotized zombies.

'Mark,' I whispered as I walked past him with the gravy. 'What are you saying? There is no normal.'

'I'm not sure whether Julio's violent. The police are outside. If we can get your mum to come downstairs and leave him up there they can go in and get him.'

'OK. Leave it to me,' I said, and walked to the bottom of the stairs.

'Mum!' I yelled. 'I can't find any savoury doilies.'

Everyone held their breath. There was no response.

'Try again,' whispered Mark, looking at me admiringly.

'Get Una to take the gravy back into the kitchen,' I hissed. He did what I said, then gave me a thumbs-up. I gave him a thumbs-up back and cleared my throat.

'Mum?' I shouted up the stairs again. 'Do you know where the sieve is? Una's a bit worried about the gravy.'

Ten seconds later there was a pounding down the stairs and Mum burst in, looking flushed.

'The savoury doilies are in the savoury doily holder on the wall, you silly willy. Now. What's Una done with this gravy. Durr! We're going to have to use the Magimix!'

Even as she spoke there were footsteps running up the stairs and a scuffle broke out above us.

'Julio!' shrieked Mum and started to run for the door.

The detective I recognized from the police station was standing in the living room doorway. 'All right, everyone, keep calm. It's all under control,' he said.

Mum let out a scream as Julio, handcuffed to a young policeman, appeared in the hallway and was bundled out of the front door behind the detective.

I watched her as she collected herself and looked round the room, appraising the situation.

'Well, thank goodness I managed to calm Julio down,' she said gaily after a pause. 'What a to do! Are you all right, Daddy?'

'Your top – Mummy – is inside out,' said Dad.

I stared at the hideous scene, feeling as though my whole world was collapsing around my ears. Then I felt a strong hand on my arm.

'Come on,' said Mark Darcy.

'What?' I said.

'Don't say "what", Bridget, say "pardon",' hissed Mum.

304

'Mrs Jones,' said Mark firmly. 'I am taking Bridget away to celebrate what is left of the Baby Jesus's birthday.'

I took a big breath and grasped Mark Darcy's proffered hand.

'Merry Christmas, everyone,' I said with a gracious smile. 'I expect we'll see you all at the Turkey Curry Buffet.'

This is what happened next:

Mark Darcy took me to Hintlesham Hall for champagne and late Christmas lunch, which was v.g. Particularly enjoyed freedom to pour gravy on to Christmas turkey for first time in life without having to take sides about it. Christmas without Mum and Una was a strange and wonderful thing. Was unexpectedly easy to talk to Mark Darcy, especially with Festive Julio Police Siege Scene to dissect.

It turns out Mark has spent quite lot of time in Portugal over the last month, in manner of heartwarming private detective. He told me he tracked Julio down to Funchal and found out quite a bit about where the funds were, but couldn't cajole, or threaten, Julio into returning anything.

'Think he might now, though,' he said, grinning. He's really v. sweet, Mark Darcy, as well as being rocky smart.

'How come he came back to England?'

'Well, sorry to use a cliché, but I discovered his Achilles' heel.'

'What?'

'Don't say "what", Bridget, say "pardon",' he said, and I giggled. 'I realized that, although your mother is the most impossible woman in the world, Julio loves her. He really loves her.'

Bloody Mum, I thought. How come she gets to be the irresistible sex goddess? Maybe I should go to Colour Me Beautiful after all.

'So what did you do?' I said, sitting on my hands to stop myself shouting '*What about me? Me? Why doesn't anyone love me?*'

'I simply told him that she was spending Christmas with your dad, and, I'm afraid, that they'd be sleeping in the same bed. I just had a feeling he was crazy enough, and stupid enough, to attempt to er, *undermine* those plans.'

'How did you know?'

'A hunch. It kind of goes with the job.' God, he's cool.

'But it was so kind of you, taking time off work and everything. 'Why did you bother doing all this?'

'Bridget,' he said. 'Isn't it rather obvious?'

Oh my God.

When we got upstairs it turned out he had taken a suite. It was fantastic, v. posh and bloody good fun and we played with all the guest features and had more champagne and he told me all this stuff about how he loved me: the sort of stuff, to be honest, Daniel was always coming out with.

'Why didn't you ring me up before Christmas, then?' I said suspiciously. 'I left you *two* messages.'

'I didn't want to talk to you till I'd finished the job. And I didn't think you liked me much.'

'*What?*'

'Well, you know. You stood me up because you were drying your *hair*? And the first time I met you I was wearing that stupid jumper and bumblebee socks from my aunt and behaved like a complete clod. I thought you thought I was the most frightful stiff.'

'Well, I did, a bit,' I said. 'But . . .'

'But what . . .?'

'Don't you mean but pardon?'

Then he took the champagne glass out of my hand, kissed me, and said, 'Right, Bridget Jones, I'm going to give you pardon for,' picked me up in his arms, carried me off into the bedroom (which had a fourposter bed!) and did all manner of things which mean whenever I see a diamond-patterned V-neck sweater in future, I am going to spontaneously combust with shame.

Tuesday 26 December

4 a.m. Have finally realized the secret of happiness with men, and it is with deep regret, rage and an overwhelming sense of defeat that I have to put it in the words of an adulteress, criminal's accomplice and G-list celebrity:

'Don't say "what", say "pardon", darling, and do as your mother tells you.'

January–December:
A Summary

Alcohol units 3836 (poor)

Cigarettes 5277

Calories 11,090,265 (repulsive)

Fat units 3457 (approx.) (hideous idea in every way)

Weight gained 5st 2lb

Weight lost 5st 3lb (excellent)

Correct lottery numbers 42 (v.g.)

Incorrect lottery numbers 387

Total Instants purchased 98

Total Instants winnings £110

Total Instants profit £12 (Yessss! Yessss! Have beaten system while supporting worthwhile causes in manner of benefactor)

1471 calls (quite a lot)

Valentines 1 (v.g.)

Christmas cards 33 (v.g.)

Hangover-free days 114 (v.g.)

Boyfriends 2 (but one only for six days so far)

Nice boyfriends 1

Number of New Year Resolutions kept 1 (v.g.)

An *excellent* year's progress.

25 Years of Bridget Jones

Life Before Bridget

'Could it be that a hitherto unrecognised literary law dictates that the less a person expects others to read a diary, the more interesting it will be?'

As I was rifling through the boxes of cuttings in the attic, I was startled to discover this piece from 1992 about writing diaries, which I had completely forgotten about. I thought how weird it was that I wrote the sentence above (which I have inserted in manner of a literary novelist, adding an earnest *aperçu* at the start as if to point the reader in the right direction, while showing off), because honestly, if I'd known so many people were going to end up reading *Bridget Jones's Diary* I would never have dared write any of it.

Now, though, as I sit, calm and zen-like with a scented candle, smugly studying my own *oeuvres*, I wonder, had I been secretly fermenting the notion of writing a diary for years, like a vat of hops beginning to turn into beer?

Dear Diary: don't tell a soul . . .

Sunday Times, 16 August 1992

LAST WEEK the humiliation of Mike Tyson continued as one of his bodyguards revealed on American TV that, at Tyson's request, he had kept a computerised diary of the boxer's conquests, covering names, dates and details of sexual encounters with 1,300 women (not including one-night stands).

The South African journalist Jani Allan might well

have found herself £300,000 better off this week if she hadn't thought fit to keep a diary of sexual exploits (imaginary or otherwise). "It was heaven. We were stoned. We made love twice," is not the sort of phrase you want turning up in your handwriting about a married Italian pilot when you are trying to win a libel case by saying you don't have affairs with married men.

And what of the Taylor sisters, jailed for life in July for the murder of Alison Shaughnessy after extracts were read out in court from a diary written by Michelle Taylor, who was having an affair with Shaughnessy's husband? "I hate Alison, the unwashed bitch," she wrote. "My dream solution would be for Alison to disappear as if she never existed."

"Keep a diary and it will keep you," is the popular phrase coined by Mae West. Keep a diary and it will keep you in prison or penury seems to be more to the point.

"Tuesday – stabbed Binky to death – that'll teach him! Felt great. Hid murder weapon in back of wardrobe. Wednesday, slept with wife's younger sister – blimey! Hope she doesn't find out!!"

Why on earth are people so insane as to write these things down? When the general public is willing to pay upwards of £14.95 to read some dreary politician's pompously self-aware journal, when even *The Country Diary of an Edwardian Lady* is one of the biggest-selling books the country has ever known, other than the Bible, isn't it obvious that nobody will be able to resist a diary full of secrets absolutely free – even if it doesn't have pictures of hedge wortle in it.

Recent history is littered with diaritic disasters. In 1979, a 35-year-old Hampshire woman went down for two-and-a-half years with her reputation somewhat tarnished after police broke into her flat, looked under her bed and found diaries containing fantastically detailed accounts not only of all the things she had been nicking from local shops, but the 51 men she had slept with over the past year, cross referenced with a list of the number of times she made love each week and star ratings for the likes of "Richard the Teenager" and "Ugly Ali".

The year before, a schoolgirl got into very hot water over comments in her diary about her English teacher. "I have lost my virginity to him, but who cares?" she mused.

Writing a brief and to-the-point diary, reminding you what you are supposed to be doing, or what you did, is perfectly normal and useful. But murder, adultery, rogering of schoolteachers and large-scale frauds do not need to be included because, even when planned well in advance, they are seldom the sort of thing which slips the mind.

It is the other confessional Dear Diary outpouring job which is the baffling one. I started doing one briefly on my home computer, as much to avoid getting on with my work as anything, filing it craftily under Gas Bills, with a decoy file called Diary, Strictly Private which, inside, said only: "Hahahaha don't be so nosy."

It played on my mind, though, ticking away in there like a time bomb. What if the computer accidentally faxed it to the office? What if I died and somebody found it while trying to get a rebate from the gas board?

Eventually, I'd had enough and wiped it – rather, I fancied, in the manner of the writer Anthony Trollope, who kept diaries for 10 years then destroyed them, writing (presumably in his new diary), "They convicted me of

317

folly, ignorance, indiscretion, idleness, extravagance and conceit." (Is that all? Huh!)

Those people who don't destroy their diaries must have some secret need or wish for them to be read, a need or wish which affects what is written in varying degrees. At one end of the spectrum is the therapeutic confessional, where the need or wish is a subconscious, complicated thing; at the other end is the diary of the politician or other public figure, where the need or wish – to be read – is the whole point of writing the thing in the first place.

But could it be that a hitherto unrecognised literary law dictates that the less a person expects others to read a diary, the more interesting it will be?

Political diaries certainly prove the point. It would be rare to find political memoirs declaring the likes of "Virginia said hello to me today. She has fantastic breasts. I hate Peter Bottomley. My dream scenario is for him to disappear as if he never existed, the unwashed bastard."

For politicians, thoughts seem to pop out perfectly grammatically formed and groomed to show the writer in the best possible light. A diary is the perfect medium for subtle propaganda, with all manner of dull nonsense masquerading as honest unselfconscious outpourings.

But if the literary law was a good one, then my recently discovered university diary would be fantastically interesting. I certainly never considered it being read by others. This is what it contained on page after page:

Yoghurt 90
Celery (2 sticks) 10
Carrots (3) 33

Egg 75
Cottage cheese 100
Pickle 10
Celery (4 sticks) 20
Box of Milk Tray 2,000
Carrots (2) 22
Chelsea buns (3) 750
Pizza 800
Chips 400
Chocolate fudge cake 380
Coffee (black) 0

A case of keep a diary and one day it will keep you in a mental institution.

I haven't been locked up yet, but the night is still young . . . so to speak.

This is a real page from the university diary I described – no social engagements to speak of but endless lists of food and calories, and the beginnings of a lifetime quest to lose that elusive half stone. *Why?* I think to myself. *Why?* While of course still determined to lose it.

APRIL 1978

26 WEDNESDAY
WEEK 17 · 116-249

12.
2.45   The
            family planning.

Alpen .	300 .
Leeks	20
Rhubarb + Sug.	50
Custard .	150
Apple	40
orange	40 .
Steak	100
Veg .	50
Banana	100
Custard	200
	~1,050

MAY

M	1	8	15	22	29		M		5	12	19	26
T	2	9	16	23	30		T		6	13	20	27
W	3	10	17	24	31		W		7	14	21	28
T	4	11	18	25			T	1	8	15	22	29
F	5	12	19	26			F	2	9	16	23	30
S	6	13	20	27			S	3	10	17	24	
S	7	14	21	28			S	4	11	18	25	

320

I always wanted to be a writer but after university was diverted into television because the BBC offered me a job. I did, during this period, write a novel for Mills & Boon entitled *Fires of Zanzibar*, but it was rejected with a devastating letter saying that neither my characters nor my story was 'up to the high standards required by the Mills & Boon reader.' I got into a petulant sulk, threw the book away and didn't write another work of fiction for seven years.

After the BBC I spent a period working as a journalist in East Africa, and then some time being a backpacker, going to India, Guatemala, Honduras, etc. After that I started trying in earnest to get into newspapers. It was rather a long road – no money and endless days waiting for the phone to ring. I wrote a piece on spec for the *Guardian* about how annoying car burglar alarms are then called them up every week for six weeks to see if they'd read it yet, but the reply was always the same: 'We'll be getting on to it soon!'

Then I started getting lucky by taking 'a sideways look at' or 'a fractured take on' things for the *Sunday Times*: the Summer Season for example, or awards ceremonies, or Crufts, or indeed diaries. I'm a huge fan of the writer Craig Brown, who had a very funny restaurant column at the paper and allowed me to fill in for him when he was away. This led to a regular gig and a golden era when I could graciously invite my friends and family for free meals. Looking back, I realize this was the beginning of pillaging these witty and generous friends and family for fictional fodder.

For my first-ever restaurant review, I took my Mum and Auntie Margaret who, with their high spirits, brightly coloured two pieces, and breezy gaiety became the inspiration for Bridget's Mum and Auntie Una. They had a baffling confidence in their world view and lack of self-doubt; probably a product of being brought up in the war and in an age before Photoshop, *Cosmopolitan* and social media. I loved their refusal to be intimidated by their surroundings, their determination to bring the 'fancy' down to earth, and their turn of phrase, heavy with post-war food metaphors. I once heard my Mum, a former 'domestic science' teacher, being patronized by a tax man and retorting, 'Listen – can YOU make a brioche?' On another occasion she bit into a profiterole in a well-regarded restaurant and said, 'Well if I'd made these, I'd have considered them a failure. I'd have thrown them away and opened a tin of pears.'

Sunday Times, 1 March 1992

Feeding Yorkshire Roses

THE BOX TREE, ILKLEY

The Box Tree in Ilkley is one of Yorkshire's poshest restaurants. Many a local legend has grown up around its poshness. One unsuspecting diner apparently received a bill so huge that he had to leave his watch and assorted valuables, only managing to retrieve them when he had emptied the bank of his life savings. According to an apocryphal story, The Box Tree's predilection for fancy cooking is said to have begun when the chef accidentally served a fillet steak with chocolate sauce instead of gravy and received such high praise from the recipient that it completely turned his head.

My mum, my mum's cousin Margaret and myself were thus slightly crestfallen to discover that lunch was only £15.95 a head (it was on expenses, after all) but were greatly encouraged to see that roast beef would be served with Yorkshire pudding and was in quite a different section of the menu from the chocolate puff ball.

Ilkley is a lovely spot (though as my mum did point out, Gerry Robertson's first wife Jean's parents had lived here and found it a bit on the damp side). The little town nestles beneath the rugged crags made famous by the popular song "On Ilkley Moor Baht 'At". Once inside though, all thoughts of natural beauty are banished by a cottagey treasure trove of unusual artefacts, oriental masks, life-sized dalmatians and Georgian pretend windows looking into alcoves containing pottery. Auntie Margaret was startled to find a porcelain cat sitting on one of the chairs, but Mum said she wasn't in the least surprised: "The last time I was here one of our party sat on a bee."

We had plumped for the second of the Sunday lunch sittings and the little lounge was mercifully bee-free and pleasantly full – a very nice young couple with a baby, several families, and a live pianist next to a cherub on a pillar, holding a clock. We were settled into some very attractive chairs in a fabric which Mum was sure she'd nearly had for her suite.

You could tell The Box Tree was very high class because they asked if we'd care for anything all the time. "Would you care for a drink before your meal? Would you care for a canapé?" The dining room had a lovely cosy feel with a lot of crushed raspberry in the furnishings. Mum was very taken with the Bergère ceiling fans.

So far, the occasion had been just a little clouded over by the plainness of the menu. Somehow from the legendary Box Tree we had envisaged caviar and foie gras sculpted into tiny replicas of Leeds Town Hall and served with real custard; weird fish and possibly even seahorses with piles of flower-shaped chips. Instead there were four simple choices for the main course: three roasts and a fish. But when the starters arrived – well, they were as fancy looking as anyone could wish for. My pimento mousse was very delicately flavoured, though the vegetable garnish caused some consternation.

"It's a leek," said Auntie Margaret.

"No it's not, it's a parsnip," insisted Mum. This was as nothing besides the furious debate engendered by Auntie Margaret's crêpe Alfredo. "I would certainly have it again and recommend it," she declared protectively. Yes, but what was in it? Spinach and onion? "There's something else in there. I'm not so sure it isn't fish," said Mum. Fortunately the waiter, who we all thought was lovely looking, was on hand to declare the mystery ingredient not so much fish as chicken. Thank heavens for the simplicity of the gravadlax, which Mum proclaimed "excellent and very nicely presented".

Plain but dainty were the words which sprang to mind with the main courses. My beef was done just right, not too pink, not too brown, with a gravy both thin and delicate. I handed the Yorkshire pudding over to the connoisseurs, who declared it a triumph – "There's an awful lot of eggs in that." Mum was very impressed with her pork. "Betty Grainge does hot pork with prunes, but I've never seen it with damsons." And Margaret was more than happy with her cod sitting on a bed of grated leeks which had "just seen a bit of hot steam". The conversation ran naturally from the cod to fish and chips. "I'll tell you who does good chips – that Mr Whatnot in Huddersfield."

And then, at last, it was time for the puddings. It was apparently Major Tinker's wife, a friend of Auntie Margaret's, who used to say "the test of a good dinner lies in its sweets" and the same is no less true of a good restaurant. There being just four sweets on the menu, it seemed only responsible to order the lot.

It was here that the service really came into its own, for the waiter, without being told, instinctively placed the sweet each of us had fancied in front of the correct party; lemon tart for Auntie Margaret, sherry trifle for Mum and bread and butter pudding for me, with the highly suspicious chocolate puff ball, which may or may not have contained pieces of fillet steak, tactfully placed in the middle. Each having been sampled by all, they were considered perfect, the puff ball delicious and entirely free of meat.

After the food we found we did care to move upstairs for coffee and truffles. There we sank into armchairs, wondering whether to send the thoughtfully provided postcards of a wintry Box Tree to the *Sunday Times*, claiming to be snowed in and obliged to stay until the bee season returned. The bill, even with pre-prandial champagne and a bottle of Pouilly-Fumé, came to £94. It fell to Auntie Margaret to sum up the satisfaction felt by all.

"I've had three courses, two bread rolls, two very rich desserts and a chocolate truffle, and I still don't feel bloated," she said. "Now that's a clever meal."

Cunning as a fox, I began to inch the restaurant column towards the overnight-stay column. Soon, myself and my best Singleton friends Sharon and Tracey (the original Shazzer and Jude) were mini-breaking away at the *Sunday Times*'s, and subsequently the *Independent*'s expense. The heady weekend described below was when I adopted the writing tic of using colourful verbs such as 'sneered' or 'slurred' rather than – as advised by Ernest Hemingway and other literary giants – a simple 'said'. I feel the advantage of the colourful verb is that it is more fun.

Independent, 1996

A night out with the girls

THE LAMB INN, OXFORDSHIRE

THE LAMB – an ancient flagstone-floored inn in the picturesque Cotswold village of Burford – is a lovely spot for a meal or mini-break. With its inglenook fireplaces, low ceilings and pretty walled garden it is cosy in winter and cool and pleasant in summer. My friends Sharon and Tracey and I were running 15 minutes late for our dinner reservation, what with having our toenails to paint and everything, but we were a little surprised – when we rang to apologise – to be told really quite strictly to come as quickly as possible. It was probably no bad thing – preventing us applying even more make-up – but it did seem odd, having rushed, then to be kept waiting for a full half-hour in the drinks lounge.

A tense lady in purple who took our order kept reassuring us that we could go through as soon as "chef" was ready, which made us giggly wondering what "chef" was going to appear dressed up as. Eventually we were led into a candlelit dining room which, with its plain walls and pale wooden floor, was atmospheric and historic-seeming – just a hint of monastery – without being fussy.

We had chosen from the Lamb's three-course dinner menu at £23, offering four choices for starter and main course and a half a dozen for pudding. No sooner had we settled when "chef" finally gave birth, as it were, and our starters arrived simultaneously, borne by two ladies looking, in their long white flouncy aprons, like Victorian midwives.

"Mmm they're good. They taste very rangy, I mean gamey," said Tracey of her warm salad of forest mush-rooms. There was a scare when we noticed the salad wasn't dressed properly – some of the leaves were prac-tically stark naked – but a species of "mushroom slime" was discovered below, which made a much more deli-cious arrangement. "The thing about mushrooms is that often the taste gets drowned in a garlicky sauce but this is just essence of mushroom. Mmm."

My tomato soup with basil was fresh-tasting and lovely, but Sharon was reserved about her salmon and smoked trout mousse – "nice, but not as nice as Marks and Spencer's" – and considered the lime and parsley dressing "a bit bland". At this point my friends became self-conscious about being "dining companions", worrying that I might gain amusement at their expense, perhaps inserting spiteful verbs to make them seem bimbos, drunks, bitch queens or metropolitan snobs. I assured them I wouldn't dream of such a thing.

When our main courses arrived we agreed that Tracey had done best on the ordering again, with her sautéed sea bass, though Sharon's honey-glazed Norfolk duckling on a confit of roasted apples and shallots and Calvados sauce came with the most things. "Well, as you'd expect, it is a bit fatty isn't it?" sneered Sharon. "It was supposed to come on a bed of apples or something," she slurred, "but this Calvados sauce is just like gravy – with a couple of bits of apples on the side." "More like a futon of apples," snickered Tracey. "I've got a Chinese vegetable mélange with ginger in it, stir-fried," she tittered. "Mmm, it's tasty and the fish is tasty."

My supreme of chicken en croute with a tomato and chilli coulis was disappointing, though in hindsight it was a stupid thing to order after tomato soup – of which the coulis was strongly reminiscent. Call me a bigot, but I don't think chicken en croute is a good idea unless the pastry is light as a nightie and lined with a mouth-watering sauce, neither of which was the case.

At this point we noticed a recurring theme: a sprig of dill garnish. Tracey suggested we should tag our dill sprigs and see if they turned up on our puddings.

"You can't go wrong with summer pudding," said Tracey decisively while I dithered between white chocolate and ricotta cream on raspberry coulis or cinnamon meringues with blueberries and crème fraîche on a blueberry and kirsch coulis. Sharon plumped for apple pecan and soured cream pie because it didn't have any coulis. "It's coulis hell here," she said. "It's got more coulis than *Jewel in the Crown*," agreed Tracey, musing. "You can't go wrong with summer pudding."

I enjoyed my coulis and blueberries, but wasn't so

keen on the cinnamon meringues; nothing wrong with the execution, they just seemed a weird idea when it came to it. Sharon took against her apple pie with extraordinary vehemence. "Yours are so glamorous and mine's a great slab like something you'd get on a community centre trolley," she said. "Ooh, look, it's got little heart-shaped coulis things," enthused Tracey over hers. "And it's the same colour as our toe-nail varnish. It's very good. You can't go wrong with summer pudding." "Tracey, are you working for the Summer Pudding Marketing Board?" said Sharon.

As we made our way back to the waiting-for-chef lounge we agreed that the food had been very good in parts only, and that the simple things worked the best (which, as Tracey pointed out, is just another way of saying you can't go wrong with summer pudding). It was a lovely place and the service had been excellent, and despite the fact that we were dressed like lascivious new divorcees in a roomful of quiet couples there had been no fuss, or "Ladies" this, that or the other.

Unfortunately, as we sipped our coffee, the others started reading my notebook and high spirits rather got the better of us. Tracey began to cough and go bright red in the face, but Sharon and I thought it was just hysterical laughter and carried on giggling. But Tracey had a choc-olate lodged in her windpipe and was not chuckling but choking to death. Then suddenly . . . she threw up very neatly on a side plate right in the middle of the coffee lounge.

"Could you take this away, please," I barked bossily at the waitress. The service, as ever, was excellent and discreet, but I don't think they'd have us back in a hurry.

I realize now that although it was all huge fun, at the time I was writing these columns we all still felt privately stupid about being single. I blame Society of course, with its narrow and outdated expectations. In fact, what we were constructing was a perfectly valid lifestyle and support system – what Bridget went on to call the Urban family – made up of Smug Marrieds, single girlfriends and gay friends. It has, in fact, been *proved by surveys* (c.f. Harvard Study of Adult Development) that this sort of nurturing, supportive community is a much bigger indicator of long-term happiness and mental health than wealth, success or the mere fact of a partner.

Sex, however, was a constant pre-occupation. There were endless 'dating lists' and in-depth analyses covering various lovers, boyfriends, flings and instances of emotional fuckwittage. I once heard that people never mind being put into your writing as long as you make them really physically attractive. It's gratifying how many people believe themselves to be characters on whom Mark Darcy or Daniel Cleaver were based. The gentleman in the restaurant review below was one of the top contenders and, obviously, incredibly handsome and buff.

Independent, 1996

Tripping the bite fantastic

THE RITZ TERRACE AT THE RITZ HOTEL, PICCADILLY

"THE MEN in London have quite a quaint custom of not giving a girl many presents." So concluded Lorelei Lee – grumpily – in *Gentlemen Prefer Blondes*, while staying at the London Ritz, before decamping to Paris to try out the "veecounts". The ghosts of fictional heroines reluctant to curl a lip at a diamond clip, however geriatric the donor, still hover so around the gilded mirrors, palms, marble and pale pink gorgeousness of the Ritz that it makes a girl walking through the bar feel shifty when a waiter says: "Can I help you?"

"I'm looking for someone tall and dark," I whispered, giving quite the wrong impression even though I hadn't even added "and rich". But far from throwing me out, the staff were so helpful and obliging I wouldn't have been in the least surprised if they had offered me a choice of four, all holding out Tiffany's boxes.

The London Ritz is 90 years old this year and, to celebrate, is being renovated with such discretion that there is no evidence of it whatsoever. As I waited in the bar for my gentleman friend (with a newspaper provided unrequested, presumably to keep a girl's eyes averted) all seemed so elegant, divine and romantic it was hard to imagine what would possess a person to meet a gentleman friend anywhere else for the sake of saving a pound or five on a glass of champagne.

The particular lure of the Ritz's world-famous Louis XVIth dining room is that one can dine on the Terrace or in the sunken Italian Garden. It being this particular summer, we had made a pact to arrive sporting a range of warm and sturdy undergarments. Even these did not promise a match for the biting wind outside, but on entering the extraordinary Belle Epoque room we were relieved. It is one of the most glamorous, seductive, breathtaking rooms imaginable, with a ceiling of blue sky and clouds, a circle of gilt fanciness suspended beneath and everywhere pink marble, chandeliers, flowers and candlelight.

It being a Friday night, a dinner dance was in progress. Such affairs in hotels can often be naff, with men with strange hair crooning "Hun forgeddubble . . . hasss . . . uh . . . woyouarrruh" and nobody else there. But here the room was full and buzzing. A jazz band with clarinet and sax was playing "Diamonds Are A Girl's Best Friend", transporting one back to the New York of the 50s. There was a delicious air of being fussed over at the highest level, with many very busy waiters and trolleys. One parked at our table, showing off a large side of roast beef. As my date remarked, it was rather like being in a Chinese dim sum market. For reasons not unconnected with the fact that starters alone ranged from £10 to £61, we opted for the set four-course dinner at £49. It was a shame there was not a lighter cheaper one since there is only so much food one can eat, especially when unexpected extra items keep on turning up. We were presented with a coffee cup of pea soup, which made us worry that next they would bring us a plate of tea.

The Ritz wine list is a stranger to the notion of value. There is nothing under £20 apart from the house wine at £17.50. We plumped for a perfectly serviceable St Veran for £25. Running hotels is expensive, but it does seem a shame that somewhere so beautiful as this should be priced out of the reach of most romantic couples, unless their expenses are being paid by a newspaper or one of them owns one. Perhaps as part of their family values campaign, the government could subsidise the Ritz, rewarding any who stay married for five years with a main course with vegetable.

The food initially promised well. My chilled tomato consommé with prawns and very tiny asparagus was gorgeous. Translucent and flavoured with lemon grass, it had the complicated, delicate flavour of the finest Thai soup. My date, however, felt his gravadlax was bland and needed a sauce. Next I tucked into warm aubergine gâteau with sweet and sour mushrooms: fine, but too rich for what was effectively a second starter. My date felt similarly about lobster and langoustine soup with morels and spaghetti. "Too many morels," he complained throatily. "Can we book a room?"

At that we thought we'd better dance, and discovered that once the band had you up, the numbers ran into each other, so it was impossible to stop. "The nearest I've come to perpetual motion," murmured my companion.

We dragged ourselves back for the main course: an excellent fillet of beef in bread and herb pastry, though the vegetables – dauphinois potatoes, sugar snap peas – were deemed too rich. My red mullet was really not worth breaking off a dance for. The fancy arrangement in a circle with celeriac and lobster did not make up for the mullet's lack of lightness and moisture and we couldn't wait to return to perpetual motion, eventually having to be summoned by the waiter for raspberry soufflé.

Having once had a traumatic experience with a raspberry soufflé myself – far from sinking, it seemed to grow and multiply like a space monster so that everywhere I looked in the flat for days there was more and more raspberry soufflé lurking – I was sympathetic about the fact that this one had sunk in the middle and had to be disguised with a blob of ice-cream, particularly as it was my fault for losing all track of time. The texture and taste was superb: and they had managed to keep it all in the dish, without letting it get out into other parts of the dining room. As if five courses (counting the pea soup) were not enough, we were presented with a miniature coffee cup of chocolate mousse and a plate of petits fours.

Dinner, dancing, water and wine came to £127, including coffee and service. Though the food was not our favourite kind, and we would have preferred more consistent expert execution and less fancy fussiness, the gorgeous environment and glittering atmosphere were out of this world. For a romantic evening out with a gentleman friend, a girl could do no finer – unless at the Ritz in Paris . . . ed?

The Diary of Bridget Jones

In hindsight I'd been germinating the character of Bridget Jones and the diary format for a long time. I had written a pilot TV show for the BBC called *30s Panic*. The protagonist's main joke was the gap between aspiration and execution, e.g.:

'I am not going to sleep with him.'
CUT TO: She is in bed with him.

Like most of my *oeuvres* at that time, it was rejected; but I used a similar character in my first novel, *Cause Celeb*, which was published in 1994 by Picador. When critics later complained that Bridget Jones was too silly, I often retorted that my first novel was set in a refugee camp in the Sudan, but nobody bought that one.

In the mid-nineties I started working at the *Independent* newspaper, which was an exciting place to be and where I was keen to make my name with my political acumen. The *Independent* asked me to write a column as myself, talking about dating and being single in London. I said no, as that would be hopelessly exposing and embarrassing. But, being extremely short of cash to pay the mortgage, I said I would write it as a fictional character. My editor Charlie Leadbeater suggested I use the first-person voice from *Cause Celeb*, which was great as I'd had lots of practice.

The column was really put together in a quite casual way. We used a photograph of Susannah Lewis, who was working as an assistant in the office. I had a friend who always talked about her friend Bridget in a funny way, so I thought Bridget was a good name. And I just picked Jones because it sounded ordinary. I didn't think about *Tom Jones* and Henry Fielding, though I pretended I did later.

Sometimes people claim that Bridget was the godmother of chick lit. But the truth is it wasn't just Bridget or me, it was zeitgeist. The fictional representation of single women had not caught up with reality. An air of shelves, spinning wheels and Miss Havisham still loitered around the world of the single girl, which was out of step with the (warning: pomposity ahead) socioeconomic reality of this demographic group.

The chances are, if you have an idea, so will thousands of other people, and hundreds of those people will be writers. I was lucky; I was writing a column in a newspaper, so my thoughts were published instantly. I got credit for a concept which lots of people were having at the same time.

It's quite weird reading this first *Independent* column back, though. It seems so random. I did always try to make it topical and include some story from the week's news, but Cones Hotline? WTF? Surely there were more important matters to write about?

Independent, 7 March 1995

Sun 26th Feb
8st 13, alcohol units 2 (excellent), cigarettes 7, calories 3100 (poor).

2pm. Why oh why hasn't Daniel rung? Hideous, wasted weekend glaring psychopathically at the phone, and eating things. I cannot believe I convinced myself I was keeping the entire weekend free to work, when in fact I was on permanent date-with-Daniel standby.

On top of everything, I open the papers to find the bloody Cones Hotline is being scrapped. Who else am I supposed to ring up late at night when I feel lonely? I love the lovely Hotline idea: whisking you straight to the heart of Cone World on a fast track. In my experience there is always some bored chap at the end of it at any hour of the day or night, only too happy to moan a little about people ringing up at 2am to order a 99 or Cornetto ("I know I know") then move on to your own problems. Maybe they should re-name it the Cones Chatline or the Cones Supportline. That would be more Nineties, I feel.

Right: work. Beginning on Ash Wednesday: "I will not fantasise about or behave ridiculously regarding Daniel Cleaver, boss of my publishing house" is to be relaunched along with the other New Year Resolutions: I will not smoke. I will get down to 8st 7, I will not recycle items from the laundry basket, I will not bitch about Perpetua but work positively with her.

8pm. Phone call alert, which turned out just to be Tom asking if there was any progress. Tom, who has taken, unflatteringly, to calling himself a Hag-Fag, has been sweetly supportive about the Daniel crisis. (He has a theory that homosexuals and single women in their thirties have natural bonding; both being used to disappointing their parents and being treated as freaks by society.)

Last Tuesday, at the *Cheapskate's Wine Guide* launch, weeks of flirtation appeared to climax. When the others were boring on about Stephen Fry ("Understandable, I mean, everyone has their breaking point", ". . . size of Kent", ". . . pathetic. I mean, we all have to learn to take criticism", "Actually, Stephen's a rurely good friend of mine"), Daniel moved behind me and murmured, "So . . . will I see you?" and then, more quietly, "I mean . . . see

339

you?" – so horny. Then he wrote "Bridget" and my home number on a cigarette packet and said "I'll call you."

11.15pm. No call. At breaking point I dialled the Cones Hotline. No reply. I understood, all those months of relentless criticism and now the press, but then, after 14 rings, came a kindly voice. We had a cursory chat about cones and then moved on to Daniel. Maybe he had lost the cigarette packet? The Hotline man, I must say, very tactfully, raised the question of directory enquiries. "He doesn't know where I live," I replied, "and there are 25 B. Joneses in the directory." Should I call him? The Hotline man thought no. "The essence of alchemy is release," he said.

Mon 27th Feb

9st (irreversible slide into obesity), alcohol units 4, cigarettes 29, calories 770 (v.g. but at what price?).

Nightmare day. I arrived in the office, to find Perpetua in hysterics. Usually, on Monday morning the smug witch is in full telephone autowitter to Hermione or Piggy about the weekend's dizzzy social whirl, and the latest £1/2m Fulham flat she's about to buy with Hugo. "Yars, yars, well it is north-facing but they've done something frightfully clever with the light." Flats were off. The whole flat thing, apparently, was based on the job Hugo was about to take up with Barings. "Darling! Go home," the whole office cooed. "Everyone has their breaking point."

I watched the door for Daniel all morning: nothing. By 11.45am I was seriously alarmed. Suddenly, I saw it all.

He had broken, of course: he'd been too successful, clever, witty, and good-looking for too long. Should I raise an alert? Go round to his flat? Quickly I was immersed in a Daniel-in-emotional-crisis fantasy: me, him, talking late into the night: "I have never, never found anyone I could say these things to before. Oh, Bridget . . ."

"Daniel? He's at the sales conference in Croydon. He'll be in tomorrow." Perpetua, coat on, suddenly bellowed and sniffed into the phone. "God, all these bloody girls ringing him up."

A French cook's knife cut through me as I reached for the Silk Cut. Which girls? What? Somehow I made it through the day, got home, and in a moment of insanity left a message on Daniel's answerphone saying (oh no, I can't believe I did this), "Hi, it's er Bridget here. I was just wondering how you are and if you wanted to go out sometime, like we said."

The second I put the phone down, I realised it was an emergency and rang Tom who calmly said leave it to him: if he made several calls to the machine he could find the code and erase the message. Eventually, he cracked it, rang to do the deed and Daniel answered. But instead of saying, "Sorry, wrong number", Tom put down the phone. So now, Daniel not only has the insane message, but will think it's me who's rung his answerphone 14 times this evening and then, when I did get hold of him, banged the phone down.

It is almost Shrove Tuesday. I shall disgust myself with my own greed by smoking 40 cigarettes instead of eating pancakes. And on Wednesday my new smoke-, fat-, and Daniel-obsession-free life will begin.

Initially I told no one I was writing the column. Then Tracey inquired casually, 'Have you seen this Bridget Jones column in the *Independent*?'

'No,' I lied, before murmuring insouciantly, 'What do you think of it?'

'It's really funny,' tittered Tracey, at which point I burst out, 'It's by me! Me! Me! Me!'

Fan letters started to arrive at the office. Some writers were clearly merely aroused by the photograph of Susannah Lewis. My favourite – mostly for its absurd formality given the subject matter – was written to the editor of the *Independent* and read:

Dear Sir,

I would quite like to shag Bridget Jones. Could you let me have her phone number please?

Yours faithfully,
[REDACTED]

At the time I thought the qualifying 'quite' was quite funny. Now, obviously, I would have been #METOO and furious about it.

I was still, however, reluctant to let my colleagues know I was behind Bridget. I couldn't understand, when others were writing so knowledgeably about New Labour and Chechnya, why anyone in their right mind would want to learn why it takes three hours between waking up in the morning and leaving the house.

Independent, 25 April 1995

Thursday 20 April

*8st 12 (yes!), alcohol units 2, cigarettes 30 (swings &
roundabouts), calories 966 (VG).*

Feel strange, perhaps unnatural, affinity with Victoria
Althorp, with her addictions and weight obsession.
Wonder if self will soon have to check into similar clinic.
But why have so many children when things are so rocky?
Is it possible to get addicted to children, too? Weight 6st
7, alcohol units 14, children 7. Hate thought of world
being full of unsuspected new pitfalls for addictive
personalities. Strangely perplexed also about Tuesday's
date with Dr Rogers. I do not think Dr Rogers, or rather
"Peter", is gay any more, for the following reasons:

1) He has an ex-long-term girlfriend.

2) After he drove me home (own car, drank only one
   glass of wine, clearly not alcoholic – unless exagger-
   ated cover-up – all excellent signs), he stopped the car
   and leaned forward to give me what I anticipated as a
   "peck". But no. It was one of those on-mouth kissettes
   with a question mark attached, followed by another. I
   was too startled to respond.

Or was it that? Had it been Daniel, nothing, even wild
pigs in the car, could have prevented me tearing the
buttons off his shirt. So why no response to Dr Rogers?
He is perfect. We are going for a walk in the country on

Sunday. Maybe he is gay but doesn't know it but my body secretly understands. Maybe I have turned frigid.

Monday 24 April

9st 3lb (better than eating disorder), alcohol units 4, cigarettes 19, calories 1234.

Depressed as do not love eminently suitable Dr Rogers with his stupid country walks. Love mad, badly behaved Daniel. Depressed also by constant lateness for work, and failure to address in-tray bulging with threats from bailiffs etc. Resolve to investigate with time and motion study on self.

7am. Get weighed.

7.03. Return to bed in sulk over weight. Head-state bad. Sleeping or getting up equally out of question. Think about Daniel.

7.30. Hunger pangs force self out of bed. Make coffee, consider grapefruit, defrost chocolate croissant.

7.35–7.50. Look out of window.

7.55. Open wardrobe. Stare at clothes.

8.00. Select shirt. Try to find black Lycra mini-skirt. Pull clothes out of bottom of wardrobe in quest of skirt. Go through drawers and search behind bedroom chair. Go through ironing basket. Go through dirty linen basket. Skirt has vanished. Have cigarette to cheer self up.

8.20. Dry-skin brushing, bath and wash hair.

8.35. Begin selection of underwear. Laundry crisis means only available pants are vast and white cotton. Too unattractive to contemplate even for work (psychological damage). Go back to ironing basket. Find unsuitably lacy prickly pair but better than giant mummy-pant horror.

8.45. Start on black opaque tights. Pair one seems to have shrunk – crotch is three inches above knees. Get second pair on and find hole on back of leg. Throw away. Suddenly remember had Lycra mini-skirt on when returned with Daniel from most recent date. Go to living room. Triumphantly locate skirt between cushions on sofa.

8.55. Return to tights. Pair three have hole only in toe. Put on. Hole transforms into ladder which will protrude tellingly from shoe. Go to ironing basket. Locate last pair of black opaque tights twisted into rope-like object speckled with bits of tissue. Untangle and purge of tissue.

9.05. Have got tights on now. Add skirt. Begin ironing shirt.

9.10. Suddenly realise hair is drying in weird shape. Search for hairbrush. Locate in handbag. Blow-dry hair. Will not go right. Spray with plant spray and blow some more.

9.40. Return to ironing and discover stubborn stain on front of shirt. All other possible shirts dirty. Panic about time. Try to wash out stain. Entire shirt now soaking wet. Iron dry.

9.55. V. late now. In despair, have fag and read holiday brochure for calming five minutes.

10.00. Try to find handbag. Handbag has vanished. Decide to see if anything nice has come in the mail.

10.07. Access letter only, about non-payment of minimum payment. Try to remember what was looking for. Restart quest for handbag.

10.15. Beyond lateness now. Suddenly remember had handbag in bedroom when looking for hairbrush, but cannot find. Eventually locate under clothes from wardrobe. Return clothes to wardrobe. Put on jacket. Prepare to leave house. Cannot find keys. Scour house in rage.

10.25. Find keys in handbag. Realise have forgotten hairbrush.

10.35. Leave house.

Three hours and thirty-five minutes between waking and leaving house is too long. In future must get straight up when wake up and reform entire laundry system.

Buy paper to discover man arrested for Oklahoma bombing was convinced the authorities had planted a microchip in his buttocks to monitor his movements. Horrified by thought of similar chip being in own buttocks, particularly in the mornings.

As the weeks flew by, the column attracted more attention, leading me from denial to incessant boasting. However, I did – and still do – hope to be taken seriously, ideally as a medical doctor or literary novelist. I was attempting to wrestle the second novel in my two-book deal to the ground – a literary exploration of cultural divides in the Caribbean called *Trouble in Paradise*. Whilst the Caribbean research had been enjoyable, the ensuing novel was sadly far too turgid to actually read. I went out for drinks at Kettner's with Georgia Garrett, my then editor at Picador, who suggested I make the Bridget columns into the second novel instead. I jumped at the idea and, even when sobered up, thought it was an easy way out of the whole turgidity pickle. The only problem was I had no plot. At the time, however, the BBC's adaption of *Pride and Prejudice*, with Colin Firth as Mr Darcy, was beginning to grip the country's imagination . . .

Independent, 18 October 1995

Thursday 12 October
8st 12; alcohol units 4 (VG); calories 1750; cigarettes 22; revision 3.5 hrs; total Instants expenditure £7, wins £3, effectively Instants 4 (VG).

Today is my interview with Richard Finch of *Wake Up Britain* for a researcher's job. I have told Perpetua I am at the gynaecologist's. I know I should have said dentist, but opportunities to torture the nosiest woman in the world must not be allowed to slip through the net. I am almost ready and merely need to complete my make-up while practising my opinions on the Portillo speech. Oh my God, who's the Shadow Defence Secretary? Oh damn, oh damn. Robin Cook? Shit: telephone. I can't believe it: terrifying telephonic teenager with patronising south London sing-song going, "Hel-*lo* Bridget, Richard Finch's office here. Richard's in Blackpool this morning so he won't be able to make the meeting." Rescheduled for next Tuesday.

Sunday

Finding it hard to concentrate on my current affairs revision as repeatedly distracted by "Stocking Filla" catalogues tumbling out of the newspapers. Particularly keen on the shield-shaped, burnished metal, "funfur"-lined Spectacles Holder Stand: "all too often spectacles are put down flat on a table, inviting an accident". The Sleekly Designed "Black Cat" Key Chain Light does indeed have a simple flip-down mechanism, as it "casts a powerful red light on the keyhole of any cat lover". Bonsai Kits! Hurrah. "Practise the ancient art of Bonsai with this tub of pre-planted Persian Pink Silk Tree seeds." Nice, very nice. Hmmm. Must press on with Saddam's Hold on Iraq.

8.55 Just nipped out for fags ready for *Pride and Prejudice*. Hard to believe there are so many cars out on the roads. Shouldn't they be at home getting ready? Love the nation being so addicted. The basis of my own addiction, I know, is my simple human need for Darcy to get off with Elizabeth. The football guru Nick Hornby states in his book *Fever Pitch* that men's obsession with football is not vicarious. The testosterone-crazed fans do not wish

348

themselves on the pitch, claims Hornby. Instead they see their team as their chosen representatives, rather like Parliament. That is precisely my feeling about Darcy and Elizabeth. They are my chosen representatives in the field of shagging, or rather courtship. I do not, however, wish to see any actual goals. I would hate to see Darcy and Elizabeth in bed smoking a cigarette afterwards. That would be unnatural and wrong and I would quickly lose interest. Hmm. Anyway. Why More Top Firms are Halting Donations to the Tories. This is not to say, however, I would not delight in sleeping with the actor Colin Firth. Sharon just called and we spent 20 minutes growling, "Fwaw, that Mr Darcy." I love the way he talks, sort of as if he can't be bothered. Ding-dong!

Monday

Ugh. Just about to watch *Panorama* on "the trend for well-qualified female breadwinners – stealing all the best jobs" (one of which I pray to the Lord in Heaven Above and all his Seraphims I am about to become), "does the solution lie in redesigning the educational syllabus?" – when I stumbled upon a photograph in the *Standard* of Darcy and Elizabeth, hideous, dressed as modern-day luvvies, draped all over each other in a meadow: she with blond Sloane hair and linen trouser suit, he in monstrous striped polo neck and mad leather jacket with *Shoestring*-style moustache. Apparently they are already sleeping together. That is absolutely disgusting.

Tuesday

I cannot believe the situation I am in. Instead of being ushered into the office to meet the great Richard Finch, who has merged bewilderingly with Mr Darcy in my mind, I was left, pouring sweat, in reception for 40 minutes, before being picked up by the terrifying sing-song secretary, sporting Lycra cycle shorts and a nose stud, who blanched at my Jigsaw suit as if in a hideously misjudged attempt to be formal I had turned up in a floor-length, shot-silk, off-the-shoulder Laura Ashley ball gown. "Yeah, Richard says to come to the conference, right," she muttered, powering off down a corridor, while I scurried after her. She burst through a pink door into a vast open-plan office strewn with piles of scripts, TV screens suspended from the ceiling, charts all over the walls and mountain bikes propped against the desks. At the far end was a large oblong table where the meeting was in progress. Everyone turned and stared as we approached. A plump, middle-aged man with curly blond hair, a denim shirt and red Christopher Biggins spectacles was jigging up and down at the end of the table. "Come on! Come on! Rosemary West," he was saying, holding up his fists like a boxer. "I'm thinking lesbian rape victims, I'm thinking Jeanette Winterson, I'm thinking *Wake Up Britain* doctor, I'm thinking what lesbians actually do. That's it! What do lesbians actually do in bed?" Suddenly he was looking straight at me. "Do *you* know?" The entire table of grunge youths stared at me. "You. You must be Bridget," he shouted impatiently. "What *do* lesbians actually *do* in bed?"

I took a deep breath. "Actually, I think we should be doing the off-screen romance between Darcy and Elizabeth."

He looked me up and down slowly. "Brilliant," he said suddenly. "Absolutely fucking brilliant. OK. The actors who play Darcy and Elizabeth? Come on, come on," he said, boxing at the meeting.

"Colin Firth and Jennifer Ehle," I blurted.

A slow leer spread across his features. "Bridget Jones," he said, oilily. "Welcome to *Wake Up Britain*. Take a seat, my darling," and then he winked.

With the nation's TV obsession with Darcy and Elizabeth in full flight, a plot solution revealed itself: why not simply steal the plot from *Pride and Prejudice*, along with Mr Darcy himself? Or rather, a mélange of the BBC's Mr Darcy, Bridget's Mark Darcy and the actor Colin Firth? My reasoning was as follows: Jane Austen probably wouldn't mind, her story had been very well market researched over a number of centuries, and anyway she was dead.

At that time the British press was full of first-person confessional columns: so much so that the satirical magazine *Private Eye* monitored self-obsession in its weekly *Hackwatch* by counting the number of times journalists used the word 'I'.

Resolved, therefore, never to use it, self. Also developed elliptical style owing to necessity of column running at 1,000 words. As journalist, accustomed to one's writing being cut by the inch, resolved instead to make column always exactly 1,000 by removing non-vital words, in manner of filling car up with petrol and making it land on exactly £20. Reading columns back, though, realize same often led to sentence over-stuffing with multiple thoughts.

Independent, 5 June 1996

Monday 3 June
9st 3 (not self's fault: manipulated by media). Alcohol units 5 (drowning sorrows). Cigarettes 22 (fumigating sorrows). Calories 3684 (suffocating sorrows in lard-duvet).

Humph. Fed up. After marvellous three days stuffing face after "too skinny" *Vogue* models furore, suddenly open papers to find Nigel Lawson diet everywhere and that idea is to try and lose third of body weight by refusing all alcohol except "fine wines". Fear if see enough photo-shoots of weird-looking yet slender Nigel Lawson he will turn into self's new role model and will find self cutting hair into short bubble curls, reading *The Economist* and trying to shove face down into neck to give impression of multiple ex-double chins. Anyway going round to Shazzer's tonight so should be able to sort out over-impressionable identity crisis with feminist ranting; though fear being unable to drink as Shazzer's leftover birthday Kwik-Save Bosnian-Muslim Cabernet Sauvignon probably does not, come to think of it, qualify as fine wine in any normal interpretation of the term.

Tuesday 4 June

9st 1 (excellent). Cigarettes 0 (unable to find window for same in mouth). Alcohol units 4 (but champagne-type wine so fine).

9am. Got bloody third degree from Shazzer last night. All Tom's fault. Since made the mistake of admitting about new self-help book, *The Rules*, had been reading last week about how to make men fall in love with you by ignoring them, not returning calls etc. Tom then spent entire week faxing me new rules. "Rule 35: when you see a man simply stick two fingers up at him and run off. How else will you know if he's truly in love with you?" "Rule 36: if you find yourself married to a man stab him with a kitchen knife like Sara Thornton: how can he put you on a pedestal if he doesn't feel he has to win you over?" There was no need to bloody well tell Shazzer though.

353

"I gather you've been practising The Rules!" she said coldly.

"No I haven't! No! No!" I gabbled gaily. "I was simply interested in them for professional reasons. I thought they might make an item for *Wake up Britain*."

"Item my arse," growled Sharon. "The Rules are profoundly insulting to women. The whole premise behind them is that men are unable to deal with women's hard-won economic power and therefore it is up to women to resolve the situation by mimicking the dating mores of pre-emancipation females to make men feel powerful and in control."

"Bastards!" I bellowed hopefully trying to distract her.

"Shazzer," bellowed Jude, loyally jumping to her feet and grabbing the wastepaper basket. "What's this doing in your Relationship Corner? Don't you know anything about Feng Shui?"

But Shazzer would not be stopped. "The whole self-help culture is the most shaming face of modern womanhood," she bellowed. "A mindless substitute for religion, feeding on the guilt and lack of self-worth, foisted on fledgling economically powerful group by a hostile male media who . . ." Fortunately she was interrupted by the doorbell and Simon, looking hideously smug.

"Yessss! Yessss!" he said, punching the air.

"What? What? You've finally shagged Isabella?" I shouted excitedly.

"No," he beamed. "But I rang her and she didn't ring back!"

There was silence.

"Well there's only one explanation isn't there?" he said, looking at our sceptical faces. "She's been doing The

Rules! Which must mean she wants to marry me!"

We practically had to shut Shazzer up with tranquilliser darts. But she does have a point. Whole dating scene has become like hideous game of bluff and double bluff with men and women so puzzled and defensive about each other that no one has first idea what is going on. Anyway, do not need men, am going to throw self into work. Oh goody, party tonight.

10pm. Loos at party. Aargh. What's Mark Darcy doing here? Have never seen him look so . . . oh my god, dark and brooding and hot. Anyway determined to ignore him and all other men, meet no one's eye and say nothing then no way can end up looking like prat.

10.30pm. Loos at party. Aargh. In complete panic. Went back into party and accidentally locked gaze with Mark Darcy. Tried desperately to look away demurely in manner of Rules but it was as if self had turned into a warm Rolo. Mark just lifted his eyebrows sexily and nodded towards the garden. What could I do? I felt as if I were being dragged out there by tiny dainty silken aliens. Once we were outside he didn't say a single word, just looked down at me lustfully for a second then kissed me till I was practically fainting. As we broke off panting I said "Stop" feebly and, it has to be said, rather late in the day – since *The Rules* say you're definitely not supposed to snog till date two or was it three and we haven't even been on a date yet. At which point we re-started kissing with even wilder abandon. Eventually he murmured into my neck, "The car's outside, see you there in five minutes," and pressed his hand down by bottom and thigh.

"But . . ." I squeaked, trying not to pass out.

"It's all right, Bridget," he murmured throatily. "You need to read *More Advanced Rules: The Rules*, volume II, pounds 6.99, Harper Collins."

"What does it say?" I said suspiciously.

"It says," he whispered, "if you're young and gorgeous it's the first day of summer and you've just had the snog of the century, it's absolutely imperative to get in his car, go back home with him immediately and fall into bed."

Oh no, oh no! Cannot stay in bathroom any longer. What to do?

Bridget's friendships have always been very important in her life, as well as to me as a writing tool. The importance of the friendship group is something I often have to fight to protect in the screen adaptations. The friends process life's ups and downs from various perspectives, allowing Bridget to be a passive observer while e.g. as above Shazzer gives the stridently feminist and – though I say it myself – quite prescient view.

The format of the column allowed me to write about almost anything, indulging in my own passion for self-help books, politics, random thoughts and passing theories, while merging them with the *Pride and Prejudice* story and the Mark–Mr Darcy–Colin fantasy hybrid. If I was developing an opinion about something or other, for example a distaste for late-nineties Tories, I could work it into the column. It was really fun.

Independent, 29 January 1997

Tuesday 28 January
9st 1 (vg); alcohol units 2 (not nearly enough to prevent heart attack: must do better); cigarettes 5 (excellent); calories 8243 (poor).

Oh no. Scary dinner party tonight with lawyer-style people. Mark Darcy says it would be a good idea to join in the conversation more instead of sitting in silence looking terrified and that it was not necessary to say "Please may I get down?" to the hostess at the end of the meal. Obviously I know that, and on the occasion when it happened it was an accident brought on by Louise

357

Barton-Forster who is an incredibly opinionated partner in Mark's law firm and the sort of woman you can imagine forcing you to eat cabbage. Anyway will make an effort to join in perhaps even reading the paper to form opinions. Hmm. Think will put different bra on.

2am Back home. Disaster. Was determined to join in but Louise Barton-Forster was hogging the entire conversation with complete gibberish "but in a sense one could argue the entire ER Emeuro Proto is a Gerbilisshew". Then heard chap at other end of the table going, "What we need to be talking about is what kind of party people actually want." As luck would have it this was a subject very close to my heart.

"I completely agree," I joined in eagerly, seeing Mark look pleased. "What people really want is back to basics." Emboldened by Mark's proud expression I went on. "The time parties were really good was when everyone was united in a common purpose, and half an hour after you arrived all the lights would be off and everyone was snogging on the floor."

Suddenly Mark burst into polite laughter which didn't sound at all like him, but which everyone else joined in. "But seriously," he said, shooting me a filthy look, "I think you're absolutely right, Nigel. If I'm going to vote Tory again I want to know my views are being a) researched and b) represented."

I stared at Mark, dumbstruck, in complete horror. Felt like my friend Simon did once when he was playing with some lovely little children at a party then their grandfather turned up and he was Robert Maxwell.

I have always feared there was something a bit odd

about Mark Darcy – but had never suspected I had been sleeping with a man who voted Tory. Suddenly felt I didn't know him at all, and for all I knew, all the time we had been going out he had been slipping off to rugby matches on a coach, and mooning at other motorists out of the back window.

Was all very tight-lipped in the car on the way home.

"What's the matter?" he said.

"Nothing," I mumbled.

"You're . . . quivering. Come on. What is it?"

Eventually he stopped the car and made me tell him.

"So I vote Tory, what's wrong with that?" he said, staring at me incredulously.

"But, but . . ." I stammered. "I mean if I voted Tory I'd be a social outcast. It would be like turning up at Café Rouge on a horse with a pack of beagles and Charles and Camilla in tow or having dinner parties on shiny tables with side plates."

"What do you vote?" he said.

"Labour, of course," I hissed. "Everybody votes Labour."

"Well I think that's patently been proved not to be the case, so far," he said. "Why, anyway?"

"What?"

"Why do you vote Labour?"

"Well because . . ." I paused thoughtfully, "because voting Labour stands for being left-wing."

He looked at me strangely.

"And socialist," I added.

"And what does that mean?"

"The workers standing together."

"Well Blair hasn't exactly been shoring up the powers

of the unions, has he?" he said. "Look at Clause IV."

"Well the Tories are rubbish."

"Rubbish?" he said, in a really nasty cold superior voice. "The economy's in better shape now than it's been in for seven years."

"No it's not," I said emphatically, suddenly realizing I had no idea what I was talking about. "Anyway they've probably just put it up because there's an election coming."

"Put what up?" he said. "Put the economy up? How does Blair's stand on Europe compare to Major's?"

"Quite left of centre," I said doubtfully. "Anyway he would rescue the NHS."

"So why hasn't Blair matched the Tory promise to increase spending on health year by year in real terms?"

Honestly. If only Jude and Shazzer had been there it would have been all right since they could have explained it is perfectly obvious that Labour stands for sharing, kindness, gays, single mothers and Nelson Mandela as opposed to braying bossy men having affairs with everyone shag shag shag left right and centre and going to the Ritz in Paris then telling all the presenters off on the *Today* programme. And that it is important to vote for the principle of the thing, not on the itsy bitsy details about this per cent or that per cent. But Mark just started up the car and drove along going on and on about pledges on VAT and Labour and the single currency to the point of utter boredom. Eventually instead of driving us back to his place, he drove straight to mine, and didn't even undo his safety belt or turn off the engine.

"Bridget," he said, "if you persist in these bigoted, ill-informed woolly liberal views I don't see how there can

360

be any future for us. I'll call you tomorrow to discuss this more calmly."

Am torn between love and my political principles in manner of Harriet Harman, Romeo and Juliet or similar. Oh my God. Am on horns of dilemma. Oooh, I wonder if *Eurotrash* is still on on the telly.

I am quite journalistic, or nosy, and I like to be part of things and see what's going on. When Princess Diana died, the column gave me a chance to explore how I was feeling, and how London was reacting, and to go down to Kensington Palace on my own in a way I might not have done without Bridget in my life, on that very sad night.

Independent, 3 September 1997

Sunday 31 August
9st 2, cigarettes 0, alcohol units 0. Instants 1 (v.sad).

10am Why am I so fat with no boyfriend all on own on Sunday morning. What is wrong with self? Am just no good. Am going to go down and get paper then have fag.

10.03am Is unbelievable. Like dream or sick newspaper April Fool. Is unbelievable. Diana Dies is just not kind of thing she would do.

10.10am Am going to put on telly and they will say it has been a mistake and she is back then we will see her coming out of the Harbour Club with all the photographers asking her what it was like.

11.30am Cannot believe it. Is so scary when is obvious no one in authority knows what to do.

12.00pm At least Tony Blair seemed to say what everyone

was thinking instead of repeating "grief and shock" over and over again in manner of parrot.

13.00pm Just feel so guilty that she was our national treasure and people were niggardly about her and she did not like being here. Is like great big hand coming down from heaven saying "if you are going to squabble over her nobody is going to have her".

13.30pm Keep having to look at newspaper headline again to make self believe it.

13.45pm Really she was the patron saint of Singleton women because she started off like the archetypal fairytale doing what we all thought we were supposed to do i.e. marry a handsome Prince and she was honest enough to say that life is not like that. Also it made you feel that if someone so beautiful and gorgeous could be treated like shit by stupid men and feel unloved and lonely then it wasn't because you were rubbish if it happened to you. Also she kept re-inventing herself and sorting out her problems. She was always just trying so hard like modern women.

2.00pm Hmm. Wonder what people would say about me if I died?

2.01pm Nothing.

2.45pm Have just had horrible realisation. Was watching television with the sound down and tabloid front page came up which looked as though it might have had actual pictures of aftermath of the crash in. Realised was horrible part of me which actually wanted to see the pictures. Clearly would not buy said newspaper even if could but. ugh ugh What does this mean about me? Oh God. Am terrible.

4pm Just keep staring into space. Simply hadn't realised how much Diana was part of consciousness. Is like Jude or Shazzer being there and full of life and giggly jokes and lip gloss then suddenly being something so grown-up and horror-filled and alien as dead.

5.45 Just rang up Magda who has been to the garden centre and bought a tree and planted it for Princess Diana. Maybe could plant something in window box e.g. um basil? Could get from Cullens.

6pm Hmm. Basil does not seem right somehow.

7pm Not sure what think about everyone going to Buckingham Palace with floral tributes. Have people always done this? Is it something naff people do to try and get on the television like camping all night outside sales, or good real thing. Hm . . . Feel want to go though.

7.15pm Think going with flowers might be a bit creepy . . . but thing is really did like her. Was like having someone in heart of authority who was same as you. Also all huffer puffers criticised her re: landmines etc but if you ask me was bloody intelligent use of mad publicity. Better than doing nothing except huffing at home.

8.45pm What is point of living in capital city if cannot join in great expressions of feeling? Does not seem very English thing to do but maybe everything has changed with the changing weather and Europe and Tony Blair and it is all right to express yourself. Maybe she has changed English stuffiness.

9pm You see she was brilliant on the landmines programme. Just as good as Dimblebys Pilgers etc.

9.15 OK am definitely going to go to Kensington Palace . . . Have not got any flowers, though. Will get some from petrol station.

9.30 Petrol station has sold out. Only things like chocolate orange and custard left. Nice but inappropriate.

9.35 Bet she would like them, though.

9.45 Have chosen copy of *Vogue*, Milk Tray, 1 Instants and packet of Silk Cut. Not perfect but everyone will have bought flowers and know she liked *Vogue*.

11pm V. glad went. Felt a bit shy walking through in Kensington in case people knew where was going and that was on own, but then when think about it Princess Diana was often on own.

Inside park was v. dark and gentle with everyone just walking quietly in one direction. Was no histrionics like on News. The bottom of the wall was covered with flowers and candles in the darkness and people relighting the candles that had gone out and reading messages.

Hope that she knows now after all the times she worried about not being good enough, look what everybody felt about her. Really all this should say a message to women who are worried about how they look and being rubbish and expecting so much of themselves just not to worry so much. Felt a bit embarrassed about the *Vogue* and chocolate and Instants so hid under flowers and looked at the messages which made you think that you do not have to be a spokesman for anything to be able to express things. The best one was copied from the Bible, I think, and it said in wobbly old lady's writing:

"When I was in trouble you cared about me, when I was in danger you tried to stop it, when I was sick you visited me, when people ran away you took my hand. Whatever you did for the poorest and smallest people I felt as if you did it for me."

Bridget Becomes A Thing

As the columns became a novel, and the novel grew in popularity, a whole new life began for me, bringing some incredibly glamorous moments with it. The interview with Colin Firth below was actually a real thing that happened and one of the highlights of that whole heady time. I was obviously in love with Mr Darcy/Mark Darcy/Colin Firth. I persuaded the *Independent* to allow me to interview Him in Rome, where He was living at the time.

It was heaven. We had lunch and a bottle of wine in one restaurant and a lot of fun. We then decided to switch restaurants and have another bottle of wine and go into character: He into Mr Darcy/Mark Darcy, with a nod in the direction of Colin, and me into Bridget. The interview you see here was pretty much verbatim. We laughed so much. It was one of those fabulous days you remember forever.

Independent, 23 March 1996

Bridget Jones reaches fever pitch

Tuesday 18 March

9am Right, am going to write up interview in Rome with Mr Darcy. Was just so fantastic. Taxi dropped me off in Roman square and thought was going to faint: just fantastic golden sunshine and huge, huge massive square full of high-up ruins and in the middle of it all Mr . . . ooh, telephone.

It was bloody Michael from the *Independent*.

"So did you do it, then?"

"Yes," I said hoity toitily.

369

"And you remembered to take your tape recorder this time, not your Sony Walkman?"

Honestly. If they cannot let a person forget a simple past mistake, then huh. "Well, you've got till lunch time tomorrow. So get on with it."

Lala. That is ages. Will just relive day for a bit. Mmm. Oh God. He just looked exactly like Mr Darcy: all smouldery and lean. And he even took me round a church with a hole in and some Adrian's tomb or other and Moses and was incredibly masterful every time I nearly walked under a car and kept talking Italian. Mmm. "Colin" is better than Mr Darcy but strangely also Mr Darcy.

6pm Writing day has not gone particularly well, though obviously needed some time to absorb what happened, and discuss impressions with peers so probably has been highly productive. Will stay in tonight. Will get bulk of it down, then fine-tune tomorrow. Mmm. Mr Darcy.

12.20am Argor eswor blurrygoofun. Shazzanjude v. jealous re Misdarcy. Misdarcymisdarcy. Oops.

Wednesday 19 March
10am Right. Does not matter if have hangover. Ooh, telephone again. You see this is what it is like when you are major profile writer: phones ringing incessantly. Was bloody Michael again: "How are we coming along?"

Bloody nerve. Is not even my deadline till lunch time, which obviously means two o'clock. Actually, really pleased with tape. Did really good thing of starting Him off with easy questions before going into Tom's meaty questions which I had written down night before despite being a little on squiffy side. Think He was really quite impressed with my line of questioning, actually.

10.15am Will just have quick cup of coffee and fag.

11.00am Hmm. Better just listen to tape back again.

Ding dong! Will just ring Shaz again and play her this last bit.

Aargh, aargh. Is 12 o'clock. Anyway no need to panic. They are not going to be back from lunch till three and is all there in head. Just need to write down. Wait till they see my Scoops.

How to start? Obviously, interview must include my impressions of Mr Darcy as well as skilfully weaving in stuff about new film *Fever Pitch*, theatre v film etc. They will probably give me a regular interview spot every week: The Bridget Jones Profile. Jones meets Darcy. Jones meets Blair. Jones meets President Marcos.

2pm How can I be expected to create if bloody Michael keeps ringing up all the time saying what I must and must not put in? Grrr . . . If that is him again . . . They have no respect for journalists in that office. None whatsoever.

3pm Harhar. "I.Am.Do.Ing.It." I said. That has shut him up.

5pm Anyway is OK. All top journalists have deadline crises.

6pm Oh f*** Oh f*** Oh f***

6.30pm Argor scareer isnruin. Argor.

DUE TO INSUPERABLE TECHNICAL DIFFICULTIES IT HAS BEEN NECESSARY TO PRINT BRIDGET JONES'S INTERVIEW WITH COLIN FIRTH AS A DIRECT TRANSCRIPT OF THE RECORDING.

BJ Right. I'm going to start the interview now.
CF (SLIGHTLY HYSTERICAL SOUNDING) Good, good.
(VERY LONG PAUSE)
BJ What is your favourite colour?
CF I'm sorry?
BJ What is your favourite colour.
CF Blue.
(LONG PAUSE)
BJ What is your favourite pudding?
CF Er . . . crème brûlée.
BJ You know the oncoming film *Fever Pitch* by Nick Hornby which starts next Friday?
CF I do know it, yes.
BJ (PAUSE. RUSTLING PAPER) Do . . . Oh. **(MORE RUSTLING PAPER).** Do you think the book of *Fever Pitch* has spored a confessional gender?
CF Excuse me?
BJ Has. Spored. A Confessional. Gender.
CF *Spored* a confessional gender?
BJ Yes.
CF Well. Certainly Nick's style has been very much imitated, and I think it's a very appealing, er, gender whether or not he actually, um . . . *spored* it.

BJ You know in *Pride and Prejudice*?

CF I do know in it, yes.

BJ When you had to dive into the lake?

CF Yes.

BJ When they had to do another take, did you have to take the wet shirt off and then put a dry one on?

CF Yes, I, I probably did have to, yes. *Scusi. Ha vinto. E troppo forte. Si grazie.*

BJ (BREATHING UNSTEADILY) How many takes did they have to do?

CF (COUGHS) Well. The underwater shots were a tank in Ealing Studios.

BJ Oh no.

CF I'm afraid so. The um, *moment* of being airborne – *extremely brief* – was a stuntman.

BJ But it looked like Mr Darcy.

CF That was because he had stuck on sideburns and a Mr Darcy outfit on top of a wet suit, which actually made him look like Elvis as you last saw him. He could only do it once for insurance reasons and then he had to be checked for abrasions for about six weeks afterwards. All the other wet-shirt shots were me.

BJ You know the other wet-shirt shots?

CF Yes.

BJ Were they you?

CF Yes.

BJ And did the shirt have to keep being re-wet?

CF Yes. They'd spray it down. They'd spray it down and then . . .

BJ What with?

CF I'm sorry?

BJ What with?

373

CF A squirter thing. Look can we . . .

BJ Yes, but what I mean is did you ever have to take the shirt off and, and put another one on?

CF Yes.

BJ To be wet again?

CF Yes.

BJ (PAUSE) You know the oncoming film *Fever Pitch*?

CF Yes.

BJ What do you see as the main differences and similarities between the character Paul from *Fever Pitch* and . . .

CF . . . and?

BJ (SHEEPISHLY) Mr Darcy.

CF No one's ever asked me that.

BJ Haven't they?

CF No. I think the main differences are . . .

BJ Do you mean it's a really obvious question?

CF No. I mean no one's ever asked me that.

BJ Do people ask you that all the time?

CF No, no. I can assure you . . .

BJ So it's a . . .

CF It's a totally brand-new, new-born question, yes.

BJ Oh Goody.

CF Shall we get on now?

BJ Yes.

CF Mr Darcy's not an Arsenal supporter.

BJ No.

CF He's not a schoolteacher.

BJ No.

CF He lived nearly 200 years ago.

BJ Yes.

CF Paul in *Fever Pitch* loves being in a football crowd.

BJ Yes.

CF Whereas Mr Darcy can't even tolerate a country dance.

BJ No.

CF Paul doesn't smoulder.

BJ Oh he did, though. That bit with the coffee cups. It's fantastic where that woman Miss Hughes is just standing there and Mr Darcy just masterfully takes the cups away and then, like, snogs her.

CF I think that might be a similarity, then.

BJ I'm not putting words into your mouth or anything.

CF No, no. Now. Can we talk about something which isn't to do with Mr Darcy?

BJ Yes. **(PAUSE, RUSTLING PAPERS)** If you had to play another character in a historical novel – apart from Nostradamus – who would you choose? **(PAUSE)**

CF Apart from Nostradamus?

BJ Yes.

CF You see, Nostradamus *is* a historical character. Nostromo, however, isn't.

BJ What?

CF Nostromo is a fictional character invented by Joseph Conrad and I didn't actually play him. I played someone else in the story called Charles Gould but, um, he's not historical either. I don't know if I've ever actually played a *historical* character.

BJ (SHOCKED) Apart from Mr Darcy.

CF Apart from Mr Darcy, yes. He's the only actual true-life real-existing historical character I've actually played.

BJ What did you have to wear when you were Nostromo?

CF Well, I wore jodhpurs and a tweed jacket and . . . boots and things.

BJ Leather boots?

CF They were leather, yes.

BJ Quite high ones?

CF They were up to the knee.

BJ Tight?

CF Fairly tight. I mean I was able to get them on and off. But, um, they were tight enough. They were for riding and um, and, er . . . and that's about it, really. They . . . it was, er . . . Yes. That's about it.

BJ You know the dance you just mentioned in *Pride and Prejudice*?

CF (SIGHS) Yes.

BJ Was it quite, you know . . . sexy . . . in real life?

CF Well. It's actually quite difficult to do acting and dancing at the same time and I think one, er, stress factor of making sure that you've reached the right place to say your next line is that, the *eroticism* isn't the first thing in your mind necessarily.

BJ Do you think it was quite an erotic series?

CF Well, some people have found it to be so. I think it's a very erotic book.

BJ Do you think the word erotic is quite an erotic word?

CF *Quite* an erotic word, yes.

BJ Mmm.

CF Yes. So. Now where were we?

BJ Are you still going out with your girlfriend?

CF Yes.

BJ Oh.

(LONG PAUSE)

CF Is everything all right?

BJ (ALMOST INAUDIBLE) Do you think small British movies are the way forward?

CF I can't hear.

BJ (MISERABLY) Do you think small British movies are the way forward?

CF The way forward to . . . **(ENCOURAGINGLY)** – to what?

BJ (VERY LONG THOUGHTFUL PAUSE) The future.

CF Right. They seem to be getting us along step by step, I think. I quite like small movies but I do also like big movies and it would be nice if we made more of those as well.

BJ But don't you find it a problem her being Italian and everything?

CF No.

(VERY LONG SILENCE)

BJ (SULKILY) Do you think that Mr Darcy has a political dimension?

CF I did speculate on what his politics might be, if he had any. And I don't think that they would be very appealing to a reader of the *Independent*. It's that pre-Victorian or Victorian idea of being the rich social benefactor, which would be very Thatcherite probably. I mean, the thought of socialism obviously hadn't entered the . . .

BJ No.

CF . . . entered his sphere. And it is clearly stated by way of showing what a nice chap he is that he is very nice towards his tenants. But I think that he'd be closer to a sort of Nietzschian figure, a . . .

BJ What is neacher?

CF You know, the idea of the, er, human being as superman.

BJ Superman?

CF Not Superman himself, no. No. **(SLIGHT GROANING NOISE)** I don't think he wore his underpants over his breeches, no. Look, I'd *really* like to get off this subject now.

BJ What will be your next project?

CF It's called *The World of Moss*.

BJ Is it a nature programme?

CF No. No, no. No. It's um, it's er, about an eccentric family in the Thirties the father of which owns a moss factory.

BJ Doesn't moss grow naturally?

CF Well, no, he makes something called Sphagnum moss which was used to dress World War I wounds and er, it's er, quite a light, er, comic . . .

BJ (VERY UNCONVINCINGLY) It sounds very good.

CF I very much hope it will be.

BJ Could I just check something about the shirt?

CF Yes.

BJ How many times altogether exactly did you have to take it off and put it on again?

CF Precisely . . . I don't know. Um. Let me see . . . there was the bit where I was walking towards Pemberley. That was shot once. One take. Then there was the bit where I give my horse to somebody . . . I think there was a change.

BJ (BRIGHTENING) There was a change?

CF (STRICTLY) There was. One change.

BJ So it was mainly just the one wet shirt, though?

CF The one wet shirt which they kept respraying, yes. All right?

BJ Yes. What is your favourite colour?

CF We've had that.

BJ Um. **(PAPER RUSTLING)**

BJ Do you think the film *Fever Pitch* was in reality all about emotional fuckwittage?

378

CF Emotional what?

BJ Fuckwittage. You know: men being mad, alcoholic, commitment phobics and just being interested in football all the time.

CF No, I don't really. I think in some ways Paul is much more at ease with his emotions and has much more liberty with them than his girlfriend. I think that, in fact, in the final analysis, is what's so appealing about what Nick Hornby's trying to say on his behalf: that, in a rather mundane, everyday world, he has found something where you have access to emotional experiences, which . . .

BJ Excuse me.

CF (SIGHS) Yes?

BJ Is your girlfriend coming to the premiere of *Fever Pitch*.

CF Yes.

BJ But won't she have trouble understanding it, being foreign?

CF Well she speaks very good English.

BJ But don't you think you'd be better off with someone who was English and more your own age?

CF We seem to be doing alright.

BJ Humph. **(DARKLY)** So far. Do you ever prefer doing the theatre?

CF Um. I don't subscribe to the view that the theatre's where the real acting is, that film's not really acting. But I find I do prefer the theatre when I'm doing it, yes.

BJ But don't you think the theatre's a bit unrealistic and embarrassing and, also, you have to sit through the acting for hours before you have anything to eat and you can't talk or . . .

CF Unrealistic? Embarrassing and unrealistic?

BJ Yes.

CF Do you mean unrealistic in the sense that it . . . ?

BJ . . . you can tell it isn't real.

CF . . . that sort of unrealistic, yes. **(SLIGHT MOANING SOUND)** Um. I think it shouldn't be if it's good. It's much more . . . it feels more artificial to make a film.

BJ Does it? I suppose it doesn't go all the way through, does it?

CF Well no it doesn't. No. Yes. A film doesn't go all the way through. It's shot in little bits and pieces. **(LOUDER GROANING NOISE)** Little bits and pieces.

BJ Has it been detrimental to your career being called Colin?

CF (LAUGHS) Well, I did ask my mother why she plumped for that *particular name* and she said, "Well, we couldn't call you Andrew because of your cousin."

BJ Oh. Do you think Mr Darcy would have slept with Elizabeth Bennet before the wedding?

CF Yes, I do think he might have.

BJ Do you?

CF Yes. I think it's entirely possible. Yes.

BJ (BREATHLESSLY) Really?

CF I think it's possible. Yes.

BJ *How* would it be possible?

CF Don't know if Jane Austen would agree with me on this, but . . .

BJ We can't know because she's dead.

CF No, we can't . . . but I think Andrew Davies's Mr Darcy would have done.

BJ *Why* do you think that, though? Why? Why?

CF Because I think it was very important to Andrew Davies that Mr Darcy had the most enormous sex drive.

380

BJ (GASPS)

CF And, um . . .

BJ I think that came across, really, really well with the acting. I really think it did.

CF Thank you. At one point, Andrew even wrote as a stage direction: "Imagine that Darcy has an erection".

(V. LARGE CRASHING NOISE)

BJ Which bit was that?

CF It's when she's been walking across the country and bumps into him in the grounds in the early stages.

BJ The bit where she's all muddy?

CF . . . and dishevelled

BJ . . . and sweaty?

CF Exactly.

BJ Was that a difficult bit to act?

CF You mean the erection?

BJ (AWED WHISPER) Yes.

CF Um, well, Andrew also wrote that I don't propose that we should focus on it, and, therefore, no acting required in that department at least.

BJ Mmm.

(LONG PAUSE)

CF Yes.

(MORE PAUSE)

BJ Mmm.

CF Is that it, then?

BJ No. What was it like with your friends when you started being Mr Darcy?

CF There were a lot of jokes about it: growling "Mr Darcy" over breakfast and so on. There was a brief period when they had to work quite hard to hide their knowledge of who I really was and . . .

BJ Hide it from who?

CF Well, from anyone who suspected that perhaps I was like Mr Darcy.

BJ But do you think you're not like Mr Darcy?

CF I do think I'm not like Mr Darcy, yes.

BJ I think you're exactly like Mr Darcy.

CF In what way?

BJ You talk the same way as him.

CF Oh do I?

BJ You look exactly like him, and I, oh, oh . . .

PROTRACTED CRASHING NOISES FOLLOWED BY SOUNDS OF STRUGGLE

Editor's note: Bridget Jones has been sacked.

The growing interest in Bridget and the ensuing change in my life created a mixture of awed gratitude and confusion in me. I myself became an object of interest to the British press which was surreal since I was part of the British press, which is how it had all started in the first place.

On one occasion, returning to my flat in Notting Hill I spied a paparazzi on a motorbike waiting for me outside. 'Honestly,' I huffed, tossing my hair indignantly. 'Why can't they just LEAVE ME ALONE?' As I got closer, though, I realized it was the delivery guy from Domino's Pizza and was really disappointed.

For a struggling freelance journalist, to manage to get a book in print at all is a great privilege, let alone to have your character become part of the culture, and to have her lexicon absorbed into the language. I got a huge thrill from these *Pile 'Em High* cartoons by Kipper Williams, and the *Mirror* front page. I always wanted to hang them in the guest toilet to impress but found it too creepy.

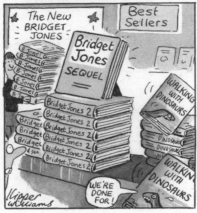

William Hague's head on Renée Zellweger's body was downright disturbing . . .

Wednesday May 9 2001

The **Mirror**

www.mirror.co.uk

(32p)

BRIDGET HAGUE'S DIARY

June 7, 2001

Nightmare! Told we're going to be left on shelf AGAIN!! Seems everyone's right. I AM useless. Hear Portillo is bitching behind my back. Plan to have 14 pints and chicken tikka massala to forget. Note to self: Remember inner poise and find proper career. Job prospects v.v. bad.

WARNING: Voting for Hague can seriously damage your health

. . . but it was still a source of pride to be on the front page.

In spite of its ageing-ness with regards to me, I'm deeply grateful that *Bridget Jones* is still being read and discussed after twenty-five years. The thought that it might be read by generations in the future is something that I would never previously have presumed to fantasize about, but now I dream that maybe one day someone will be stealing *my* plot, without realizing it's actually Jane Austen's.

Bridget in the 21st Century

I tend not to read my own books (once I've written them, obviously) or re-watch the movies, but a couple of years ago I took my children, Dash and Romy, to see a screening of the *Bridget Jones's Diary* movie as it was being shown with a live orchestra. I was shocked at the casual sexism in every scene, which an unenlightened Bridget just put up with as part and parcel of having a job. Honestly, in this day and age all of Bridget's bosses would have been fired and shamed on the spot. Solemn Feminists could get angry about what Bridget put up with, but the fact is, I didn't write the diary as a sociological treatise. It became widely read because there was recognition. It was reflecting a reality, not creating it. When my goddaughter, Scarlett Curtis, was putting together this edgy collection of essays about Feminism, I was pleased to be part of it, and wrote this entry in Bridget's voice.

Monday 16 April 2018
9st 2. Alcohol units: 3. Instagram followers: 167.

"That was the most sexist, horrifying, disgusting movie I've ever seen," ranted Shazzer. "If John Travolta made that now, he'd *never fucking work again*."

We had just got to the end of a 40th anniversary screening of *Saturday Night Live*. It was an invitation from Jude's investment bank in a sedate screening room with drinkies and canapés.

"NONE of them would ever FUCKING work again!" Shazzer bellowed, as the credits rolled, and people made to leave their seats. "Did I actually hear the word 'cunt' seven times??"

"Shazzer. Shut urrp," hissed Jude. People were staring. Tom, meanwhile, was smiling at them as if to say, "Everything's lovely! She's our patient," ignoring the fact that he was wearing a tight white three-piece suit and high heels.

"John Travolta sat in the front seat of the car while they *gang-raped* his ex-girlfriend whose only crime was to have some sort of sexual desire and admit to it!" Shazzer continued to yell. "And what does he do when he actually wins the Goddess Virgin Anti-Whore-girl of his dreams? He fucking tries to rape her! Princess Diana *danced* with John Travolta, for fuck's sakes! At the White House! And not the fucking Trumpian White House, either!"

"Let's get her out of here," said Jude.

It was all very unnerving, I thought. We clattered down the stairs. *Saturday Night Fever* was a cult classic, surely, like *Grease*. We'd gone to have a laugh and sing along to the Bee Gees in very high voices, not to have our youthful sense of right, wrong and gender understanding turned upside on its head, leaving us feeling like duped idiots.

"But wasn't this the uncut version?" said Jude. "And wasn't *Saturday Night Fever* known for being a deliberately provocative piece, exploring the dark side of youth culture. And the whole 'cunt' . . . Oh hello!" Our host and Jude's CEO, Johnny Carruthers, was coming up the stairs.

"No, it fucking wasn't!" yelled Shazzer, barging past him. "*Saturday Night* Fucking *Fever* was known for everyone thinking John Travolta was hot, the Bee Gees were cool, and it was a charming teenage dance frenzy. But ACTUALLY, that movie was a celebration of the worst kind of profound, misogynist sexism when women are treated with utter contempt and casual violation."

By this time we were weaving through cars and rain across the Soho street and pushing our way into the warmth and crowded coziness of Kettner's.

"AND WE FUCKING DIDN'T FUCKING NOTICE because we are an OPPRESSED RACE!" finished Shazzer, as we got through the door.

"Shhhh," I said, suddenly flashing back to shushing Shazzer in exactly the same manner and bar, twenty years ago, when she went into a feminist rant in front of someone Jude fancied and I said "Shhhh! There is nothing so unattractive to a man as strident feminism." This, I insisted and still maintain, was a *multi-layered ironic joke*.

"We women are only being treated like shit because we are a pioneer generation, daring to rely on our own economic power," Shazzer had yelled that night. "In twenty years' time, men won't even *dare* start with fuckwittage because we will just laugh in their faces and they will all just be kept in *kennels* as *pets*."

It is twenty years later now. Men are not, generally, being kept in kennels as pets, but everything has both changed and not changed.

"Shall we get ourselves a bol of Chardonnay?" said Tom.

11.30pm Back home. Children are asleep. Just having a little nightcap and looking back through old diaries from 1996. The strident feminist thing *was* a multi-layered ironic joke! At that time, I felt like "a Feminist" was another intimidating thing you were supposed to be: along with thin, in a relationship, a mother, running your own business and gliding smoothly from person to person at parties like Tina Brown. Solemn Feminists like Camille Paglia and Germaine Greer seemed to be always telling us off, for being less Feminist than them, and for trying to combine some sort of economic independence with the reality of finding men attractive and wanting to love and be loved, keep a job, pay the rent and just sort of *manage* without pissing everybody off too much to continue.

But it was also the era of Susan Faludi's marvellous treatise, *Backlash*, where (even though I never actually read it but – epic Feminist fail! – Mark Darcy did), Susan Faludi flagged up that our faltering steps towards gender equality were being stamped upon by movies like *Fatal Attraction*, and that hideous quote from *Time* magazine saying a woman over the age of 40 was statistically more likely to be killed by a terrorist than find a husband. And look at my mother's dreaded Turkey Curry Buffet! Uncle Geoffrey and even Smug Married couples my own age were still saying, "Why aren't you married?" and "Tick-tock-tock tick-tock!" when I was only 32. It was as if I was some freakish Miss Havisham figure who was going to end up dying alone and being found three weeks later half eaten by an Alsatian, so much so that I felt moved to say, "It's because actually underneath my clothes my entire body is covered with scales," because that's what they actually suspected, or made me feel like.

We all got angry, and I seem to remember that leading to a time when being a Feminist started to lose its capitalization and go without saying. You wouldn't go around asserting that you were "a Feminist" because that seemed like an insult to all the other women around you. Things weren't perfect but, to draw the general from the particular, no one would dare ask a 32-year-old woman why she wasn't married anymore, because it would sound ridiculous. Single women in their thirties were Singletons, not Miss Havisham.

We're not talking about the real gender equality issue here – the developing world, women living below the poverty line who are not trying to avoid being insulted, but rather raped, mutilated, killed or starved. We're talking about reasonably well-off women in the developed world. And on that level, in the decade after I first wrote those diaries, things were not at all perfect, but we seemed to be doing better. Gender equality issues were at least being aired, progress was being made.

"You thought!" as Billy, my 12-year-old son (see? shove your tick-tock up your arse and smoke it, Uncle Geoffrey) – says all the time.

2am Still reading my diaries. OMG. Trump. Weinstein. The last two, three years have seen a Backlash bigger than anything Susan Faludi could have imagined and a corresponding wake-up call, telling everyone exactly how well we aren't and weren't doing, and turning our view of the past on its head.

What did I put up with, in the days of these diaries, without even knowing I had the right to not put up with it? Talk about #METOO. Mr Tits Pervert! (AKA the head of our publishing house, Mr Fitzherbert) Ieuwwww. I just accepted that part and parcel of having a job was that my boss would stare freely at my breasts, not know my name, and ask me to put a tight dress on to make an idiotic speech. I suppose I did eventually turn around and tell them all to shove their job, but then I walked straight into another one with Richard Finch. And said Richard Finch – who gave me my big break in television – still spent his entire time trying to get shots of my bum or my tits and generate ratings by humiliating me on camera (not that that was particularly difficult, let's face it). None of that could happen now. Mr Fitzherbert and Richard Finch would lose their jobs, no question. No studio would touch *Saturday Night Fever*, as it was written, with a bargepole.

And "feminism" is once again – as Billy would say – a Thing. It's a different thing. It's not appropriated by solemn, self-righteous intellectuals. It's everywoman's now.

11.45pm Just googled "Feminist Clothing" and got 24 million results: sweatshirts, jewellery, hats, mugs, badges, with every tone – angry, witty, playful, self-mocking, and, yes, it's finally acceptable, multi-layeredly ironic: "Pro Choice, Pro Feminism, Pro Unicorns." "My Marxist feminist dialectic brings all the boys to the yard." "'I really want to marry the guy that whistled at me from his car.'– No One, Ever." "Eve was framed." "Fuck your patriarchal bullshit." "Has anyone tried turning the US on and off again?"

Though I'm still not sure we could get away with Shazzer's favourite line "Anyone who could actually sleep with Harvey Weinstein deserves an Oscar." Will just have another little snifter of wine.

Midnight Probably quite right too, because thass sexist against. The sexual attraction at work's not simple and looking back I's did sexually harass Daniel Cleaver. But, thas different because I fancied him and, er, I was a woman and he was a man? It was resiprocal? Also, it was really boring in that office and we wanted to have fun. Crucially, I wouldn't have dissed another man professionally for not being attractive. Its not just people treating "attractive" women as sex objects that's the problem, it's what that means when they're "not" – and there's no one better to

396

explain THAT, than our eSTEEMED US president, Mr Trump. Am gon google cut anpaste.

1997 in *Esquire* re: the media "You know, it doesn't really matter what [they] write as long as you've got a young and beautiful piece of ass."

1997 Miss USA contest "If you're looking for a rocket scientist, don't tune in tonight, but if you're looking for a really beautiful woman, you should watch."

2006 re: Rosie O'Donnell "If I were running The View, I'd fire Rosie. I'd look her right in that fat, ugly face of hers and say, 'Rosie, you're fired.'"

April 2015 "If Hillary Clinton can't satisfy her husband what makes her think she can satisfy America?"

September 2015 Re: Carly Fiorina "Look at that face. Would anyone vote for that?"

12.15am Pah! Actually maybe I'll post those quotes on Instagram.

12.20am Ugh. The only good thing that can be said about all terribleness is that it makes people rise up and own their opinions, instead of juss checkin Instagram follower.

Shit I just lost 4 followers. Why? Dids I have Trumpian followers? Maybe, as Tom says, my whole feed needs to have a uniform pallet. Not just random things of this that and the other. And I should just post pictures of calm interiors in quiet neutrals and greys that read white and stuff. Hmm.

Anyway, t point is, about Harvey Weinstein, *Saturday Night Live*, I mean *Fever*, etc. is that all this hideousness had come out of the woodwork in Hollywood – but whereas books and things reflect what is happening in the world, Hollywood movies DICTATE IT and MOULD what people think. And these SEXIST FUCKWITTED BASTARDS are in charge of MAKING THE MOVIES! Fuck them! I'm going to screenshot this and POST IT ON INSTAGRAM.

12.30am Humph. No wonder everyone thinkst 70 year old men can play successful romantically viable parts whereas any woman over the age of 45 apart from MerylS Streep, or "unattractive" has to be some sort of OPPRESSIVE STEREOTYPE. Xactly, nagging mothers, resentful ex-wives, villainesses, icy corporate no-characters. Hollywood men stars are 30 YEARS older than their women-stars and if it's the other way round that's the subject of the WHOLE MOVIE like *The Mother* or *Film Stars Don't Die in Liverpool*. Pah! Thas the new thing – women sex-ageism. Women of Age – the new culturally OPPRESSED MINORITY.

Tuesday 17th April 2018
11 stone. Alcohol units: 167. Instagram followers: 3

Prepared breakfast for the children, gaily pretending head was not hurting and did not desire to be sick in oatmeal. Was still fired up by messianic new feminist fervour.

"Billy," I said. "Tonight, we're going to watch *Thelma and Louise*."

"What?"

"I want you to learn about how to treat women and that what happens if you don't treat them as equals and . . ."

"I know about *Thelma and Louise*, Mummy," said Billy. "Are you talking about sexism and gender inequality?"

"Yes," I said slightly sulkily. "It really is the scourge of the future and . . ."

"You thought. That's just for old people," he said. "If you're our age, Mummy, sexism just isn't a Thing."

Maybe there is hope in the new generation. Or maybe I should take away his Instagram for trying to insinuate that I am somehow not 32.

I still write the diary sometimes, if there's something interesting going on or something I feel indignant about. Brexit was a classic example of the latter but not the former. It's amazing how little we all actually know when skewered on subjects. There's a lot of fuzzy knowledge around. But in 2019, Brexit took fuzzy knowledge to a whole new level.

Sunday Times, 26 March 2019

Monday 25th March
Stockpiled items: French white wine 18; toilet rolls 48; mini-breaks 2; Fray Bentos pies 6; panic attacks 2; no. times checked signatures on petition 24 (better) (but 24 times per minute undeniably obsessive).

3am Awake in usual Brexit cold sweat when remember after years-long assumption that someone somewhere knows what they are doing, realization that no one is in charge or has first idea about anything.

7am Just turned on telly. Unbelievable. A million people marched in streets last weekend, 1,000s per hour signing petition and is as if nothing happened. Still politicians wandering Parliament Square slagging each other off in endless stream of incomprehensible gibberish to any news camera that will listen: "Vote on a series of meaningful, indicative votes, to amend the way to a *favoured outcome*, cross-dressing Brexit, 12th April, 22nd June, customized unicorn exit Brexit etc. etc."

Don't they realize WE DON'T HAVE THE FIRST IDEA WHAT THEY'RE TALKING ABOUT, what they're objecting to, what's in the deal or what it will mean for us because no one can be arsed to explain it? Suspect they don't understand it either. Even researching online unsustainable as hypnotizingly boring in manner of Theresa May speech.

7.15am Completely terrified again. What will we eat? Will there still be the National Health? What about goats cheese and French outfits? Maybe all our bank accounts will be seized like in Greece. Will we still get cable? Will our passports work? Can we still go on holiday? Can we watch European football? What about mobile phones? Will Grazina the cleaner have to go back to Lithuania. Are we going to run out of wine?

Tuesday 26th March
Alcohol units 12 (must start to ration) Stockpiled items: toilet rolls 47; bottles of French wine 20; small car 1; no. times checked signatures on petition 22 (per minute – better).

1am Argor was blurry goofun night with Jude Shaz 'n Tom and have completely solved Brexit with our plan . . .

7am . . . though cannot entirely remember what plan was.
    "Backstop? Bastards more like!" Shazzer was ranting, downing a glass of Chardonnay. "Stupid, smug, self-interested . . . it's political FUCKWITTAGE – pass me some of that pizza will you?"

"Bastards!" I yelled happily, "Fuckwittage! Shall we get another bol wine?"

"I don't know what to do. I don't know what to stock-pile." Tom was flapping around. "I think Xavier's going to have to go back to Spain."

Jude was being annoyingly smug and pro-Brexit. "If we tell Europe we're staying it'll be like breaking up with someone then asking them to take you back. And then they can't resist punishing you. The people voted to leave so that's what should be happening. Pass me a dough ball?"

"That's ridiculous," exploded Tom. "It was the hottest night of the year! It was June. Everyone was plastered. More people googled 'What is Brexit' the next morning than ever before."

"People vote on symbols," I concurred. "They voted in because they wanted nicer food and pavement cafes and they voted out because they didn't want refugees. We all thought Theresa May was actually going to explain it to us when she did her address to the nation – not just slag off her colleagues."

"They should do a jolly show, like Comic Relief where they explain it in a user-friendly manner," said Tom.

"Oh please. Like, I'm a Politician Get Me Out of Here?" sneered Shaz.

"We need a leader," I said, fired up with messianic fervour, "someone everyone trusts, who's not self-interested, has vision and eloquence, can cut the crap and communicate with the population, rather than with a small group of traumatized, sleep-deprived politicians. There's a whole self-help movement about minimizing admin – yet the country has mired itself into an admin black hole. Also look at the Xmas Gatwick Drone Fiasco – it took three days to call the army in. What if a major disaster had happened and they were still blarblarblar Brexit? We need a hero who will rise – like Winston Churchill, or Russell Crowe in *Gladiator*."

Suddenly had overwhelming sense that perhaps *I* was that leader.

"Perhaps it should be . . ." I said, dropping my eyes modestly, "me?" They all looked at me, mouths open.

"If I came to power," I said, "I would stand up and say to the nation, 'Look!'"

"'Look?'" said Tom. "Is that it?"

"No! 'Look. We know it's a mess and nobody under-stood what they were voting about. So we're going to have another vote but first I'm going to EXPLAIN the whole thing perhaps in an entertaining TV show! Then everyone has to take a multiple choice test – like with driving tests in America or citizenship here – and if you get enough questions right then you can vote in or out.'"

"Er, Bridget," said Tom, "why should anyone listen to you?"

"Because I would be the Prime Minister," I explained, patiently.

"Right, right. But just say there was some element of urgency. And you hadn't yet been voted into power in the next two weeks, who would . . ."

"Well it can't be any of the politicians," snapped Shazzer.

"What about Holly Willoughby?" said Tom. "It would be nice to have someone who at least has a blowdry, and an edgy beachy wave."

"No," said Shaz. "Nelson Mandela?"

"Dead."

"What about David Attenborough."

"People might think he's biased because of the animals and the environment. We need someone else as well."

"Joanna Lumley?"

"Yes!" we all exclaimed.

It was perfect! Joanna Lumley wouldn't indulge in PROPAGANDA. Joanna Lumley wouldn't say the Common Market was costing 34 billion pounds on the side of a bus just so she could be the next prime minister.

"Wait!" I said excitedly. "What about the Queen?"

"Perfect! The Queen is the soul of integrity and loves her country and is about to be played by Olivia Colman. The Queen and David Attenborough and Joanna Lumley!" cried Tom.

Thus, the solution to the Brexit crisis came to us quite naturally like a Buddhist miracle. The Queen and David Attenborough and Joanna Lumley shall go on TV and explain everything and then everyone gets to vote as long as they can answer a simple questionnaire correctly. Even though we had quite a few bottles of Chardonnay we managed to draw up the quiz there and then!

Brexit questionnaire thing

What is the main point in the deal which everyone is arguing over:

a. Brexit

b. Backstop

c. Common Market Two Zero

d. A customized union

e. A customized unicorn

f. Who gets to be the next prime minister

If we leave the EU on a hard Brexit we will have to pay:

a. 40 billion pounds

b. 60 billion euros

c. 40 billion trillion euros

d. 70 billion squillion trillion million euros

e. Nothing it'll all be free trade and marvellous

f. The firstborn child of every family

Backstop is:

a. When all the lorries get stuck at Dover and turn the motorways into a giant car park

b. A soft Brexit in Ireland. Or a hard-boiled egg

c. No border between Irelands

d. Stopping refugees getting into the backs of lorries

e. Obsessive stockpiling of toilet paper

If we leave Brexit that will mean:

a. Nothing because you can't leave Brexit because Brexit *is* leaving Brexit

True or false. If we leave Europe that will mean?

a. Everyone will be richer and free and Britain will be great again

b. We won't be able to go on mini-breaks any more

c. They will activate emergency bunker under the Ministry of Defence

f. Planes can't fly over Europe

g. Ireland will be rent asunder

h. Grazina will be spending her entire time on the 40p per minute Brexit helpline

i. Grazina will have to go back to Lithuania

Which of the following is the current state of the nation and which is the title of a self-help book:

a. When Things Fall Apart

b. The Land of Indecision

c. Living With Uncertainty

d. The Life Changing Magic of Minimizing Your Admin

e. How to Reason With a Delusional Person

f. The Subtle Art Of Not Giving A Fuck

If above questions are too difficult there could be a catch-all question instead i.e. do you want to:

a. Never have to say or hear the word Brexit again

b. Just make it all stop

If answer to both is yes then simply tick the Remain box and it will be like the whole bloody nightmare never even happened.

Think will go to Parliament Square and see if anyone will interview me!

What a tragic waste of time and energy all that was. If we had known what lay ahead with Covid-19 would we ever have got so mired in Brexit ? It's almost unbelievable that exactly one year to the day after I wrote the Brexit piece we went into lockdown, and I found myself writing Bridget columns again. As my friends know, I'm a terrible poser and go on and on about how I'm actually a *journalist* when it happens to suit my image.

When lockdown happened, our family was living close to Camden Town, between three major hospitals. It felt like being in a war zone. There were helicopters overhead and sirens all the time. It was difficult to write about the epidemic in Bridget's voice because it was so sad, but it's always appealed to me to try and tread the dainty line between comedy and tragedy because I think, at root, they're very close and have an almost kinetic relationship (Durr! There I am, posing again!) It took me ages to write this diary and I was really proud when the *Sunday Times* flagged it on the front page in a banner headline, though Tom did point out that it was considerably smaller than the banner which read: 'Getting Back into the Garden'.

Sunday Times, 29 March 2020

Thursday March 26th

Times per hour googled Coronavirus: 247. Nuisance calls to elderly neighbour to see if needs anything: 7. No. of Uber-like texts from Volunteer Helpline calling self to arms: 0. Minutes spent opening hilarious viral videos and forwarding to everyone I know: 2457. Times sniffed hyacinths to check if have lost sense of smell and have

Coronavirus: 282. Minutes de-cluttering and reading classic literature: 0. Minutes staring at wall aghast with mouth open: 4765. Calories: 8765. Alcohol units: 12. Work done: 0. Exercise: 0. (V. bad.)

7am Just woke up. Right. Time go to work and get some coffee and croissant.

7.01am Oh my god. OH MY GOD!!! Life as we knew it is over and we are in midst of the Apocalypse.

7.02am Calm and poised. It is those who have inner strength and calm who will get through. Like me.

7.03am Gaaah! Someone is FaceTiming. Maybe Boris telling me to get under the bed and stay there.

8.00am Was Miranda. "Waxing," she whispered shiftily.

Peered at screen. She was indeed developing uni-brow and handlebar moustache. "Don't tell anyone I'm even thinking this, but you do realise we're going to revert to nature? No hairdresser, no nail salon, no waxing . . ."

Grasped table, as more wheels continued to fall off the bus of everything have hitherto taken for granted.

"Sh** I've got to go!" she said. "Zoom meeting in hideous close up. Why did audio calls choose the moment we turn feral to become obsolete and rude?"

"Me too," I said. "Zooming with Sit Up Britain at 9. Talk later."

7.30am Oh God. Right. Am not going down rabbit hole. Am going to be completely ready for meeting: online yoga, boiled egg and put on actual clothes and wash "hair" – i.e. weird thing on head – and figure out camera/mute issue.

7.45 How can everything completely change in such a short space of time? Was it only last week we still went to pubs and actually interacted with live people?

Just spooling back through week's diary . . .

DAY BEFORE LOCKDOWN

Sunday March 22nd
4pm Just back from walk on Primrose Hill with the friends. Scary: everyone with same gob-smacked expression. Too many people but felt rude veering away from others. Ooh goody FaceTime.

"Just going into the village, darling, I want a cobbler!" – my Mother. "This fancy sourdough you brought is rock hard!"

Grrr wish she wouldn't be so bloody fussy about the groceries I saintly deliver.

"Mum. You're over seventy – you're not allowed out."

"I'm not over 70, darling! Well, at least I don't look 70, and my physical age is 43."

"Mum . . ." I said, dangerously.

"Anyway the point is, Una and I have got sticks."

"Exactly. You're elderly."

"No. Two metre sticks, so if anyone comes too close we'll rap them."

4.50 10 minutes to Boris time. Really like that he talks to us every day. It's not a question of anyone being perfect or doing everything perfectly. It just makes you feel like we're all part of the same thing.

6pm He is right. It is time to be responsible. Am going to start right now!

11pm Argor es war blurry goo FaceTime tonight with Tom, Shaz, and Miranda crisis analysis. "Iss like the Old Testament," I explained. "God hath decided to purge us with fire, floods and pestilence."

"Yes! For destroying the beautiful planet!" slurred Shaz.

"He saw our over-mini-breaking and SMOTE us!"

"Smote, Bridge?"

"Yes! There was a locust plague and I've got ants in the cereal."

"That's because you're a rubbish housekeeper."

"It's like Noah's flood. We need to set up some sort of ark and take two of each species with us."

"Nooo! That's exactly how the whole thing started: a crocodile on top of a wolf cub on top of a peacock on top of pangolin."

"I needs PURPOSE. I want to help. I could deliver food for people. I could cook!"

"Noooo!" yelled Tom. "Your cooking is the last thing we need. Go to sleep."

Monday March 23rd
Just went up hill again. Everyone is walking nicely apart so the headmaster won't close the parks and make us stay inside.

5pm Oh no! Boris is not on. I bet he's drinking whisky in the bath and making up speeches like Winston Churchill.

7pm Boris is speaking to the nation at 8.30. Have lurch in stomach like when you're going out with someone and they text, "can we talk?"

9pm We are in lockdown. Is this really happening? What were we thinking before? All the time we wasted worrying about nothing, the Brexit years with everyone dithering about details nobody understood in the first place and now earth-shattering decisions are being made on an hourly basis and we're losing everything. What were we thinking?

Tuesday 24th March

It's the silence which is so eerie. It's so unreal when the sun is shining and the daffodils are out. It must be like being in the Home Counties in First World War when the bodies and injured people started coming home. Feel like the crying NHS workers on the web are the first hint of the hell which is going to break loose.

Text message: GOV.UK.ALERT CORONAVIRUS. New rules in force now. You must stay at home.

Unreal. There's a siren and a helicopter. If I go outside will I be shot?

Stop, must not catastrophise but maintain positive rousing wartime spirit (i.e. start drinking before Boris comes on).

Have always just wanted to watch telly in pyjamas

eating ice-cream. But so confusing that by doing nothing you're doing your duty.

Have shameful sense of relief that for once this is not one of my own self-inflicted dramas.

Maybe should make certain areas in home be special and only use on special occasions. Like, um, the shower?

Shelf in fridge just fell out and the milk bottle burst. Was about to chuck rest of milk away like I usually wouldn't when thought "Nooo! That's the last of the milk!"

Just turned on *EastEnders* repeat and had judgemental frenzy at them going to pub and embracing. Wanted to yell, "No! Stay home! Protect the NHS."

Want to stop looking at WhatsApps so I can grieve for what the world's lost and what I've lost. OMG though have you seen the one with the glamorous mum going on about Distance Learning. Hilarious!

Weird how quickly you accept the new reality, like frogs in boiling water.

Wednesday 25th March
6pm "Oh f***," said Miranda. We were trying to sign up as NHS volunteers. "I've entered an old Tinder verification code instead of the volunteering one. Oh wait, this is the Red Cross."

Suddenly noticed Shaz on screen but holding a sign saying, "Help!" Like a Melania Trump meme. She held up another saying "I can't hear!"

Grrr technology! Cannot navigate NHS signup. Why would it think I'm a robot? How am I going to be any use as an NHS volunteer if I can't even figure out how many squares have a fire hydrant in?

412

2am Yay! Have done it!

Today again. Thursday 26th March
8.45am Must stop reading diary and get ready for Zoom meeting. Ooh goody FaceTime: Tom, Shaz and Miranda.

"Right. We need leadership and a press conference on grooming. It's a self-esteem issue."

"Yes!" I enthused. "Going feral should be re-branded as support for the NHS."

"Your Country Needs Your Uni-brow!" said Tom. "Princess Kate should get one."

"Stay Home. Have Roots. Support the NHS!" I said. "Maybe Boris could get dark roots!"

"Wait," said Tom. "Not waxing means no bikini waxing. Does that mean, like, giant bushes will be back in fashion?"

"What about people who've had them lasered?" panicked Miranda.

"Aargh! An outdated lady garden!" said Tom.

"This is a biblical apocalypse of inestimable seriousness! How can you be so flippant?" roared Shaz, corona-sanctimoniously, ruining the call.

Humph. If you don't laugh you'll cry. We all know a really terrible time is coming. You have to look for the good in dark things and there are good things:

- All the rubbish we got caught up in – carbon emissions, waste, over-choice, fake perfection – being taken away from us as if by wise dolphins.
- Countries and companies are realising they can ditch red tape and in-fighting and get things done quickly.
- 400,000 people volunteered to help each other in 24 hours.

- People are realising the important things are community and kindness.
- There are clear waters and turtles in the Venice canals and . . . gaah! Sit Up Britain Zoom is starting and am still in nighty with mad hair.

Never mind! Will mute camera and quickly wash hair while Richard Finch is blathering intro.

Richard's voice boomed out, "Bridget – for fuck's sake we can all see you in the shower. Charming as it is this is not appropriate behaviour in an apocalypse."

It really is all going marvellously.

Friday 27th March
11.15am OMG Boris has got coronavirus now. BoJo nooo! We need you.

It was quite tricky doing this for the *Sunday Times*, which was a weekly paper, because the News Review 'went to bed' – as we (smirks) journalists say – on Thursday for publication on Sunday. When one is at the cutting edge of news, things may happen in between. By the Friday morning of the column above, Boris had been diagnosed with coronavirus, managing in a ludicrous sketch-like manner to infect the Health Secretary and Chief Medical Officer – who'd all been telling us to stay far apart – at the same time. All we managed to squeeze in on the subject was the last line of the column.

I carried on with the diary and meant to do another column for the end of lockdown but then lockdown just didn't really . . . end. There wasn't the giant party we had all dreamed of. It was the beginning of much confusion. I had, though, FINALLY managed to get a position as an NHS volunteer – practically a doctor! Whilst not quite the full-on medical role I had imagined it did give me something to write about.

I was also getting a lot of questions as to whether Mark Darcy was based on the new Labour leader Keir Starmer. Sir Keir is my local MP and I'm a huge fan. When Boris and Sir Keir started sparring at Prime Minister's Question Time, they were just too much like Daniel Cleaver and Mark Darcy for me to resist.

Sunday Times, 24 May 2020

Wednesday 20th May

11.30am Totally Confused re: lockdown. World seems completely bipolar: one minute glorious and hot, next minute grey and freezing; one minute everyone paranoid and shouting at others for getting too close, next minute making out on rugs in bikinis. It's like Brexit: half the people I know are Remainers and still won't leave the house; the others are getting bootleg mani-pedis and drinking mojitos in Borough Market. On top of everything else I've just got all my summer clothes out and they've shrunk.

Noon Shazzer and Tom just FT'd: "You watching PM's Questions? Boris's hair is CRAZY!" Mmm. Love Sir Keir and Boris standoff – like watching Daniel Cleaver and Mark Darcy fight in the old days. Is classic clash of ideologies: Daniel/Boris attempting to smooth-talk everything with public-school quips and charm and Mark/ Keir Starmer, the soul of integrity and decency, calling him on truth and ethics and so buttoned up you just want to rip his shirt off and . . . phaww.

"Sir Keir is going to blow," panted Shaz.

"He's like a caged beast or tiger," I gasped. "Any second he'll say, 'All right Johnson, outside.'"

"And they'll fight in a fountain."

"Bridget," Tom burst out indignantly, "Sir Keir Starmer is a highly respected QC who did, admittedly, purchase his mother a donkey sanctuary but is not a 'caged tiger'. You've been watching too many Tiger Kings."

"Normal People more like," growled Jude.

"It's a war effort," said Tom. "They shouldn't be fighting."

"Someone's got to call this," exploded Shaz. "We're not a success, with the worst death rate in Europe, when no one knows what the f*** is going on with tracking and testing. The care home thing is a scandal. Everyone in

Europe except us can go on holiday because no one will have us!"

"Yo, Boomer!" grunted a low voice.

"Gaah! Got to go," I panicked. "One of the teenagers has come off its devices."

What is happening? Both teenagers are at large now. Maybe I've completely spaced on a mealtime or they're trying to make me do something embarrassing for a TikTok. Also I am NOT a baby-boomer.

Obviously when lockdown started I was marvellous with the teenagers, dancing, baking, collecting empty toilet rolls to make an Instagrammable ping-pong route downstairs, but we quickly realised to survive we need to stay within our designated areas apart from specified occasions: meals, facetiming Granny, outbreaks of corona despair etc.

"Can I have friends over in the garden?"

"You're absolutely right to ask that question," I flannelled wildly, like a politician skewered on *The Andrew Marr Show*, while trying to remember the rules re gardens.

"Can Amanda come?" said Mabel.

"Well! We are outlining a staged and measured . . ."

"How come four-year-olds can go to school and we can't? Four-year-olds lick people."

Remembering Tom's advice to assume control (Tom is a child psychologist so used to such crises) I announced, "Zoomers! Return to your devices. Save mental health. Return TO your devices."

It worked. They are quiet again.

The Zoomers act cool, but some nights they creep in, tearful, wondering will we ever see Granny again? Are you going to die, Mummy? What will happen to everything? All I can do is cuddle them to sleep and go down and open the wine. If this happened to just one person the fuss would be incredible. But it's everyone. Everyone's in shock and exhausted, including the politicians. We need to be kind and help.

4.00pm Feel so fat. I've got to get out of the house and stop eating chocolate. Maybe the army could coax everyone back to work if they set up pop-ups to suck out everyone's fat.

4.05pm Oooh! NHS email. When the crisis started I was wild with *Dad's Army*-style enthusiasm, volunteering for anything I could, imagining self as land girl. I got endless humiliating rejections: "The quality of entrants has been unusually high this year etc." Finally managed to get a Zoom interview but a few minutes in, the lady said: "Can I just ask: where are you?"

I peered at the screen. Zoomers had changed the background so it looked like I was in front of a wind machine in the Bahamas.

"We'll get back to you," she said and rang off. Had to google Harry and Meghan to feel better about self.

4.10pm I got the job! I'm an NHS volunteer! I have to show up to the hospital tomorrow afternoon! I'm helping. No more chocolate!

5pm Tom called – shall we get take-out margaritas from the pub to celebrate?

"Mummy, if you're going out, can we? It's so hot!"

"OK but social distancing. Remember Edna in the street is 90."

"Should I wear a mask?"

"Yes you must, except, er . . . if you can't," I tailed off.

"But, Boomer, in what circumstance can't you wear a mask?"

"Can I get an ice-cream?"

"Just . . . just . . . Stay Alert," I finished desperately as we approached the pub where Tom was distancing.

"I'll get you a margarita," said Tom as they scampered off.

Primrose Hill was like summer of love. Groups of people drinking, dancing, making out. Someone had set fire to the grass with a joint. Only policemen in sight were two officers strolling elegantly on horseback.

"Everybody is so YOUNG," said Tom. "It's horrifyingly Darwinian."

It did indeed have the air of Noah's Ark after the flood, rainbows everywhere. They just needed to release a couple of giraffes from the zoo and the vision would be complete.

Magda suddenly facetimed, hysterical: "I've just been raided by the police."

WTF?? Jeremy has not allowed Magda out since lockdown except a walk round the block once a day because he thinks lifting the lockdown is insane.

"Jeremy went to the doctor's so I scarpered to the hairdresser's garden to do my roots. The police raided and I had to come home with the foils in. Oh f*** he's home bye."

Just then a video popped up from Miranda's friend in Hackney who was IN the pub. "It's OK we're socially distancing. Oh shit, the police! Get in the cupboard."

Next who should walk past but Jude – in corona melt-down – with Shazzer. "Rebecca just facetimed from a paddle board in Gloucestershire," said Jude, "mono-loguing about her fantastic lockdown doing sunset yoga, making sourdough starter with the kids and Mia has been making facemasks for the homeless on a 3D printer. I feel I've been rubbish at lockdown like those people who had a bad war. The only place I've gone over the top is my bra."

"Call the police," yelled Shazzer. "Report Rebecca."

"You can't report someone for giving lockdown FOMO."

"Why would you talk to someone in the country anyway? Everyone knows you have to stick to your bubble with people on the same emotional plane."

"Is that Rishi Sunak?" gushed Tom, pointing to a fit guy in a hoodie. "I'd like to see HIM in a fountain with Keir Starmer."

"It's not him," slurred Jude, who works in finance, except that, currently, like the rest of us, she's lost the ability to get dressed before three.

"What confuses me," I said, "is what actually IS money? Rishi Sunak keeps giving six squillion pounds out. Where from? Are there gold bars hidden under the floor?"

"They print it," said Tom, airily.

"But there's no point in printing money because you can't use it any more. Even on Deliveroo."

"Well it's possible real trend growth will come to the rescue," began Jude, "once the cyclical downturn is reversed. Oh f*** it . . . shall I get some more margaritas?"

"Maybe money just IS, like technology: or – as Pink

Floyd said – it's a gas," said Tom. "Unless you haven't got any."

"Boomers!"

It was the teenagers. Wearing masks. Socially distancing.

"Mummy, why are you not sticking to the rules? There are four of you and Edna is having a party with six people in the garden and she's 90. Can we have a party?"

I looked at them wearily. I just don't know any more.

I don't know if children can spread it to adults. I don't know if it spreads outdoors. I don't know if masks don't work. I just want someone to either tell me what they know or go back like it was before when we all knew we had to stay indoors and it was really simple. Apart from lying on the hill with margaritas.

Thursday 21st May

Arrived, inspired, at the hospital, at last joining the war on Covid and, crucially, on Fat. Shown into my "office". Was stuffed from floor to ceiling with donated chocolates, Cadbury's creme eggs and fizzy drinks.

"Your job is to guard it," said my new boss. "And organise it into these trolleys for delivery to the wards. It's OK to eat what you want – that's your reward for volunteering."

Confusing as ever. But as I left I saw a long line of exhausted nurses at the end of their shifts – queuing for small bags of donated fruit and veg.

It just doesn't seem right – so many of us furloughed in the sun, no tracking and trace in place, the NHS staff still slogging it out, cleaning Covid wards for a backlog of normal patients, waiting for the next wave, which might well come from everyone milling about in the sun. I do hope Mark Darcy keeps on at Daniel Cleaver and they make sure money raised by Captain Tom goes straight to the one group of people who do seem to know what they're doing through all this, with a big fat bonus in their pay packets. And a creme egg.

Ah. As I look back and realize how much I've seen and learned and how many self-help books I've read I think, 'Why not write a self-help book myself? Perhaps one called *Bridget Jones's Guide to Life*!'

Then I remember that I already did that, when the first movie came out. Perhaps not as exhaustive as I might like but there are some very useful tips in there.

To Create a Pleasingly Ordered Bedroom

Expecting attractive bedroom visitor? Plagued by things all over floor? Simply follow easy step-by-step guide to transform your most intimate space into impressively ordered enclave.

1 Push all things under bed.

2 Some persistent items may still protrude
tellingly from under bed.

3 Push persistent items further under bed.

4 There.

Terrine of Venison with Juniper and Pistachio Nuts

SERVES 10–12

This is just about the easiest terrine in the world to make because you can buy the venison and the pork ready minced. The result is a lovely, rough country pâté. Serve it with thick slices of toasted country bread, and an excellent accompaniment would be the Confit of Cranberries on page 43.

[handwritten: meat]
[handwritten: see insides of sausages or just chopped tin of anchovies]

1 lb (450 g) minced venison, available in large supermarkets	1 heaped teaspoon chopped fresh thyme *[handwritten: use lettuce maybe]*
1 lb (450 g) ready-minced pork	2 rounded teaspoons salt
8 oz (225 g) rindless smoked streaky bacon	*[handwritten: 12]* 6d oz (175 ml) dry white wine *[handwritten: Murmurs]*
30 juniper berries, crushed	1 fl oz (25 ml) brandy
1 rounded dessertspoon mixed peppercorns	
4 oz (110 g) ready-shelled pistachio nuts *[handwritten: or peanuts]*	
¼ teaspoon powdered mace *[handwritten: eh?]*	

You will also need a 2-lb (900-g) loaf tin 7½ x 4¾ x 3½ inches (19 x 12 x 9 cm) deep, preferably non stick, or a terrine of 3-pint (1.75-litre) capacity.

Pre-heat the oven to gas mark 2, 300°F (150°C).

[handwritten: chop everything up + shove in a bowl]

First of all, place the venison and the pork in a large bowl then place the bacon slices on a board stacked on top of one another and cut them into thin strips about ⅛ inch (3 mm), then add these to the bowl. After that crush the juniper berries quite coarsely with a pestle and mortar, add these to the bowl then crush the peppercorns, also quite coarsely, and add these. To deal with the pistachio nuts all you need to do is chop them in half then they can go in along with the thyme, mace, salt and then finally the wine and brandy.

[handwritten: if time if not just mix it up + a bit]

Now you've got quite a lot of mixing to do, so either use your hands or take a large fork and thoroughly combine everything. Cover the bowl with a cloth and leave it all to marinate for about 2 hours, then pack it into the loaf tin or terrine and cover the surface with a double thickness of foil, pleat the corners and fold it under the rim. Now place the terrine in a roasting tin and put it on the middle shelf of the oven, then pour in about 1 inch (2.5 cm) of boiling water from the kettle and let the terrine cook for 1¾ hours. After that, remove it from the oven, leaving the foil on, then after 30 minutes place two 1 lb (450 g) weights on top or the equivalent in tins of tomatoes or something similar. When the terrine is completely cold, place it in the fridge with the weights still on top and leave it overnight to really firm up. Don't forget to take it out of the fridge about an hour before serving, and serve cut in slices.

◇

Weight-Loss Tips

Always wear 3-inch heels when weighing . . .

. . . to create impressive weight to height ratio.

Remember to subtract weight of shoes from total.

Then experiment with your scales' responses . . .

. . . simple hand pressure can reduce weight by several
pounds. There.

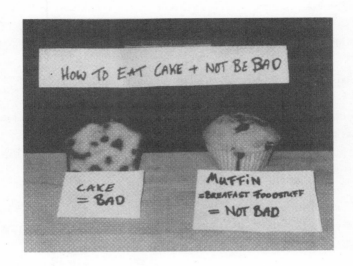

Useful Terms and Words for Practical Living

Aargh aargh.

Answerphone substitute for normal human partner.

Bunny boiler hateful poison concept suggesting that if a woman is thirty-six and unmarried she is going to start murdering other people's husbands and boiling their children's rabbits.

Commitment phobic person who insists on describing anything from shag to fourteen-year relationship as 'just good friends'.

Communal changing room hateful place always containing the girl who looks fantastic in everything and swings around smirking at your thighs, flicking her hair and doing model poses in the mirror saying: 'Does it make me look fat?' to her obligatory obese friend who looks like a water buffalo in everything.

Daniel fuckwit that I used to go out with.

Emotional Fuckwittage annoying behaviour by fuckwits, e.g. saying will ring then not ringing, shagging others then not calling them, being in relationships with others then saying it's not a relationship, going out with people for twelve years whilst insisting they don't want to get too serious, refusing to go on mini-breaks, etc. etc.

Fuckwit person (man) who does emotional fuckwittage.

Fuckwittage (the French pronunciation) verb: fuckwitted behaviour.

g. good.

Gaaah! expression of shock on discovering self forty-five minutes late for work, or love interest forty-five minutes early for date.

Humph useful expression for showing disgruntlement.

I rarely used word normally replaced by 'self'.

Jellyfisher person who drops little verbal stings into conversation which you hardly notice at time but leave you feeling hurt afterwards whilst not pinpointing exactly where came from, e.g. 'Just seen some great trousers, well, unless you have cellulite jodhpurs, of course.' (Portuguese Man of War variety.)

Jude lovely Singleton friend with whizzy job in the City: better at dealing with collapse of the Yen than commitment-phobic non-boyfriend Vile Richard.

Karma v. important but incomprehensible concept.

Lettuce rare foodstuff which uses up more calories to chew than it contains.

Mentionitis when someone's name keeps coming up when

not strictly relevant, e.g. 'Rebecca has a car like that', or 'Rebecca likes fish', thereby suggesting said person performing Mentionitis has crush on said Rebecca. Especially if one is paranoid.

Mini-break important rite-of-relationship-passage involving stay of not less than one and not more than three nights in country house/hotel/fisherman's cottage, near pub by river (ideally with open fire) in country, e.g. Cornwall or similar. Mini-breaks clearly demonstrate that a man has sufficient romantic interest in you to come away from football and thus that you are having a relationship and not just shagging.

Natural look only achieved for date after several hours of farming techniques – harvesting, crop-spraying, filing, waxing, plucking, exfoliating, etc. Never actually let yourself revert to nature or you will end up with a full beard and handlebar moustache on each shin.

One-Four-Seven-One telephonic device which adds to excitement of being single but also doubles misery potential on arrival home: no-number-stored-on-1471 misery adds to no-message-on-answerphone misery, or number-stored-turning-out-to-be-mother's misery.

Pashmina pretentious scarf thing but, more importantly, pashmina is platonic friend who makes you feel small because you know you want to shag him more than he wants to shag you.

Pashmarried platonic friend whom you used to go out with and is now married with children, likes having you around as memory of old life, but makes you feel like mad barren pod-womb imagining vicar is in love with self.

Pashmincer platonic friend who you fancy but unfortunately is gay.

Pashspurt 'platonic friend' who keeps making passes then getting cross when you say you just want to be friends.

Quince fruit-type thing beginning with 'q' unlike any other words can think of.

Re-tread hideous poison concept generated by misguided journalist that thirty-something girls are the sort of girls you wanted to go out with when they were in their twenties and they wouldn't and now you can go out with them but don't want to. Said misguided journalist now happily ensconced with thirty-something girl plus baby thereby proving whole concept was load of old bollocks.

Self-control alien concept, not necessarily desirable – look at Pol Pot.

Shazzer lovely Singleton friend: top radical feminist except when sobbing in sheep's voice over boys she met in gym.

Singleton replacement for poison outdated word 'spinster'.

Smug Married annoying married person who says things like 'Why aren't you married yet?' 'How's your love life' and 'Can't put it off for ever, you know, tick-tock, tick-tock.'

Tom best gay friend who always greets self with 'Bridget, you've lost so much weight.' Which is nice.

Urban family select group of Singleton friends who perform function of old-fashioned blood family only do all communication over phone or e-mail unless involves Chardonnay.

Valentine's Day purely cynical commercial enterprise unless you get one and then it's a marvellous vehicle for people to show their appreciation of others who more than deserve it: rather like awards at award ceremonies.

v.g. very good.

Why frequently asked question, e.g. Why do Smug Marrieds/fuckwits do this? Why?

X person who should never go off with anyone else but remain celibate to the end of their days in order to provide you with a mental fallback position.

Zen something which, when you look at life, can be applied to anything: Zen and the art of shopping, Zen and the art of blow-drying, Zen and the art of VAT returns, etc. etc. It is all a question of flow rather than struggle. But Jude says not to mention this to Shazzer as she thinks it is bollocks.

I still am a great believer in Zen even though Shazzer thinks it is bollocks. And as I sit surrounded by all newspaper cuttings and items I wrote so long ago and through this wild ride with Bridget I think to myself – what have I learned? What further *aperçus* would I like to share? For example:

Life is so much more fun when you accept the mess it is and all of us are and just rock and roll with it.

The only value in striving for perfection is to laugh at the very idea.

You're only ever going to get things a percentage right.

And where, today through realizations such as these, has Flow and Zen thus brought oh shit what is that smoke?

Oh f*** oh f***! The fire alarm is going off. What is happening? The original Bridget Jones columns are on fire. Is the bloody scented candle.

Helen Fielding
September 2020

Permissions Acknowledgements

Grateful acknowledgement is made to the following for permission to reprint the articles and excerpts listed:

'A Christmas Poem', *Serious Concerns* © Wendy Cope, 1992. Reprinted by kind permission of Faber and Faber Ltd.

'The Diary of Bridget Jones' (7 March 1995), 'Bridget Jones's Diary' (18 October 1995, 30 October 1996, 29 January 1997, 7 May 1997, 3 September 1997) and 'Bridget Jones reaches fever pitch' (29 March 1997) © Helen Fielding, 1995–97. Originally published in the *Independent*, *Independent on Sunday* and *Independent* Magazine

'Dear Diary: don't tell a soul . . .' (1992); 'A stately Sunday with mother' (1995); 'Bridget Jones's Brexit diary' (2019); 'Bridget Jones's Coronavirus diary' and 'Bridget Jones's lockdown diary' (2020) © Helen Fielding, 1992–2020. Originally published in the *Sunday Times*

'Bridget Jones's Feminism Diary' © Helen Fielding, 2018. Originally published by Penguin Random House in *Feminists Don't Wear Pink* by Scarlett Curtis, reprinted with permission

Daily Mirror front page (7 May 2001) © Mirrorpix/Reach Licensing

'Pile 'Em High' cartoons © Kipper Williams 1997. Originally published in the *Sunday Times* and reprinted with permission.